Miles Apart

Feel Me

K M Walker

Copyright © 2019 K M Walker
All rights reserved
First Edition

NEWMAN SPRINGS PUBLISHING
320 Broad Street
Red Bank, NJ 07701

First originally published by Newman Springs Publishing 2019

ISBN 978-1-64531-554-4 (Paperback)
ISBN 978-1-64531-555-1 (Digital)

This book is a work of fiction. Names, characters, places, and incidents are products of the author's imagination or are used fictitiously. Any resemblance to actual events or locales or persons, living or dead, is entirely coincidental.

Intended for mature readers.

Printed in the United States of America

Dedication

THIS BOOK IS DEDICATED TO my wonderful husband, who laughed when I was in deep thought with the "book stare" as I wrote *Miles Apart*. Thanks to my mom, my two daughters, other family members, and friends (past and present) who became my sounding board, as I spoke about the series. Thank you to real musicians, who write, compose, produce, and perform, to bring music to life and brighten the colors of the world around us. God is love.

Chapter 1

I grabbed the handle to the back hotel door but found it locked. I quicken my pace to the front, focused on the sidewalk, and made sure I didn't fall.

Two white Cadillac SUVs were parked under the awning. A small, unmoving crowd blocked the entrance. I pushed my brown-rimmed glasses into place on my nose and shook my head in irritation about being delayed by the commotion of people who gathered to gawk.

The crowd watched the parade of people emerge from the parked vehicles. I extended my apologies, squeezed between two gentlemen, and stepped close to the door.

A burly man and I grabbed the silver front door handle at the same time. I tried to pull it open, but he held it shut. I let it go as he stood tall and shook his head at me. He towered over me and stretched his other arm to the closest opened car door. His stance blocked my view of the people who moved behind him. The crowd swayed, and someone pushed me into the man.

"I'm sorry," I blurted as I grabbed his bicep to keep from falling on him. Like an idiot, I reached to feel his foot. "Did I hurt you?"

"Just my toes, ma'am." He hissed with sarcasm. He let go of the door handle and brought his foot to his hand. He squeezed his toes, returned to his stance, and commanded, "Step away from the door."

He had broad shoulders and a thick neck. His dark-gray eyes matched his dark, graying hair. A thin shaven, salt-and-pepper beard outlined his face. He stared down his nose at me. He thrust his giant hand toward my face to indicate for me not to move.

"I need inside. Please?" I pleaded with wide eyes.

"You're going to wait," he said with furrowed eyebrows.

"It would take one quick second. I'd use my ninja-like skills so you wouldn't see me if you blinked." I smiled, but he scowled.

He stood firm as did his expression. He sized me up with his piercing eyes and tightened his lips.

"If you think you can without me taking you down, go for it," he challenged.

"Seriously?" I asked forcefully, and my smile faded. The first Cadillac pulled forward, but I pressed, "Five quick steps is all I need. Please."

"Not on your life," he growled.

"Oh, come on. Five freakin' steps," I exasperated and threw my head back in frustration.

"Take it easy," a low, tranquil voice said from behind this giant man.

A shorter man, who was a famous musician, peered around the tall gentleman. I became starstruck when I stared into the megastar's eyes.

"What's the problem?" the musician asked.

"She wants to get inside, but we don't have time to deal with groupies," the tall, muscular man explained but kept his piercing leer glued on me. "I need to get you away from this crowd and find out why the back door was locked."

I stared at the tall man and was offended by how he assumed I was a groupie. I didn't divert my eyes from the harsh glare he held on me. I challenged him to an intense staring contest, determined not to shift my sight or blink.

If he looked away first, a small personal victory over this intimidating man would be mine. He wanted his own reward. His eyes widened as if he accepted my invitation. In a locked gaze, we both stood our ground.

"Why are you in a rush?" the rock star asked me.

"I have a class to attend, and I'm not a groupie," I said sternly as I glared at the giant.

"Where are you from?" the celebrity asked.

"The south," I replied and smirked at the giant without blinking.

The crowd surrounded us and murmured behind me. They moved in close to see who emerged from the last SUV. Someone yelled. The stocky man blinked and turned his attention to the distraction. My smile grew wide at the victory.

I blinked the dryness from my eyes then shifted my focus to the celebrity. His glistening smile widened as we held eye contact. My cheeks flushed.

A well-known, talented musician, songwriter, artist, and actor stared at me. He looked gorgeous. He was a few years older than I but didn't age like an ordinary person.

He removed a pair of sunglasses from the top of his head. He ran his fingers through his shoulder-length, thick, wavy black hair. He dressed to perfection in his green silk, long-sleeve shirt with silk black pants and designer black tennis shoes.

He folded the sunglasses and placed one earpiece in the V-neck of his shirt. It laid above a long gold chain necklace. Out of nervousness, I smirked and felt like a peasant in the presence of a king because of his notoriety.

"You have a strong accent," the celebrity said, dragging out *strong*. "What class is held at a hotel?"

"Prostitution. We're learning how to use a new bra for swiping debit cards," I said.

"This hotel is a little upscale for prostitutes," he said with his full kissable lips.

He gazed into my eyes as he tapped the bigger man on his shoulder. The giant stepped to the left and blocked us from the crowd.

"We work the best corners at the best hotels." I held my dumb smile.

"That's where the money is," the musician flirted.

"I apologize for the sarcasm and cliché, but I'm late for a tax class. How long is this procession gonna take?" I inquired with a tilted head.

"We need to get to your room before reporters show," the giant remarked to the famous musician.

"Let's go." The celebrity held his hand out to me while people gathered around us. He introduced himself with arrogance and a smile. "I'm Teddy Nafton. I know you've heard of me."

I gently shook his hand. A soft electric shock ran up my arm as if we rubbed our feet on a carpet and touched each other. I've seen him in music videos, award shows on television, and pictures of him in the entertainment section on the Internet. They didn't reveal how breathtaking he looked in person.

"Once or twice," I teased and held his hand while we stepped into the lobby.

"We need to get everyone ready for the shoot," a short, slender, black-haired woman stated.

She pushed her black-rimmed glasses on her nose before she patted Teddy's arm. She turned on her heels and followed the band members to the elevators.

Teddy nodded but didn't look away from me. He wouldn't release my hand.

"I'm Beth." I smiled.

I wanted to keep my cool and not be an obsessed crazy fan. I loved his music and had listened to him for years. He was a household name. He topped the Board Charts many times throughout his career, and his acting was impeccable.

"Is your foot okay? I'm sorry for steppin' on it," I said to the tall gentleman.

"I'm fine," he grumbled.

"Gene Hartford." Teddy pointed to him, and I shook Gene's offered hand.

The crowd gathered around us and mumbled incoherently. Gene blocked us once again while I turned my attention to an event message board at the top of the stairs.

Taxplus Class
Second Conference Room
Downstairs

Teddy noticed my stare and read the board, "Do you work for the IRS?"

"No, sir. I own an accounting firm and would love to stand here and chat, but you have bigger and better things to do. I don't mean to be rude, but I need to go."

"May I walk you to class?" he asked.

"No, Teddy," Gene informed. "We need to go to the room. I need to do a sweep before the photoshoot."

"Yeah, yeah." Teddy waved his hand in the air to dismiss Gene, then asked me, "Well?"

"That's up to you, but I need my butt, in a chair, in that room, learning stuff." I pointed toward the stairs as my southern accent grew stronger with every sentence I spoke.

Teddy smiled, turned to Gene, and advised, "The shoot can wait." He looked back at me. "I'm going to walk Ms. Beth to her class. Is it Ms. or Mrs. Beth? I don't see a ring on your finger."

"I don't see one on you, so either you're not married, or you're a player." I smiled.

"I'm not married, and why would you say I'm a player?" Teddy asked with a smirk.

"I know your type. Guys like you are players." I chastised myself for flirting.

"You read too much entertainment news," he remarked.

"Not about you," I playfully snipped.

He laughed, stared into my eyes, and I smiled wider. His gaze mesmerized me.

Everything and everyone around us disappeared from my view. In my mind, Teddy and I stood face-to-face in a dark room with a bright white spotlight revealing us as he held my hand. I felt as though he wanted to tell me his life story, but I broke our stare and glanced at the carpet.

"Not married," I answered, and my face flushed.

"Shall we?" He held his hand toward the stairs for me to take the lead.

"Thank you," I said.

"Are you staying at this hotel?" he asked as Gene followed between the crowd and us.

"No," I said.

We stepped to the table outside the conference room. A slender young lady stood from her chair and stared at Teddy. She ran her hands through her short black hair, flattening it against her head.

"Oh, wow. Can I help you?" she blushed.

"I need to sign in, please," I said to her while Teddy stared at me.

Her sights remained on him, but she pointed to the pen and pad on the table. I signed the paper while Teddy repeated my name.

"Beth Chambers."

"Yes, sir," I said.

The lady held her hand out to Teddy and beamed, "I'm Trudie."

Being a gentleman, he shook her hand. "I'm Teddy, and this is Beth Chambers."

She clasped his hand with both of hers. She shook her head back and forth for a split second and came out of her trance.

"I spoke with you on the phone, Ms. Chambers." She nodded at me. "You're from Arkansas, right?"

"Yes, ma'am. Sorry, I'm late," I said.

Trudie smiled and let go of Teddy's hand. She handed me a book and a stack of paper, wrapped in cellophane.

"You can find a seat in the front. The first break will be soon, and lunch will be served at twelve-thirty," Trudie explained.

"I appreciate it." I juggled the thick book and papers in my arms. Teddy reached to take the book from me, but I held it tight against my body. "I got this, but thank you."

He cast his big brown eyes to the floor, like a puppy whipped with a newspaper. "Okay." He raised his eyes to me. "I wanted to help."

I smiled, and my knees grew weak with the intoxicating smell of his cologne. I wanted to touch his smooth, olive cheek, but I refrained. I looked at the carpet from the embarrassment of my thoughts. I walked close to the door and turned to him.

"Thank you for walking me to class, Mr. Nafton, and Mr. Hartford. It's been a pleasure meeting you, gentlemen. Good luck in Colorado," I said.

"Would you care to have lunch with me?" Teddy asked, and I gave him a puzzled stare.

The offer surprised me. I hesitated and recalled Gene and the woman stating earlier he had prior commitments. Not wanting to interrupt his plans, I shook my head to decline his offer.

"I'll arrange everything," Teddy said.

"Don't you have things to do?"

"Yeah. Lunch with you," he mused.

I stared into his pleading eyes. Anxious yet guilty for interposing, I said, "Fine, but not in your room, and I'm a vegetarian."

"You got it," he said, then nodded. "Thank you, Ms. Chambers."

"Ms. Chambers," Gene said with a serious expression and nodded.

I stepped through the doors. Rows of tables and chairs filled the space. I took my seat among approximately 150 people. The speaker paused and pointed to the projector to show which page I needed. I opened the cellophane from around the stack of papers, finding them to be examples of new tax forms. I settled into my chair and listened to the speaker.

After an hour of class, we were dismissed for a short break. I gathered my purse and stepped outside the hotel, into the sunlight. I walked to a bench under a shade tree. I lit a cigarette and replayed in my mind the encounter with Teddy. I questioned my actions and words I exchanged with him.

A few people from class stepped outside and lit their cigarettes. I finished mine and listened to the conversation from a few women who discussed the new tax laws. I didn't want to think about tax season at that moment. I walked into the hotel, downstairs into the conference room, and sat at my table.

I looked at my wrinkled T-shirt and jeans, then shook my head. I was embarrassed by my appearance. My long brown hair was bunched on top of my head and held with a clippie. My makeup-free face, along with my brown-rimmed glasses, made me appear like an old-time school teacher.

Time quickly past, and the speaker jarred me from my daydreams. He informed us we had one hour for lunch break. Voices in the room grew loud when people walked toward the door. Gene stood in the doorway and peered in to locate me. I made my way through the crowd to join him.

"Good afternoon, Mr. Hartford." I intertwined my arm through his offered arm.

"Good afternoon, Ms. Chambers. Please call me, Gene, and thank you for this. He's excited." He led me through the crowd.

"Call me Beth, and he's not excited."

"You'd be surprised." He patted my hand.

Several people from the class formed a line in the lobby for lunch, which was provided by the accounting association. We passed the crowd, turned right, and walked a short corridor. He guided me left, through metal double doors to the back of the kitchen.

Three gentlemen in white coats and black slacks stood around a small table. We walked close to them when Teddy stepped around the corner. He carried bowls in his hands, abruptly stopped, and looked at me.

"Is this okay?" Teddy asked, and I nodded with a smile. "Are you learning a lot?"

"Not much," I said as he sat the bowls on the table. "I've had a preoccupied mind, so thanks."

"Because of me?" He pulled a chair out for me and pointed to the seat.

"Yes, and thank you." I sat and laid a napkin in my lap.

My pulse quickened with excitement. Teddy sat in the chair across from me and smiled.

"You've been thinking about me?" He shook his napkin and placed it in his lap.

"It's hard not to," I said while Gene shooed the three gentlemen away. "You're serving the food?" I asked Teddy, and he nodded. "Don't you have people to do this?"

"I can't cook, but I know how to serve." He smiled, and Gene stood against the wall behind him.

"Looks great." I beamed and reminded myself to remain calm as I looked at the Caesar salad.

"I worked hard organizing this," Teddy stated with a wave of a hand.

"You did a wonderful job. Picking up the phone and calling someone must have caused you to sweat," I said, and he chuckled. I couldn't stop smiling, and my cheeks blushed. "I'm going to apologize now, but I need to cut lunch short to make a few phone calls."

"I don't mind if you want to make your calls now. I would like to have your full attention before you go…learn stuff." He smiled.

"Please, excuse me," I said with a heavy southern accent.

He nodded then leaned back in his chair to wait for me. I stood from the table, took a few steps from him, and called the office. No problems existed at the time, so I ended the short conversation with my employee. I texted my brother to let him know what time class would adjourn then returned to the table.

"How is everything?" Teddy inquired when I sat across from him.

"Okay," I said when my phone buzzed.

"Do you need to answer that?"

"It's a text from my brother. No biggie." I replaced the napkin in my lap.

"What is his name?"

With a puzzled expression and a stupid smile, I asked, "Scott, but why would you want to know?"

"Are you staying with him?" Teddy asked.

I tilted my head and squinted my eyes. "Small talk. It's hard, isn't it?"

"Yeah," he said.

"Did you enjoy the shoot?" I giggled.

"Why is that funny?" he asked.

"Being from the south, a shoot entails people shooting cans or deer. I can't envision you dressed in camouflage and shooting anything, much less, dressing a deer. You may mess up your manicured nails." I joked.

"You don't think I can shoot?" he smiled, and I shook my head. "I can shoot anything with a camera in my hand."

"You're lame," I laughed.

"The tour promos can wait, so I canceled the shoot," he said.

"That's cute how you think you're important enough to be on a cover of a magazine," I flirted.

"The world revolves around me." He winked, and I laughed again. "Tell me about your business."

"There isn't much to tell. It's an accounting firm my mother started some time ago, and I took over when she retired."

I turned the lettuce in the bowl with my fork. How do I gracefully eat a salad without getting dressing all over my mouth?

"How long have you been managing it?" he asked before he took a bite of salad.

"Several years." I concentrated on folding the lettuce with my fork.

"You don't like talking about yourself."

"I'm not used to talking about myself. I'm a private person with a boring life, so there isn't anything to say," I said.

"You don't see the light of day from January to April?" he questioned.

"Right." I smiled. "You're a singer of some sort?"

"I like to dabble in music."

"Dabble, huh. It would be nice if you made it big one day," I teased.

He chuckled, stared into my eyes, and said, "You're changing the subject."

"Look, Mr. Nafton." I broke our stare and laid the fork in the bowl.

"Teddy, please," he corrected me.

"Fine, Teddy. I'll be straight with you." I looked at him eye to eye. "I can't figure out why you wanted to eat lunch with me. I'm a boring accountant and am not in the entertainment industry, so I don't get this." He tilted his head and smiled. "You intimidate the crap out of me. I don't know if you intended to watch me squirm for your amusement, but that isn't cool. Maybe you're bored and wanted someone to eat lunch with, but I…"

"Bored? I'm never bored. I always have something to do or people around me. I find you," he hesitated, searched my eyes, and changed the subject. "You didn't mention meeting me when you made your calls. At least, I don't think you did. The conversation would have lasted longer. Have you texted or called people about me?"

"I'm not into gossip, and besides," I smiled, "what would be the point? Your life doesn't affect mine."

He and Gene laughed while a ringtone from a cell phone echoed in the kitchen. It wasn't mine, so I waited for one of them to answer. Teddy smiled as the ringing stopped.

"You fascinate me. Most people I meet, want something from me, or they tell the world, they met me. All you've wanted to do is run in the opposite direction. You do know who I am, right?" Teddy asked.

"You're not all that." I looked in his big brown eyes and felt at ease while his gaze held mine.

"You don't know who I am," he said with wide eyes and a slight laugh.

"I'm sorry. Sarcasm runs in the family." I blushed. "I do know who you are, but I didn't mention you because I don't want anyone to know MY business."

"I appreciate the protection of my privacy."

"I didn't do it for you." He and Gene chuckled as the phone rang again. I said, "If you have phone calls to make, I can leave."

"They can wait," Teddy said.

Gene pulled his phone from his pocket and answered it. He listened, leaned into Teddy's ear, and whispered something.

"Have Rick show her to the room," Teddy said.

"Do you need to go?" I asked.

"No. I'm enjoying the company." He studied my reactions as Gene returned to his position behind Teddy.

"Why the lunch? How many times have you eaten lunch with people who stepped on, I'm assuming, your bodyguard's foot?" I asked and returned my attention to the salad.

"This is a first. Not many people call Gene out." He looked at Gene.

"No, especially with ninja skills," Gene confirmed.

"I like your accent." Teddy smiled.

"I'm entertainment for you?" I asked, in a playful manner.

"Yep," he said and took a bite of salad. "After you apologized to Gene, you two got into the staring contest. I couldn't help but laugh from you challenging him."

"You're laughing at me as well?" I widened my eyes and held my smile.

"Yep."

"She's not like the others," Gene mumbled.

"I told you," Teddy said to him.

"Excuse me?" I asked, but neither responded. I pointed at Gene, squinted my eyes, and said, "I won the contest."

They laughed, and Teddy said, "You need to eat before you go…learn stuff." He mocked. "I imagine you want to smoke during the break."

"Wait. What?"

"I watched you walk outside when you took the morning break," Teddy said.

"I didn't see you, so are you a stalker?"

He pointed to the salad. "No, but eat. Afterward, you can call everyone you know and tell them how you had a marvelous lunch with me."

"Changing the subject, are we?" I asked and waited for a response. He didn't say a word but smiled. "You're not as wonderful as you think. I've seen better." I chastised myself for flirting.

He reached across the table and held my hand. Our fingers touched, and the jolt of energy made my body tense.

"I haven't," he grinned.

The heat in my cheeks redden my skin. I looked at the table.

"I need to quit," I said.

"Quit what?" he asked, but I didn't respond. "Are you changing the subject?"

I pulled my hand from his, picked up the napkin from my lap, wiped my mouth, and said, "Yes."

He leaned back in the chair and said, "I quit smoking with lollipops, and I kept the guitar in my hands. When I felt the urge, I played. Quitting is hard, but one of the easiest addictions I had to break."

One, huh? I remembered the entertainment news stated, he had many women in and out of his life through the years. Maybe he referred to being addicted to women or had an issue about being alone. I didn't want to be nosy, so I didn't ask for him to elaborate.

"What brings you to Colorado?" I inquired.

"A concert on Saturday night. How long have you been in town?"

"A few days."

"Are you here only for the class?" he asked before he took another bite of salad.

"And to visit my brother and his wife. Killing-two-birds-with-one-stone kind of thing."

"How is that?"

"Free room and board for the week."

"You think like an accountant."

"I am one."

"How long are you staying?"

"A few days," I said, being vague. "And you?"

"Not sure." He settled in the chair and studied me. "You're not a fan of mine?"

"I don't have time to be a fan of anyone's." I took another bite of salad.

Music was a big part of my life. I listened to different artists and genres, but Teddy's style always intrigued me. I collected his CDs and attended several of his fantastic concerts in the past. He captivated his audience with energetic performances, but I didn't want to admit any of this to him. I started the charade of not being a fan, and I didn't want the embarrassment of admitting I was one.

"But you have heard of me," Teddy smirked.

"Once or twice." I gleamed and hoped lettuce wasn't stuck in my teeth.

We ate in silence for a minute and stared into each other's eyes. My mind raced with questions, but I didn't want to pry. Teddy socialized with famous people and was well-traveled. He was prestigious, elegant, and sophisticated. I was a country hick from Arkansas. He and I lived in different worlds.

"Can I tell you something?" he asked.

"Sure," I said hesitantly and wiped my mouth.

He leaned into the table as if to tell me a secret. I leaned in to meet him, and he reached for my hands. I held his. The intense energy returned to my body.

"I dreamt of you," he said.

"You're a musician, and you can't come up with a better line?" I smiled.

"You think I could, but nothing beats the truth," he said. "Your beautiful green and gold eyes confirm what my dreams have told me all these years."

"What have they told you?" I asked.

"That I would meet the woman of my dreams, which is you," he said.

"You're full of it." I blushed.

"When I stare into your eyes, everything around us fades. We're left standing in a spotlight, holding hands," he said, and my smile faded. Goosebumps ran across my skin as he continued. "I'm comfortable with you."

I broke his gaze, stared at the floor, and knew the comfort he referred to between us. He rubbed my fingers as the electric shock coursed through me.

"I know this sounds strange, but when you stepped on Gene's foot, I caught a glimpse of your eyes. I felt your sincerest apology," he said.

I pulled my hands from his and straightened in my chair. How did he know about us standing under a spotlight?

"I didn't mean to make you uneasy," he said.

"I'm good." I smiled. I needed out of his presence and to focus on class. "I enjoyed this, but I do need to step out and call my daughters. One is babysitting my dogs, and I need to check on them."

"You didn't tell me you liked dogs. I'm a cat person, so we wouldn't get along." He laughed and dismissed me with a wave of his hand.

"I can't associate with a disgusting cat person. I'm 100 percent a dog person. I think cat people are weird." I, too, laughed at the stupidity of the conversation. We stood from the table, and I said, "Thank you for lunch. I wish you luck with the concert."

"I hope to see you again." He stepped close to me and held my hands. Another charge of energy jolted throughout my body. "Can I have a hug before you leave?"

"Oh, I guess." I rolled my eyes as if his request was a bother.

We embraced. A stronger electric shock coursed across my body and caught my breath. My skin tingled from his touches on my back. He held me close to his body. I closed my eyes and felt his heartbeat. I inhaled the soothing scent of his clean, refreshing cologne, and enjoyed being in his arms.

My body heat rose, and for a few seconds, I imagined his lips on mine. I pulled away, shook the idea from my mind, and stared into his big brown eyes. I needed to leave him to stop myself from any more inappropriate visions in my imagination.

"Thanks again," I said in a quiet voice, turned to Gene, and said with a stupid smile across my lips. "Thank you, Gene."

I placed my purse on my shoulder and stared into Teddy's eyes. The few glimpses of dancing lights I saw in his orbs, baffled me. I smiled, nodded, and left the kitchen.

I walked to the corridor then leaned on the hall wall across from the kitchen. I closed my eyes, and my heart raced. What caused the intense sensation across my skin with his touch?

The door swung open. Teddy stepped in front of me while Gene followed behind him.

"I need to see you again," Teddy said and pinned me against the wall. He came inches from my body. "I don't want this to end."

"You are a songwriter, Mr. Rhyme Guy." I felt the same, but movement from the crowd in the lobby caught my attention. I looked to the side of him and pointed, "You can sing your new song to the people behind you."

He glanced at the entrance of the hallway. A crowd from the conference stood in place. People held plates of food while some held glasses and watched us. No one said a word.

"I need to see you again," he whispered and turned to block my view of the spectators.

His fame didn't captivate me as much as the way his touch sent waves of pleasure through my body. His eyes drew me in with the return of the sensation of comfort. We shared a strong and sudden connection, but why?

"We have something. Do you see and feel it?" he whispered with a smile.

I diverted my eyes, rationalized the difference in our lives, and said, "You and I both have jobs to do. I would suggest you do yours, and I'll do mine. Thank you again for lunch."

He stepped from me, bowed his head while I moved my wobbly legs past him. I walked the corridor to the open lobby.

"Beth!" he exclaimed. I looked at him. Gene stood by his side and held the kitchen door open. Teddy smiled and confidently stated, "I'll see you again."

I smiled and took a few steps backward before I turned. I ran into a short, plump woman who grabbed my arms to stop me from falling into her.

"Hey." She smiled.

Teddy's laughter bellowed behind me. I laid my hand on her arm and apologized.

"I'm sorry, ma'am."

"It's okay, sweetie." She patted my hand but stared at Teddy.

I focused on the crowd of people in front of me. They stood motionless and gawked. I excused myself through the group, went up the stairs, and low voices murmured behind me as I ascended.

Once up the stairs, I retrieved my phone from my pocket. I glanced up in time as a tall, beautiful blonde-haired woman and myself were about to collide. I darted to my left.

"I'm sorry," I resounded.

She frowned when I stepped around her. I returned my attention to the phone and opened the front entrance doors. Outside on the bench, I lit a cigarette and made my calls.

With those completed, I walked into the hotel and made a pit stop in the bathroom. Trudie was drying her hands with paper towels. Her eyes caught mine through the mirror, and I smiled.

"Ms. Chambers," she said and leaned against the sink.

"Please call me, Beth," I politely said, then walked into a stall and closed the door.

Underneath the metal door, different pairs of shoes by several ladies passed in front of the stall door. The ladies' voices echoed off the tile walls. Their presence made me uncomfortable as Trudie continued to speak.

"I didn't know Mr. Nafton booked rooms at this hotel when I scheduled the conference. He surprised me when you two stood at the table this morning," Trudie faced the stall door while I watched her feet. "I'm embarrassed about how I reacted to him. He's gorgeous, and I love his music. I've been a fan since his third album. Did he say anything about me to you?"

"No," I snapped, and wished she would leave.

"Teddy Nafton is here?" a different woman asked.

"He's staying in this hotel." Trudie's voice veered in a different direction as she walked from the stall.

"I saw him and the band members this morning." Another woman beamed. "Did you know his concert sold out the first day tickets became available?"

"A few radio stations are giving them away, but otherwise, you can't get your hands on them," a second lady explained.

"What's he like, Beth? Did you have a nice lunch with him? What did you talk about?" Trudie asked.

I opened the stall door and looked at her as if she had grown an extra head. A tall woman stood at a sink, washed her hands, and looked at me through the mirror.

"You two were together in the hall," she said.

I walked to the sink, turned on the water, and washed my hands. Through the mirror, I glanced around the room. A round-bodied woman opened a stall door. She walked to the sink next to mine.

"I saw you with him," she said.

I dried my hands and didn't utter a word while the women gathered around me.

"Do you think you can get tickets to his concert?" Trudie asked.

The women confined and smothered me, so I grew irritated. How did Trudie have the audacity to question me regarding him?

"No, ma'am," I said with disdain.

"But you had lunch with him," the tall lady said.

"I don't know him," I rebuked.

I moved my arm between the tall woman and Trudie to part them. I excused myself and left the ladies in the bathroom. I fumed at the idea of Trudie questioning me. I would not have the nerve to ask someone for a favor because they knew a celebrity.

I walked into the conference room to my seat. A single white rose laid on top of my book. I glanced around the room but didn't see Teddy or Gene.

I smiled, and my frustration calmed. I gently picked up the flower and smelled the sweet scent. I sat in the chair while a few people focused on me as they prepared for class.

I held the book and flower tight against my chest and walked outside as class adjourned for the evening. A refreshing scent from the breeze in the air rejuvenated me.

Scott's car was parked on the side of the hotel. I walked to it and noticed him not inside. I looked around before I tried to open the car door. Finding it locked, I hoped I had the correct vehicle. I leaned on it and searched for him.

"Hey," Scott blurted as he walked from the building.

I smiled at the thought of him taking a week of vacation from work to spend with me. His belly slightly protruded over his khaki shorts. His red T-shirt swung as he walked toward me. His flip flops clip-clopped as he walked. His graying, dark brown, short hair gently blew in the light breeze while he smiled through his goatee.

"Were you waiting on me inside?" I asked and pointed to the hotel.

"Yeah, but are you ready?"

"Yeah."

He unlocked the car, and we sat. He turned on the vehicle, and music blared.

"Sorry." He adjusted the sound and drove from the hotel.

"Where's Carol?" I asked.

"She's at home. Do you want to go out for dinner or stay in?" he asked while I looked out the window.

"It doesn't matter. Sorry to have kept you waiting, but I didn't think you would look for me."

"It's okay. How was your day?"

"Fine. Did you have a good day off?"

"I bought a snowblower," he said excitedly in his southern accent.

"A snowblower." I laughed.

"It's a big deal here. The snow gets deep."

He explained the size and capabilities of the equipment. He beamed with joy and enthusiasm, describing his newfound treasure.

I loved my older brother, who made me laugh with his sarcasm. We teased each other, which could have caused the laugh lines around his green eyes.

He pulled into his neighborhood and pointed at my tax book that laid in my lap.

"Where did you get the flower?" I didn't respond, so he asked. "The IRS doesn't give out flowers, so who?"

"Someone I met today. It's no big deal." I didn't want to explain Teddy to him at that moment.

"Was it from a guy?" he asked and pulled into the garage.

"No, a llama," I said sarcastically. I stood then looked at him over the hood of the car and smiled. "Don't be an ass. Remove yours from my business, please."

"I have to look after my baby sister," he said as we walked to the door.

"Your baby sister can handle her own." I smiled, patted his arm then we stepped into the house.

Chapter 2

The alarm rang. I tapped the snooze on the phone for a few minutes of solitude. Teddy's eyes, smile, and touch returned to my thoughts. I opened the music app on my phone and hit the play button. I shut my eyes, listened to his sultry voice sing, and imagined being in his arms. He twirled me as we danced under a spotlight.

The snooze alarm rang again and brought me out of the fantasy. I turned off the beeping and walked into the bathroom while music played.

I stared in the mirror, and single, short, gray hair stood from my brown bangs. I scrunched my nose and twisted my fingers around it.

I plucked the hair from my head and ran my fingers over my green eyes. I pulled the skin back to relieve the one subtle wrinkle, which formed in the creases.

I'm too old for someone like Teddy Nafton. I'm ordinary, and he is manicured and pristine. I shook my head at the sight of my reflection. I twisted my hair into a bun, clasped it with a clippie, and slipped my glasses on my nose.

I dressed in a blue T-shirt and jeans, shut the music off, shuffled upstairs, and into the kitchen. Music from Scott's phone, filtered through the room while eggs and bacon sizzled in pans on the stove. Scott twirled a spatula between his fingers as he sang the song.

"Morning," I said.

"Morning. Breakfast?" He acknowledged me, and I shook my head. I opened the refrigerator and peered inside. "I'll go to the store and get you a few sodas while you're in class."

"Thanks. Where's your coffee?" I smiled, and he poured me a cup.

Carol descended the stairs as her little black and white dog, Pelt, followed. Makeup perfected, she wore black dress pants and heels, which helped her to appear taller than her five-foot stature. A pink satin blouse accented her hazel eyes. Her long, dark-red hair was pulled into a ponytail and swung as she took a step.

She was a housewife who liked to sleep in, so it shocked me to see her awake this early. I stirred sugar in the coffee and stared at her.

"What are you doing up?" I asked.

"I'm helping your brother cook," she said and poured a cup of coffee.

"You're weird." I smiled and assumed they had a special day planned.

I walked out the back door and stepped onto the porch. I sat on one of the three lounge chairs, which stood next to a firepit.

The house was among many that outlined the twelfth hole of their community golf course. The view in their backyard was two sandpits, a pond with tall cattails, and geese surrounding the water. A golfer's nightmare.

Scott held a plate in one hand and coffee in the other while Carol opened the door for him. We sat on the chairs and watched two golf carts stop on the green.

"How early do they play?" I asked.

"Some like to get out here at daybreak," Scott said then took a bite of eggs.

A robust man stood from a golf cart as his passenger pointed in the direction of his ball, which landed by the pond. Geese basked in the morning sun by the water and watched the men. The animals must have been accustomed to players. They didn't move when the gentleman walked near a few in search of the golfers' ball.

He stepped close to a goose, waved his arms, and the animal gave chase, honking at the man. He ran to the other side of his golf cart for protection from the feathered enemy. Laughter filled the air from two other gentlemen in another golf cart, which parked behind the one.

The goose honked a few more times and waddled back to the pond. The man yelled at his companions.

"That thing could have killed me. I get a drop," the heavy-set gentleman stated."

"In the sand," one of his friends yelled, and we laughed.

"Last day of class," Scott said as we watched the men.

"I can't wait to relax," I said as Pelt ran to the door and barked.

"You sure you don't want any breakfast?" Scott asked and walked to the door, then the dog ran inside.

"I'm sure. I'll be ready to leave after this cigarette," I said as Scott disappeared into the house. "I love the new place, Carol."

"Thank you. It took some time getting to know our way around town, but after four months, our neighbors are like family. I feel at home," she said and lit a cigarette.

The back-sliding glass door opened, and Pelt darted outside. Scott emerged, followed by Teddy and Gene.

"What the hell?" I was shocked, and my heart raced.

"Good morning," Teddy smiled.

"Morning," Gene grumbled.

"Please explain," I demanded while Scott laughed.

"I'm to take you to class," Teddy said and stood in front of me. "I brought you this." He held a soda toward me. "Scott said you drink these in the morning."

"Thank you, but…you're a stalker," I teased.

"No. I'm Teddy Nafton." He smiled and winked at me.

"What does that mean?"

"I can make the earth move and rock your world." He smirked.

"Not my world, and you're not all that," I reminded him.

"Yeah, he is," Carol said and stood beside me.

"It's nice to meet you, Mrs. Tarman," he said.

"It's an honor to meet you, Mr. Nafton," she said, shook his hand then he introduced her to Gene.

My head spun. Was I dreaming? Teddy Nafton casually walked through my brother's house to take me to class?

Scott stood next to me, laid his arm on my shoulder, and said, "I have their tag number, so be cool. Let me know when you arrive to class."

"How did you find out about him?" I asked.

"When I picked you up from the hotel, I walked inside to wait on you. Mr. Gene stood by the door and asked if my name was Scott."

"You two look like siblings," Gene said and pointed at us.

"I confirmed, and he told me about your lunch meeting. I followed him upstairs and met Mr. Nafton. We spoke for a few minutes, then arranged this," he said, and I punched his arm.

"You could've told me you knew," I said to Scott as he rubbed his arm.

"Why didn't you tell us about him?" Carol asked as she held Teddy's arm.

"You know why, Carol," Scott said. "That's how Beth operates. She keeps everything to herself. Remember the divorce? She didn't tell us for months."

"Are you ashamed of me, babe?" Teddy asked.

I slowly shook my head and stared into his big brown eyes. Black magnetic dust as if on an etch-a-sketch formed a word in my thoughts.

"*Hi.*" The sound of his voice played in my mind.

I tilted my head and stared into his eyes. Did his lips move?

He shook his head and smiled. I could live in his eyes forever.

He was a beautiful man in his sky-blue shirt and pants. A small gold chain laid on his chest.

He was in shape from performing on stage. He chuckled, held my hand, and I blushed from imagining him shirtless.

"Everyone, call me Teddy, and this is Gene." He continued to stare at me and asked, "Would it be okay if we took you to class?"

"Thank you, but this is weird. You drove from the hotel, to pick me up, to drive back to the hotel," I said.

"We're going to get to know each other," he stated firmly. I didn't say a word but stared at him while he shifted his weight. A few moments of intent staring and no words, he tensed, glanced at Scott, Carol, Gene then back to me. He smiled. "If it's okay with you."

"You are a stalker." I laughed.

"I'm not…"

"Thank you, Mr. Nafton." I smiled to help ease him. He laid his hand over mine. I enjoyed the comfort of his touch. "I can't believe you're here."

"I am," he said.

"Want breakfast?" Scott asked the men.

"No, thank you," Teddy said but didn't take his eyes from me.

"Let me gather my things. Excuse me," I said and walked past him. Scott followed me into the house, leaving Carol, Gene, and Teddy outside. "I can't believe you, Scott. What did he say to you?"

"I told you," he said. "Why don't you let me into your life?"

"You have to contend with things here," I said and walked to the downstairs door.

He grabbed my elbow, spun me, and said, "The family and the business are not yours alone to carry. I'm here to help."

"I know," I said.

"He seems like a nice guy, but superstar or not, I'll take him out if anything happens to you."

I rolled my eyes at him, then walked downstairs. I gathered my purse and tax book, then met Teddy and Gene upstairs at the door. We walked to the SUV, and Gene opened the car door.

"Do you want me to drive?" I asked Gene.

"I can do it, Ms. Chambers. Thank you," he grumbled.

"It's Beth, and you're not a morning person, huh."

"No, ma'am," he said as we sat in the car.

"Did y'all rehearse late last night?" I asked, and Teddy nodded. "Aren't you tired, or do you always get up this early?"

"They always rehearse late and no. He doesn't get up early," Gene snapped.

"Please excuse, Mr. Morning Sunshine. He's in a bad mood." Teddy smiled at Gene.

"Like you're happy in the morning, mister, I will not get out of bed before noon," Gene said. "This is a rarity to see him awake at this time, Beth. I must hand it to him. He's two for two."

"That's right, man. Don't forget about yesterday," Teddy said defensively. "I might have slept on the plane when we left Michigan, but I was awake when it landed."

I like the way they spoke with each other. They were friends instead of employer and employee. I felt relaxed to know they cared for each other.

"I want to know you," Teddy said and held my hand. "I hope you give me a chance."

"We'll see, but you haven't impressed me, yet. I don't know if you can hold my attention." I flirted.

"Be my guest at the concert tomorrow night. I'll get your attention." He smiled.

"I've been to a few of your concerts. You were born with a guitar in your hand."

"You're saying I have talent," Teddy said as Gene sat quietly.

"No, I'm not." I smiled.

"When did you attend?"

"Years ago. It looked like you knew what you were doing."

"You're a fan." He shoulder bumped me.

"No. I'm not." I laughed.

"I can have a car get you, Scott, and Carol around six for dinner tomorrow night. Come to my show and let me impress you, babe." He smiled.

"You don't have to call me babe." I blushed.

"You don't like that term? I can think of something else."

I thought a moment, took my hand from his, waved it in the air, and replied, "It's better than what you could call me."

He chuckled at my expression then asked, "Do you have any more siblings?"

"Yes, sir. I have an older sister back home and one who passed several years ago. I'm the baby of our family, and Scott is the oldest."

"I see who I need to get approval from."

"Approval for what?" I asked with raised eyebrows. A few seconds of silence and gazing at one another, I smiled. "You don't know the half of it, Mr. Nafton." The longer I stared into his eyes, the more comfortable I felt. "It's not his approval alone you need, but twenty-five to thirty others. My family is huge, and we are close. Some say we're strangely close. Not southern close like cousins marrying cousins, but we've had people outside the family tell us it's unusual."

"Anything weird?" he asked and lowered his head along with his voice.

"No. I mean, we all speak to each other at least once a week, if not once a day."

"You have your own entourage," Teddy said.

"You could say that. I'm famous, you know."

"I thought I've heard of you. The Southern Beth."

"The Southern Ninja Beth," I corrected him.

"Yeah, about those ninja moves. I might need to see some of them," he playfully said.

"I can't show 'em to you. They're ninja secrets." I smirked.

"I knew I would like you." He stared at me. "Scott said you aren't seeing anyone."

"I don't have time to see anyone and quit talking about me to him," I said in shock.

"No time?" he chuckled.

"I'm a busy woman," I said seriously but wanted his focus off me. "Where's your girl or girls?"

"Avoiding the subject because it's about you." He was right, and he widened his smile while I awaited his response. "I don't have a girl per se."

"You aren't dating anyone?" I asked.

"What about the concert?"

"Changing the subject?" I squinted my eyes at him.

"I'll arrange everything." He smiled.

"You're bad at changing the subject." I laughed as he adjusted himself in the seat. "I need to check with Scott and Carol. We're planning a day at Pikes Peak."

"I hope you pick me over a mountain, or I'm doing something wrong," he said.

I stared into his brown eyes, wanted to jump with excitement, and scream, "Yes, I want to come to your concert, get to know you, and live in your gaze." But I kept my cool and calmly said, "We don't want to impose."

"It's not an imposition. I would love to have you…join me," he chuckled.

The scent of his cologne made me relax, and I enjoyed being in his presence. "It's fine with me if Scott and Carol want to go."

"They already said yes."

"You asked them before you asked me?"

"I knew you would say yes." He smirked.

I smiled, rolled my eyes, and said, "Thank you for the rose yesterday."

"You're welcome."

My face blushed. I scorned myself for flirting with him.

"Well, Mr. Nafton. What do you want from me? I'll tell you anything." He stared at me, and I said, "Let me reiterate, I will TELL you anything. Not DO anything."

"How long were you married?" he asked.

"You have to start there, huh," I said, and he nodded. "I'll make this easy for you. I met my husband when I was sixteen, pregnant at seventeen, married at eighteen, and was so for twenty-seven years. He fell in love with someone else because we grew apart or some bullshit like that, but either way, we divorced. I have two daughters and three granddaughters who are my everything. I've been divorced for a few years and no. I'm not seeing anyone, nor do I want to at this point in my life. Does that help?"

"Yeah," he said. "How old are the kids, and what are their names?"

"Lucy is my oldest, and she's twenty-eight. She's marrying Ellis next year, and they have two daughters. Sadie is eight years old. Kara is nine months. My youngest daughter, Danielle, is twenty-two. She's married to Colby, and they have a daughter named Gabi, who is eight months old. I won't leave out my two baby bichon dogs. Izzy is five, and Olly is one. Now you know my life, and I mean all my life."

"You don't look like a grandma." He stared at me. A few seconds passed, and his eyes widened as if he had a revelation. He grabbed my hand and said, "Oh, wow. You're a grandma."

"Do you wanna stop the car and let me walk now?" I asked.

Gene smiled at me through the rearview mirror.

"No. You're a beautiful granny, but you don't look old enough," Teddy said.

"Thank you. I had my kids young, and they had theirs young. Also, I'm not a granny or a grandma." I corrected him. "I'm a Mimi."

"A Mimi?" he smiled.

"Yeah. Granny sounds old." I smiled. I never heard that Teddy had children, so I asked Gene, "Do you have kids?"

"I have two boys. Tyler is seventeen, and Bart is fourteen."

"Ewe, teenagers. I feel for you. I like kids. We have a lot of them in my family," I chuckled.

"Aren't you going to ask if I have any?" Teddy asked.

"I don't remember hearing you do, and I can't see you having any." He held my gaze and pouted. "But, I will ask. Do you have kids?"

"I do." He beamed and squeezed my hand that he wouldn't let go. "Since you're a fan, you know my band Five/Ten."

"I'm a fan of theirs, but not yours." I smiled.

"Kyle is my son," he said bluntly.

"Your drummer?" I asked, and he nodded. "Why or how have you kept him out of the public eye?"

"Back then, we didn't worry about social sites or the Internet. Honestly, I didn't know he existed until he was seven. His mother, Katrina, notified me about him when she was diagnosed with cancer. She wanted to make sure he would be taken care of, if and when she passed."

"That's awful, but this is playing like a soap opera," I remarked.

"My attorneys informed her to get a DNA test to prove Kyle was mine. You would not believe how many women claim they're carrying my baby." He smiled. "She agreed to the test, and it came back positive. We shared custody before she was murdered."

"Kyle lived with me from then on. I protected him from the public. He never told anyone he was my kid, and I never told him not too. I didn't care if the world knew once he became old enough to care for himself."

"Oh, wow, you're a dad," I said with wide eyes.

"Yeah, I know," he proudly said. "I like kids and dogs and cats."

"Me too." I hesitated. "Kyle didn't find her, did he?"

"No. He spent the weekend with me when she died."

"That must have been hard on you both," I said.

"They never found her killer, and sometimes it gets to him. Authorities said it was a drug deal gone bad, but…what drug deal is good?" he asked, which made me slightly smile because of his expression. "The cancer caused her a lot of pain, so she bought pills off the street and ran with the wrong crowd."

"That's sad, but why did she wait until Kyle was older to inform you? You'd think you being who you are, she would've wanted a piece of the pie," I said.

"She said she didn't want him raised in the spotlight." He rubbed my fingers and said, "I'm proud of Kyle. He works with his own band along with me. He's a busy guy, and he's making a name for himself."

"I'm dumbfounded." I stared at him for a second. "I'm kind of sad for you."

"Why?"

"You didn't get to see him take his first step or hear his first word. You missed the best years. I'm sorry."

"I didn't know how special those years were until Gene had his boys. I got to see them crawl and walk."

"Why are you telling me this?" I asked.

He grew quiet and stared into my eyes for a few moments. "You didn't tell Scott and Carol you met me."

"It's none of their business," I said.

"Have you told your kids about me?"

"No. They're grown, and I don't want to give a play by play of my life. I'm not…" I stumbled, trying to think of a reasonable excuse. "What is there to say? I met Teddy Nafton?" I asked in a funny voice.

"Well, yeah. Are you sure you know who I am?" He laughed.

"I didn't mean it like that." I smiled. "I'll be on vacation as soon as this class ends, which means I can relax and not answer to anyone. I can enjoy the rest of my time here in peace."

"Where in Arkansas are you from?"

"You're observant." I smiled and let go of his hand. "I have a question for you."

"Changing the subject." He shook his head.

"I am." I smiled.

"This is my time to grill you, but go ahead."

"Why me?"

"What time is it, Gene?" Teddy asked.

"We should arrive in fifteen minutes. You'll be on time, Beth," Gene informed.

"Are you changing the subject?" I asked.

"No," he said with a slight smile.

I could melt in his eyes and wanted his touch, but I broke our stare, looked to the floor of the car, and asked again, "So…why me?"

"Why not?"

"I'm not worthy. You're you, and I'm me. We have nothing in common," I said.

"What makes you think that?" he asked, tilting his head.

"Do you know who you are?" I widened my smile.

"I know who I am. Do you know who you are?"

"You're avoiding the question altogether." I laughed. "I'll let you off the hook, but I have one more for you."

"Ask me anything."

"Are you sure you don't have a girlfriend?"

"I'm not seeing anyone seriously."

"You have a new woman every day of the week. I've heard about you celebrities. Especially, you musicians."

"I stopped that mess last week," he said, which made me laugh. "I'm joking. That's not how I operate." We smiled at each other. "You were supposed to talk about yourself. Instead, I told you about me. How do you do that?"

"Do what?" I asked, loving the sight of his eyes.

"Make me feel so comfortable, I want to tell you my secrets. That's one reason it's you."

"You make me feel the same, except I don't have secrets, and that's not a good enough reason." My cheeks ached from grinning.

"Everyone has secrets, Beth. They might not be as big as what I told you, but you have them. I'm the one to get them out of you," he said.

I blushed, knowing he wanted more from me. "Teddy." I placed my hand on his knee and felt the charge between us. "Thank you for everything. Yesterday and this morning were great, but..." He looked at my hand, rested his on top of mine, and our eyes met again. "I'm not looking for a relationship or a one-night stand. I have a lot going on in my life, and I don't have time for either. I can use a friend, but that's all I'm offering. Do you understand?"

He smirked and said, "Yes. That's all I want from you right now. You're easy to talk too. I want to know you and show you a good time with no strings attached." He added, "And your phone number would help."

I looked into his eyes. Sadness and loneliness rushed over me. I shook the feelings from my thoughts then slightly nodded. I reached into my purse and pulled a business card from my wallet.

"That's my cell number." I gave it to him.

"They're here, Teddy." Gene turned into the parking lot of the hotel.

"This early?" He looked out the window.

"I need a plan," Gene said.

"Dammit." Teddy reached for his phone.

Several people stood around the front door. Some held cameras while others spoke on their phones.

"Reporters?" I asked.

"I said no media, Shelly," Teddy said into the phone while Gene drove past the hotel.

"Take me a few blocks from here. I'll walk," I said.

"No," Teddy said and held my hand. He raised the phone to his ear and said, "Find out who told them our location." Then he hung up.

"You know who it was," Gene said.

"I can walk a block or two," I said as Gene drove to the back parking lot of the hotel.

"We'll think of something," Teddy said to me.

"Drop me off here." I glanced out the window and didn't see anyone.

"I'm sorry," Teddy said.

"It's part of your life, not mine," I said. "Please let me out, Gene."

"I didn't mean for this to happen," Teddy said as Gene stopped the car.

"It's okay. They're here for me. They follow me like I'm some kind of superstar," I joked.

"That was lame." Teddy smiled.

"I know." I winked at him. "Thank you for this morning."

I gathered my book and purse as he said, "I want to apologize for yesterday. I shouldn't have stepped out of the kitchen after you, but…" he looked at the floor of the Caddy. "You had several stares and a few questions about me."

"Are you spying on me?"

"It's protection," he murmured.

"What?" I asked.

"Nothing." He looked at his clasped hands. "I drew attention to you. Once I did, I thought you were going to have a hard time being you know me." He raised his eyes, looked at me, and tilted his head. "I'm not making things any better because of the reporters waiting outside of the hotel."

"I don't know you," I said.

"You will," he said.

"I can take care of myself, so it's all good."

"I bet you can." He gently rubbed his finger across my cheek. I jumped as the shock of electricity came from his fingertips. "You do feel it."

I blushed and bowed my head, "I need to go."

"This is another reason it's you," he said in a serious tone. I slipped the seat belt off, fumbled for the door handle, and he asked, "Are you going to be okay?"

"Yes, sir." I opened the door, stood, and looked back at him. "Thank you again," I said, and he nodded at me. I smiled then walked to the front hotel entrance.

Chapter 3

Teddy vanished into the hotel. A few reporters went to their vehicles. Others sat on a half wall by the front door, but none followed him inside.

I walked inside and down the stairs. A small crowd surrounded the table in front of the conference room. A sea of people parted, and a muscular man guided Teddy from the table.

"Learn stuff," Teddy said and winked at me in passing.

I shook my head, smiled, and walked to the table. Trudie stepped behind it and held a clipboard toward me.

"You can sign in here, Ms. Chambers."

"Thank you."

I signed the sheet, handed it to her, then she said, "Follow me, please."

She led me into the conference room and pointed to a seat next to the back door. I thanked her, placed my book on the table, and thought it strange to have her escort me.

"They have donuts if you prefer them," Gene said and sat two sodas and cookies on the table.

"Um, thank you, but what are you doing?" I asked.

"Joining you for class." He sat in the chair next to me.

"Why? Did Teddy tell you too?" I asked while the speaker stepped to the front of the room.

"Open your eyes, honey. People saw you with him yesterday. I know they were talking about you two. I'm good at observing people. It's mine and Rick's job. We take it seriously," he said.

"Who is Rick, and you guys are watching me?" I asked with wide eyes, being offended.

"He's Teddy's other bodyguard, and yeah. People are wondering who you are and why you were with Teddy. I'm here to make sure everything goes smooth today."

"Let's get started," the speaker stated, and the lights dimmed, so we could see the projection screen.

I found a piece of paper in my book and wrote:

You need to be with Teddy.

I showed Gene, and he took the pen from my hand:

I'm okay, but if I snore, elbow me.

I smiled and wrote:

Get rest. I'll be okay.

Gene looked at it, shook his head, then pointed to the speaker to tell me to pay attention. I slumped in the chair, folded my arms across my chest, and knew he'd won this dispute.

My phone vibrated to alert me to a new text.

Did you make it okay? - Scott

Yeah. - I texted.

If you need me, call.

My mind swirled with thoughts of Teddy. Why did he think HIS bodyguard needed to be with me? Over an hour and a half into class, my phone vibrated once again with a text:

It's Teddy. How are things?

I'm mad. Gene needs sleep. - I texted.

I want him with you.

> *You don't have to take care of me. I'm a big girl. I won't hurt you and tell any secrets. I don't want to feel like a prisoner, nor do I want to keep Gene from his job with you.*

After several minutes, he texted back:

It's not your call. I'll see you at lunch.

Not my call? I grew irritated with him thinking I needed a babysitter, so I texted:

I can handle things.

Learn stuff. Later, babe. - He texted.

Fifteen minutes before the morning break, Gene leaned into me. "If you want to step out, we need to do it now."

I followed him to the lobby, walked past the table, but Trudie stopped us. She embraced me.

"Thank you, Beth. Teddy gave me two VIP tickets, so I'll see you tomorrow night."

"Oh, man," I said disapprovingly and broke her embrace.

"Thank you for saying something to him." She beamed.

"I didn't," I said then stepped into the bathroom while Gene waited patiently by the door.

I hoped she wouldn't follow, so I could have a minute to myself. What does Teddy and Gene think will happen to me? I'm a nobody.

I washed my hands, then joined Gene. We walked through the downstairs lobby. He guided me past the kitchen and out a back door. The daylight hit my eyes, and I squinted. We walked to a shade tree, and Gene leaned against it. He reached for a pack of cigarettes in his pocket.

"I didn't know you smoked," I said and lit my cigarette while my phone rang.

I answered, and Lois, one of my employees, asked about a client's tax folder. During our brief conversation, Gene held my elbow, guided me close to him, and faced me toward the building. He stood in front of me while I spoke with her.

I finished the call and tapped on Lucy's number. While the phone rang, I asked, "What are you doing?"

"Placing you in the shade," he said and glanced around.

I gave him a weird glare as Lucy answered on the second ring.

"What's up?"

"How are the kids and dogs?" I asked.

"Everyone is fine. The dogs aren't eating their food, but they're drinking. Should I be concerned?" she asked.

"I bet they'll be okay, but lay off the treats. If they don't eat in the next day or two, worry."

"I'm going to put you on speaker. Talk to them and let me see what they do."

"Okay." I played along. "Are you ready?"

"Go," she said.

"Hey, Izzy. Hey, Olly. What are my babies doing? Are you being good?" I asked in a funny voice.

Lucy laughed. "They're looking at the phone and turning their heads at the same time. Not in the same direction, but at the same time. That's funny."

"Don't let Ellis beat you guys up," I said in the same funny voice, and Gene smiled.

"They went into Kara's room." Lucy laughed and took me off speaker.

"Keep me posted on their eating habits," I said. "I have to go to class, but is everything okay?"

"Yeah. Danielle and Gabi came over last night. We were on the Internet to get Christmas ideas for the kids. The top story was Teddy Nafton touring again. He's playing in Denver tomorrow night. Since he's your favorite, ask Scott to take you," she suggested.

The color left my face. I stared at Gene and laughed nervously.

"Scott doesn't want to take me to see him. He doesn't like Teddy."

"You never know. I wish I could go."

"Hopefully, he'll tour in Arkansas. We could have a girls' night out with you, Danielle, and me." I dug a hole for myself with her.

"He's starting a tour with his new album, and since it's been a while, it's creating a buzz. I'll keep an eye out for him coming here." Thankfully, she changed the subject. "Are Scott and Carol settled in their new house?"

"Yeah. It's beautiful. I'll tell them you said hi and call if you need me," I said, trying not to sound nervous.

"Take pictures and relax."

"I will. Love you."

"Love you too. Bye," Lucy said, and I ended the call.

Gene placed his hand on my shoulder. "Is everything okay?" I explained what Lucy said. "Why didn't you tell her about him?" he asked with a puzzled expression.

"I choked, but it's not a big deal, right?" I looked for Gene to guide me. "Teddy will be a thing in the past come tomorrow night. I go home, tell both girls, get yelled at, have a good laugh, and move on."

Gene smiled, patted my shoulder, put his cigarette out, and moved his hand to my back. "We need to go inside."

"Okay." I put my cigarette out.

He didn't remove his hand until we stood at our seats in the conference room.

"Do you want something to drink?" he asked.

"No, thank you, but go ahead," I said.

"I'll be right back."

I retrieved my phone, then a short bald man stood over me in front of the table. "Can you get me tickets for Teddy's concert?"

"Pardon me?" I asked when Gene returned. The man repeated his question. "I don't think so," I said. He stared between Gene and me as he sat at a few tables from us.

"You're bringing attention to me by being like a freakin' bodyguard, Gene," I said.

"I am a freaking bodyguard. Let's get through this day."

I turned my attention to the text I typed and sent it to Danielle. I didn't pay attention to the speaker. I immersed myself deep in thought about Teddy and now the kids.

Gene snored. I bumped his arm. He shifted his weight then fell back asleep in the chair. An hour slipped by before Gene jumped and reached for his phone.

He looked at it and whispered, "I'll be right back."

He left the room, and my phone vibrated with a text.

How's class? - The text read from Teddy's number.

Boring. Gene needs sleep and I hope you did. - I texted.

Not yet. Please forgive me, but I can't meet you for lunch.

Nope. You blew it, Mr. Brown Eyes. I'll never eat again.

Ha. Ha. Ms. Sexy. I bet I could get you eating grapes in bed. - he texted.

With you? I don't think so. Your not my type. I like grapes, but they're not my favorite. - I texted.

With who and what is your favorite?

Quit flirting and take care of what you need to. I have to learn stuff. ☺

Lol. Your right. I'll see you later.

I waited for a few seconds to see if I would receive another response but didn't. I saved his contact information into my phone and texted:

Noah Parker and bananas.

"We need to leave in ten minutes for lunch," Gene whispered as he sat next to me.

I nodded and was glad to leave class a few minutes early. After I stacked papers and organized my space, he held my elbow and signaled for me to get my purse.

Trudie told us to have a good lunch when we passed her station. Gene led me up the stairs, out the front door, and we stopped in front of the hotel, under the awning. He held a car fob in the air and pushed a button. A black SUV blinked its lights.

"Come on." He led me to a Cadillac.

He opened the passenger door. Five white roses and one single red rose with a note attached, laid on the seat. I picked them up and sat in the car while Gene closed the door.

"Do you want a veggie burger? I know a place," he said.

"That's fine, but where did the car come from?"

"Aren't you going to read the note? Most women are suckers for flowers." He backed out of the parking spot.

"I'm not one of those women." I waited for him to answer as he pulled into traffic.

"The car came from Teddy. He texted me to get the key from the front desk. I grabbed it and made sure reporters were gone."

"Do you want me to drive?" I asked with a smile.

"No."

I shook my head and opened the note, which read:

Five beautiful roses for five people I hope to meet someday.

One red rose for my babe. See you tonight.

Teddy

"That was sweet." I liked the flowers but felt strange, receiving them from him. "Does he get his way all the time?"

Gene turned into a fast-food restaurant and asked, "Do you want to eat here or carry it to the hotel?"

"The hotel, if you don't mind." I glared at him and repeated my question. "Does he?"

He ordered lunch, and after a small argument of who was paying, he won and drove us to the hotel. He saw my frustration from no response.

"Yes, Beth. He's Teddy."

"He's a spoiled megastar," I said with disappointment.

"To a degree," Gene said with a smile. "Several people will agree with whatever he wants, but a few of us tell him no."

"How much are VIP tickets?"

"Why?"

"He gave Trudie two because of me," I said.

"No, it wasn't. Teddy does that kind of thing." Gene watched my expression.

It saddened me to owe anyone anything. "He wouldn't have if we hadn't met."

"Wow," Gene looked at me, quizzically. "It's okay."

"I'll figure it out." I dropped the subject and settled in the car with my lunch. "How did you and Teddy meet?"

"Have you been to any of his afterparties?" I shook my head and took another bite of my burger while he explained, "I worked as a bouncer at one of his afterparties in Virginia. My boss, at the time, placed me next to the stage. Some guys got drunk, started a fight, and I took them both out with a few punches. Me and another guy grabbed them and hauled them outside. I returned to my post, and Teddy never missed a beat."

"After his set, he said to come work for him, and he would double my pay. That was a lot of money for a guy my age. I was twenty-six, no family, and wasn't married. I had nothing holding me there. I quit my job, packed, and have been working for him since."

"That's cool. He's lucky to have you not only as a bodyguard but as a friend," I said.

"A guy like Teddy has to be selective with his friends. He's had several people who he thought were his friends, turn on him, especially after he made a name for himself," Gene said.

"He works hard. No man I know deserves the fame and fortune more than him. As you know, there are many famous people like him, yet there isn't anyone like him. I would never do anything to hurt him, and I would stop anyone who tried. I love him like a little brother. He's part of my family."

"You protect family," I smiled.

"I can't believe you didn't tell your daughter about him."

"I know, right?" I couldn't believe it myself. I stared at Gene for a second and asked, "Is this a get-to-know-Beth day? Are you taking notes for him?"

"I'm keeping my eyes on you," he said.

"What kind of grade do I have?"

"D minus. It'll take a lot for you to make an A plus in my book."

"That's a high bar, Gene. Unfortunately, I won't be around to make the grade."

"We'll see." We finished lunch, crinkled our wrappers, and placed them in the bag. "I guess it's time to head back to snoozeville. Smoke first?"

I nodded, took the last sip of soda, and placed the roses in the cup. "Can you crack the window, please? I don't want the flowers to wilt."

"Okay."

We stepped out of the car, lit our cigarettes, and I asked, "What does your wife think of your work?"

"She married me when I was doing this, and she knows I'll retire or die doing this."

"What about your boys? How are they with Dad being gone? I would like to see pictures." I raised my eyebrows and looked at him.

He laughed, pulled his phone from his pocket, and tapped on his photo app. "The boys are used to my work schedule. Teddy makes sure we have family time when he tours. Shelly, his manager, schedules his concerts, so we're home on all holidays. Teddy will fly the family to us on occasion, or if we request. If we travel during the summer, the whole family can join us."

I looked at pictures of his handsome sons and beautiful wife while we spoke about them. I put my cigarette out and patted his arm.

"It's nice to know you, Gene. Thank you," I said.

He led me into the hotel and downstairs to the conference room. Everyone from class sporadically walked into the room. As soon as I sat in the chair, I realized I hadn't signed in for the afternoon class session. I stood to go out the doors when Gene placed his big hand on my shoulder and stopped me.

"I have to sign in, or I won't get my credits," I said impatiently. "If I don't get those, I can't prepare taxes. If I can't prepare taxes, I don't have a business. Do you see where I'm going with this? I don't want to move in with you, Gene."

"Please wait until class starts."

"Okay." I set my purse on the floor and looked at my book. "Gene." I elbowed him in the side.

I pointed to the book. Names, phone numbers, and messages were scribbled and addressed to Teddy, on two pages I left exposed.

"That's weird," I said.

"That's nothing. At least, a few asked for you to give him their number." He leaned back in the chair.

The speaker stepped in front of the room, and the lights dimmed. We were an hour in the afternoon session. Gene slept the best he could in the stiff chair. I needed to go to the bathroom, sign the sheet, and I would be back in a few minutes. I slowly stood, so not to disturb him.

I stepped to the table outside the door, signed the sheet, and walked into the restroom. The bathroom door opened, and footsteps clapped on the tile while I stepped out of the stall. I was surprised to see a man leaning on a sink.

He was a foot taller than me with a big beer belly. He was young, and his black beard and hair looked scruffy around the edges. He wore dark-blue dress pants and a white button-down shirt with the top four or so buttons, unlatched, revealing a thick, black, hairy chest. He stepped close to me.

"Can I help you?" I asked with the stall door against my back.

He stood an arm's length from me and asked in a gruff voice, "Can you introduce me to Teddy?"

"No." I tried to squeeze by him, but he lightly grabbed my waist.

"I would like to meet him," he insisted.

"I can't help you." I placed my hands on his arm, pushing, but couldn't get free.

"You can, and you will. Call him," he demanded and tightened his grip on my waist while he blocked my exit.

"I can't," I said forcefully and stared into his dark beady green eyes.

The door swung open, and Gene appeared. He stepped close to us.

"Let go of her, buddy," he growled.

The man removed his arm from my waist and held them in the air. He stepped a few feet from me.

"No harm. I need to meet Teddy. I have a demo for him," the guy said.

"That's not going to happen, mister," Gene snarled, held my elbow, and turned us to the door.

"Thank you," I said in a low voice as Gene escorted me out of the bathroom.

He held tight to my elbow and led me to the seat in the conference room. He pointed to it.

"Don't move," he said in a low forceful voice

I felt like a child scorned by her parent. The man who was in the bathroom walked into the conference room. He stared at us and sat at the front table. I trembled, suddenly aware of how knowing someone famous could put me in danger.

"How did you know he was in there?" I whispered to Gene.

"I didn't. I was mad that you left, so I walked out. Trudie pointed to the bathroom. It was dumb luck I walked in when I did." He glared at me.

He pointed to the speaker for me to drop the subject. I turned my gaze to the front of the room. The afternoon went fast.

The last break came, but I didn't move from the chair. Gene walked to the back of the room and retrieved two water bottles. He sat one in front of me as a lady walked past and dropped a piece of paper on my book. Gene retrieved the paper, read it, and handed it to me.

You're not Teddy's type. Have him call me. 720-555-8794. Greta.

"This is ridiculous," I said.

"This is normal. People react to celebrities in different ways," Gene said.

"Teddy's the celebrity. Not me."

"Most of these people saw you guys together, briefly. Imagine if you were photographed and seen with him regularly."

"Let's don't let that happen," I said.

Trudie came to our table. "I'll understand if you need to leave early. You signed in, Beth, so you'll get your certificate. I'll bring it tomorrow night. You have the material, so read it."

"Thank you," I said.

Gene retrieved his phone, typed something, and said, "We'll leave once class starts."

Fifteen minutes past, and he motioned for me to gather my belongings. He held my elbow, and we walked out of the conference room.

"Do you want me to drive?" I asked with enthusiasm while we walked to the car.

"No," he said bluntly and opened the door for me.

I sat in the car, and as he sat in the driver's seat, I asked, "What do you think that guy would have done if you hadn't shown?"

"I don't know." He pulled out of the hotel parking lot.

"I could have handled it." I smiled.

"I didn't see you use any ninja moves," he chuckled.

"The situation didn't escalate to the point of using them." I laughed.

I stared out the window for a second, and asked, "How does this Rick guy play into the bodyguard role for Teddy?"

"Teddy has always had two bodyguards. Years ago, we fired my co-worker and hired Rick temporarily to help with a concert. At an afterparty in Memphis, while Teddy was playing, a woman rushed the stage, and Rick stopped her. Once we had her outside, we found a pair of scissors in her coat pocket. She said she wanted a lock of

Teddy's hair. Rick proved himself to us that night, so like me, he's been with Teddy ever since," Gene explained.

"I can't get over people wanting so much from Teddy," I said.

"Some people want him to acknowledge them while some may want to hurt him because of the music he produces. Some want to thank him because he affected their lives in some way. Others may want something physical from him. Like the guy in the bathroom. All he wanted was for Teddy to hear his music in hopes of getting a record deal," Gene said.

"Has he ever been hurt by one of these crazy fans? I mean, has he put you in a situation like I did today?"

"Not intentionally. We've had close calls. He's been doing this for a long time, so he knows what he's dealing with when he goes into the public."

"I'm glad I haven't told anyone about him after what happened today. I meant it when I said I'm a private person." I turned my attention on the passing street signs.

"You impressed him because of that. He feels he can trust you," he said.

"I'm not trying to impress anyone, but my business is my business, his is his, and yours is yours."

He nodded, turned the car into Scott's subdivision, and asked, "When do you leave Colorado?"

"In a few days and not looking forward to the plane ride. I hate flying," I said. "When do y'all leave?"

"When Teddy says, go," Gene said.

"What the hell?" I asked, seeing another Caddy in Scott's drive.

Chapter 4

"Are you going to tell Teddy about the incident?" I held Gene's arm before he opened the car door.

"I don't hide anything from him, so if he asks, I'll have too," he said.

He came around the car and took the book from my arm.

"I can carry it," I said.

"You get the flowers." He pointed.

"I can do that, along with four sacks of groceries, a bag of dog food, and a kid under my arm." I smiled.

"Good for you, but today, carry your purse and flowers." He smirked and closed the door behind me.

We walked inside. Carol, Scott, Teddy, two women, and a gentleman sat in the living room. Teddy rose from the couch and embraced me.

"How was class?" he asked as the electricity flowed between us.

"Thankfully, it's over." I pulled away and looked at Gene, who stood behind me.

"Did you learn anything?" Teddy teased Gene but kept his arm draped over my shoulder.

"I know what a 1099-K is now," he said with no enthusiasm.

"I'm shocked. I thought you only saw the back of your eyelids," I said.

"Those are pretty flowers." Carol pointed at them.

"Thank you, Teddy." I hugged him once more, but he held me longer. I closed my eyes and enjoyed his scent and touch. "They're beautiful, but they don't make up for Gene being my spying babysitter. Not to mention Trudie's gift."

"She told you?" he asked.

"Yes. How much do I owe you?"

"Nothing. I had them lying around."

"You're a stalking liar," I teased and walked to the kitchen.

I added the flowers to the one from yesterday, which was in a vase. I got a cold soda from the refrigerator and grabbed my cigarettes out of my purse.

"Does anyone want anything to drink?" I asked.

"No thanks," Teddy answered for everyone, but stared at me and smiled. "Wouldn't you prefer a banana?"

"I'm good." I blushed.

He draped his arm on my shoulder again and said, "Let me introduce you. This is my manager, Shelly Manning, my guitarist, Susan Certs, and my bodyguard, Rick Landerson."

"It's nice to meet you," I said to Shelly as I shook her hand.

Shelly arrived with Teddy at the hotel and reminded him of his shoot. She stared at me, emotionless. She wore jeans and a yellow T-shirt with a white sweater.

I looked at Susan, then shook her hand.

"I've heard of Susan Certs. Your wonderful, and it's nice to meet you," I said.

She was a small, shy girl with shoulder-length, strawberry-blonde hair. Her face showed a few freckles dotting her nose. Her thin lips and blue eyes gave her an innocent essence. She wore jeans, a blue T-shirt, a matching blue baseball cap, and a loose jean jacket. Her small frame made her look like a teenager, but she could play the guitar with the best.

"Mr. Landerson," I said and shook his hand.

"Call me, Rick." He smiled.

He was the gentleman who led Teddy to the hotel stairs, but now I got a good look at him. He was more muscular than Gene, but not as tall. He was thinner, a little younger, and he sported a buzzed military haircut with a small amount of brown hair protruding from his scalp. His clean-shaven, square jawline, held a slight smile across his thin lips. His tiny, dark-brown eyes looked me over.

"What's going on?" I asked and walked to the back door.

Teddy reached around me, slid the door open, and said, "Noah Parker, huh."

"All the way, baby," I flirted then walked outside.

"I met him once. He's an ass," Teddy said as he followed me.

"He has a fine one, but I doubt he is one," I said and leaned against the porch railing, as everyone joined us.

"You would be surprised." Teddy stood next to me with his hip touching mine.

"What are y'all doing here?" I asked as I felt electricity from Teddy's touch.

"I'm offering you and Carol a shopping spree. You can purchase outfits for tomorrow night's show. Shelly, Susan, and Rick will help you," Teddy said.

My smile faded, and I looked at Carol. She bowed her head to avoid eye contact with me. I shook my head and turned to Teddy, who brightly smiled.

"It's on me," he sang and raised his eyebrows.

"Thank you for the offer, but I'm not going to take your money. Also, I hate shopping. I'm grateful for your kindness, but I'm going to decline," I said.

"I told him you don't like going." Carol waved her hand at me.

"What do you not like about it?" Teddy asked with a puzzled expression.

I smiled so as not to hurt his feelings. "Everything. The crowds, trying on items, and overpriced clothes."

"I've never met a woman who hates to shop," he said.

"I like buying things for the grandkids or my kids, but as far as I go, I like it if I can sit in my underwear at home and purchase things from the Internet. I can complain in the privacy of my own home."

"I would like to see that one day," Teddy said.

Carol stood on the other side of me and made me feel like a Beth sandwich. "Can we please go?" She sounded like a little girl.

"It'll be fun and won't take long." I looked at her over my glasses. "We can go to a toy store."

I stepped from between Carol and Teddy. I placed my hand on Teddy's arm and felt the jolt of energy I liked with every touch.

"I don't want you buying me anything. I owe you because of Trudie. I love the offer, but I won't take your money," I said.

"You don't owe me." He held my hand on his arm, leaned close to me, and continued in a soft voice while Carol joined the others by the firepit. "It's one outfit with no strings attached."

"I told him you would complain," Scott said from across the porch.

"Scott will get lonely being here by himself." I looked at my brother.

"He's coming with us to the arena. We'll meet you for dinner," Teddy explained. I stared into his eyes and thought about the money I owed him for the tickets. I didn't say anything, but he said, "The tickets were a nice gesture I wanted to do for Trudie. You don't have anything to do with that, so you don't owe me." He swung our hands back and forth. "Let me treat you to a good time. Please?"

"You already have," I whispered.

"No, I haven't. Are you always this stubborn?" he asked.

"I'm not stubborn. I'm determined."

"Come on, Beth," Carol pleaded.

I gave in and nodded in defeat. Teddy squeezed me into his side, then turned his focus from me to Gene.

"You get to sleep." Teddy smiled at him.

"In a bed? Oh, thank you, sir. Thank you," Gene said dramatically.

"Are you guys ready?" Teddy asked and shook his head.

Everyone nodded, so we stepped inside. Teddy held my hand until we reached the front door. He turned me to face him, and I studied his calming eyes.

"You haven't slept much today, have you?" I asked.

"How do you know?" he asked.

"You look tired," I said.

"I have to condition myself for tomorrow," he said.

I let go of his hand, embraced Gene, and said, "Thanks for today. Get some sleep."

He whispered, "Teddy was right. You're easy to talk to." He held me at arm's length and said, "Thank you, Beth." He kissed my cheek and opened the door.

Teddy stood in front of me, stared into my eyes, and asked, "Did anything happen today that I should know about?"

"Nope. Just tax stuff." I diverted my eyes to the floor and thought about the guy in the bathroom.

He placed his hand on the cheek Gene kissed, lifted my face, and I held my smile. "Hmm." He studied my eyes for a few seconds and said, "I'll see you at dinner." He kissed my other cheek, walked out the front door, and to the car.

Scott followed Teddy but stopped in front of me. "Are you okay?" I nodded, even though I felt confused and overwhelmed. "If you need to talk, call me."

I shut the door behind Scott. Everyone stood behind me and stared.

"Can I gather a few things before we go?" I asked.

Shelly nodded, so I walked to the downstairs door. After I descended, I turned right, stepped into the bathroom, and brushed my hair. I balled it back up on my head and clasped the clippie. The upstairs door opened and closed. Footsteps patted the stairs.

"Ms. Chambers," Shelly called while she stood on the last step.

"Yeah," I said, stepping to her side, but made her jump. "I'm sorry, and please call me Beth."

"You startled me. Call me, Shelly." She smiled.

"What can I do for you?" I asked.

"I wanted to speak with you alone for a moment," she said.

"Would you care to have a seat?" I pointed to the big sectional couch in the entertainment room.

"No, thanks. This won't take long," she said. "You've impacted Teddy in a way I can't explain. There is this…what word am I looking for…" she said in thought. "Calm. No. Happy. No." Frustrated, she said, "There's something different about him after he met you. It's hard to explain because you don't know him, but it's kind of like you uplift him."

"That big ego of his keeps him uplifted," I chuckled.

"I'm going to come right to it. What are your intentions with him?" she asked.

"If you're hinting I'm out for gain, I can assure you, I'm not. It's great how I met a star, but it doesn't change my life, or his and I don't expect it too. Teddy seems like a good guy. A diva, so to say, but all in all, a decent person," I explained.

"He is a diva, and yes. He has a big ego, but I love him like a brother." She stared and pointed her finger at me. "If you hurt him…"

"You have no worries," I assured her. "Would you like to finish your threat?"

"You get what I'm saying but one more thing," she said as we walked to the stairs. She placed her hand on my arm. "I'm asking that whatever happens between you and him, please do not post pictures or anything on social media."

"I won't," I said.

"We need to protect people like his managers, lawyers, roadies, and even his band members. Think of him as being a multimillion-dollar business. We don't want any bad publicity to jeopardize the business."

"I understand."

"I appreciate it," she said, and we ascended the stairs.

Everyone waited for us in the living room. We walked to the car, and Rick held the door open.

"Do you need me to drive?" I smiled.

"No, ma'am," he said before I sat in the seat next to Carol.

We drove to our destination as Shelly explained about a few stores she wanted us to visit. While she spoke, I shifted in my seat and looked at Susan, who sat in the third row.

"How did you come to play in the band?" I asked Susan.

"Four years ago, I played in a rock band. We were jamming in a small downtown bar in the Salt Lake City area. Teddy and his group walked in around two in the morning. They sat in the back corner and listened," she said, then continued.

"After our set, Gene asked me to join Teddy. I went to his table, and Teddy asked if I would audition for him, so I said, yeah. We scheduled a time for me to go to Michigan, I auditioned, and have been with him since. It's not a glamorous story, but kind of cool. You wouldn't think a person like Teddy would show at a bar to listen to a local band, but he does. He likes to play the local scene from time to time."

"How long have you been playing?" I asked.

"Since I was eight. My dad thought it was a good idea to teach me a musical instrument, and I loved the guitar, so the rest is history."

"You're wonderful. I can see why Teddy chose you."

"Thank you."

We were at the mall in no time. Rick drove the car to the front door, stepped out, and I swung the door open.

"That's my job, ma'am," he said as he walked to the car door.

"Call me Beth, and we can walk to and from the parking lot," I said.

"I'm doing my job, Beth." He pronounced my name with attitude.

I walked to the door, wanting this to be over. Noise from shoppers echoed through the building, and Shelly pointed the way to a store. I went straight to the sales rack, thumbed through the clothes, but found nothing. Rick and I waited in front of the store.

"Couldn't find anything?" Shelly asked, joining us.

"No." I watched Carol and Susan.

Neither Carol nor Susan found anything, so we resumed our hunt. I walked past a children's store and stopped everyone.

"Can we go in there?" I asked and pointed at the store.

"Yes," Shelly said with a smile.

We shopped while Shelly and I spoke briefly about our families. I found several outfits and a few toys for my three grandbabies.

As I placed the items on the checkout counter, Shelly stepped to my side. She pulled a credit card out of her purse. I put my hand on top of hers to stop the transaction.

"Please step away from the register." I smiled and retrieved my wallet.

Shelly looked at me with sad eyes and said in a low voice, "I was told to use this for anything you want, which includes gifts for your family."

"I won't buy a damn thing if you use that card. I'll walk to the car empty-handed. I won't owe anyone." I handed the cashier my credit card.

She stepped a few feet from me and raised her phone to her ear. The cashier completed the transaction and bagged my items when my phone sounded with a text.

Please play nice. - Teddy texted.

I didn't respond. I placed the phone in my pocket, walked to Shelly, and said, "If we're to get along, we need to come to an understanding. I agreed Teddy could buy me an outfit for tomorrow night, but anything else I find, I'll take care of myself. Deal?"

"He said…" I gave her a hard look and stopped her words. She cleared her throat then said, "He said anything, Beth. Don't you get it?"

"Please, Shelly?" I asked.

She looked at Rick, who smiled, then she looked back to me and said, "Deal."

"Thank you." I felt relieved.

Shelly regained the lead of our group when we left the store. Carol and I pulled clothes out of bags and showed each other our treasures. Shelly stopped us in the middle of the mall and faced us.

"We have a few more stores," she said.

"Oh, man," I complained.

"You enjoyed the last one," she said.

"These are for my grandbabies. I like them a whole lot," I chuckled.

"They're better than the big kids," Carol joked.

We followed Shelly into the next store and the next.

After the fifth, I looked at her and said, "No luck. It's time to give up."

"One more," she said, but I rolled my eyes. "Please?"

"Fine," I said.

Susan intertwined her arm through mine, gave me a slight tug, and laughed. I peered at her, and a picture came to my mind.

"Are you dating, Kyle?" I asked.

"No," she said and scrunched her nose.

"Okay." I smiled.

Pictures flashed in my thoughts of her and Kyle, embracing and laughing. Another one of them kissing.

"You and he aren't dating?" I asked.

"No, we're not." She smiled while we stepped into the store.

"Wait here." Shelly held her hands to us.

"You saw Susan and Kyle in your mind?" Carol asked me, and I nodded.

"We're not dating," Susan said with a slight grin.

"Okay." I smiled.

A young, tall, robust woman with short, bright-green hair greeted us at the door. Shelly introduced us as Susan leaned her head between Carol and mine.

"This might be a *Pretty Woman* experience," she said, and we laughed.

"Please follow me," said the green-haired woman.

She led us to a small area in the back of the store. A couch sat in front of three full-length mirrors.

"Who's first?" the saleslady asked.

I pointed to Carol and held Susan's hand. Both of us walked to the couch while I twirled my hand in the air.

"Dazzle us." I smiled.

"Okay," Carol smirked.

The saleslady circled Carol then said, "Please come with me."

"I hope you two are going to buy something," I said.

"I'll be in stage clothes all night," Susan explained.

"You need to splurge and get something nice. What if you meet Mr. Right?" I winked at her.

"I agree with Beth. You need to treat yourself on occasion. You're after her," Shelly said to Susan and pointed at me.

"You're going after Carol," I said to Shelly.

"We don't have time. We're to meet everyone for dinner," she said.

"Not acceptable." I smiled.

Carol came in and out of the dressing room with different outfits. Susan and I clapped if we liked it and booed if we didn't. Shelly smiled a few times, especially when I stood next to Carol and pretended to be a seamstress.

After several outfits, Carol walked out of the dressing room with a calf-length soft tan and white print skirt, a white button-down blouse, and short tan heels. It accented her dark-red hair and looked simple but flattering.

"I like that," I said.

"I do, too," Carol said and swayed her hips.

"It suits you." Susan nodded with approval.

Shelly clapped, and I looked at her. I smiled and clapped.

"Good. We agree. Shelly, you're next," I said.

"You or Susan go," she protested.

"I'm not moving." I folded my arms across my chest and settled on the sofa.

Susan sat next to me, folded her arms as well, and informed Shelly, "You're next, girl."

"Fine," she said.

Shelly went to the back with the saleslady while Carol joined Susan and me on the couch. We clapped and booed while Shelly came in and out of the dressing room with different outfits. We agreed on a black, spaghetti-strapped dress with a teal cardigan and low flat black shoes. It was perfect for her small stature.

"You don't want heels?" I pointed at her shoes.

"I need comfort," she explained.

"Let me help you tomorrow night. I can earn my keep," I said.

"Your job is to enjoy yourself." She gave herself one more glance in the mirror, then her eyes caught mine. "You're up, Beth. I'll walk you back."

The saleslady escorted me into a small room. Clothes hung on the walls.

"Try those on. Don't ask why, but stay with red," Shelly said to me and slipped into her changing room.

I said through the wall, "That makes no sense. Red is not my color."

"You want to help?"

"Of course." I ran my hands through the clothes.

"Don't ask questions and trust me," she said.

"Trust you. I don't know you," I said and sifted through the outfits.

Three outfits caught my attention. I tried on a red dress that buttoned down the front. I wrapped a big black belt around my waist and walked to the couch area.

"Here we go." I looked in the three mirrors then said, "Never mind."

"What's wrong with that?" Carol asked.

"I know what I want. I'll be right back," I said.

I wanted pants for comfort when dancing. I closed the door, thumbed through the clothes, and found the outfit. I dressed in what I thought was decent and walked out for the ladies to see.

"I love that," Carol said.

"Will this do?" I asked Shelly.

She walked around me and nodded. "It'll be perfect."

"I'm done. Susan, you're next." I beamed.

I changed and handed the saleslady the outfit and shoes. Susan walked through the changing room doors.

"Make yourself pretty, girl," I said.

Carol, Shelly, and I waited on the couch when Susan came out. She bowed then faced the mirrors.

"That's pretty," Carol said.

"You're a beauty queen. I'm jealous," I said, and she blushed.

She wore a light blue and green dress with a thin dark-blue belt. The top of the dress came off her shoulders and revealed her soft skin. She wore three-inch dark-blue heels, which matched the dress perfectly.

"That wasn't bad," Susan said and swayed as she looked in the mirror.

Shelly clapped so Carol, and I followed her cue. Everyone was satisfied with their choices. Susan went to change while Shelly went to the front of the store to take care of business.

"I can't believe I'm saying this, but it was fun," I said to Carol.

"Yes, it was." Carol agreed.

Once Shelly and Susan joined us, we spoke about the shopping trip. Rick retrieved the car, picked us up, and drove from the mall. Shortly after, he pulled into a hotel parking lot.

"What are we doing here?" I asked.

"We changed hotels," Susan said. "To get away from reporters and Teddy wanted to be close to…"

"The arena." Shelly finished Susan's sentence.

Chapter 5

GENE WAITED FOR US AT the front door of the hotel as Rick stopped the car. One at a time, we climbed out, gathered around Gene while Rick parked the Caddy.

"Sup," Gene said playfully.

"Sup." I laughed. "You got some well-deserved sleep."

"Yes, ma'am." He held his elbow out for me. "Come with me, please."

He guided me into the hotel as the others followed. Through double doors of the lobby, a sign on the wall read: *Conference room*, with an arrow pointing in the direction we walked. I rolled my eyes, shook my head, and smelled a wave of food before we stepped through another set of doors.

Two rows of three tables sat in the room. Fifty to sixty people mingled with one another. Gene guided us to a table, pointed to a seat for Carol on the other side of Scott. Kyle sat across from me. Susan took her place next to him, then Gene sat next to me.

"Beth, this is Kyle Jenkins," Gene said.

"It's nice to meet you." I nodded.

He resembled Teddy with his big brown eyes, dark, curly, shoulder-length hair, and smooth olive complexion. His nose and mouth were thinner than Teddy's.

"You're the Beth, I've heard about." He smiled.

Teddy's bass player, Thad, walked to the table, leaned past Susan, and said to me, "No wonder Teddy is smitten. You're cute."

"No, she isn't," Scott said, and they laughed.

"I'm Thad Lowell," he said and shook my hand. He was a tall gentleman with blond hair and thick, black-rimmed glasses.

"Nice to meet you," I said as he sat at the table.

I stared at Teddy, who walked into the room. He spoke with his pianist, along with another gentleman. A beautiful, dirty blonde-haired, thin woman hung on Teddy's arm and glanced around the room.

She was taller than he, by an inch or so, makeup perfect, and not a hair out of place. The length of her hair hung to her shoulder blades. Her bangs were pulled back and held with a big green butterfly hair clasp. She wore light green slacks with matching colored shoes. Her long silver earrings dangled while she elegantly tossed her head as she laughed at something Teddy said.

She must have been cold. Her nipples were visible through her white silk shirt. Her breasts forced the material to stretch across them. An oversized light green unbuttoned shirt hung loose on her shoulders.

"Mark Roberts plays piano, and the other gentleman is Teddy's producer slash photographer, Keith Berigo," Gene explained.

"The blonde trophy girlfriend is Carissa," Scott said to me. "Stop staring at her. I've stared enough for both of us."

She looked familiar, but I couldn't remember who she was or where I had seen her. Regardless, she was someone special to Teddy, by the way, she clung to him.

"You look like shit," Carol said to me, and we laughed.

"Wow," I said and returned my focus to the woman. "She's breathtaking. Look how she's dressed and then look at us. We're so country." I looked at Scott.

"You are. I'm city folks now." He smiled.

"Yeah, right. You're in jeans and a T-shirt with something spilled on it. What is that?" I pointed to a small stain on his shirt.

He lifted the material, licked the spot, and said, "Chili from last week."

Gene, Kyle, Susan, Thad, and we all laughed. Rick stepped through the door.

I returned my attention to Carissa's smooth demeanor as she held Teddy's arm, and they walked to the table. I had not consciously seen her in magazines or the entertainment industry, but something was familiar about her. My eyes widened as I remembered almost running into her at the hotel.

She was young and beautiful. She was perfect for Teddy. The opposite of me. Teddy caught my eyes, slightly shook his head at me as if he read my thoughts.

"I can't get over how flawless she looks," I said.

"She's beautiful," Scott agreed.

"She's not what she seems," Gene whispered.

"She's elegant, young, and graceful. They look happy, so what more could she be for him?" She stared at me as I asked Gene, "Have you seen me?"

"Yes, and you're better. Carissa is a model. She appears flawless, but she isn't. She had a shoot here in Colorado and decided to meet Teddy," Susan said, getting into the conversation.

Teddy sat at the head of the table with Carissa on his right and Mark taking the seat on the left. What does Teddy want with me when he has her? I'm the last person on Earth who needs to associate with him. There is no way I belong with this group of people.

"Let's pray, please," Teddy said and stared intently at me.

After prayer, Gene told me people's names and their professions as they sat at the tables. The backup singers, dancers, and horn section of the band, not to mention a few roadies, sat for the meal. I felt insignificant being around these talented performers and asked myself, why am I here?

Several people emerged from a side door, carrying plates of food. A gentleman placed a plate of filet mignon in front of me. I closed my eyes and shook my head. I opened my mouth to say something, but Gene reached for the gentleman and whispered something to him. The waiter removed the plate and apologized.

"I'll eat it if you don't want it," Scott said.

"You're gross." I elbowed him and looked at Gene. "Thank you." The man returned and placed a rice dish in front of me. "That's better. Thank you."

I looked around and caught Teddy staring at me. We made eye contact, and he smiled before he returned to the conversation with Mark and Keith.

"You don't eat meat?" Kyle asked me.

"No, sir."

"That's weird," he said.

I took a bite and studied Kyle. "Teddy tells me you have a band of your own?"

He finished chewing and said, "Yes, ma'am. Have you heard of The Smashing Men?"

"I can't say I have."

"We play heavy rock. We're about to release our second album and tour the UK next fall," he said.

"How did you get hooked up with Teddy?" Scott asked.

"He helped us get the band together. He likes different music styles, so he opened his studio to us and helped record the albums. Smashing Men isn't well known yet, so I'm working with Teddy until it takes off."

"I wish you all the success," I said.

"Thank you, Ms. Beth." He smiled.

"Did you ladies finish your shopping?" Scott asked.

Carol looked at me from across Scott. "Yeah, but you know your sister. It was like dragging a cat to bathwater. She fought us all the way."

"I did not," I exclaimed.

"Y'all bought for the kids, didn't you?" Scott asked. Carol and I bowed our heads and grew quiet. "That's what y'all do."

"You don't eat meat, and you don't like to shop?" Kyle asked.

"She's weird," Scott said.

"I learn from my elders, dear brother," I countered.

"I'm not that much older than you."

"You knew Moses back in the day," I teased.

Kyle laughed at our verbal sparring and said, "I like to see siblings get along."

"You should see our family," Scott said before he stuffed the last piece of filet in his mouth.

I wiped my mouth, leaned back in my chair, and said, "I'm full."

"Full of..." Scot said.

"Scott!" I exclaimed. "We're eatin' with fancy folks."

"Make room for dessert," Gene said.

The wait staff walked through the door once again and moved around us, as though they danced. They gathered empty dishes, then sat dessert plates in front of people. Gene pointed to me.

"What are you doing?" I asked him.

A woman stepped to my spot and sat a plate charger with a bowl in front of me. It consisted of a half banana lying on top of a mixture of fruits.

A photograph laid underneath the bowl. I lifted it to see a picture of the famous Noah Parker with horns drawn on his head, blacked-out teeth, and glasses scribbled on his face. A bubbled caption from his mouth read: *I'm an ass.*

I laughed hard, and everyone looked at me. Gene, Kyle, and Susan guffawed while I glanced at Teddy as he laughed. I looked to his right. Carissa glared at me. I nodded at her, but the burning cold stare she held never left her face. She gave a scorned look at Teddy. I took a forkful of banana then toasted Teddy before taking a bite.

"What is that about?" Scott asked while Teddy smiled and nodded in my direction.

"Nothing," I said with a big smile.

"Teddy said you would like that," Gene said.

"Your boss is crazy," I said.

"I like Noah," Susan said.

"Me too. He's a wonderful singer and nice to look at," I confirmed.

After an insightful conversation and dessert completed, Gene patted my leg, I bounced.

"In a minute," he said.

"I didn't say anything, and you don't have to go with me. I mean, is there a ritual Teddy performs after a meal?" I asked in a whisper.

"No. You can go if you want." He smiled.

"Go where?" Kyle asked.

"We have a few smokers," Gene said.

Kyle placed his fork in his bowl, stood, and looked at me. "I'll go with you. Come on."

"Are y'all going outside?" Carol asked.

"Yep," I said.

I pushed my chair back to stand. Scott reached around to help, but I fell back in it. At this moment of all times, my klutz gene had to show itself.

"Had too much to eat?" Scott smiled while everyone around me chuckled.

"Shut up, Scott." I glanced at Teddy, who smiled.

"I'll lead the way." Gene stood from the table.

Kyle looked at Susan and asked, "Would you care to join us?"

"Why, yes, I would." She stood from the table.

The five of us walked out of the room to the back of the hotel. When I reached the fresh air, the crisp breeze whisked through my hair.

I observed Susan, who stood close to Kyle, and they whispered to each other. I walked to them.

"Y'all do make a cute couple," I quietly said.

"She knows," Susan said to Kyle.

"Why did you tell her?" he asked.

"Please forgive her. She can see things some people can't," Carol said and patted my shoulder.

"I told her we weren't," Susan said in a delicate voice.

"I'll leave it alone," I said, then waved my hands in the air to dismiss the subject.

"Told ya," Carol said.

"Did you pick up on it?" I asked her.

"No. I was busy making sure Ms. Thing's boobs didn't land on her plate." She laughed.

"Sorry, Gene," I said in a louder voice, not sure if he heard Carol.

"That happened once. I laughed so hard, soda came from my nose." Gene smiled. "She was pissed that we laughed. Do you two remember?"

Kyle and Susan nodded at Gene. I stared at the young couple again. A picture flashed in my mind of them getting married, which made the smile return to my aching cheeks. Kyle held my stare for a minute or so while I took a drag from my cigarette, not saying a word.

"Okay, okay. Yes, we're together. Gene!" He pointed to him. "Don't tell Teddy. I don't want him to freak out."

Gene walked to him and smiled. "It's not my place." He turned his attention to me, patted my shoulder, and said, "Good call. I didn't see that coming."

"We would like to keep it that way, please," Susan said. "I don't want Teddy to worry if I'm going on tour with Kyle."

"The plot thickens." I smiled again at them. "I don't know you guys, but I think if you tell Teddy, he'll...,"

"You're right, Ms. Beth. You don't know Teddy or us," Kyle interrupted.

"I didn't mean to offend you, so I apologize," I said.

"No offense taken," Kyle said. "We're here to protect Teddy, and I don't want a groupie..."

"Don't call her that," Gene said as I was going to say something. "She's not a groupie."

"Thank you for acknowledging that, Gene," I said then looked at Kyle. "I'm not after Teddy, so there isn't a reason to protect him from me. I don't know why I'm here except..." I looked at Carol and asked, "Why am I here?"

"There's a reason for everything, Beth. Like how you see these two." She pointed at Kyle and Susan, then said, "Your and Teddy's friendship will be revealed."

"Are you a fortune teller or something? I don't believe in ghosts, witchcraft, or voodoo shit," Kyle said.

"Carol is, and my ancestors were, but not me," I joked. "That's why Carol has been part of our family forever."

"Your mom pays me well to stay with your brother," she said, and we laughed.

"You guys are nice, but I don't want Teddy to know," Susan said.

"It's not my story to tell," I said.

"She hasn't told her daughters, she met Teddy." Gene pointed at me.

"What?" Kyle asked.

"Thanks, Gene. Let's turn the attention back to me. You're a butt, sir." I smiled then looked at Kyle. "No, I haven't, and yes, they are fans of you, guys. Lucy commented about y'all playing here. She said Scott, and you need to take me." I pointed at Carol.

"She gave you the opportunity to tell her, and you didn't?" Carol asked.

"No," I said.

"I can't believe you," Carol said.

"Who meets a superstar and doesn't say anything to anyone?" Kyle asked.

"Beth!" Carol exclaimed.

"Y'all can leave me alone," I said and looked at Susan and Kyle. "Speak with Teddy about you two. He'll understand." I changed the subject.

"Do you think he suspects anything about us?" Susan asked.

Carol shook her head. "He has other things on his mind if you get my point. Huh, Beth?"

I smiled, and Gene walked to Susan, put his arm on her shoulder, looked at me, and said, "I guarantee Teddy doesn't know, and yeah, Carol. He has other things on his mind, but it's not what you think."

"How long has this been going on?" I pointed between Kyle and Susan.

"A year," Kyle and Susan said at the same time.

"I'm happy for you both," I said.

"A year? Man, I'm slipping," Gene said.

We visited for a little longer, then Thad, Mark, and Keith joined us outside. Gene formally introduced us.

Mark had a broad smile with thin lips, small green eyes with crow's feet forming in the creases. He shook his round face when he laughed, and his long brown ponytail blew in the wind.

Keith was a tall skinny man with short spiked red hair. He had beautiful light blue eyes, a big white smile, and a few freckles on his cheeks.

We joked with one another and spoke about the concert. They told us a few road stories as the night fell on us. I retrieved my phone, noticed it was getting late, and turned to Carol.

"We need to get Scott and go home."

"Is it that late?" she asked, and I nodded.

"No need to rush off. I'm enjoying this," Susan said.

"Me to darlin', but you guys have to perform tomorrow," I said and walked with Gene into the hotel.

We stepped into the conference room. People stood in little groups, speaking with one another. Teddy, Carissa, and Shelly were in a conversation. We joined Scott, Rick, and a few others. We informed Scott we were ready to leave. Gene whispered to Teddy, and Carissa turned her glare on me once again.

Gene held my elbow and led me to the door. I looked at Teddy as Carissa hung on his left side. She gave his shoulder a noticeable squeeze, and her stare burned a hole through me.

"Thank you, everyone. It was a nice dinner," I loudly stated, but stared at Teddy.

He removed his hand from the small of Carissa's back. He waved at me, then Gene, and I walked out the door. I linked my arm through Gene's arm, and he laid his hand on mine.

"What's wrong, honey?" he asked.

"Not a word from Teddy." I laid my head on his lower bicep.

"He's dealing with something right now, so don't take it personally."

"Oh, I'm not." I smiled, then asked, "Do you want me to drive?"

"No." He laughed and patted my hand.

Once we were at the house, I sat my purse on the counter and retrieved my phone and cigarettes. I stepped onto the back porch. Scott lit the fire in the pit while Carol sat in a lounge chair. The blue, red, and yellow colors danced around the coals of the flame in the pit. It burned low, and I warmed my hands.

"What did you do with Teddy while we shopped?" I asked Scott.

"We watched Carissa get dressed." He smiled.

"That's not funny, dumbass," Carol said, then shoulder bumped him.

I rolled my eyes at both and said, "She's beautiful. Teddy said he wasn't seeing anyone seriously, but he's lying. She looked like his girlfriend."

"I don't think they're serious. She wasn't with him all day. She showed at the hotel before dinner," Scott said.

"Maybe we're entertainment for him or his muses," I said.

"You're more than a muse to him. I saw the look on his face when Gene informed him of what happened in the bathroom today," Scott said then took a sip of beer.

"What happened?" Carol asked.

"I was speaking with Teddy in his suite when Gene woke and joined us in the sitting room. Teddy asked how the day went, and Gene said it was okay, trying to be nonchalant. Teddy mentioned he thought something happened, but he didn't know what. He wanted an answer, so he asked Gene once more. He explained to Teddy about the guy in the bathroom and how he put his arm around you, blocking your exit," Scott said.

"It wasn't a big deal," I said.

"It could have been if Gene didn't come in when he did," Scott said, scooting to the edge of his seat. "Look, Beth. I like Teddy and the rest of the gang, but you need to be careful."

"I understand," I said.

"Anyway, Teddy got pissed and paced the floor for a few minutes. I spoke to Gene, and he didn't think the guy would have done anything to you, but he was glad he showed when he did. Gene told Teddy how he likes you, and he thinks you could have taken care of yourself if the guy didn't overpower you. We spoke about you for a few minutes," Scott explained.

Carols eyes widened, and she asked, distressed, "Why would someone want to hurt Beth?"

"I'm cute, and they're jealous." I wanted to lighten the mood.

"Gene said, sometimes people want to get to know celebrities so bad, they latch onto whoever is associated with them. This guy wanted to get a demo to Teddy," Scott said to Carol then looked back at me. "Teddy promised me nothing would happen to you, but we have to be careful as well. No posting pictures with Teddy anywhere, Carol. No blabbing to the neighbors you met him and no telling the kids. I mean it," Scott said forcibly. "There's crazy people in this world, and thankfully, Beth, you're okay."

"You're being overdramatic," I said.

"Wow. You could've been hurt," Carol said, not letting go of the conversation.

"No, I couldn't have," I said.

"It's not like Arkansas. You can't carry your gun here when you fly," Scott chastised.

"I know. I would never put you in danger, and if I thought for one millisecond you were, I would do everything in my power to change it."

"I'm not worried about us." Scott stood, looked down at me, and said, "It's you, so please be careful."

"I ain't scared," I said with confidence.

He walked to the door. "You wanna another soda?"

"No, I'm fixin' to go to bed," I said, putting my cigarette out.

Carol stood and hugged me. "We love you, girl."

"I love y'all. See you in the morning," I said.

I opened the door at the same time Scott returned to the porch. "Night."

"Night," I replied.

I walked downstairs. I brushed my teeth, turned lights off, and crawled into bed. My mind raced with thoughts of Teddy. I wanted to hear his voice, so I plugged my phone into the charger and opened my music app. I scrolled to one of Teddy's songs.

True Love played. I closed my eyes and imagined him singing to me while I stood next to a piano. I drifted to sleep with the vision, dancing in my thoughts.

The phone rang, and I quickly sat up.

"Hello!" I belted.

"Did I wake you?" His sultry voice sounded in my ear.

"Teddy?" I asked, looked at the phone, and saw the caller ID. "What are you doing?" I slammed my body against the bed and pulled the sheets up under my chin.

"Sorry, but I couldn't sleep. I wanted to hear your voice," he said.

"That's weird."

"What?"

"I'm embarrassed to tell you, and it's late. You need to be asleep."

"Are you okay?" he asked.

"I'm fine. How are you?"

"I'm sorry I didn't get to speak with you. It's a long story about Carissa and…"

"No explanation is needed," I interrupted. "Why are you on the phone with me when you have a girlfriend? I asked if you had one."

"I don't," he quickly said.

"It looked to me, you do. Where is she now?"

"In the other room. She's leaving in the morning. I didn't want to draw attention to her changing rooms this late at night, so I'm taking the couch."

"It's not my business, Teddy," I said.

"I hate how we didn't get to speak."

"It's okay. Get rest. You need energy for the concert."

"I wanted to apologize about today or, well, yesterday. Gene said you encountered a weird guy because of me. I shouldn't have drawn attention to you."

I rubbed my eyes and said, "That's okay." I waited for a few seconds then said in a lower voice, "I don't have to be at the concert. I don't want to cause rifts between you and your girl. She's beautiful. I can see why you're with her."

"She's not as beautiful as you. I want you…" He stumbled with his words then said, "I mean, I want you to join me."

"I know you asked to be nice, so I'm letting you off the hook."

"There is no hook for you to let me off, so please come. Let me show you a good time."

"You already have, and I thank you," I said before I fell silent and thought about our worlds being different. "You have a girlfriend who you need to pay attention to, so show HER a good time. Don't worry about us. Meeting you was enough for me."

"You don't worry about *the girl*," he said, raising his voice with aggravation. "Meeting you isn't enough for me. I want more."

"You don't know what you want," I said. "All I'm saying is if you change your mind about us being there, it's okay to tell me. I won't be upset or stalk you. I'm not even a fan, so you're safe from me. Now, Noah is a different issue." Why am I flirting on the phone to a taken man?

"Again, with Noah," he said.

"The plate thing was funny."

"He is an ass," Teddy said, which made me laugh.

"Watch what you say about him. He's my guy, but I don't know this Teddy Nafton dude. I'm not sure if he's any good."

"I'm the best," he said.

I grew quiet for a second before I said, "I don't have to see you, to hear you, so I don't have to be at the concert."

"You don't want to see me perform?" he playfully teased.

"It would be fun, but I won't lose any sleep if I don't," I said.

"I will," he said.

"Teddy…" I wanted to tell him how I enjoyed speaking with him. I loved the feel of his touch on my skin, the playful banter between us, but he interrupted my thoughts.

"Tell me what embarrassed you," he said in a soft voice.

"Are you changing the subject?"

"I'm admitting that I am, so tell me," he said.

"I wanted to hear your voice tonight, so I played your music until I fell asleep."

"You ARE a fan." He laughed.

"No, I'm not. I like your voice and music," I jibed, "but that doesn't mean anything."

"What song were you listening to?" he asked.

"I don't want to tell you."

"I can guess."

"I don't want to be here all night, so it was *True Love*.

"That's your favorite?"

"No," I said.

"You don't have to defend yourself to me because guess what?"

"What?"

"I'm a fan of yours."

"Why do you do this to me?" I asked.

"What do I do?"

"Take my breath away, all the time."

"Tell me how I do that."

"I'm not getting into it."

"So, if *True Love* isn't your favorite, what is?"

"I'll keep that answer to myself," I said as my cheeks ached yet again from smiling.

"I'll get it out of you. Sorry I called so late. Go back to sleep, babe," he said. I liked him calling me that, but I would never admit it.

"I'm fine. Are you sure you're okay?"

He paused for a moment, then said, "Yeah. You calm me, so thank you for answering the phone. I'll see you later."

"If you need to talk, I'm here," I said, not wanting to hang up.

"Thanks. Goodnight."

"Goodnight." I hung up.

How could I sleep now? Did I dream that conversation? I checked the phone for the last number called, and it was Teddy's. I didn't want our conversation to end, but I closed my eyes and replayed his voice in my thoughts until I drifted to sleep.

Chapter 6

I COMPLETED MY SHOWER TO prepare for a lunch outing with Scott and Carol. I dried and wrapped my hair and body in separate towels.

I opened the bathroom door, walked into the entertainment area, and quickly grabbed the towel around my breasts. I held it tight and froze in my steps. Teddy, Shelly, Rick, Gene, Carol, and Scott stared at me as the shock of seeing them made my face blush, and my eyes widen.

"Beth!" Gene exclaimed as he quickly turned and faced the wall.

"Good morning," Teddy said with a wide smile as he looked me over.

"Sorry. I led them down. I thought you would be dressed by now." Scott laughed.

"You're an ass, Scott," I said and quickly walked to the bedroom door.

"Are you changing?" Teddy asked.

I walked into the bedroom then shut the door behind me. I shook from embarrassment. Teddy Nafton saw me wearing nothing but a towel. I smirked, closed my eyes, and envisioned his lips on mine as he glided his hands across my back. He danced with me close to the bed, then laid me across the mattress.

I shook the thoughts from my imagination and dressed. I picked up the wet towel from the floor but left the other on my head. Everyone sat on the couch and waited for me.

"I'm sad you dressed," Teddy said. He stood, embraced me, and whispered in my ear. "I liked where my imagination was taking us."

I blushed, thinking about what I saw in my mind. He chuckled, and I stepped from his arms.

"What are you doing here?" I asked again.

"To treat you and Carol to a day at the spa before the concert," Teddy said.

"Can I speak with you for a moment?" I asked.

"Sure," he said.

"We'll give you guys a second." Scott took the hint and motioned for everyone to follow him.

I walked into the bathroom, hung one towel, and dried my hair with the other while everyone ascended the stairs. I balled my hair up with a clippie, then stepped into the entertainment room. I looked at Teddy with frustration.

"Why are you upset?" he asked.

"I don't want you to treat us to the spa," I said.

"You don't like spas?" he asked while I stepped into the bedroom.

I retrieved my phone and cigarettes then rejoined Teddy. "I appreciate the offer, but I don't want anything else from you. The clothes, dinner, and concert are enough."

"I want to show you a good time."

"It's enough." I widened my eyes at him.

"No, it's not. I'm trying to make up for yesterday." He wrapped his arm around my shoulder.

"Nothing happened." I stepped out of his arm.

"Then last night."

"Nothing happened," I loudly said and turned to the stairs. "You don't owe me anything, but as of right now, I owe you a lot."

"You don't owe me." He followed.

I stopped on the first landing and gazed into his brown eyes. I felt happiness, excitement, and aggravation, all at the same time.

"What do you see?" he asked, holding my stare.

I furrowed my eyebrows, concentrated on his beautiful big eyes. "Elated, yet saddened," I said quietly. "I'm confused." I looked to the floor, shook my head, and said, "I don't know."

"You will." He pulled me into him.

"I will what?" I smelt his enticing cologne then stepped from him.

"Open your eyes."

"My eyes are open."

"Let it happen naturally," he said.

"What are you talking about?"

"You'll believe it when you see it," he said, then led me up the stairs.

We walked through the living room and out the back door. We joined everyone on the back porch, and the conversations stopped.

"Is everything okay?" Scott asked.

"Yeah," Teddy said. "Okay, ladies. Have fun. Shelly, take care of them." I gave him a stern look, and he pointed at me. "Not this one. She can take care of herself."

"Um, yeah, I can, but I don't like this." I glared at him.

"Please play nice, Beth," he said and turned to Scott. "Would you like to come to the arena with us?"

"Sure," Scott said.

"Ladies." Teddy embraced me once again. "I'll see you tonight."

"Do you always get your way?" I asked agitated.

He laughed, then squeezed my arm before he disappeared into the house. I watched through the sliding glass door as he, Scott, and Gene walked out the front door. I lit a cigarette and stepped to the railing of the porch. I leaned on it with my elbows, stared at the pond, and thought about how to keep up with the amount of money I owed Teddy.

"I'll get ready. Do you want to grab lunch?" Carol asked.

"I lost my appetite," I said.

The back door slid open then closed. Shelly leaned next to me, holding a tablet and clipboard tight against her chest.

"Are you okay?" I asked her.

"It's concert day," she said.

"Why are you here? Your fingers look like mine when I board a plane. I grip my computer bag until my knuckles turn white."

"I'm doing my job," she said.

"I'll get my things." We walked into the house, and I said to Rick, "I can drive."

"I got this." He smiled.

Rick pulled into a parking lot, stopped the car at the front door, and I waited until he opened my door. The Denver Salon was in front of us.

"We can get tortured now," I said.

"You don't like spas?" Shelly asked as we stood in front of the door.

"I don't like people doting over me," I said.

"You're in for an awakening," Shelly said while Rick laughed. "Manicures, pedicures, and facials. The works. I didn't get to schedule a massage because of the time."

"We don't have to do this at all," I complained as we walked inside.

"Yes, we do," Shelly said.

"I'm Liza. You must be Shelly," a pink-haired, tall, young woman said to her.

"Yes." She pointed to us. "This is Carol and Beth."

"We're ready for you, ladies. Follow me, please." Liza smiled.

Carol and I looked at each other, grabbed Shelly by the arms between us, and she asked, "What are you doing?"

"You're having this done, too," I said.

"I need to make calls," she said.

"Hey, Liza. Can you fit Shelly in too?" I asked.

"Sure," she said.

"See Shelly? Relax today," Carol said while we followed Liza to the back of the room.

We stopped at three chairs, and Liza walked to the last one. She tapped her hand on each chair.

"Carol here, then Shelly and Beth here," she said.

Three people emerged from a side room on the right of us. A heavyset, gentleman, about six feet tall, stood behind me. A shorter, thin woman stood behind Carol while a robust woman stood behind Shelly.

"I'm Nat," the one behind me said in a low strong voice.

"Nice to meet you, Nat." I smiled.

He draped the neck drop around me and asked, "What are we doing today, sweetie?"

"The works," Shelly answered for me.

"Okay, honey. Let's see what you have." He took the clippie from my thick, straight light brown hair, which hung to my waist. "Oh, my God. You have beautiful hair, girl. Look at this, Latasha, Mona."

"Wow, Beth. Why don't you wear it down?" Shelly asked.

"I can't have it in my face when I'm working, so I usually have it in the clippie or a ponytail."

"What would you like for me to do?" Nat asked.

I pulled my head from his hands and said defensively, "I don't care if you color it, style it, layer or trim it, but please do not cut the length."

"Okay, sweetie. No cutting the length," he said with his hands in the air.

"Sorry." I turned in the chair then noticed Shelly looked at me. "I don't want to be one of those grandmas with short gray hair. It'll happen in my life, but not yet."

While the three stylists brushed, tugged, and cut our hair, we spoke about the grandkids, the kids, and husbands. It was relaxing for us to get to know Shelly, but we never mentioned Teddy. She told us about her three children, with the youngest being the same age as my oldest granddaughter. We laughed at the fact we were the same age, yet I was a grandmother.

"What are you ladies doing tonight?" Nat asked.

"We're having a girls' day and night out by going to a concert," I said.

"I know who you're going to see." Nat perked up.

"We're all going. I have seven people in my group," Latasha quipped.

"I have nine," Mona chimed.

"There are six of us," Nat said. "I can't wait. I stayed on hold for an hour to buy the tickets the first day they went on sale. I couldn't believe it sold out as fast as it did, but we are talking about the fine, one and only…Teddy."

"He's okay," I said.

"Okay?" Nat asked with wide eyes. "Sweetie, he is the best. I would love to have five minutes alone with that man. I'll show him how to entertain."

"He is hot, hot, hot!" Mona sang.

"Oh girl, I'm going to do your hair where it won't go flat before the show. Teddy baby will definitely notice you after he notices me." Nat placed his fingers to his chest, which made me giggle. "Where are you sitting tonight?"

"Ask her." I pointed at Shelly and smiled from ear to ear.

Carol looked at me and laughed. Shelly shifted uncomfortably in her chair. She gave me a look that could kill, but I held my smile.

"Where, Mrs. Shelly?" Mona asked.

"We're on the floor," she said with no emotion.

"We're on the floor. Maybe we'll see you there," Latasha excitedly said.

Nat pulled his ticket from his front pocket. "We're in row eighteen. Beat that."

"I can't remember which row we're in," Shelly said and held her glare on me.

Carol and I laughed while Nat explained what he wanted to do with my hair. We made plans to meet before the concert when my phone rang with a text. I retrieved it from my pocket and saw a message from an unknown number.

Who is this?

Who is this? - I texted back.

After twenty minutes of no response, I gathered it was the wrong number. The rest of the afternoon was filled with coloring, cutting, manicuring, pedicuring, plucking, and all kinds of things. By late afternoon, we were ready to leave with rollers in our hair.

Shelly texted on her phone then paid for our services while Nat gave me a tight hug.

"See you tonight, beauty," he said.

"See you tonight, cutie. Can't wait to see you dolled up for the man. If you meet him, send him my way," I said.

We walked outside, got into the car, and Shelly said, "We'll take you to the house, so you can rest before dinner. It'll be held at six-thirty. You both be ready."

"Aren't you going to get ready with us?" I liked Shelly. She worked hard and was focused, but she needed to relax and enjoy the show.

"No. I'll see you tonight," she said.

"Get pretty. Teddy might notice you," I said, trying to sound like Nat, which made us laugh.

I turned the TV off, grabbed my phone, and hit my music app. I tapped the play button and the sultry voice I was becoming more infatuated with, sang to me. I walked past the big-screen TV and wrap around sofa to the bathroom.

I looked in the mirror at the tightly wound rollers in my hair. I brushed my teeth, retrieved my makeup bag, and got ready for our big night.

I dressed in my new red and black pinstriped slacks with two-inch black heels. I wore a mid-arm length, black sheer asymmetrical overshirt. Designs were cut out on the front, to reveal a red spaghetti-strapped undershirt. I stepped in front of the mirror and was satisfied with myself.

I grabbed my purse, placed my cigarette case in my left pants pocket, and my phone in the right. I walked up the stairs, went to the refrigerator, and got a glass of tea.

"You look good, sis. Clean up real nice," Scott said as he stood at the bar.

"So, do you," I said. He wore a light teal dress shirt and dark khaki slacks. "What? No chili stains?"

"I save that shirt for the real important fancy meetings," he said in a heavy southern accent.

We walked to the back porch, sat on the outdoor couch, and spoke about the many golf balls that hit his house. The back door opened, and Carol posed in the entryway.

"Woohoo. You look good, woman," Scott exclaimed.

"You look beautiful." I clapped.

"We're gonna party tonight," Scott said and took her into his arms.

Carol blushed and said, "Thank you. You both look good."

"Thank you, Carol, but it's picture time," I announced.

I retrieved my phone from my pocket. We took pictures of each other as if it was prom, then the doorbell rang.

"I'll get it," Scott said, leaving the porch.

After a few minutes, he and Gene joined Carol and me outside.

"Hey," I said and embraced Gene.

"You look stunning." He let me go and walked around me. He stopped, held his elbow out for me, and said, "I'll be honored if you would please be my date for tonight."

I squealed like a schoolgirl, placed my arm through his, batted my eyes, and said, "I would love to be your date, sir. Can I drive?"

"You know the answer." He smiled.

"You look good," I said.

He wore black slacks, a white shirt, and a thin black tie. Not much different than what he usually wore.

"Thank you," he said. He made a big production of how Scott and Carol looked wonderful then said, "We had better get on the road."

He guided us to a limo, and my eyes widened along with my smile. I excitedly said, "I can drive if you want."

Gene laughed, shook his head, and opened the back door for me to get inside. Once everyone was seated, he drove toward the arena. I looked around the car and could not believe the size of the interior. I sank in the leather seats.

"Are you sure you don't want me to drive?" I asked him.

"You would have us lost in no time."

"How many times have you driven in Colorado?" I asked.

"More than you," Gene said.

I looked around the spacious vehicle and said, "I've never ridden in a limo."

"You're sheltered." Scott laughed. "I ride in them all the time."

"Yeah, right," Carol sneered.

"Why a limo, Gene?" I asked.

"For style and effect." He smiled at me through the rearview mirror. "You are to enjoy yourselves tonight, so I hope you have fun."

"I've had more fun these past few days than I've had in a while," I said.

We drove past the front entrance of the arena, and I peered out the window. People formed long lines at the front door.

"I can't believe all these people," Scott said.

"How do they do this?" Carol asked.

"Teddy lives for the stage and music. He gives the fans his all, and the band follows his lead," Gene said.

He stopped the car in front of big metal doors. He got out, opened our door, and held my elbow.

"Don't bring me down tonight, Gene. You better be ready to dance." I smiled.

He laughed and held the metal arena door for us. We entered and walked down a hall. We turned right, and Gene opened another door for us. Rows of tables in the center of the room and more tables lined the walls with food, plates, and utensils placed in buffet style.

People from Teddy's group spoke to one another. Gene properly introduced some to us, but when Susan saw us, she gave Carol and me a hug.

"You ladies look good," she said as she let me go.

"Thank you," Carol said.

"Your hair is beautiful, Beth." She pulled my hair over my shoulders and let it fall over my breasts.

"Thanks. You look great. Are you ready for tonight?" I asked.

"Nerves are setting in. I don't know why Teddy thinks we need to eat before a concert. Sometimes I can't."

"You're great, and you got this," Carol said and hugged her again.

Teddy and Carissa joined us in the room and spoke with Shelly. Teddy stared at me as Carissa hung on his arm and glared at me.

Shelly left Teddy's side and walked in a hurry toward us. I grabbed her arm before she got away.

"Hey, girl. Where's the fire?" I asked.

She threw her arms around me and said, "Sorry. It's last-minute crap. You look great," she said and clapped a few times as she walked out the door.

"You know what to do when she comes back," I said to Carol and Susan.

Gene led us to a table that had drinks in buckets of ice. He waited for my order.

"Water, please."

I stepped backward, out of the way for Carol and Scott. I tripped and felt an electric charge as Teddy quickly put his hands on my shoulders. He stopped my momentum from hitting the floor.

"Clumsy even dressed beautifully," he said.

"Thank you, sir." I blushed. Carissa was by his side. I looked at her and said, "Good evening. I'm Beth."

I held my hand out to shake hers. She looked at it, then back at me, not taking my hand. She held a snarled expression, looked me over, and never said a word. I pulled back my unshaken hand and looked at the floor.

Teddy placed his finger under my chin and lifted my face to his. He looked into my eyes. *You're beautiful.* The words appeared in my thoughts. Did his lips move? I tilted my head then realized his lips hadn't moved.

He smiled then walked away with Carissa hanging on his arm. Did I read his mind, or did he read mine? Can Carissa feel the electric shock from him? Does Teddy have a magic touch?

Carissa looked back at me as they walked to the front of the room. I scolded myself. I flirted with Teddy in front of his girlfriend. I was embarrassed by the infatuation I had for him. Carissa felt threatened by me. I needed to explain to her how I wasn't interested in him. Once this night passed, he would be gone and never think of me again.

Teddy looked back at me, shook his head, and mouthed the word 'no' while Shelly walked through the door. I regained my senses and elbowed Carol. She, Susan, and I clapped.

Shelly looked stunning in her new outfit. She stopped, looked at us three, and smiled. Teddy clapped, which in turn made everyone applauded.

"You go, Shelly," I cheered.

She blushed. The clapping faded, and she bowed her head from embarrassment. She joined us and gave Carol, Susan, and me a hug. She looked at Teddy and waited for him to speak.

Carissa didn't express any emotions or clap. She continued to glare at me and clung tight to Teddy's arm as he addressed the room.

"Before we pray, I would like to say a few words. Mrs. Shelly, you are the glue that holds us together, and sometimes we forget what it is you do. You're gorgeous and tonight…relax. You deserve it.

He continued, "Beth…thank you for reminding us who is important. You bring the sun's rays into a room as you enter the door. Carol, Scott, and you have shown us wonderful hospitality. Thank you. I hope you all are ready to party."

Kyle, Keith, Thad, and Mark yelled, "Party. Party."

"Let's say grace." Teddy laughed.

After prayer, Gene brought me a plate and directed me to the table, which was filled with veggies, fruits, bread, and cheeses.

"Thank you, Gene. You're a wonderful date."

"Yes, I am, and please tell my wife. She forgot over the years," he said.

"I would love to have the chance," I said.

"I bet you will," he said, then left to put meat on his plate.

I walked toward the table to take my seat, but Teddy stepped in my path. I looked behind him to see where Carissa had gone. She sat at the table with her arms folded and glared at us.

"You look scrumptious tonight. I love your hair," Teddy said, pulling the right side around to drape over my shoulder.

I lowered my head and said in a soft voice, "Thank you for the outfit and spa day."

He raised my head with his finger and looked in my eyes.

"No glasses?"

"Contacts." I smiled.

I swam in his eyes, then words formed in my thoughts. *Can you hear me?* I leaned in close and concentrated on his full lips. Did that come from him? I felt baffled, but I smiled and thought the word, *Yes*.

"We'll work on that," he said, then walked away.

My smile faded. Work on what? What did he mean? Gene joined me and pointed at two seats available between Carol and Shelly.

Once seated, Carol leaned into me and said, "This is cool."

"Yeah, it is," I said.

Gene sat between Shelly and me, but she leaned in front of him to speak with me. He stood and laughed.

"Oh no, you don't. I know what you're going to do."

He switched Shelly's and his plates around, so she could sit next to me. Susan and Kyle sat across from us with Teddy once again at the head of the table and Carissa on his right.

"You look great," I said to Shelly.

"I want to thank you, Beth. You're a caring person," she said.

"No problem, girlfriend." I waved my hand in the air like Nat. We ate for a minute, but Susan wasn't eating. I pointed to her plate.

"Eat." I insisted.

"I don't have the stomach for food right now," she said.

"I understand, but you need your strength. You can't be passing out on stage. If I have to come up there, you all are going to be in trouble," I said, then stood from the table.

I retrieved a roll and brought it back to her. Teddy watched me and smiled. I sat the plate in front of Susan.

"Please eat," I said.

"Do you always watch out for others?" she asked.

I smiled, blushed, and looked at my plate. I didn't have much of an appetite. Before show jitters. I felt anxious for everyone.

"How long before we go to our seats?" I asked Shelly.

"We'll go out front in twenty to thirty minutes, so you can find them," she said.

"Thanks."

We completed dinner then spoke about the tour with the band members. Shelly walked out of the room. After a few minutes, she came to us with a clipboard and tablet in hand.

"It's time, guys. Come with me," she said.

I hugged each band member then said, "Good luck."

Teddy appeared behind me and asked, "What? No hug?"

"Your girl is sitting at the table," I said.

"No, she isn't. I need a hug from my girl," he said, then held me tight as the energy flowed between us.

"I'm not your girl," I said, not wanting to let him go.

"You are," he said and squeezed me tight.

"She's glaring at me," I whispered in his ear and smelt his wonderful cologne.

"Ignore her," he said.

"It's hard too." I rubbed his arm, then said, "Thank you. This is amazing."

"Do I have your attention?" he asked.

"No," I said and stared into his eyes. "I'm lying. You do."

"You haven't been amazed yet," he said with confidence.

"Let's go," Shelly said and took my arm.

"Good luck, everyone," I said out loud, and Teddy looked at the floor in thought.

"Thanks," People yelled back at me.

Carissa held a blazed stare on me. I wanted to speak with her, but Shelly pulled my arm as Gene walked behind me. Scott and Carol followed us to the side of the stage.

"Do we need to wait on Carissa?" I asked.

"She doesn't like to go to the floor," Shelly said and pointed to a leather chair that sat on the side of the stage. She led us down three stairs to a door, then paused. "If you need the restroom or drinks or fresh air, please tell Gene. I don't want you to enter or exit without him or myself. It's going to get crazy back here."

"You're not joining us?" I asked with disappointment.

"Maybe once I have everyone settled," she said and nodded.

Gene placed an earpiece in his left ear, and I said, "Now I understand the date, Gene. You're using me, so you can keep an eye on Teddy and the others from the floor."

"You, ma'am, will never be used. You're too smart for that," he teased.

He placed his hand on the small of my back and guided us to our seats. Metal bars separated twenty or so metal chairs from the rest, which lined the spacious floor. Gene pointed to the front row.

"Hate to do this, but I need to seat you in order." He walked to the last seat and pointed. "Scott, Carol, Beth, and then me. I don't mean to treat you like children, but there is a rhyme and reason."

"That scares me," I said.

"You're in good hands, Beth. Nothing can touch you tonight," he said.

"Beth! Carol!" Familiar voices called.

Carol turned and said, "Nat, Latasha," then we both waved.

"Can we go see them?" Carol asked Gene in a small voice.

"Mother, may we?" I asked, batting my eyes.

"Yes." Gene smiled.

Carol looked at Scott and said, "I'll be right back." She grabbed my hand, and we walked through the chairs to the bars.

They were waiting on the other side, and Nat said, "You win. You have better seats." He looked at me and moved his figure in the air for me to spin, so I did. "Your hair looks good, girl."

"I have you to thank." I gave him a hug with the bar between us.

"Hey," Mona said, joining us.

"You're next, Carol. Spin for us, girl," Nat said, then she spun. "Looking good."

"So do y'all. Are y'all excited?" I asked.

"This is going to be great, but where's Shelly?" Mona asked.

"I don't know where she ran off to," I said.

"She must be getting drinks," Carol said, and we pretended to look for her.

"Oh," Mona said and searched for her as well.

"Where are y'all sitting?" Carol asked.

After they pointed out their sections, Nat excitedly said, "Ladies, if Teddy talks to you, slip him my number."

"We'll do," I confirmed, then gave each other hugs and returned to our chairs. I sat next to Gene and said, "I could go for a drink stronger than water.

"What? You're a drinker?" Gene asked.

"All the time. What do you think I put in the soda cans?" I asked.

Scott looked at me and said, "If you drink a cup of anything, we'll have to peel you from this floor, sis. You don't drink."

"I've had a few crazy days and would like to relax. I need to get my groove on to keep up with Gene."

"Would you like to come with me and get the ladies something?" Gene asked Scott.

"Sure," he said.

Gene spoke into his earpiece cord, then said, "Let's go."

They walked to the door, then paused. They disappeared while Shelly held the door open. Five people joined our section, and Trudie came to me.

"Beth." She hugged me. "It's nice to see you again."

"It's nice to see you." I smiled.

"I had your certificate, but that lady said to give it to her. I hope you don't mind." She pointed in the direction of Shelly.

"It's in good hands," Shelly said as she walked to us and tapped her clipboard.

"Thank you, Shelly, and thank you, Trudie, for bringing it," I said then introduced Carol.

Trudie introduced her husband, Mike, and proceeded to ramble on about how long it took them to get ready. I laughed at their expressions. She was one of those people who always had something to say about everything. She was kind and had a great sense of humor.

Gene and Scott returned with drinks for us. Gene handed me a big plastic cup with Teddy and Five/Ten's tour name, *Dance With Me*, written on the front.

"A drink for the beautiful lady," he said.

I took a sip, and it about knocked me on my butt with a strong taste of bourbon mixed with soda. I glanced at the cup to see writing in blue ink:

Have a blast.

"Teddy made it for you. I told him you got loose when you drink," Scott said to me.

"I don't have to drink to get loose." I laughed. "Did he make it?"

"Yep," Gene said.

The lights dimmed. People clapped, yelled, and chanted Teddy and Five/Ten's name. Anticipation built within me as my grin never faded. People's voices lowered while they waited for the talented musicians.

Chapter 7

A BEAM OF BLUE LIGHT revealed Teddy. He stood on stage with his back to us and guitar in hand. The arena came alive with the screams and cheers of the enthusiastic audience. The band played low-toned music, and Teddy didn't move from his spot for several seconds. He played a fast guitar riff, which made the roars and whistles of the crowd grow louder.

The music vibrated as the lights danced and brightened my surroundings. People danced, sang, and laughed. Excitement filled the air, and in unison, the crowd sang Teddy's song with him.

Teddy and the band performed several songs with the same energy as the first. Teddy brought his hands to his side to direct the sound level of the music to soften in a methodical low beat. He introduced the members of Five/Ten. One by one, they played a solo upon introduction, and the crowd loudly applauded.

Teddy bowed, and lights went black. I reached for my drink, plopped in the chair while Gene sat beside me.

"He keeps people on their feet," Scott said.

"He's a great entertainer, but don't tell him I said that." I smiled.

"Are you ready for another drink?" Gene asked.

"No, we're good," Scott spoke for us.

After a brief break, the overhead lights dimmed. People stood next to their seats and waited. The lights came on, and Teddy sat at a grand piano. He winked our way and played a soft melody that made the crowd cheer.

I leaned on Gene and took my shoes off as Carol leaned on Scott and did the same. We danced, sang, and laughed. Sweat poured down my back. Energy hummed throughout the arena until the set ended, and the stage was clear of musicians. I took a long hard drink from my cup, slurped the last sip, and shook it to hear the ice move.

"All gone," I said.

"I need to use the restroom," Carol announced.

"May we be excused?" I asked Gene, and he nodded.

I grabbed my shoes and cup. Gene spoke into his microphone. A few seconds later, Shelly stood at the door. He led us to the back while Shelly stayed in the area with the VIP people. We walked the hall, past the empty leather seat, and Susan came from the bathroom. She gave me a quick hug and walked to a dressing room.

"You're doing great," I complimented.

"Thanks. You, too. I saw you dancing." She laughed.

We turned to go into the restroom, but someone tugged gently on my hair. I turned and saw Teddy walk to a door across the hall. He placed his hand on a doorknob and winked at me. He opened the door, and I caught a glimpse of Carissa. She stood next to a chair with a frown on her face and arms folded across her chest.

I joined Carol in the restroom. We came back to the hall, and Gene handed me the same cup. Black inked words were written next to the previous words:

I like it when you dance.

"Teddy didn't sign it, so maybe I can pass it off being Noah Parker's handwriting," I teased, and Gene laughed.

We walked to the little door next to the stage. Carissa sat alone in the leather chair. The band walked onto the stage while Teddy waited for his cue. He smiled at us, then joined the band.

Carissa lifted her eyes to me. She frowned as I stepped in front of her.

"Care to join us?" I asked with enthusiasm.

"No," she said loudly, but firmly.

"Are you sure? It's fun out there." I wanted to be friendly.

"I'm sure." She continued to stare at me. "Beth, is it?"

"Yes, ma'am." I held my smile as Gene stood by my side.

She uncrossed her long legs, stood from her seat, and adjusted her black miniskirt on her thighs. The black high heels helped her tower over me by several inches. She cast her glare on me.

"I hope you don't have plans with Ted."

"I don't. I'm enjoying the evening," I said as my smile faded.

"Good. He leaves with me tomorrow." She kept her piercing blue eyes locked on me.

I tilted my head and said, "I'm sorry if I upset you, but there's no need to worry about me coming between you two. I'm enjoying the music and savoring the night before things return to normal."

"You won't come between us. I'll make sure of that." She leered down her nose and studied me.

"Let's go, Beth," Gene said and tugged my elbow.

Carissa stared at me until we walked to the door, which Shelly held open. I grabbed her arm and smiled.

"Are you going to join us?"

"In a minute," she said.

I nodded and went to my seat. I took my shoes off, placed them in the chair, and looked at Teddy.

I understood if Carissa was threatened by me. I didn't mean to flirt with him, but when I looked in his eyes, it came easy for me. I need to help Carissa, and him reconcile tonight. I'll speak to her after the concert and convince her I won't come between them.

"It's not your call. It's mine. I am yours, so don't be blind," Teddy ad-libbed into the song he sang and looked at me.

I laughed, and he continued to ad-lib lyrics when he sang *Fire In Your Heart*. His facial expressions, body movements, and words had the audience roaring with laughter and yet captivated by his dance moves.

We danced and threw our arms in the air, enjoying ourselves. I spun to my left, and Shelly stood next to me. I smiled, grabbed, and swayed her hand. She smiled as she moved her hips and danced as Teddy finished the song then went into the next.

After a few more, Teddy left the stage, and the crowd chanted, "Teddy. Teddy. Teddy."

Shelly smiled and said, "That was fun." She patted Gene on the arm. "You're pretty good at this, old man."

"I haven't enjoyed a concert in a while. Thank you, Beth," he said, and I nodded.

"Y'all havin' fun?" I looked at Carol and Scott.

"Hell, yeah," Carol said while Scott took a drink of beer and nodded at the same time.

"I didn't know you knew Teddy's music, Scott," I said.

"I bought some the day we met him and have been listening to it ever since." He laughed.

I pulled my phone from my pocket and noticed I had a text from Danielle:

> *Hey, Mom. We're at Lucy's having a bonfire. I'll call you in the morning. Dogs are great.*
>
> *Have fun.* - I texted.

"Is everything okay?" Shelly asked.

"Yeah. The girls are having a bonfire. I won't hear from them until tomorrow."

"Is Helen there?" Carol asked, inquiring about her daughter.

"You know she is," I said.

The lights dimmed, and the crowd fell silent. All turned black except a small white light shining behind Teddy to reveal his silhouette, center stage. He held the guitar, strummed a few cords, and the crowd roared to life. The spotlight shifted and showed him.

My mouth opened wide as I blinked several times and looked at Carol for answers. She looked at me then we both looked at Shelly and Gene. They studied my reaction, but I focused back on Teddy. He looked in our direction, smiled, and the crowd sang with him an old song, word-for-word.

"The red," I said out loud, and Shelly held my hand.

Teddy wore a long-sleeve untucked red silk shirt and thin black tie. His black tennis shoes blended well with his black silk pants. The band members remained in their original stage clothes.

"What's going on?" I asked Shelly.

She leaned into my ear and spoke loudly. "In about twenty minutes, all VIPs will be brought to the stage. Once you are there, you'll walk out first and join the band. Dance as hard as you have been."

"Does everyone know the plan?" I panicked.

"Yes. Gene will bring you to the door when it's time," she confirmed and let go of my hand.

"Shelly!" I exclaimed and reached for her as she turned to walk away. She leaned into me. "I can't do that. I'm klutzy, and I don't want to embarrass him."

"You'll be fine." She patted my arm and left us.

I studied Teddy on stage. He was calm and professional. Sultry, sexy, witty, and full of grace and style. I glanced at Carol. She put her arm around my shoulder.

"You're going to be fine," she said in a loud voice.

"Don't leave my side," I yelled at her, and she nodded.

I finished my drink while Teddy played another song. Gene put his hands on my hips and swayed them back and forth to get me in the mood to dance. I moved my body and kept the rhythm as my nerves settled.

After several more songs, Gene held my elbow. He motioned with his head for us to walk to the door while Shelly held it open. I retrieved my shoes and cup from the chair, and we followed him.

I smiled at Carissa, who sat in her leather chair and glared at me. Gene held my cup while I leaned on him and put my shoes on. Shelly lined us up as if we were going outside for recess, then she leaned into my ear.

"When I say go, walk to the line on the ground next to the piano. Do you see it?" she loudly asked.

"Yeah." I nodded.

I glanced past the stage, and butterflies danced in my stomach. The crowd clapped, cheered, and sang along with Teddy until the song ended.

He sat at the piano and played an upbeat melody. I motioned for Carissa to join us, but she didn't move or take her eyes off me.

"Go, Beth," Shelly said, and Gene nudged me.

I walked on stage with Carol following. Teddy caught my eyes. He smiled while he sang and nodded his head back, as to say we were to join him. I danced to the beat, and his smile grew wide. We held eye contact. I forgot there were twenty thousand-plus people in this space. He held my hand. The electric charge coursed down my body as we touched.

He directed me to sit next to him on the piano bench. He pulled his hand back, so he could continue to play. His fingers moved elegantly across the keys, creating a beautiful sound. I glanced at Carol and the others, saw they danced behind the piano, then gazed back at Teddy. He smiled and sang the ending of the song, then the music led into a slow melody.

I recognized the song and closed my eyes for a second. I remembered my vision from the other night. I opened my eyes.

Teddy stared into them while the words to *True Love* poured from his lips. I glanced behind the piano. The other VIPs stood on the side of the stage. Panic rushed over me.

Shelly motioned with her hands for me to stay seated. Teddy held my hand, stood from the piano bench, and I followed him with my eyes. He pulled me up, spun me toward him while Mark slid into his spot to take over the keys.

Teddy pulled me close into his body, kissed my cheek between singing the lyrics, and my skin tingled while our bodies pressed against each other. I forgot about the crowd while we danced. He dipped me, twirled me, then pulled me close into his body before he completed the song.

We stopped moving. He kissed my cheek again before the lights faded to black. The crowd's applause reverberated through the building.

"Thank you, Denver, and God bless," Teddy said. The audience roared louder with approval. He lowered our hands from his chest and said into my ear, "Don't let go. Follow me step for step."

The music continued to play while he guided me off stage. Once in the hall, he hugged me. His damp clothes clung to him, then he held me at arm's length.

"Sorry. Did I get you sweaty?" Teddy asked.

My face blushed. Shelly, Gene, and the others gathered around us. I glanced at the leather seat but didn't see Carissa.

"That was great," Shelly exclaimed.

"I thought I was going to be with you guys the whole time," I complained.

"You two took my breath away," Carol said and pointed to Teddy and me.

"I don't know how you guys do this," I said.

I leaned into Teddy while he laughed. The scent of his cologne and sweat blended attractively. He was sexy and irresistible.

"The fun isn't over." He kissed me on the cheek. "Shelly, could you show our guest into the dining area?" He brushed his finger across my cheek and said, "I'll join you in a few minutes."

"Right this way, please," Shelly said and led us into the room.

"Shall we?" Gene asked, presenting his elbow to me.

I took my cup from him as we entered the room. Food, fresh plates, and more drinks sat on the tables. Scott walked to the drink table and got a beer. I left Gene, joined Scott, and hugged his neck.

"Thank you for this evening," I said.

"It wasn't me. This all happened because you ran into Gene. It's been fun, and you looked good on stage," he said.

"Beth," Trudie called from behind me. She and Mike joined us. I introduced Scott to them, then she said, "You and Teddy looked great dancing. How long did you practice?"

"We didn't," I said, while Gene walked our way.

"You had to have. You guys were in perfect sync. It was like you became one with each other," she said.

"Would you two care for something to eat or drink?" Gene asked them.

"Really?" Trudie asked.

"Sure. Help yourself and please excuse us," he said, held my elbow, and led me from them. "Now, girl, how is your drink? Would you care for another?"

"Show me the way. I'll get it." I shook my empty cup.

"I'll get it. Go mingle, you little rock star." He smiled and took my cup.

I stood with Carol and Scott while we glanced around the room for a few minutes. We spoke about Teddy and the band being wonderful entertainers.

My plastic cup was held in front of my face. I recognized the hand holding it. I smiled and turned to see Teddy. He looked clean and refreshed in a different outfit. I took my cup from him and read what he wrote.

Thanks for the dance.

My smile grew wide, and I said, "You could have filled me in on what was going on, but now I understand the reason for the shopping trip. You had it planned all this time."

"Guilty." He smiled, then turned serious. "I didn't know you could sing."

"When did you hear me?" I asked.

"You harmonized with me on the last chorus of *True Love*," he said.

"I'm sorry. I was comfortable, and I guess I got into the song. I hope no one else heard."

"You were great," Teddy said.

"You're a natural," Gene said. "You can also dance. You were moving and grooving."

"How do you do this so calmly?" I asked Teddy in a flirtatious voice.

"Music is my passion," he said.

"Teddy!" Shelly said from behind Carol. "Will you come with me and meet these people, please?" she asked. "Sorry, guys."

He held my hand, and we followed Shelly. "I'm not doing this by myself, ma'am."

"These people are here to see you, not me," I said before we stopped in front of Trudie and Mike.

"Do you remember Trudie?" Shelly asked Teddy.

"I do. It's nice to see you again," he said, then held his hand out to Mike, "and this is?"

"This is my husband, Mike," Trudie introduced. "I was telling Beth earlier, you, and she melted together while dancing on stage. You put on a great show."

"You're a wonderful entertainer. Thank you for the tickets," Mike said.

"Thank you for the compliments. I'm glad you enjoyed the show," he said to them.

We excused ourselves. Shelly led us to the other VIPs. They stared at Teddy and didn't pay attention to Shelly or me. Teddy shook everyone's hands as they spoke about winning the tickets from a radio contest.

The door across from us, behind the guest, opened. Carissa stepped through and caught my attention as we held eye contact.

"Are you all coming to the afterparty?" Teddy asked the group.

"Yes, but can you do us a favor?" Donna, a VIP, asked.

"Depends on what it is," Teddy held his famous smirk.

"Will you sign our badges?" she asked, then held the badge she wore around her neck.

"Sure," he said and turned to Shelly to retrieve a marker.

He noticed Carissa by the door. He shook his head at her before turning his concentration back to the group. He signed the badges while Trudie, Mike, and the others rushed over to get his autograph. The rest of the band members signed the badges as they gathered in our group and spoke with one another.

Carissa turned on her heels and stepped out of the door. I diverted my eyes to the floor and felt confused. Why isn't she standing with Teddy? They were in a relationship, and I don't belong with him.

He held my hand and squeezed it, which brought me to look in his eyes.

"You do," he whispered. I gave him a puzzled glance, then he said to the group, "See you at the afterparty." He led me away from them. "Carissa and I aren't together."

"It looks to me that you are," I said.

Carol, Scott, and Gene met us across the room. Gene handed Teddy a drink.

"Mr. Teddy drinks?" I asked.

"Mr. Teddy has one drink after a successful show." He smiled.

"It went flawlessly," Gene said.

"This one was tough. I was afraid the shitty day would have ruined the concert," Teddy said.

"You had a bad day?" I asked.

"Somewhat, but you've been the highlight." He brushed his finger across my cheek.

"Carissa should be with you."

"No," he said quickly. "But, I do need to go to my dressing room if you will excuse me."

He left us, then Gene said, "We have time to smoke. Do you want to step outside?"

"I have to make a pit stop if y'all don't mind," I said.

"Me too," Carol chimed.

The effects of the bourbon and coke made my head spin. I held Carol's arm and leaned into her as we entered the restroom.

"Please don't let me do anything stupid tonight." I walked into the stall.

She yelled through the door. "What classifies as stupid, Beth? Toilet paper hanging from your butt or dancing the funky chicken? I need guidelines."

"You know what I mean," I said and stepped out of the stall. I walked to the sink, washed my hands, and looked at her in the mirror as she emerged from a stall.

"You pissed Carissa off," she said, washing her hands.

"I didn't do anything." I spun to face her while I dried my hands. "All I did was ask her to join us. She said no. How is that pissing anyone off?"

"She got mad when you and Teddy danced. She jumped from the chair and watched y'all for a few seconds then stormed down the hall," she said.

"Well, that's stupid. It was only a dance. I know they're fighting, and I don't want to go to the afterparty if it's going to cause more crap between them. I need to speak with her, go home, and let them be."

"You have to go to the afterparty!" Carol exclaimed. "Who cares what she thinks. Like you said. Teddy Nafton will be a thing in the past come tomorrow. Let's have fun tonight. I'll help monitor you, and I'll kick ya' if you do something stupid."

When we walked out of the restroom, Gene and Scott waited with our drinks. We went to the metal doors, but I lagged. I pulled Gene's arm while everyone else stepped outside.

"Can I speak with you?"

"Anytime, honey. What's up?" He leaned into me.

"I don't have to go to the afterparty. If it's going to be a problem, I can get a cab to take me home. I know Carissa and Teddy are arguing, and I need to leave," I explained in a low voice.

"She'll be okay, but I want you at the afterparty," Teddy said from behind me. I faced him, and he said, "Sometimes she doesn't want to dance." He looked at Gene and asked, "Are we ready?"

"I was taking Beth to smoke, then we'll load the cars. I'll get your things," he said, then left us in the hall and went into Teddy's dressing room.

"I'm sorry about you and Carissa. Maybe I shouldn't have said anything to her during the concert, but if I speak to her, maybe I can help."

"Carissa and I are not together. I didn't know she was going to show tonight, and I didn't want to cause a scene with an argument in front of the crew. She's gone, and I won't be seeing her any longer." He smiled.

"I don't want to be the cause of a breakup, so you better be truthful with me."

"You're not, and all I can do is be truthful with you." He held my gaze then pointed at the door. "Can we go and have a good time, please?"

He led me outside to meet the others. I lit my cigarette, and Gene pulled Teddy to the side to speak privately.

"Did you tell him?" Carol asked as she and Susan joined me.

"Tell who what?" Susan asked in a low voice, and Carol explained my situation. "You can't leave," Susan quietly said. "Carissa is full of herself. She makes Teddy's life worse for the wear. It's been a publicity thing between them, so we all knew they weren't serious. He's calmer and smiles more when you're with him, so please join us?"

"He told me he wanted me there, so I guess I'm going," I said then took another drink.

"He likes you, and we like him liking you," Susan said, but I rolled my eyes at the thought of Teddy and me.

"You did well," I said to her.

"So did you. You and Teddy glowed when you danced," she said.

Gene motioned for everyone to gather around him, and I asked, "Do you need me to drive?"

"No," He, Scott, and Carol said at the same time, which made everyone laugh.

I sulked and sipped my drink. Teddy smiled and held my hand. He led me to the limo, then opened the door.

"Ma'am." He studied me for a second, tilted his head, and asked, "Are you pouting?"

"Thank you." I climbed into the car. "And no, I'm not," I said in a sad voice. "I've never driven a limo." We slid into our seats.

Carol leaned into the car, looked at both of us, and asked, "Can I hitch a ride?"

"No. We were about to have sex when you rudely interrupted. I don't think you wanna see that." I smiled.

"Wait a minute." Teddy held his hand in the air. "Let's not be hasty. She could join us if she wishes."

"You couldn't handle us both, Teddy." She sat in the limo.

Scott sat, and Teddy teased, "Hey, Scott. I tried to talk your wife into a threesome with Beth and me. Is that okay?"

"That's fine with me. I've had thirty-two years of touching her. I don't like doing it anymore, so someone else needs too," he sarcastically said and laughed while Carol punched his arm.

"You're gonna get it," I sang.

"I got it years ago," he said while Gene drove from the arena.

I took another drink then asked, "You know what upsets me, Teddy?"

"Oh, man." He smiled and shook his head. "What?"

"The other VIPs received a badge, right?"

"Yeah. We didn't get one," Carol agreed.

"The other crappy thing is, he signed them," I said to Carol.

"What? I could have sold that online." Scott joined in the conversation.

"He must like them better than us, or he's cheap," I said, then took a few sips of my drink.

"I would say cheap. He didn't have any imported beer at the show," Scott said.

Teddy chuckled and shook his head like this was the most stupid conversation of the night.

"I am cheap," he said. "I saved two bucks a necklace not giving them to you, plus I do like the other VIPs better. They come and go out of my life, but I have a feeling you people are needy. It's going to be hard to get rid of you."

"Scott," he continued. "I had an idea you would sell yours online for more chili and golf balls. As for you, Beth Chambers, you would lose yours, even if I outlined it in diamonds. I saw how you lay your shoes everywhere."

"They're always right where I leave 'em." I lifted my foot in the air the best I could and grinned from ear to ear.

Gene pulled the car into a parking lot behind a tall building. The band limo was in front of our car, and it stopped. Rick stepped out of the first limo while Gene opened our door. The band members followed Rick, and we were to follow Gene. Everyone stood from the limo except Teddy.

He grabbed my hand and said, "Sit with me for a second."

"Is everything all right?" I asked, concerned.

"Yeah." He smiled. "I want a moment with you."

He became silent but stared at our hands. He was in deep thought, so I withheld my voice while he rubbed my fingers. I became rigid and motionless so as not to disturb him.

"Would you relax?" He let go of my hand and placed his on my knee.

"I'm trying, but I thought you needed some quiet time before we went inside." I smiled.

"I make you nervous." He snickered.

"Um, no," I said even though he was right.

"Liar," he said.

The light from the street lamp shone into the tinted car. He stared into my eyes. He moved his hand from my knee to my cheek, as though he was going to say something.

"Are you ready?" Gene interrupted, peering inside.

"Yeah." Teddy smiled and rose from the car.

He held his hand out to help me. I handed him my cup, then took his free hand. I stood, but fumbled, plopped back in the seat on my butt, and he laughed. Embarrassed, I chuckled and scolded myself for being a klutz. I felt grateful I landed in the car and not on the pavement.

"Too much to drink?" he asked.

"Not yet, but now you know my secret. I'm not graceful."

He held his hand out to me and said, "Try again." I stood out of the car with his help.

I blushed as he guided me into the building. With the doors shut behind us, music played. A small walkway led to the stage on the left of us and straight ahead, down two steps, was the dance floor and bar area.

We joined the band members who lined the wall next to the stage. Teddy leaned against the wall and held my hand. He guided me to stand in front of him, with my back against his chest. He laid his chin on my shoulder as Gene blocked our view of the dance floor.

"What are you doing?" I asked.

"Feeling you," he whispered in my ear.

"When do you want to go?" Shelly asked Teddy.

"Let's do it," he said, then tightened his grip around my waist.

I faced him, giggled, and said, "Not with you."

"Not here and not yet." He laughed.

The band followed Rick to the stage. The crowd screamed with excitement. The building came to life when a gentleman introduced Five/Ten. Teddy hugged me before he joined the band.

Chapter 8

Red velvet rope barricaded a space from the rest of the crowd. Gene unclasped a section and led us to a few couches. The other VIPs joined us as they sat at bar tables and on a few different couches. The stage was to our left.

"What if I want to dance?" I asked Gene.

"Go dance," he said. "I'll latch it when Teddy and the band join us. You're not that important."

"Thanks a lot." I laughed.

"I'm joking. I have you covered." He laughed and squeezed me into his side.

Teddy and the band performed while Gene left with my cup in his hand. People danced as though we were back at the concert. Shelly sat next to me.

"You take care of everything," I said to her.

"Someone has to," she said.

"You do a wonderful job," I said.

"Thank you."

Gene set my cup on the coffee table in front of me. Two waitresses served everyone else drinks.

"Thank you, Gene."

"You're welcome," he said.

He patted my shoulder then stood next to the opened section of the restricted area. Rick stood on the other side of the roped area and observed the surroundings. Four husky, tall men worked as bouncers and stood close to the stage.

The crowd grew in numbers and filled the dance floor. The building was at its capacity.

Carol stood and grabbed my hand. She informed us she needed to go to the bathroom.

"I got this," Scott said to Gene. "Come on, ladies. Y'all pee more than a racehorse."

"It's called dancing and drinking a hell of a lot, Scott," Carol said.

"Yeah, Scott." I wanted to defend Carol.

We followed him to the back of the establishment. Women were in the restroom, applying makeup, checking their hair, and clothes when Carol and I entered.

We overheard several women scheming how they were going to conquer Teddy. One woman stated she wanted to get as close as she could to the stage, then flash him in hopes of drawing his eyes in her direction.

"He's not into that kind of thing anymore," another lady told the young girl.

"Be smooth and get your number on stage. That's what I'm going to do," a lady said and adjusted her boobs in her bra.

"Most men like boobs, so write your number on yours, then flash him. That'll get his attention," I said while I washed my hands and got into their conversation.

"Maybe you're right," the boob adjuster agreed.

"I need to find a marker. You guys have a great time," I said to the room full of women before we left.

"You're so bad, Beth." Carol laughed while the door shut behind us. "He doesn't care about those gold diggers."

"It's funny listening to people talk about him. They only want one thing," I said as we met Scott outside the men's bathroom door.

"What one thing is that?" Carol smirked.

"You know what I'm talking about."

"Like you haven't thought about it?" she asked.

My face turned red, and I said, "I have for a brief minute or… five, but I'm not like that. I know I'm not going to see him after tonight, plus, he has a girlfriend who suits him better."

"You should hear what some of the guys say around the urinals," Scott said while we walked to the couches where Teddy and the band were sitting for a break.

"What?" I sat next to Teddy, who held his hand out for me to join him.

"They want him too." Carol and I both giggled at Scott's comment.

"What are you talking about now?" Teddy asked and held my drink cup.

"How you are popular with both the females and males," Scott explained loudly because of the music from the local band playing behind us.

"Thanks to Beth, y'all are going to get some boob action tonight," Carol said.

"Really?" Teddy asked me.

"Not from me," I giggled.

Carol explained what happened in the bathroom, then Teddy asked, "Where's that marker, Shelly?"

"You're funny," I said.

"I asked for your number too soon," he teased.

He leaned in front of me and handed Carol and Scott a VIP necklace. I looked at him with a sad face while Carol and Scott thanked him and watched my reaction. Teddy stared at me for a few seconds, then placed one around my neck. I bounced in the seat, held it in the light, and read what he signed.

My Dancing Queen
Teddy

"Thank you," I whispered in his ear then hugged him.

"I can't believe a plastic necklace makes you happy."

"I've had the time of my life, and I do thank you." I stared into his eyes.

Gene stepped behind Teddy and whispered into his ear. He acknowledged the information and leaned into me.

"I need to leave you for a minute," he said.

He and the band members followed Rick to the stage. They played an upbeat, fast-paced song. I sang and danced in my seat as

Shelly laughed at my movements. I couldn't sit any longer. I pulled Shelly, Carol, and Scott out of their seats and went to the dance floor.

We moved to the groove and laughed when one of the women flashed Teddy. He laughed, then looked at me. I pointed in her direction and held a thumb up to him. He smiled but kept eye contact with me throughout the rest of the song.

Once he finished the set, Teddy introduced the local band. As they took to the stage, we convened on the couch.

"Boob action. Did y'all see it? Did you get her number?" I asked Teddy.

"I couldn't make it out," he said.

"555-4728," Scott said, and everyone laughed.

Teddy leaned into me and said, "I love to watch you dance."

"I love to hear and watch you perform," I said.

"I can perform well." He brushed his finger across my cheek.

"Music." I blushed and chastised myself for flirting.

Teddy and I stared into one another's eyes. If he was an available man, I could fall for him. My imagination revealed his lips on mine as he made love to me.

"You guys sound great," I said to stop the thoughts in my mind.

"Thank you," he said and took a sip from his glass, but continued to gaze at me.

"Quit staring at me," I said.

"I can't help it. You're beautiful," he said.

"Thanks, but so is Carissa," I said.

"Stop worrying about her. You can't be the cause of a breakup when there wasn't a relationship to break up," he said. "Relax and have a great time tonight."

"I already have," I said.

His big brown eyes captivated me. I wanted to kiss him, but I couldn't. He belonged to another woman, but if they were together, why is she not by his side?

"Exactly," he said.

"What?" I asked.

"I don't want her," he said.

He leaned into me, but I sat back from him. I looked at the floor in thought. Don't get comfortable with him, I told myself.

"I'm going to play with the local band, so go dance." He smiled.

He and the band went to the stage. The rest of us went to the dance floor. Shelly and I were grooving when someone tapped my shoulder. I spun into a tall strawberry blond-haired gentleman.

"May I have a dance?" He held my shoulders.

"Sure," I said.

He placed one hand around my waist. We moved in place while I held onto his shoulders. He spun me, and I laughed.

"I'm Randy," he said when he drew me into his body.

"Beth," I shouted over the loud music.

"Nice to meet you. Are you here with anyone particular?"

"A group of people. How about you?" I asked.

"Same," he said. "Did you go to his concert?"

"Yeah. How about you?" I asked as Scott and Carol danced next to us.

"Yeah, but we left early to get here. I hate fighting the crowds and traffic," he said, then pointed at Teddy. "He's good, isn't he?"

"Yeah," I said while Teddy stared at me.

"Where are you from?"

"The south," I said while we danced.

"Tennessee?"

I smiled, then asked, "Are you from here?"

"Yeah. How long are you in town?"

"A few days."

Gene held his stare on me. Scott walked Carol to the couch then he patted Gene on the shoulder.

"You're sitting in the VIP section?" Randy asked.

"Yeah," I said.

"Do you know him?"

"No. He's guarded."

"Would you care to join me for drinks?" he asked.

Scott walked to us, tapped Randy on the shoulder, and asked, "May I?"

"We're sitting over there if you want to join me," Randy said in my ear and pointed to the back of the bar.

"Thank you," I said while Teddy ended his song and sang another.

"I didn't need to be rescued," I said and danced with Scott.

"I beg to differ, little sister."

"I need a drink," I said.

Why did he think I needed help? It was a dance in a crowded room. What could have happened? I walked to the section while Gene frowned at me. I took the longest, hardest drink I could handle, but gave myself a brain freeze. I held my head in my hands and stomped the floor a few times.

"That's what you get," Scott laughed.

"What did I do?" I asked him and rubbed my head.

"You can't dance with strangers," he shouted. I gave him an evil glare. "We don't know who knows you are with Teddy or who saw you with him on stage. It's like tax class."

"I can handle my own," I said offensively and leaned against the back of the couch.

"Not on my watch," he said.

Teddy stood the guitar in a stand, walked to me, and grabbed my hand. He led me to the small hallway toward the back door and stepped in front of me, face-to-face.

He held my shoulders, backed me against the wall, and pinned me. With his lips inches from mine, he stared into my eyes.

I broke our stare and looked toward the dance floor. Gene stood a few feet from us and blocked my view with his back. I gazed at Teddy, and he searched my eyes for a good minute.

"What am I going to do with you?" he asked.

"I don't know. What do you want to do with me?"

His smile widened, and we continued our staring contest.

"How's the brain freeze?"

"Fine." I smiled, raised my hand to his cheek, and felt his smooth skin.

The electricity between us grew. My body tingled with anticipation of our lips meeting, and our bodies pressed against one another.

I wanted it to happen. I moved my hand and held onto his waist. He grabbed the nape of my neck as if he was going to pull me into his lips, but he stopped.

"You're fuzzy."

"What does that mean?" I asked. With no response, I whispered, "Are you mad?"

"Ted!" A woman's voice said from the other side of us.

"No, babe," he said. "Do me a favor and stay close to Gene or Scott, please."

"Yeah, I screwed up. Scott called me on it."

"Ted!" the woman's voice yelled once again.

"Good," he said to me before he let go of my neck.

Carissa glided down the hall toward us. A tall, muscular gentleman walked behind her. Teddy stepped from me, and Gene stood beside us.

"What are you doing?" Teddy asked her with aggravation, punctuating his words.

"We can work this out," she said while she glared at me.

Teddy held his finger toward her. He continued to look at me as if he was going to say something.

"Y'all do need to reconcile," I said. "I don't want to come between you two." I stepped under Teddy's arm and looked at Carissa. "Nothing happened, and nothing will. I'm sorry." I looked at Teddy and said, "I'm not a person who comes between a couple."

"Damn right, you aren't coming between us," Carissa said and placed her hand on Teddy's shoulder.

He jerked from her touch, then held my elbow. He turned me to Gene then kissed my cheek.

"You have nothing to do with her and me," he said to me then looked at Gene. "Please take Beth to her seat."

Kyle and Shelly walked past Gene and me. I looked back as Gene guided me. Teddy held Carissa's arm and spoke with her. He, Kyle, and Shelly guided her in the opposite direction of us. Gene made sure I stood next to Scott, then he left to join Teddy.

I sat on the couch and reached for my full cup. I took a long drink and watched the local band while Carol stared at me.

"What?" I asked.

"Are you okay?" Carol asked.

"Yes. Our worlds don't mesh, and I shouldn't be here," I said.

Everyone came back to our area. Teddy stood behind the couch, leaned into Scott, and whispered something.

"Keep an eye on your date, Gene," Teddy said and patted my shoulder.

"We'll do," Gene assured.

Teddy ran his hand through my hair before he returned to the stage with Five/Ten and the local band. They played wonderfully for several hours while we drank, laughed, sang, and danced in our group.

I pushed the thought of Carissa from my mind and got tipsy from the alcohol. I took a break and watched drunk people dance in the most awful ways. Some people sat and sang with Teddy while a few others continued to party.

In the early-morning hours, Teddy thanked everyone for letting them play. He sat on the couch next to me, leaned with his elbows on his knees like his energy was spent. I rubbed his back, felt the sweat through his shirt, then laid my head on his shoulder.

That's it. I'm lit like a Christmas tree. I hope someone can help me to the car. I lifted my head from his shoulder but continued to rub his back. I chuckled and decided the alcohol brought down my inhibitions. Given the opportunity, I might have gone home with Randy, so as not to be alone.

"I wouldn't have let you," Teddy said, and I looked at him.

"Excuse me?" I asked.

"Are you ready to leave?" Teddy yelled to everyone but held eye contact with me.

"I'm good to go." I stood, swayed, and focused, putting my shoes on.

"You got it?" Teddy asked as he held my shoulders.

"I think so," I said, then stomped my feet on the floor to make sure my shoes were secure.

Scott came to my side to help, but Teddy said, "I got her. Get your woman." Then pointed to Carol, who swayed while she stood.

Scott leaped a step and helped her, laughed at the both of us, and said. "You guys can't keep up."

I waved at Trudie and Mike while Teddy wrapped his arm around my waist to help steady me. We walked the hall to the back doors when I held up my cup.

"I don't want to lose this." I tried to find my VIP necklace but fumbled. "Or this."

Teddy held it for me to see. "I won't let you lose it. Do you have your shoes?"

"I sure do." I stopped in the hall, looked at my feet, and held my right leg up.

"You're doing well, Beth." He smiled.

Once outside, the cool air felt refreshing, hitting my face. I leaned my head back to feel the nightly breeze.

"I had a lot of fun." I slurred my words.

"That's great, babe, but I need to get out of the wind," he said with his hands on my shoulders. "Let's walk to the car."

"Oh, your voice!" I exclaimed." Man, you gotta be careful with that weapon."

He helped me into the limo and slid in while everyone else spilled into the car. Gene closed the doors, took his place in the driver's seat, and turned on the engine.

"Hey, Gene," I blurred.

"What?"

"I'm going to let you drive." I leaned my head against the chilly windshield.

"Thanks for giving me permission," Gene said as everyone laughed.

"Did you see them, Shelly?" Teddy asked.

"We're on it," she said. "Gene?"

"We got this," Gene said.

"On what? Got what?" I asked and tried to make sense of what they were discussing. "What?" I asked once again.

"Nothing. Are you okay?" Teddy placed his arm around me and pulled me to him.

I laid my head on his shoulder and said, "Fine and dandy, Mr. Tandy." I raised my head. "I can rhyme like you do. Hey, maybe you need me to help you write a song." He and Scott laughed. "I can do it. I'm great at writin' songs. Ain't I, Carol?"

"Fine as pig hair." She laughed and laid her head on Scott's shoulder.

"You'll be home in a few minutes," Teddy said and guided my head to his shoulder.

I smelt the scent of cologne mixed with his sweet-scented sweat. This man was irresistible. I loved the energy that ran through my body with his touch. He draped his arm around me, and I softly nuzzled my nose into him.

My body tingled, and I kissed his neck. I tasted the salt from his skin. He touched my cheek, and I kissed him again. He leaned his head to mine and stopped my lips from contact.

I quickly moved and tried to focus on his eyes in the dark. "I just did that, didn't I? I'm sorry."

"Don't be," he quietly said with his hand on my cheek. "What am I going to do with you?"

"What do you want to do with me?" I whispered then closed my eyes to get my bearings.

He guided my head to his shoulder. I wanted his touch all over my body, but I argued with myself in my drunken thoughts.

This man had his own life with a beautiful girlfriend by his side. I won't be a man stealer, and she didn't want to let him go. He needed to make up with her.

"Stop arguing with yourself," he said and stroked my hair.

"How did you…" I sat up.

"You're fuzzy," he said.

"You're a nice guy, Teddy. Thank you for a magical night. I hope you and your girl have a great life," I said.

He leaned his head on mine and said, "I hope WE do too."

Chapter 9

I WAS MELANCHOLY WITH NO contact from Teddy since the afterparty. I questioned myself as to whether I should have called him. I could have texted to thank him properly, but I didn't want to cause trouble between him and Carissa.

I reached for the phone, but the cup and VIP necklace on the nightstand, next to the bed, caught my attention. Instead of the phone, I picked up the cup. I turned it in my hand and smiled at the last thing he wrote:

I had a wonderful time.
Teddy
(Not Noah Parker)

I pulled the cup to my chest and grabbed my phone. I had a missed text from the early-morning hours. I opened my music app first, hit play, and heard his voice. I snuggled under the covers then opened my text app. Words from the unknown number:

Are you Babe?
Who is this? - I texted.

I rubbed my eyes and stretched. Teddy's sultry voice sang a slow ballad then I received another text from the same number.

Leave him alone or you'll regret it.

I don't adhere to threatening words, nor will I be intimidated by a stranger. I smiled and texted:

What kind of threat is that? Be more creative next time or at least tell me who you're talking about.
You know it's Teddy and you'll be stopped by whatever means. It would be easier for you not to cause any scenes. – Unknown.

Your rhyming does not show creativity and we are not together for me to leave him alone. – I texted.

I waited for a response, but within a few minutes, I rose from the bed. I showered, dressed, and walked up the stairs. I went to the refrigerator, got a cold soda, then stepped outside on the back porch.

I sat on the love seat, lit a cigarette, and watched a mother goose tend to her babies. They swam in the pond behind the cattails. The back door slid open.

"Morning. Do you want to get breakfast on the way?" Scott asked.

"Morning. I'm not hungry," I said. "When are we leaving?"

"In about an hour," he said and took a sip of coffee.

"I love it out here."

"It's peaceful," he said, and the back sliding door opened again.

Carol held a flower bouquet in one hand with her arm intertwined through Teddy's. The band members, Shelly, Gene, and Rick, followed. Scott stood as I moved to the edge of the seat and stared at them.

"Hey," Teddy said and held more flowers.

"We didn't hear the doorbell," Scott said and grinned at me.

"Pelt barked, so I looked outside, and it was them. I greeted them at the door, so Beth wouldn't be alerted." Carol smiled, then asked me, "Surprised?"

I nodded, and Teddy sat next to me. He handed me a bouquet of six beautiful white roses.

"What are y'all doing here?" I asked him.

"Going to Pikes Peak," Teddy said.

"Y'all left yesterday," I said and smelled the flowers.

"No. We're here," he chuckled.

"You're lame." I snickered and looked at Scott. "You knew they were going with us?"

"I was going to tell you last night, but when I went downstairs, you were asleep on the couch with your head on the tax book. You were calling out Teddy's name. Teddy! Oh, Teddy!" Scott teased, being dramatic and raised his hand to his chest.

"What are you, like five?" I asked him while everyone laughed.

"That's okay, babe. I dreamt about you last night," Teddy said, and shoulder bumped me.

"I didn't, but thanks for the flowers," I said to him. "You decided to go with us to Pikes Peak, and no one could have told me?"

"After we spoke last night," Scott said and pointed between himself and Teddy. "We thought it would be fun to surprise you."

"It worked, but where is everyone else?" I asked as the band members, Shelly, Gene, and Rick sat on different outside furniture and around the patio table.

"Everyone went home except for who you see," Teddy said.

"Y'all have a tour, so shouldn't you be…oh, I don't know. Touring?" I asked.

"We have time before our next gig," Kyle said.

"We haven't lined out all the venues so, we decided to take in a few sites," Thad said.

"You leave tomorrow evening." Teddy held my hand, and I nodded for confirmation. He asked, "How would you feel about us hanging with you guys and getting to know one another?"

It was my fault, they stayed in Colorado. I came between Teddy and Carissa as well as kept Gene, Shelly, and Mark separated from their families.

"Whoever wanted to leave, left yesterday. You're not keeping anyone from anything," Teddy said. "As far as Carissa goes, you didn't cause us to break up."

"How did you know what I was thinking?" I asked.

"I know more about you than you think," he said.

"I've had a combined three-hour conversation with you; therefore, you don't know me," I said.

"Don't be too sure. I know you're a fan. You want me," he smiled.

"Noah Parker, but wanting you? Umm, I don't think so." I smiled. "When are y'all leaving Colorado?"

Teddy glanced at Scott, then back at me, and asked, "May I speak with you privately?"

"Sure," I said, then we walked to the door.

"You got this," Scott said and patted Teddy on the back.

I glanced at Scott, then Teddy, and I walked into the kitchen. He leaned against the counter while I added the flowers to the vase with the others.

"Thank you. These are beautiful, but don't waste your money on flowers for me," I said.

"You deserve beautiful things," Teddy said, and I rolled my eyes at him.

"I wanted to text you, but I chickened out. I had a wonderful time at the concert, even though I'm embarrassed how tipsy I got at the afterparty." I smiled and arranged the flowers.

"Tipsy?" He laughed. "I wouldn't say tipsy. You were flat out drunk."

I blushed, brushed my fingers over the flower petals, and said, "Sorry. I hope I didn't do anything stupid."

"You wouldn't keep your clothes on."

"I hope I did, but that would explain why the next morning, I woke in my bra and panties." I leaned against the opposite counter.

"Shelly helped you into bed." He blushed.

"Thank goodness." I breathed a sigh of relief, then bluntly asked, "Where's Carissa?"

"She went to California for a shoot," he said.

"Why didn't you go with her? You were to work things out with her."

"Carissa and I aren't exclusive. Her and my relationship were companionship and had been on and off for years. She liked the publicity I offered, so she was upset to see it go. *The Teddy and Carissa Watch*." He shook his head and looked at the floor. "It's over and will be no more."

"I've never heard of *The Teddy and Carissa Watch*," I said.

"Hum. I thought you were a fan." He studied me.

"Told you, I'm not." I smiled.

"You may not have read about me, but you know my music; therefore, you listen to me, therefore, you're a fan." He analyzed.

"I like your voice and music, but that's it." I flirted. "What's this watch?"

"The media would run stories of her, and I being an on-again, off-again romance. Carissa loved the spotlight, so she fed them stories, which created *The Watch*. It was to keep our names in the public."

"Well, I can't offer anything except friendship. I'm sorry about the other night. I didn't mean to come onto you and make you uncomfortable," I said.

"You didn't." He snickered. "It's refreshing to meet someone who stands by her beliefs and family values. You're independent."

"I do what I have to do, and that's it. If you need more than friendship, go after Carissa," I said.

"I know where I want to be."

"No more flirting. I'm sorry about doing it." I smiled.

"I like the flirting." He blushed.

"I'm glad you picked up on it. It's been a while." I continued to flirt. I scorned myself, stop it, Beth.

"You're doing it right." He smiled wide.

My imagination played in my mind of him lying in bed, under the covers, wide awake, staring at a ceiling. Loneliness rushed over me, but why? I wasn't lonely.

"Are you sure you want to hang with us?" I asked.

"More now than a minute ago."

"Is this why you wanted to speak with me?"

"Why do you guard yourself?" he asked.

"I have a lot to protect."

"What?"

"The girls, my grandbabies, family, business, and dogs. That's what my life consists of, and they're my world. Your and my worlds don't match, and they never will, so why are you here?"

"You'll see with time."

"See what?" I asked and raised my eyebrows. With no response from him, I said, "The fact that you're a good guy? Not because of your fame, but you're genuine. I hope you find what you're looking for, so don't waste your time on me. You need to be calling your girl."

"Do you think you're a waste of time?"

"For you, yes, sir," I said.

"I have my work cut out."

"I'm not a challenge, so don't work on me." I felt offended.

"You said you protect your kids, grandbabies, family, and business, not to mention the dogs. Dogs, Beth. Not once did you say you were protecting yourself, but that's a form of it. Your heart was broken, and you're scared it will happen again, so why bother handing it to someone. Am I right?" he asked, moved close to me, and held my hand.

The energy grew between us, and shivers ran down my spine. My imagination showed how he and I were in a tender embrace and a passionate kiss. Reality slapped me in the face. His life and goals were different than mine.

"It took a while to rebound from the first heartbreak. I don't want to go through that again. I don't know what you're looking for, but I need to tell you." I evaluated my emotions. "I'm scared of you."

"Why?" he asked.

"My life is an open book, so it's not a secret I've only been with one man my whole life. The thought of being with any man scares the hell out of me, but with you, it's easy to imagine…"

"Beth…" He interrupted.

"Listen." I continued. "You need to focus on your girl. You've been around the block several times, and you don't want me. I'm too old, and I have baggage."

"The math puts you at forty-four or forty-five pending on your birthday, so you're not too old. I know math."

"Have you seen the women you date?" I snickered.

"Yeah," he said. "I'm older than you."

"But you date, girls my daughter's age."

"You've thought about you and me in that way?"

"What way? A one-night stand that's now turning into what, three?" I asked.

"I don't want a one-night stand with you. Don't think it's not tempting, but I want more, and you want more, as well. I'm to give you time for you to see what we have together is special," he explained.

"You don't know me," I said.

"If you let me in, you would see…"

"No. Let's drop this," I said.

"You have control issues. Lots of bricks making up that wall of yours," he said.

"Yeah. Run now." I smiled while I looked at him over my glasses.

"I'm not running. I want to know what I'm dealing with."

"I might need to know what I'm dealing with," I said. "You sending Gene with me to tax class, tells me that YOU have control issues."

"I'm used to taking care of people." He smiled.

"The last thing I need is someone trying to control or take care of me, so please don't play bodyguard. I can take care of myself."

"I'm not your bodyguard unless you want me to be," he said, and I laughed.

The back door opened, and Scott said, "Sorry to interrupt. I'm getting a few drinks."

"I'll consider it." I held Teddy's stare, not paying attention to Scott.

"I have the qualifications," Teddy said.

"You aren't ready?" Scott asked me.

"I'll get ready," I said. "Thanks for the talk, Teddy."

"I'm not finished," he said.

"You didn't…" Scott said.

"No," Teddy interrupted him. "I need a few more minutes."

"Well, come on," I said and led Teddy downstairs. "Is everything okay?"

"Yes, but I have a proposition for you," he said.

"Shoot," I said and went into the bathroom for my contacts.

"When does your flight leave?"

"I have to be at the airport at seven. Why?" I asked while he stood in the small hall. I leaned on the doorframe of the bathroom, smiled, and waited for his response. He hesitated and stared at me. "What? The famous Teddy is scared to ask something?"

"I want to take you home." He blurted then took a step back.

"I'm not going to hit you, but I don't understand. I have a ticket."

"I know, but I own a plane and could fly you home. I want to meet your family, and it's more comfortable instead of a commercial flight," he said to convince me it was a good idea.

I moved to the entertainment room and sat on the couch in thought.

"That's a strange request. Why would you want to meet the family? I haven't told them about you."

He walked to the opposite couch and sat on the other end. "I like you and want to be a part of your life. I want to know everything about you, including your children and grandkids. I want to see your world."

"You need to go home to prepare for the tour, plus, how do you know we'll speak after today? I'm not that friendly." I felt unsettled with his offer.

"You are, and we'll speak every day. We want to do this," he said.

"It's now WE?" I shook my head.

"I spoke to everyone. They're excited to meet the rest of your family, including Shelly, Gene, and Mark. We won't bother you. We have a hotel in mind."

I walked into the bathroom in thought. I pulled my hair into a ponytail then placed a contact in one eye. I stared into the mirror and felt confused. He needed to focus on the tour and didn't need to waste fuel and time on me.

"Are you going to say anything?" he asked from the other room.

"Don't the others want to go home?" I leaned against the bathroom, doorframe.

"They want to relax before things get crazy," he said.

"I don't get it." I returned to the bathroom mirror and placed a contact in my other eye.

"Look, babe," he said and walked to the bathroom door. "We're friends."

"It's too early to tell." I looked at him through the mirror.

"You're beautiful, smart, funny, and I could live in your eyes forever."

"Why would you say that?" I asked.

"It's true," he said. "If I were to ask any other woman to fly her home and walk her to her doorstep, she would jump at the chance to show me off to her family."

"I'm not..."

"I know you're not like other women, but think of me as a rich friend who wants to spoil you, except you're making it difficult." He smiled.

"My world is boring." I applied blush, and mascara then turned to the doorway. Teddy blocked me from exiting.

"Let me decide." He held my shoulders.

I looked at the carpet and said, "I haven't told the kids about you. It's hard for me to grasp that someone like you is wanting to be friends with someone like me, especially when you have someone like Carissa hanging on your arm. You have all the friends in the world. With a snap of your fingers, they'll appear, so why me?"

"Why do you ask that?" he asked.

"My brain can't comprehend the reasoning. I'm a nobody."

"You aren't a nobody. If it's the money, I'll buy the ticket from you. I don't expect anything from you."

"Is that what you think? That's it's about the damn money?" I pushed my way past him and became angry. I stopped at the stairs and looked at him. "I don't want to owe YOU."

"And you won't," he said.

"The money and time you're wasting on me is too much."

"You're not a waste."

"We can speak on the phone until we decide if we're going to be friends."

"I said, friends. Nothing more yet." He held my hand.

"Yet?" I asked and took my hand from him. "There isn't going to be more."

I ascended the stairs as he followed. He grabbed my elbow and stopped me before I opened the door. With my back against the wall, he leaned in close.

"This is a nice gesture, not a handout. It's been difficult to contain myself around you, even now, while you're being stubborn." He stared into my eyes for a second, lowered his voice, and said,

"I think about you all the time. The first day I caught a glimpse of you…last night…this morning. I can't get you off my mind. I see wonderful thoughts when I look into your eyes. I want your heart and head in agreement. You need to understand that what we have between us is special. Your trust issue is keeping you from seeing the truth."

"What truth?" I gave him a puzzled glance, but he didn't respond. I angrily said, "I'm not after your money, so if you think I am, I don't want any part of you. I can take care of my own, and I don't need anyone to lean on. I'm not looking for gain, or be the cause of your and Carissa's separation, so the answer is no, Teddy. No handouts. No nothing. I appreciate the offer, but no."

I ducked under his arm and opened the door with him on my heels. "I'll be ready in a few, guys," I said to everyone as they sat throughout the kitchen and living room area.

I walked to the back porch, stepped into the sunlight, and stared at the geese in the pond water. I was a charity case for him. Time or money didn't mean anything to him. I was a business owner, and my time was valuable. Finances didn't come easy for me, and I worked hard for every penny I earned. I faced problems with family, money, and clients, whereas Teddy, was carefree. I lit a cigarette, and the glass sliding door opened, then shut. Teddy walked to me.

"I could offer you anything, Beth. Say the word, and I'll hand you the world," he said.

"I don't want the world." I stared into his eyes and physically felt my heart hurt. Words formed in my thoughts.

Do you hear and feel me?

I tilted my head, and he asked, "You do, don't you?"

"If our lives don't intertwine today, and our friendship isn't built, you go your way, and I go mine without guilt," I said.

"Ms. Rhyme Girl," he chuckled. "Together, you and I have a destiny. It is to intertwine our lives and live in harmony."

"Really? You had to rhyme." I laughed.

"That's my job," he winked.

I wanted to get to know him, but his life and Carissa waited in Michigan. His existence consisted of wealthy friends, no time frame, and beautiful women who threw themselves at him. My life involved grandchildren who threw up on me.

"It's been a wonderful experience to have met you all, and y'all are welcome to my house anytime when you're in town for a purpose," I said.

"You are a purpose." He wrapped his arms around me and pulled me close. I relaxed in his embrace. "I'm not wrong about you."

"What does that mean?" I stepped out of his arms.

"Are we going today?" Scott asked impatiently. "You two finished with your little tiff?" He pointed at me and said to Teddy, "I told you she would get pissed. Most women would jump at the chance, but not her."

We stepped inside the house, and Teddy told him, "You're right. She's stubborn."

I spun and gave them both a look that could kill. I pointed at Scott then at Teddy and said, "Y'all stop talking about me behind my back. I ain't dead. You talk about me when I'm dead."

"Fine." Scott raised his hands in the air.

"You're an ass, Scott. Now go to the car." I pointed to the door. I was agitated. He knew Teddy's plan and didn't tell me.

"After you, Godfather Junior." Scott bowed his head and held his hand toward the front door.

"Stop it," I said as he laughed. We walked outside. Two black SUVs were parked in the driveway, and I asked, "No, limo?"

"I'm not driving a limo up a mountain," Gene said.

"Do you want me to drive?" I asked Gene.

"Get in, Beth." He held the door open for me.

Teddy and I sat in the third row while Scott and Carol sat in the second. Gene drove while Shelly rode in the front seat. The other SUV carried Susan, Kyle, Thad, and Keith while Rick drove, and Mark sat shotgun. It was going to be a beautiful day going to Pikes Peak.

Chapter 10

"Why did you call Beth, Godfather Junior?" Teddy asked Scott.

"You have to ask her to give me permission to speak." He smiled.

"You're an ass." I thumped Scott on the back of the head, and he chuckled.

"Our mom is the original Godfather. She's the one who holds the family together. Beth will be her successor once the Godfather baton has been passed," Scott said.

"Which hopefully won't be for a long time," I said.

My phone rang, and I looked at it. I saw the name, panicked, and hung up.

"Who was that?" Carol asked.

"Lucy."

"She's going to call back until you answer," she said as my phone rang again.

"Please be quiet," I asked everyone then answered. "Hey."

"Beth wants you to be quiet, Teddy," Scott shouted.

"Shut up," I whispered sternly.

Teddy smiled, leaned next to the phone, and asked, "Do you want me to be quiet?"

"What are y'all. Seven?" I asked them.

"Who was that, Mom?" she asked.

"Do we need to stop before you lose service?" Teddy boomed, and I lightly hit his shoulder.

"I'm going to have to call you back, Lucy," I said to throw her off the subject.

"Are you okay?" she asked.

"Yeah, but…"

Scott reached around the seat to grab the phone. Teddy helped wrestle it from me, then held the device to his ear, and smiled.

"Hi," he said.

"Good," Scott said to me.

"This is Teddy."

I reached to get the phone back, but Carol spun in her seat. She raised her hand and intervened my hand.

"They need to know, Beth," she said.

"I was going to tell them when I got home," I said, then threw my hands in the air from defeat.

"Teddy Nafton," he paused. "Yes, the singer. You're Beth's oldest, right?" He paused again, then said, "A date." He held the phone from his ear while she screamed. "She's right here. Hold on." With wide eyes, he handed me the phone and said, "She's a spitfire."

I held the phone next to my ear, and she asked loudly, "*The Teddy Nafton?*"

"Why didn't I get that response from you when we met?" Teddy asked me.

"Yes, it is," I said to Lucy then looked at Teddy. "You were in my way."

Lucy excitedly asked questions, but I interrupted to calm her. "Okay, honey. I'll fill you in later tonight. We're driving to Pikes Peak, and I might lose service."

"You know *The Teddy,* and now you're on a date with him?" she demanded.

"This is not a date," I said.

"Yes, it is," Teddy sang, and I shook my head.

"Then what is it?" she asked.

"He's a stalker," I quipped.

"I am not." He laughed.

"Did you go to his concert?" she asked.

"Yes."

"Have you told Danielle?"

"No. I'll call her as soon as we hang up," I said.

"Y'all are friends?"

"We're getting to know one another to see if we want to be friends," I said and smiled at Teddy.

"Let me talk to him," she said.

"I'm going to put you on speaker." I pushed the button. "Scott and Carol are here along with Shelly and Gene." They all said hi at the same time.

"Hi, guys. Mr. Nafton, how do you know my mother, and is this a true date?" she asked.

"We met several days ago and hit it off. For the time being, I agreed to be friends, but yes. She agreed to go out with me today, so this is a date." He smiled.

"Stop the car and let me out." I joked.

"You met *The Teddy* several days ago and flat out lied to me about the concert," she scolded.

"Why does everyone refer to you as *The Teddy*?" I asked him.

"That's who I am," he said proudly.

I shook my head and said, "Yes, Lucy. I'm sorry for lying. I don't want to get into this right now. I want to call your sister before we lose service."

"Fine, but WE WILL talk," she said factually. "It's nice to speak with you, Mr. Nafton."

"Please call me Teddy." He looked at me. "Hey, Lucy, would you help talk your Mom into letting me bring her home tomorrow? I want to meet you all."

"Are you serious?" she yelled. "Hell, yeah. What's your problem, Mom? How close are you guys? We need to meet this dude. What if he's not Teddy, the singer? You could be going senile in your old age."

"I can verify he's Teddy, the singer," Scott said as we laughed.

"I thought he was Teddy, the actor," Carol teased.

"I thought we picked up some random guy off the street, dressed him like Teddy, and called him Teddy," I said. "Lucy, honey. I'll talk to you more about him tonight. I have to call your sister."

"I want proof, so can you take a picture of you and him together and send it to me?"

"If you promise not to post it on social sites or send it to your friends or the rest of the family. Keep this between your sister and us. No telling anyone. You know I don't like attention or questions," I said.

"I promise. No social sites, no friends, no family," she confirmed.

"I will after I speak with Danielle. Kiss the kids for me. Love you."

"Call me tonight. Love you, Mom. Bye, y'all," she said.

I hung up, scrolled the screen, and found Danielle's number.

"I can't believe you guys. Y'all are asses." I complained.

"Hey, Mom," Danielle answered.

"Hey, sweetie. How are things?" I asked, and Teddy smiled as if he won a victory.

Gene pulled the car to the shoulder of the road with the mountain view in front of us. "Do you have service, Beth?"

"Yes, Gene. Thank you."

"Who are you talking to?" Danielle asked.

"That's the reason for this call. A few seconds ago, I spoke with Lucy and told her about Teddy Nafton."

"*The Teddy*? What's up with him?" she calmly asked.

"Why does everyone call you, *The Teddy*?" I held my smile on him.

"Fine, Teddy Nafton," she rephrased her question.

"He's here with me. Is it okay if I put you on speaker?" I asked.

"Yeah, but how, when, and where…what's going on?" she asked in a level-headed manner.

I tapped the speaker button on my phone. "Danielle, this is Teddy. Teddy, this is my youngest, Danielle."

"Hi, Danielle," Teddy said.

"Carol and Scott are with us along with Gene and Shelly."

"Hey," everyone said at the same time.

"Hey. Is this really Teddy Nafton? Did you get to meet Five/Ten?" she asked.

"Yeah. It's me, and she likes me more than them." He smiled.

"Five/Ten are awesome, but Teddy can't sing," I teased.

"That's bullshit," Danielle said. "You've been a fan of his since you were a teenager."

"No, I haven't. You're mistaking him for someone else," I said as he laughed.

"You have all his CDs," she said.

"You're grounded, Danielle," I snapped.

"Thank you for verifying that she's a fan," Teddy said. "I have a favor to ask of you, Danielle."

"What?" she asked.

"Please help me convince your Mom to let me come with her to meet you guys tomorrow." I rolled my eyes at him.

"You want to meet us?"

"Yeah."

"Well, yeah," she said excitedly. "You have to let him, Mom."

"That's not going to happen."

"Let me make sure I have this straight. You met Teddy Nafton, and now he wants to meet your kids, and you said no?" she asked. "That sounds like you. You're going senile, old woman." We laughed, then she asked, "Are you sure it's Teddy?"

"I don't know any other," I chuckled.

"Yes, Danielle. It's Teddy Nafton. We went to his concert," Carol said.

"Why didn't you tell us, Mom? You couldn't say, 'Oh, by the way, I met Teddy Nafton?' Saturday night, Lucy and I got online and went through his tour dates. We were going to surprise you with concert tickets in Memphis for your birthday."

"There isn't any need for that now." Teddy beamed.

"I wouldn't go if tickets were free," I teased.

"Liar," Danielle said.

"Danielle!" I exclaimed.

"How and when did y'all meet?" she asked.

"We met a few days ago, but I don't want to get into this now. We're going to the mountain, and I've stopped two cars. I'll call you this evening and tell you everything," I said.

"Fine, but Teddy Nafton is sitting next to you? Where's the band?" she asked.

"He's sitting close enough for me to smack for starting all this, and the band members are in the other vehicle behind us," I said.

"Please help me convince her," Teddy said.

I shook my head as she said, "We'll convince her, but I need proof."

I explained to her what I told Lucy then said, "I'll send it in a few minutes. Give Gabi kisses from me."

"I will."

"Love you," I said and hung up.

"Danielle is more like you," Teddy observed.

"She's a logical thinker, and Lucy is a free thinker." I smiled. "They're as different as night and day."

"That's for sure," Carol said.

"Yours are too," I said to Carol then raised my voice for Gene to hear. "Thank you, Gene." I looked at Teddy. "Happy now?"

Teddy's gorgeous smile glistened, and he said, "Yep. We'll convince you."

"That's not going to happen," I said. Gene pulled the SUV into traffic, and I looked behind us to see the other SUV followed. "I stopped everyone."

"Yes, you did, Ms. Princess. Can we have some fun now?" Scott asked.

I opened the camera app on the phone and said, "I could shoot you and Scott."

"I'm going to be part of your life," Teddy said assuredly.

"No, you aren't." I smiled and hoped he would. "Would you mind a quick picture?"

"Now, you want one." We made silly duck faces and took a selfie. He and I approved then I sent it to the kids. "The kids can't convince you?"

"No." I rolled my eyes at him once again.

"Quit rolling your eyes," Teddy said.

"I'm checking for spiders above my head."

"Scott, help me out. Convince Godfather Junior to let me do this," Teddy said.

"I can't talk this thing into anything." Scott pointed at me.

"You can't have your way all the time." I smiled at Teddy. "I want to stop talking about it and look for Bigfoot." I stared out the window.

"Let's find a bigfoot," Teddy agreed to change the subject.

We drove up to the mountain, looked for Bigfoot, and laughed at the thought of one existing. Trees were toppled in the woods. We claimed Bigfoot threw them on the ground when he became jealous of his Bigfoot woman having an affair with the Yeti who lived on top of the mountain.

A lake and a gift shop were on the mountainside. We pulled into the parking lot, which consisted of two other vehicles. No one was outside, so we decided to look at the beautiful scenery.

I stepped out of the vehicle, and a few chipmunks sat on a rock, a couple of feet from us. I called one to me then Carol called one. They took a few steps toward us, sniffed the air, then scampered off.

Once the band members joined our group, I said, "I want to apologize for making us stop earlier."

"No problem," Kyle said and patted me on the shoulder as everyone followed his lead.

"Isn't it nice?" Teddy asked, held my hand, and pointed at the lake.

"Yeah, it is." I admired the scenery.

We stared at the brilliant blue water. Teddy draped his arm over my shoulder. Suddenly, he grabbed me with both hands and acted as though he was going to push me into the water. Scott joined in with the fun. They both picked me up like they were going to throw me in, which made me squeal.

A few more vehicles pulled into the parking lot. People stood from their cars and walked to us as they got phones from their pockets or purses.

Before the small crowd reached us, Teddy and the band members formed a tight circle around me. I laughed as they guided me the few feet to the vehicles. We were securely seated, then Gene drove to the summit.

Midway up, a sign caught my attention. I pointed to it, and Scott explained the history about the spot, Devil's Playground.

"We need to hike the trails the next time you visit. My neighbors said, during electrical storms, lightning strikes the boulders," Scott said.

"That's interesting," I said.

The further up we drove, Scott became our guide. He told us how the trees didn't grow on top of the mountain because of lacking oxygen. We neared the peak when he pointed out the window.

"There's snow," Scott said.

"Wow," I said.

"We had an early one this year," he said while Gene pulled into the parking lot at the peak.

A hundred or so cars were parked in the lot, and people walked around. Small crowds flowed in and out of a restaurant and gift shop, which stood on the far right of the summit.

Teddy stepped from the vehicle and held my hand. We walked around the car, and he leaned against the side. He pulled me to lean my back on him using the SUV to block us from spectators. I wrapped my arms around his arms while we enjoyed the beautiful view.

Shelly, Carol, and Susan joined us. Shelly asked if I wanted to go with them to the shop. I declined and relaxed in Teddy's embrace as they walked from us.

"This is nice," he said and placed his chin on my shoulder.

"Are you flirting with me? We said no, flirting." I laid my head on his shoulder.

"I might be, or it's the thin air," he said and slowly rocked me.

We looked at the trees underneath our view. In the distance, freeways, and a few buildings stood in the landscape. They looked like little toys. The colors of browns, golds, and greens, blended to create a beautiful scene.

Not a cloud was visible in the blue sky. Snow-covered giant boulders and rock formations, but it wasn't uncomfortably cold.

"It's beautiful," I said, and Scott balled snow in his hand. "Don't do it!" I pointed at him and moved out of Teddy's arms. Scott smiled, and I said in a stern voice, "Don't."

He threw it at me, hit me in the leg, and I yelled, "You're so childish." I scooped snow into my hand, while Teddy laughed and took a few steps to the side of me.

I threw it at Scott, missed him, and it set off a snowball fight. Kyle, Thad, Mark, and Keith balled snow in their hands and fired rounds at one another before they turned their attention to me. All five of them pinged me with the cold icy missiles, making me laugh and go after more snow to take my revenge. With my jeans soaked, I aimed at the guys as they ducked behind boulders or the SUV.

"Chickens," I teased.

"What would you do if you had a foot of snow?" Teddy laughed.

Scott and I looked at each other and said at the same time, "Build an igloo." We smiled and said, "Jinx." Then I said, "Stop it, Scott."

Teddy, Gene, and Rick laughed, then someone from a distance said, "That's Teddy and Five/Ten." I looked in the direction of the voice, and strangers walked our way.

"The fun is over," Teddy said and winked at me.

"I'll get the girls," Rick said.

"Let them shop. We'll be okay," Teddy said.

He backed up to the vehicle while the strangers joined us. He nodded to my brother. Scott held my shoulders and led me from the commotion.

Gene stood on one side of Teddy while Five/Ten stood on the other, and Rick protected the band members. The crowd grew, and someone loudly announced the celebrities were on the mountain.

Scott guided me away from the crowd toward the gift shop. I pulled him to a stop.

"What the hell?" I asked him and didn't want his protection.

"He doesn't want you mixed with all that, Beth," he said.

"I don't either, but are you, my bodyguard, now?" I asked angrily.

"I've always been your protector, sis. Let's hang here for a few minutes."

"Is this why everyone gathered around me at the lake? Was it to protect me?"

"Since the dude in the bathroom gave us a small scare, we don't want anyone to associate you with Teddy. We devised a plan that if something like this happens, either they will guard you, or I would," he explained.

"How are we going to get into the vehicle?" I asked as a crowd grew in numbers around the SUV.

"When Gene or Teddy gives me the signal, they'll keep the fans busy while we get in on the other side. That's why Gene parked as he did," Scott said.

"I can't believe y'all planned this," I said.

People asked for autographs and pictures. Teddy and the band members smiled and signed their names to whatever the strangers held out to them. Rick and Gene kept their arms extended in front of them to keep the people from getting too close.

It was my fault for the crowd. We were loud and drew attention to the snowball fight. I didn't consider the repercussions of us having fun.

A few minutes later, when Shelly, Carol, and Susan emerged from the shop. Shelly saw the number of people surround the SUV and stopped by us. Susan ran to Kyle and made her way to his side.

"Car now. You know what to do," Shelly said to us then walked to the crowd.

Scott helped Carol and me into the SUV. As Teddy signed autographs and thanked people, Gene held the car door open and blocked the inside view of the vehicle. Once Teddy was inside, Gene shut the door. People peered in through the tinted windows while Shelly sat in the front seat, and Gene sat in the driver seat.

"Is everyone in?" Gene asked into an earpiece. After a second, he said, "Let's move."

"That's my life," Teddy said and laid his arm around my shoulder.

I was speechless at how fast the crowd and commotion escalated. Teddy patted Scott on the shoulder.

"Thanks, man," Teddy said.

"No problem. She's my dumb little sister." He looked at me.

Shelly turned in her seat, looked at Teddy, and scolded. "Why didn't you send someone in to get me? We could have been out of there way before the crowd grew. You know I hate those situations. There had to have been over a hundred people."

Gene chuckled and said, "No one was in danger. It's good for people to see them off stage." He looked in the rearview mirror and said, "You did well, Scott."

"Thanks," Scott said.

"You okay, Beth?" Carol asked me.

"Yeah." I looked out the window to comprehend how Teddy could live without privacy.

Teddy held my hand, and I looked in his eyes. Words formed in my thoughts, *Are you okay?* I thought to myself, *I'm fine*. The word *Good* popped into my thoughts, and he smiled. We drove down the mountain until Gene found a small trail on our right.

He pulled in and said, "I want to make sure everyone is okay. We have drinks in a cooler in the other SUV."

"That was awesome," Kyle said as we stepped out of the vehicles.

"No, it wasn't," Shelly said as she got out of the car. "That was crazy." She pointed at Teddy. "You're in trouble. We have to monitor the news again."

"It'll be okay." He patted her shoulder.

"We're dealing with reporters at the hotel now, and I bet we'll have more," she said, then held her phone in the air to find service, and everyone laughed.

I sat on a boulder, a few feet from the group, and lit a cigarette. Carol joined me. After a minute of sharing the big rock with her, Gene handed us each a soda.

"Are you okay, kid?" he asked me in a low voice.

"Yeah. Thanks for the drink," I said while Teddy interacted with the band members.

"You're not saying much," Gene said and sat next to me on the boulder.

"I never thought people would stop someone and ask for autographs and pictures," I said, and Teddy looked at me. "I know they do, but I was comfortable and didn't think about Teddy and Five/Ten being celebrities. Why did they come? It's my fault people surrounded them. We were loud with the snowball fight."

"It wasn't your fault," Gene said. "This happens most of the time when they go into the public. Teddy is recognized more than the others. He's been at this for some time, so he knows what the consequences are. As you would say, 'this isn't his first rodeo'."

"It's sad," I said.

"Sad for Teddy? The man has everything," Carol said.

"He lost his freedom to his career. It's sad if you think about it," I explained. "Walk a mile in his shoes. He can't piss behind a bush without someone wanting to take a picture. He has to live in his own world to have peace."

"That's my girl. C minus." Gene smiled and patted my leg.

"I never thought about it that way. He has everything he could ever want," Carol said while Gene joined the others.

"Except freedom," I said.

I rose from the boulder. Teddy and I walked to each other. I tightly embraced him.

"What is this?" he whispered.

"You looked like you needed a hug," I said then held his hand before we walked to the others. I asked loudly, "Anyone have jerky? We need to find Bigfoot."

"There is no such thing," Kyle said.

"You guys are in the wrong car. I'm glad I'm in the fun car," Scott said then sang John Denver's, *Rocky Mountain High.*

I joined in as did Carol and Teddy. We swayed while we sang as loud as we could. Everyone, except for Shelly, sang. We laughed while we loaded into the SUVs and took our seats.

"You need me to drive, Gene?" I asked.

"No. I want to get off this mountain in one piece," he responded.

"Ye of little faith," I said.

"Yep. I sure do." He laughed.

Chapter 11

Gene drove down the mountain, taking the switchbacks fast and hard. We laughed and slid on the seat as far as we could with seat belts across our laps.

My phone sounded with text after text, as we moved to the bottom of the peak. Seven messages came through from Lucy and Danielle. I read Lucy's messages and received a few more from Danielle as Teddy watched me text. He laughed at the conversations, the girls and I held.

Shelly's phone rang, and she answered. She turned in her seat and looked back at us.

"You made the news, Teddy," she said.

"That was fast. I'm surprised anyone has service. We're not even off the mountain," Gene said.

"Are we good?" Teddy asked.

"We're trying to find out," she said.

"Is everything okay?" I held his hand.

"They're doing damage control," he said.

"They?" I asked.

"You're speaking with Marcy, right?"

"Yeah," she confirmed.

"Marcy is Shelly's right hand," Teddy explained.

"You must trust them."

"With my life. Their damn good attorneys and managers. I try not to get in their way, but sometimes I protest. For the most part, I listen."

"Yeah, right," Shelly said to him.

"I didn't know you were an attorney, Shelly. Is that why you're uptight?" I smiled.

"I tell her to chill, but she doesn't," Teddy said.

"I'm not uptight," she said. "We have a situation."

"A situation?" Teddy asked.

"Pictures of you are out, and there may be more to come. The media is saying you're vacationing here before the big tour begins."

"Are there any with Beth and me?"

"We're looking," she said.

"What about the hotel?" Teddy asked.

"We don't know how many. You should be happy they're mentioning the tour."

"Y'all can hang at the house," Scott said.

"I appreciate it, but I don't want to impose." He patted Scott's shoulder.

"Thanks," Shelly said into her phone. "They have a few of you with Beth. Marcy is trying to get them pulled. More reporters are waiting at the hotel. It looks like you lost the freedom you wanted."

"Damn. I want those pictures, Shelly. I mean now. I don't care if it takes an interview, just make it happen," Teddy said.

"This isn't only local news," Shelly said.

"Crap!" I exclaimed. "I don't want to answer my client's questions about you. I like a quiet normal life."

"Marcy sent me the pictures. You can tell it's Beth in a few," Shelly said and passed her phone to Teddy.

He looked at them as the phone rang. "Hey," Teddy said. "The fourth through the seventh need to go. Any that shows her identity." He paused, looked at me, and said, "Thanks, Marcy."

He showed me the pictures. Several were of us at the lake as we stood by the water when we played, then a few were when we faced the group. Some revealed us looking toward the lake with Teddy's arm around me, and my back faced the camera. In a couple, you could see my clothes when the band surrounded me, but my face was obscured.

"Marcy will call you in a few minutes once she has details of what we need to do," Teddy said and passed her the phone.

"I'm sorry, Teddy. You coming today wasn't a good idea," I said.

"We're okay. I knew people would take pictures. I was trying to protect your identity." He smiled.

"Thank you. People are crazy," I said.

"I'm sorry," he said. "I know you're referring to the guy in the bathroom."

"Among others that questioned me about you," I said. "You're popular."

Gene pulled the car off the road and typed something into his phone. After a few seconds, Rick passed us, then he followed.

"What are you doing, Gene?" Teddy asked.

"Rick has a plan," he said.

"It's hard to believe you can't vacation anywhere without having your name plastered on the news," I said.

"Sometimes we make it and sometimes we don't. It all depends on how many calls go into the stations. I guess they're having a slow news day," Teddy said.

Gene followed Rick into a small secluded park. We passed two parked cars near the entrance. We went further back until we reached the end.

No other cars or people were in the area. Big boulders blocked vehicles from entering the grassy section or the small walking trails, which led into the wooded area.

A big swing set, slide, teeter-totter, and monkey bars stood in a mulch barrier, near the tree line. Several picnic tables stood sporadically in the grass.

"We need to stretch our legs and regroup," Gene said.

Everyone emerged from the vehicles. Shelly motioned for them to join her. She informed them of the situation at the hotel with the reporters.

Teddy and I stood next to the vehicle, and he said, "Some adventure, huh."

"This is my fault," I said.

"It isn't. I could have stayed at the hotel, but I wanted to spend the day with you," he said. He walked to the front of the SUV, followed by Scott, Carol, and myself.

"I'm glad you joined us, but is it always like this?" I asked.

"For the most part. In our line of business, we need the reporters, but they can make life crazy at times," he said.

"Here's the situation," Shelly said, walking to us.

"Oh great, another situation." Teddy sat on a boulder and took a drink from his soda.

"Yes, Teddy," she said with her hands on her hips. "As you know, cameras are flooding the hotel. Someone from Carissa's group let it leak, you two are fighting because of another woman." She looked at me. "You're the other woman."

"What the hell! What about the concert? Has her name been fed to the media?" Teddy asked.

"Nothing so far with either, and we are looking," Shelly said.

"I'm sorry, Beth," Teddy said with concern.

"It's not about me. I'm not the other woman. I don't even like you." I smiled to calm him.

"You are now. Reporters want pictures of the other woman. Local news and *Blizz Entertainment* have the ones from the lake, so there is proof of another woman existing." Shelly faced Teddy. "*Blizz* is filmed here. They and the local news, want an exclusive with you. You give them one, and they'll stop digging into the story. They don't have her name, so we're safe for the time being."

"Dammit," he said and closed his eyes.

"You know how it works," Shelly said.

"I'm not worried about the interviews." He looked to the ground. "She called the media."

"Who? Carissa?" I asked, and he looked at me. "I told you…"

"This isn't about you," Teddy said.

"Yeah, it is," I said.

"We'll take care of this," he said then looked at Shelly. "Find out if she's still here."

"I will, and we'll try to combine the interviews with no exclusives." She laid her hand on his shoulder. "If you want to keep Beth out of the spotlight, you two cannot be seen together in public. Scott and Carol's house has now become a refuge for you two, and that is if we can get there undetected."

She sat next to him on the boulder. "I'm sorry, Teddy. I told you from day one this was going to be hard. I don't know if we can keep her out of it. We'll do our best, but Arkansas will be your salvation to spend time together unless you can convince her to come to Michigan."

"Carissa is starting the rumors to keep the watch alive, but she doesn't know where Beth lives," Shelly continued. "Her and the reporters think your next stop is Seattle, so she or her group can't call the media and point her out in Arkansas. We can protect her in Michigan."

"What did you say the first day?" I asked and looked between them.

"Can I speak to you privately for a minute, please?" he asked me.

"Sure," I said, and he held my hand.

"Find her," he said to Shelly then led me to the tree line.

"Can you explain what Shelly referred to?" I asked.

"Since the first day we met, I wanted to get to know you, but I wanted privacy. Shelly said, 'You don't get privacy, so be ready for the whole world to know her.' I told her we could keep you out of the news, but she doubted me. What I didn't anticipate was Carissa trying to keep the watch alive, but we'll stop her," Teddy said.

"Are you lying to me about Carissa?" I asked.

"No. I go after what I want, and that's you," he said.

"Friendship," I said. "I'm not looking for fame or fortune, Teddy. I want my family and business safe from the media."

He stepped from me, studied me for a moment while I thought to myself how bad I wanted to be close to him. I gazed into his eyes, and pictures formed in my thoughts as if I daydreamed.

We danced, laughed, and held each other, becoming inseparable. I broke the stare and looked to the ground. He clasped my hand and led me to the group.

"I need ideas. I don't want to give her up, as long as she'll speak to me," he said to Shelly.

"I'm not a dog." I smiled.

"That's not what I mean." He laughed then pulled me into his side. "I don't want this to end. You're the one, and I want to know your world. Let me take you home tomorrow."

"No," I quickly said.

Shelly looked at me, then at Teddy. "You can't come and go from the hotel. Not like we were doing over the last few days. The reporters will follow to get the picture. Marcy confirmed that Carissa checked out of the hotel this morning, but we don't know if she started the story of the other woman."

"Offer stands to stay at the house," Scott said.

"Let's have a picnic and think about what to do," Gene said and looked around the parking lot.

I leaned close to Carol and said quietly, "There's swings."

Teddy let go of me, concentrated on the topic, while he and Shelly glanced around to see how much traffic surrounded us. Carol and I quietly made our way to the playground.

I sat on the swing, pushed myself, while Susan walked to us. She sat on a swing. The others stood by the SUVs and discussed a plan to escape reporters.

"They're having a grownup talk." I smiled.

Teddy located me, smiled, and shook his head. I swung higher, as did the other two girls.

"What are you guys going to do?" Carol asked.

"They'll think of something. They know how to negotiate with the media," Susan said while she swung.

"This isn't worth it. He's stressing over things he shouldn't. With Carissa by his side, pictures, and reporters wouldn't be a concern. Poor Shelly is about to lose it," I said.

"You heard him. He's not letting you go," Susan said.

"I'm not his to let go," I said and swung higher.

All three of us women giggled like school-age girls seeing who could go the highest. Teddy walked to us, and I dragged my feet until I came to a stop.

"You're such a kid," Teddy said and stepped behind me.

I spun my swing around, wrapped my legs around his, and asked in a playful mood. "What's going on, froggy?"

"Froggy?" he asked and held onto my legs.

"Yeah. I could have called you seahorse, but I saw a frog over there, and he threw me off. I wasn't creative." I pointed to the ground, and he chuckled.

"We're going to picnic while we wait on Marcy to call about the interviews," he said. "Scott and Shelly left to get pizza, leaving Gene and Rick on picture duty."

I unwrapped my legs and looked up at him with wide eyes. My smile faded.

"You let Scott drive and not me?" I asked.

He laughed, turned me around, and pushed me softly. "You'll drive someday."

"No, I won't, dang it. You do like Scott bestest," I said in a pouty little girl's voice, which made Carol and Susan laugh.

Teddy moved to the front of me and grabbed my extended legs. He stopped me in the air, then let my legs drop to the ground as he held the chain above my head.

He straddled my knees, stared into my eyes, and asked, "What am I going to do with you?"

I took a step back, stood with my breasts against his chest, and asked, "What do you want to do with me?" He touched my cheek. He was going to kiss me. I smiled to ease the tension, and said, "I'm challenging you to a race across the monkey bars."

He studied my eyes for a second and said, "You're on."

"I'll judge," Susan said and ran to the monkey bars while Carol, Teddy, and I walked behind her.

Teddy and I stood next to each other. We grabbed the bars over our heads.

"Are you sure you want to do this?" he asked.

"I've been doing my yoga, son. I'm a ninja, kung fu, yoga master, so I'm ready," I said confidently.

"Ready. Get set. Go," Susan said.

Teddy and I raced across the bars. I kept up with him halfway but laughed hard because of him ribbing me. I let go and landed on my feet.

"What was that little girl?" He laughed and stepped into me.

"You're a punk." I smiled and pushed him back.

"Yoga, huh. Ninja skills." He hugged me.

"One more shot," I said and stepped out of his arms.

"Let's do this," he challenged.

The other band members walked to us while they pointed and laughed. Teddy and I stood side by side and stared hard into one another's eyes. We enjoyed the playful banter, but both took the challenge seriously.

"Ready. Get set. Go," Susan said, and we took off.

Teddy and I grabbed bar after bar, stayed in unison until the middle. He took the bars two at a time, moved ahead of me, but I let go and laughed again.

"That was so not fair. You knew I was winning, so you cheated," I said.

"Me a cheater?" He laughed. "No way. I don't cheat."

"You took them two at a time," I complained but chuckled.

"That's not cheating," he said.

"I'm a girl. I might have broken a nail. Don't you feel sorry for me?" I asked with a wide smile.

Teddy clapped the dirt off his hands and said expressionless, "No, I don't," then embraced me. "You want to go for round three?"

"I don't want to show you up," I said and tightly hugged him.

"That is the funniest thing I've seen in a while, old man," Kyle said as he patted Teddys' shoulder.

"You want a piece of this?" Teddy asked, and I stepped back.

"Let's go." Kyle accepted his challenge.

They stood side by side, and Susan said, "Ready. Get set. Go."

They took off across the monkey bars taking them two by two. They completed the race, then teased each other over who touched the last bar first. Kyle declared himself the winner, but Susan sided with Teddy. My cheeks hurt from the laughter, especially when Mark, Thad, and Keith challenged each other.

We had the best time playing outside like we were in elementary school. Carol, Susan, and I decided to play on the other equipment and left the boys to their macho monkey bar game. Susan joined Carol on a teeter-totter while I sat atop a slide. A car pulled into the park.

Gene saw the car then calmly walked to Teddy's side. He whispered something in his ear. Teddy slowly walked to me and held his hand out for me. The band members walked to a picnic table with their backs toward the parking lot.

"Would you care to go for a walk?" Teddy asked.

"Sure will," I said then rode down the slide.

I wiped my butt and took his hand while he said, "I don't see you as the kind of woman who worries about breaking a nail."

"I'm not," I said while we walked hand in hand to the tree line. "I didn't want to embarrass the great Teddy Nafton by beating you on the bars. You know I would kick your ass on the swings."

"I bet you would," he said.

He gently pushed me against a tree. He pinned me then brushed the back of his finger across my cheek.

The energy intensified between us. My nerves came to life with anticipation of a kiss. He blushed then stepped from me.

"We aren't going to make it as friends," he said.

"You don't think so?"

I couldn't stop thinking about the touch of his full lips on mine. My nerves danced, and my stomach tightened. I argued with myself if I wanted his touch. Carissa wanted him, so I can't fall for him.

"You're wrong. You can," he said.

He leaned in to kiss me, but I pulled my head back and felt confused. He studied my eyes.

"Not yet," he said.

"It can't happen," I said and looked to the ground. "I'm flattered, but you have a life in Michigan. I'm sorry I'm giving you mixed signals, and I need to stop."

"Look in my eyes," he said.

He smiled while I held his stare. In my mind, time stood still. The scenery and noise faded around us. Different emotions rushed over me. My imagination showed me darkness, then suddenly, a bright yellow light shone on Teddy and me. A slow-motion movie played in my thoughts of him pulling me close to his body. He held my face in his hands, then Gene yelled loudly, in the distance, which brought me to reality.

"Stay there," Gene said.

"You saw it," Teddy said quietly.

"I don't know what you mean." It was too much trouble being with a man like Teddy.

"You will." He embraced me. "Your heart is telling you to give me a shot, but your head tells you to stop. You need to let your heart lead."

"Or my heart is telling my body, I haven't been with a man in a while. I need to leave my emotions out of this and buy some batteries," I joked.

"I'll supply them, but I have to supervise what you do with them." He smiled and held my hand.

"I know what to do with them," I said while Scott got out of the car, and Gene sat in the driver's seat.

"If you need help or supervision, my offer stands." Teddy laid his arm on my shoulder and guided me to the car.

"There are too many people, so change of plans," Gene said. "We're going to Scott and Carol's to eat, then we can think the hotel thing through and talk about the next step. Marcy and Shelly have been speaking."

We sat in the vehicle, and Teddy stared at me.

"What?" I asked him.

"Thanks for showing me a great time today," Teddy said and held my hand.

"Thank you for risking an interview for today." I rubbed his fingers.

We rode in silence for a few minutes, and I stared out the window. I thought about the almost kiss.

I liked Teddy, but my rational thinking reminded me of the differences in our lives. I looked forward to going home. Distance would be on my side, and I could resume my ordinary, structured life.

I pulled my phone from my pocket. I checked my missed text messages and answered them.

"Can I see your phone?" Teddy asked.

"No way, man," I said.

"Please?" He looked at me with big sad brown eyes.

"Why do you want it?"

"I want to see the pictures you took on top of the peak," he said playfully.

"I'll show you," I said, then we viewed the pictures.

"I'm surprised you got to take pictures, Beth," Scott said.

"Shut up, Scott," I said.

"Why do you say that?" Teddy asked.

"Her music uses all her memory. She has to copy her pictures to her computer then delete them off the phone to make room for more. She'll give up her pictures for her music," Scott said.

"Yeah, well, you don't know me, Scott," I said quietly.

"Really? How many songs do you have?" he asked.

"I have some," I said defensively.

"Let me see," Teddy said and looked at me with big puppy dog eyes.

"You know what? Take it, you big baby," I said and handed him the phone.

Teddy scrolled through the music app. I shook my head and felt embarrassed from all his music on my phone. I looked out the window and blushed.

Scott always teased me about my music catalog, so I knew this encounter would be no different. I mentally prepared myself with comebacks to spew toward Scott.

"Beth likes music," Teddy glanced through my list. "She likes MY music. You are a fan."

"With your first big hit, she played your album over and over," Scott said. "The weird thing is she can name the song by listening to the first few seconds of it being played."

"I do listen to other musicians, so scroll." I reached for the phone, but Teddy held it from me.

"You're right. You have others, but you need to delete Noah Parker's," he said.

"Don't you dare. I like him," I said.

"Let's test your knowledge." Teddy smiled.

"I don't want to play this game," I said.

"Come on, Beth. Show the man. Find a song, Teddy. Any song." Scott egged him on.

Teddy tapped the play button. Three seconds of the song played, then he paused it.

"Well?" Teddy asked.

I rolled my eyes and said, "*Back again.*"

"I'm impressed. Let's try another." He repeated the same action, then waited for me to name the song.

"Would you give me the phone, please?" I asked.

"She might not know this one. It's from my new album," Teddy said.

"She knows it," Scott said with confidence.

"*Dance With Me,*" I said. "Now, can I have my phone?"

"Is it the music on your phone, you know, or is it other random songs?" Teddy smiled.

"It's a game we play when we camp. Watch," Scott said and held his phone up.

"Scott Tarman. This is not something we have to do right now." I was embarrassed at the stupid games we played.

"Name Game, Beth. Ready?" he asked.

"You need to be in on this, Carol," I said while she laughed. Scott played a song for three seconds. I asked, "I thought you were going to pick something other than Teddy's?"

"What was it?" Scott asked.

"*Let's Groove Tonight,*" I said, and my face flushed while Teddy smiled.

"Okay. Try this," Scott said.

"Why? You're the one who knows all the words to *Rocky Mountain High,*" I said.

"You sang with me," Scott informed me.

"The…chorus," I chuckled. "Fine." I listened to the music for three seconds and said, "*Cali Girl* by Boris. I don't listen to only Teddy. I have different moods, you know."

"What kind of mood are you in to listen to me?" Teddy asked.

"A pissed off one," I said, and everyone laughed as Gene turned into Scott and Carols' suburb.

"You like me bestest," Teddy said and smiled from ear to ear as he used my word.

We stepped into the house and relaxed since we didn't have to worry about pictures or reporters any longer. We waited on pizza to be reheated, and I retreated to the back porch. After several minutes of me enjoying the solitude, the back door slid open.

"What are you doing?" Teddy asked.

"Listening to the stillness in the air," I said.

"You would think I said that," Teddy said.

"Fore!" We heard in the distance, then the whack of a golf ball.

Soon, golfers appeared on the green while Teddy sat on the love seat beside the firepit. I leaned against the railing and studied the way he looked. I admitted to myself how I liked him. He caught my eyes and slightly smiled while I thought about how Carissa should be at his side.

"No," he said, then held his hand out for me to join him.

I walked to the love seat. He held my hand, and the shock made me tense.

"I like you." He smiled.

"I like you. Not because of your fame or what you do for a living, but, I feel…" I hesitated. "You need to figure out what you want. You wouldn't have to worry about reporters with Carissa standing next to you. Y'alls life fits better together than yours and mine ever would."

The back door opened, and Shelly stuck her head outside.

"Pizza is warm, and beer is here. Would you like for me to make you guys a plate?"

"No, thank you, Shelly. We'll be a minute," he said, not taking his eyes from me. "You're wrong. You and I will fit into each other's worlds perfectly and create OUR own world." He smiled big then asked, "Can I tell you a story?" I nodded as he rubbed my fingers.

"A few days ago, I met a woman in front of a hotel. The moment I looked in her eyes, I could feel her frustration toward us. Mostly toward Gene, but I felt her emotions. I shook her hand, and a rush of energy coursed through my body. That's what sets you apart from others for me, Beth. You're a whirlwind that swept into my life, and I like it. Analytical thoughts come to you quickly. Your brain doesn't stop, does it?"

"You feel a shock when we touch?" I asked.

"You feel it too," he said as if it were normal.

"That isn't logical, Teddy." I gave him a bewildered look.

"No, it's not, but this is why Carissa is not the one for me. You are. Soon you'll see and feel what I do, then you can't deny us. You keep yourself guarded, but you need to trust me." He stood and helped me up. He embraced me and said, "I want the whole package with you."

"I feel bad for you and Carissa," I said.

"Don't," he said and moved a strand of hair from my forehead. "Let's eat."

He led me into the house where the noise of people's laughter filled the rooms along with the aroma of pizza. Gene pointed to the counter.

"Your pizza is right here, Beth. I have to keep the animals out of it."

"Oh yeah, we all want vegetarian pizza," Scott said.

"What kind do you want?" I asked Teddy.

"I can get it," he said.

"Sit, please," I said.

"I'll take a slice of yours," he said and sat next to Keith at the bar.

"I bet you would," Keith said to him.

"That's not what I meant." Teddy laughed, then glanced at me. "Well…" He winked at me then asked Shelly, "What did you find out about the interview?"

"Interviews," Shelly said.

"You couldn't get the stations to combine them?" he asked.

"No. Local is wanting one in the morning, going live, and *Blizz* wants one Wednesday afternoon to run that evening," she said.

"This is because you asked them to pull pictures?" I asked.

"It's part of it. Both have agreed to no exclusives, but you guys have to perform. It's a good plug for the album," Shelly said.

"We can't go to Arkansas," Mark said while Teddy stopped eating and looked at me.

"Ha." I was victorious and relieved Teddy wouldn't waste jet fuel on me. "I leave tomorrow evening," I sang in a little girl's voice.

Teddy held my stare and said, "Cancel *Blizz*."

"No. You have a job to do, and you will do it," I said.

"I can take you home Thursday," he said.

"I have to work."

"We wanted a few days to relax before all hell broke loose, but I guess hell found us," Thad said sadly.

"I wouldn't mind you guys coming to Arkansas to see how we roll. My door is open to y'all, but you have a tour to promote, so your place is here," I said.

"What do you want me to do, Teddy?" Shelly asked.

He glanced at his plate and took a minute to process his next move. He spun the seat and faced everyone in the living room.

"It's free publicity, so if you guys want this, the interviews are a part of it. You all know the game but haven't played it, so how bad do you want it?" he asked.

The band members looked at one another, then Kyle said, "This could be our year."

"Let's go for it," Mark said.

"Horns and back-ups aren't here," Teddy said.

"We can do this on our own," Susan said.

Everyone agreed, then Teddy looked at me. Sadness rushed over me, but I was confused with the emotion. I was happy he wouldn't waste time on me.

"You can't have your way all the time, Teddy. Focus on your job. Once it's complete, you guys come out and play. We're fun people, so I'm extending an invitation to you all after the tour," I said.

"That's better than slamming the door in my face," he said, then asked Shelly, "What time did we make the news?"

"Hold on," she said and grabbed her phone.

"You all can hype this by going to the hotel and waving at the cameras," Keith said.

"Use this to our advantage," Thad said.

Shelly had her phone pressed against her ear and said, "You had a sixty-second segment on the six o'clock news. They're rerunning it at eleven. *Blizz* is advertising the interview late tonight and tomorrow. Everyone is mentioning the tour and album, so Marcy is working on a commercial plug with your approval."

"What time are you calling the kids?" Teddy asked me.

"Danielle will be at Lucy's in an hour. Don't feel like you have to speak with them if you need to take care of business," I said.

"Y'all are welcome to hang here if you want to watch the news report," Carol said.

"What time do they want to interview in the morning?" Kyle asked.

"Eight," Shelly said.

"This is cool," Susan said.

Teddy and I held our gazes on one another, then he said, "You guys go to the hotel and wave. I want to speak to the kids, so I'll stay."

I stepped to the porch to let them plan the interviews. Carol joined me outside, and we spoke for a few minutes. Teddy and Scott emerged from the house.

"Scott, Shelly, and Rick are going to the hotel to evaluate the situation. Everyone else is going with Gene," Teddy explained.

"You don't want to go wave?" I asked, and my phone dinged from my pocket.

"No, but I do need to make a few phone calls. Are you sure it's okay if I stay?" Teddy asked Scott and Carol.

I glanced at my phone and saw a text from the unknown number.

Time's up.

I didn't immediately respond.

"You're always welcome here," Carol said.

"You're not going to ask me if I mind?" I asked him.

"No. I know what your answer would be," Teddy said, and I laughed.

"She doesn't have a say anyway." Scott smiled. "Do you need to use my office?"

"No, but thanks," he said, and Gene came to the door.

"Are you ready, Scott?" he asked.

"Yeah."

"Don't let anyone follow you guys back," Teddy stressed.

"We got this," Gene said before they left.

"Will you excuse me for a moment?" Teddy asked Carol and me.

We nodded, then he walked into the house. I thought about the words from the unknown number. I needed to know who was texting me. Also, what time would be up, and why?

Who is this? - I texted.

Chapter 12

Teddy paced the living room floor while he spoke on the phone. I mouthed the word 'sorry' for interrupting as I rushed by him. I closed the downstairs door behind me. I went to the bedroom, plugged the charger into the phone, and laid across the bed. A chill jolted me up, and Teddy called my name from the entertainment room. My phone rang as I walked to the doorway and peered in, but he wasn't there.

"Yeah," I answered.

"What's going on?" Mom asked.

"Nothing. How are things there?" I asked and sat back on the bed.

"Fine, but I had an urge to call you, so talk."

"Everything is good. Scott and Carol have a beautiful place and can't wait for you guys to come for Thanksgiving," I said.

"Yeah, yeah," she dismissed me. "I was going to tell you this when you got in, but I dreamt about you last night. This urge is about the dream, so who are you running from, and why?"

The family learned to listen when Mom had significant dreams about us. Many times, they had come true, or they represented something important in our lives. We didn't take her dreams lightly.

"No one, but do tell," I said.

"I stood in the office parking lot and saw you sitting in your car. You were in the turning lane at the red light, near the office. There were no other cars around, and music blared from your stereo. I saw you through the window. You sang, and car danced. A black SUV with dark-tinted windows pulled up next to you."

"Whoever it was, tried to get your attention by honking over and over. Your car blocked my view of who it was," she said. "The light changed green, and you turned left. The SUV went straight as the windows rolled up. Who did you meet?"

"I met several people," I said. "The dream has no meaning. I love music, and the SUV was trying to get my attention to turn it down."

"You're wrong. You had a strong connection with something or someone in the SUV," she said. "You let it go."

"Maybe that's the next car I'm going to buy," I chuckled.

"There's more to it. I can feel it," she said.

"There isn't more to anything. I'll be home tomorrow and back in the office Thursday," I said.

"Don't believe me, but you'll see. Someone needs you, or you need them," she said. "Tell Scott and Carol, we love them. I'll see you at the office, Ms. Doubty Doo."

"Sounds good." I laughed then bid my goodbye.

Mom was a smart woman. She raised us, four kids, practically on her own. I've wondered how she could see things about us before they happened. Could she have seen Teddy in her dream? Was he the one in the SUV?

I sat on the couch, plugged the charger into the phone, and called the kids.

"Hey," Lucy answered.

"How are things?" I asked.

"Fine. Let me put you on speaker. Is he with you?" she asked, filled with excitement.

"He'll join us in a few. Who's with you?"

"It's just us," she said.

"Good. I don't want to overwhelm him with everyone, and I don't want questions from the family," I said.

"It was hard not to say anything to them, but we didn't. Danielle had a good idea to Skype. Can you do it?" Lucy asked.

"Let me get the computer," I retrieved it from the bedroom.

I connected into Skype when a fresh glass of tea was sat on the coffee table in front of me.

"Perfect timing. Thank you. Did you get everything lined out?" I asked Teddy.

"You're welcome, and yes," Teddy smiled.

"They decided to Skype. Is that okay?" I asked.

"Yeah, but it makes me more nervous."

"You don't get nervous," I said.

After working several minutes on the computer, the kids appeared on the screen. Sadie sat on the floor in front of everyone as they sat behind her on the couch. Her small framed body and blonde hair bounced as her blue eyes sparkled.

"Mimi," she squealed. "When are you gonna be home? I miss you."

"I miss you, princess, but I'll be home tomorrow night."

"Good. Can I have a sleepover when you come home?" she asked.

"We'll see, baby," I said. "Are you missing more teeth?"

"Yep. I pulled that one by myself today," she said and pointed to the newest gaping hole now occupying her smile. Teddy and I chuckled when she asked, "Who's he?"

"She's cute," he said, and shoulder bumped me.

"This is my entourage," I said and pointed to the computer. "I'll go from left to right. That's Ellis, my soon to be son-in-law, Lucy, my oldest, and she's holding Kara. Hi Kara," I said, and my granddaughter smiled as she stuck a finger in her mouth.

"Next is Danielle, and her husband, Colby, who's holding Gabi. Hey Gabi," I said to the baby. "And we can't forget, Sadie." She waved. "Everyone, this is Teddy Nafton."

They all said hi and hello, then Lucy said, "Teddy Nafton is sitting next to our mom."

"I am," he said.

"Y'all tell us the story," Danielle said.

I explained a brief story then said, "Long story short, here we all are."

"I know you, Mom. What else?" Lucy asked. "Mr. Nafton, this woman does not know how to tell a story. She starts it but leaves out details."

"She's leaving out a concert and an afterparty," he said.

"See?" Lucy asked, then exclaimed, "Mom! You owe us for not telling us about him."

"Okay. Dang big mouth," I said to Teddy and leaned into him. "There was a concert, then an afterparty," I laughed. "Oh, and today we went to Pikes Peak."

"Beth," Teddy said to me then asked the kids, "Has your mother always been calm and cool?"

"You mean no emotion at times?" Lucy asked. "Yes." Lucy and Danielle said at the same time.

"She gets tunnel vision and can turn off her emotions like no one else can. We've all seen it," Danielle said.

"And felt it. If she doesn't have control of the situation, she figures out a way to get it. If she can't, she shuts down," Lucy said.

"I do not. Can we get back on the subject, please?" I asked.

"See what we mean?" Lucy asked while we laughed. "She's not that bad, but she does like control."

I rolled my eyes at them and started the story once again. We spoke with everyone for an hour when a commotion came from upstairs. It sounded like a herd of cows had walked in through the front door. Teddy excused himself to investigate.

"Is he gone?" Danielle asked.

"For a few minutes," I said.

"I like him," she said.

"I didn't expect him to be funny," Lucy said.

"He's nervous about meeting you guys."

"Is he coming here?" Colby asked.

"No. They have an interview with *Blizz* later in the week, so Lucy, can you get me from the airport?" I asked her.

"Yeah. I hate how we won't get to meet him or the band. I was looking forward to it," she said.

"So were they, but they need the publicity to promote the album. I told them to come to the house after the tour, and we could play," I said.

"I hope they do," Danielle said.

"We'll see if we're still on speaking terms, once I leave," I said.

"It's cool how you're a groupie," Lucy said as Teddy rejoined me.

"Who, Beth? A groupie?" Teddy asked and sat next to me.

"Yes, sir," Lucy said.

"I've met my share, and she is not," he said.

"Thank you," I told him.

"Oh, dude, I bet you have some stories," Ellis said.

"A few," he said with a smile.

"We noticed online you're not touring Arkansas," Lucy said as my phone rang with a text.

"You guys have major cities surrounding the state, but we might change that," he said as I picked up my phone from the coffee table.

"If you do, you can hang with us," Danielle said.

"That would be a great time for y'all to play in our backyard," I said before I glanced at the phone.

"Thank you for the invite," he said.

I swiped the screen. The text was from the same unknown phone number.

It doesn't matter who I am. Eyes are watching. No more games. Tell him to leave NOW!

I quickly texted:

I can't make him do anything.

"What's going on, Mom?" Lucy asked.

"Nothing," I said and sat the phone on the coffee table. "Y'all want to see Carol and Scott's house?" I asked to change the subject.

"Sure," Danielle said.

"Let me see if I can do this." I unplugged the charger from the computer.

I showed them the downstairs area, then Teddy guided me up the stairs. The band members, Shelly, Gene, Rick, Scott, and Carol, sat either around the kitchen bar or the dining room table. I introduced everyone.

"Did Mom knock out your teeth, Sadie?" Scott asked.

"No, Uncle Scott." She giggled then pointed to her mouth. "I pulled that one."

"You're brave," Carol said.

"I'm going to show them your upstairs if that's okay," I said to Scott.

"Sure. I'll model it for you," he said.

He waved for me to follow as everyone watched us walk to the stairs. I moved the computer so the kids could see him. He belly-crawled up the first three steps.

"These are the stairs to my love nest," he said seductively, then moved his hands across the carpet.

"You have got to stop," I said as everyone laughed. "Get your boy, Carol."

"I don't want him." She laughed.

I showed the kids the upstairs pool table, office area, bedrooms, and bathrooms. I came back to the kitchen and involved them in our conversation. Eventually, my computer battery blinked to indicate it was running low, and our time was short.

"Okay, guys. It's time to say goodnight," I announced and picked up the computer.

"I wish we were there," Lucy said.

"Me too, baby," I said and walked downstairs with Teddy by my side.

"We'll see you tomorrow, Mom," Danielle said.

My eyes watered, and I said, "If I survive. I miss you, guys."

"We miss you," Lucy said.

"It was nice meeting you, Mr. Nafton," Ellis said.

"It was nice meeting you all," Teddy said, and we sat on the couch.

Teddy draped his arm over my shoulder, and we said our goodbyes. I wiped my eyes as Teddy guided my head to his shoulder.

"The kids are wrong. You do have emotions," he said and ran his fingers through my ponytail. "The girls look like you."

I smiled and said, "I miss 'em. Isn't it stupid? I've been gone a little over a week, and you would think I haven't seen them in several months."

I shut the computer off, stood, and reached for the phone. I missed a text when we were upstairs.

Figure out a way, BABE. – Unknown.

"Do you know this number?" I asked and showed him the phone.

"You shut down like that?" He tilted his head in my direction.

"Shut what down?" I asked.

"I see what the girls are talking about," he said.

"I'm not as bad as they say. I just want to know if you knew this number," I said.

"How many messages have you received?" He stood to get a better view of the screen.

"A few."

"Why didn't you tell me?"

"I assumed it was a wrong number. It's nothing for you to be concerned about," I said.

"I don't know phone numbers. Hold on." He pulled his phone from his pocket, tapped on the screen, and asked, "What is it?"

"917-555-8715."

"It's ringing," he said. "917 is a New York area code." With no response, he hung up. "It's no one in my contacts."

"Why is everyone back?" I asked.

"They wanted to watch the news here."

We walked upstairs, arm in arm. We joined everyone in the living room. Scott explained how the band members escaped the hotel undetected. Gene waited in the car in front of the hotel as if he were to pick up Teddy. The reporters were disappointed when Shelly walked to the car instead of Teddy and Five/Ten. The band snuck out the back of the hotel while Rick and Scott picked them up.

Scott noticed the time and asked, "Do y'all want to watch the news downstairs? There's more room."

"Sounds good," Carol said.

"I'll grab a few chairs," Scott said.

"I'll help then I need to see you, Gene," Teddy said.

"We got this," Gene said and motioned for him to stay with me.

I joined Carol on the back porch, leaned against the railing, and she said, "It's ridiculous how we miss the people who get under our skin, isn't it?"

"Yeah," I said and lit a cigarette while Teddy joined us.

"What do you think, Teddy?" Carol asked.

"Dang, Carol. Third-degree?" I asked.

"It's cool. They're good kids," he said.

"Has Beth told you about Sadie?" Carol asked.

"What about her?" he asked while Gene came to the back porch and sat on a love seat.

I told him a brief story of Sadie being born an extreme preemie. "Lucy developed preeclampsia when she was five months pregnant. The doctor had to take Sadie in hopes to save Lucy.

Sadie weighed one pound and eight ounces. Lucy had complications and stayed a week in ICU. Two weeks in the hospital, Lucy left with no baby in her arms. That was hard."

"That was a rough time on the entire family, but the girls were strong," Carol said.

"Sadie was born with two holes in her heart, and her lungs weren't fully developed." I continued. "She had two brain bleeds. I never prayed so hard in my life than I did during that time. My girls put a good scare in me."

"How long was Sadie in the hospital?" Teddy asked.

"Four months. She came home wearing a heart monitor, which weighed more than her. She was three pounds, and the doctors said they couldn't do anything else for her. We would have to give her time and keep praying, so we did. She's small for an eight-year-old, but she can see and hear. She's vibrant and strong."

"And can sing," Carol said. "She has a wonderful voice."

"Sing, huh?" Teddy asked.

"Yep." I smiled, feeling proud of my family.

"She's your little miracle," Teddy said.

"Thank you for letting me talk about one of my favorite subjects. I love my babies."

He placed his hand on my cheek and said, "I want to know the world, I'll be a part of someday."

"Dammit. I let you in, didn't I?" I was mad at myself for having feelings for him.

"Why is that bad?" he asked and raised his hand in the air.

"We've got to get downstairs. The news is fixin' to start," I said to divert attention from me.

"There's the term fixin' again. Where does that come from?" Teddy asked.

"I don't know. I've always said it," I said as Carol walked inside.

Teddy stepped into my personal space, and our bodies touched. He held my cheeks with both hands then kissed me on the forehead.

"Do not change, Beth Chambers. I like your 'fixin' and 'learnin' stuff'."

"Your family is close," Gene said, and Teddy led me to the loveseat.

"Yes, we are, but we need to get downstairs."

"We have a few minutes. May I borrow your phone, please?" Teddy asked.

I pulled it from my pocket and handed it to him while Gene asked, "What's going on?"

"Texts on Beth's phone," Teddy said.

"It's no big deal," I said.

Teddy and Gene read the messages. Gene got his phone, dialed the number, and let it ring.

"I tried calling, but the voice mail isn't set up," Teddy said.

"The news is about to come on. We need to go downstairs," I said and held my hand out to take the phone.

"Ask who it is, again," Gene said and handed me the phone.

"Happy now?" I asked after the text was sent.

"I don't like the threats," Teddy said, looking at me.

"They aren't threatening," I said.

"It didn't come up in your contacts?" Teddy asked Gene.

"No," Gene said. "Let me know if you get a response."

"I will, so can we go downstairs now?" I asked.

"Yes, ma'am." Teddy stood and held his hand out to me.

We joined everyone. Teddy sat on the couch, but I sat on the floor.

"There's room for you next to me," he said.

"I'm okay here." I looked at the TV and felt nervous about the idea of getting comfortable next to him.

He tugged my ponytail, so I glanced at him. He motioned for me to join him, but instead, I moved between his legs with my back against the couch. He held my ponytail in his hand, softly twirled it a couple of times, and sent chills down my spine. He gazed at me with a slight smile.

"What story are we?" he asked, but we didn't break eye contact.

"The fourth or fifth," Shelly said.

Everyone spoke about advertising the album, but I turned my attention to the TV. My concentration eluded me as thoughts of how I needed to get away from Teddy. He made it hard not to like him as his fingers rubbed the nape of my neck.

Teddy leaves tomorrow, once and for all. I promised myself to stop my emotions for him. He wrapped his hand tight into my hair and gently pulled my ponytail. I tilted my head and stared at him upside down.

"You can't stop this," he quietly said and released my hair.

Did I say something out loud? He twirled my hair once again. Another chill coursed down my back, and I shivered. He chuckled, and I settled between his legs, then listened to the TV announcer.

"Teddy Nafton and Five/Ten performed in Denver, Saturday evening, filling the Pepsi center to the maximum capacity. He and Five/Ten (pictures of the band, signing autographs flashed on the screen) are in town taking in the sights of our great state. (The picture of Teddy by the lake flashed, then another with him signing autographs by the SUV while we were on the summit.) They will join us in the morning for an interview and to perform a few songs. Tune in here for your morning rush."

"That will be exciting," one news anchor told the other.

They moved to the next news story, and we all clapped. Thankfully, there were no pictures of me.

"And it begins," Thad said.

"Do you know how many songs we are to perform?" Teddy asked Shelly.

"I'm not sure, but I'll call Marcy. I'll also get the time for Wednesday," she said and placed the phone against her ear.

"With no backup singers or horns, which songs are we performing?" Teddy asked the band. They tossed around names of songs while Teddy listened then asked, "What songs, Beth? You know them better than these jokers."

"I'm not deciding." I smiled.

"New or old?" Teddy asked everyone.

"One old and one new. Give people a taste of the new album, but let them know where we came from," Mark said.

"Marcy is finding out more details for *Blizz*, but for local, you'll have eighteen minutes from interview to however many songs you want. You'll need to speak, and they require a commercial break between interview and songs."

"If we did this right, we could interview for three to four minutes and squeeze in three songs," Teddy said, then asked Scott, "May I borrow a guitar?"

"You can use both," Scott said.

Teddy stepped over me. He helped Scott retrieve the instruments from the wall, then handed one to Susan.

"Anyone want anything to drink?" I asked then received the drink orders.

"I'll help," Shelly said and followed me.

"They need to go to the hotel and rehearse," I said and walked into the kitchen.

"They can't. Gear is packed and ready to go to the station in the morning," she said.

"What can I do to make things easier for you, guys? Y'all are going to be hitting it hard."

"We will, but Teddy is seasoned. He knows what he's doing," she said. "When Teddy and Gene spoke about you, my impression was not good. I was ready to come between you two, but do you know what sets you apart from others?" she asked, and I shook my head. "The look in your eyes in the children's store when you refused his money. I thought you were going to hit me."

"I was," I confessed.

"You showed me what you're about, and you have my respect and friendship if you want it. You don't take handouts, and you stand beside your beliefs and family. I respect you," she said.

"Thank you, Shelly. I can use a friend, but I don't like to be the cause of problems. It's too much for him to worry about being seen with me," I said.

"You're not a cause unless you turn your back on him. I like seeing him happy, so please give him and us a chance to get to know each other."

We gathered the drinks, and Shelly stopped with her hand on the downstairs doorknob. "This is why I love my job. Listen."

Teddy's soothing voice echoed through the house. He played the guitar flawlessly. I smiled from the thought of him.

"Teddy gets the same peaceful look when he speaks about you." She pointed at me. "Except when he's arguing with Carissa about you."

She opened the door, and the music grew louder. We descended the stairs and stepped into everyone's view. Teddy stopped in mid-song.

"What about stipulations?" he asked Shelly.

"They agreed. No personal questions," she said.

He smiled, grabbed my hand, and said, "I wish you could join us."

"I won't be watching. I'll be sleeping." I smiled.

"I'm sorry, Beth, but unless you two want the exposure together, it would be risky. If there was a picture of you, Carissa could point you out to the media. She has them eating out of her hand," Shelly said then leaned into Teddy. "Carol and Scott can come. They don't threaten her."

"Do you want me to ask them?" Teddy whispered in my ear as he embraced me.

"If you want to drag them along," I whispered.

Kyle took me from Teddy's arms, squeezed me, and said, "We'll bring you back a T-shirt."

Teddy asked Carol and Scott if they would like to join them at the station. Scott didn't answer but stared at me.

"If you want to go, please go. I'm okay," I said.

"We would love to have you two," Teddy said.

Scott looked at Carol and said, "Let's do it."

"I'll text you when they're getting ready to go on," Shelly said to me.

"I appreciate y'all trying to include me, but you don't have to keep me informed. These people are grown." I looked at Teddy and said, "Well, most of them."

"Come here." Teddy led me to the couch.

I turned sideways to watch him play. I closed my eyes, melted into the couch, and heard the soft melody of their new song, *Streams*.

Susan strummed a faster riff and led them into the older song, *Reconcile*. Teddy sang, and once he completed it, Gene read the time from his phone.

"We'll end with *Dance with Me*," Teddy said to the band. "We have an hour before we perform, so we'll rehearse after gear is set."

Teddy rested his head on my chest, held my hand, and rubbed my fingers. He held my hand on his chest, and I felt his heartbeat. I studied his hands while everyone spoke about the interviews.

How can he play these instruments with precision? Would his fingers be as meticulous on my body? I rubbed his fingers. My body yearned for his touch. My brain told me to stop my feelings for him, so I pulled my hand back. I pushed his shoulders and raised him off me.

"There's the wall." He looked at me.

"It's getting late, and you guys have an early morning. Gene said you're not a morning person," I said.

"I can take a hint." He smiled then looked at Shelly. "We've worn out our welcome."

I hit him lightly on the shoulder, pulled him against me, and hugged him. I kissed his cheek and said, "You have not, but you do need rest."

"This wall will fall," he said and stood. He helped me from the couch, and we walked to the stairs. "Let me know when we're ready. I need to talk to Ms. Thing, so if you all will excuse us." He led me to the back porch, turned me to face him, and said, "You have no idea how bad I want to kiss you."

"You don't know what you want." I took a step from him.

"Yeah, I do."

"Why are you talking to Carissa about me?"

"Who told you?"

"It isn't important. Forget I mentioned it, but you need to figure out your heart. You have a lot of people who love you. Your family, friends, and fans. Your life is full. There isn't enough room for anyone else."

"That's a bunch of crap. If something is on your mind, tell me. I'm not that good yet," he said.

"What does that mean?" I asked. "It doesn't matter. I'm not a nosy person, but I have a question for you. If I'm out of line, tell me, and I'll drop it."

"You can't be nosy, so ask."

"The day we met, and we were eating lunch, Carissa was the one who you wanted Rick to take to your room. She was here to see you. She stayed by your side until the concert, so did you split up with her because of me? Be honest."

"No, and I didn't know she would be here. She had a shoot and took it upon herself to surprise me. When I got to the room, I told her to leave, which set off an argument," he said.

"Then y'all made up the next day, which tells me you have doubts about leaving her." He stared at me but didn't say anything, so I continued, "She was with you the following night and at the concert, so you two have something."

"You're wrong," he said. "Before she left, she asked if I was going after another woman. I informed her that no matter the reason, we were not officially together, and it wasn't her concern. She said if I broke it off with her, she would go to the reporters and thrust the other woman in the middle of the media frenzy."

"I wanted privacy so you and I could get to know one another, but Carissa was insistent. She had three days in Colorado, so she stayed in a different hotel. She was supposed to leave the morning of the concert. She had a shoot in California, so I thought she left. I didn't know she would show. I tried to make her understand how we need to go our separate ways, but she wouldn't listen."

"I didn't want to be the headline on the entertainment section with a scandal, so I let her stay. She said she would leave at intermission, but as you know, she didn't."

"When I saw you at the concert, I could no longer contain myself. I wanted to touch, hold, and kiss you along with…" He stopped midsentence, smiled, then said, "Carissa and I fought. Again, I told her it was over, and she needed to leave. Rick showed her out after the performance. The last time I saw her was when she showed at the afterparty. She called several times and showed up at the hotel to see if you were with me. Once she saw you weren't, she left."

"So the unknown texts could be coming from her," I said.

"I don't know what phone she's using," he said. "Have you received any more?"

"No," I said, and people's voices filled the living room. "I don't think it's anything to be concerned about."

"Who here has your number?" he asked.

"You, Scott, Carol, and I guess Trudie from the Accountants Association. Did you give it to anyone?" I asked.

"Gene, Rick, and Shelly," he said. "Will you please let me know if you receive more?"

"You're overreacting, but okay."

"Excuse me, but we're ready," Shelly said after she opened the back door.

Teddy stared into my eyes and said, "One more minute, please, Shelly."

"Okay," she said and left us alone.

"I'm not confused with my emotions. I know who I want. You can speak to me about anything and at any time. Day or night. All you need to do is think of me, and I'm there for you. I'll tear down this wall, brick by brick, to open your eyes, so you can see what I see."

"I see just fine," I said.

He embraced me, and I wanted more from him. Pictures formed in my thoughts of him gently kissing me, trailing his lips down my neck while he held me in his arms.

"Someday," he said and released me.

"Where did that come from?"

"You." He smiled and held my hand. We joined everyone in the house, and he asked, "Well, Shelly?"

"Carol is going to let us borrow her car. You, Gene, Kyle, and Susan will be in the SUV. You keep the cameras busy while Rick gets us into the hotel, through the back door," she explained.

"Thank you, Carol," he said, then shook Scott's hand. "Thank you, Scott."

"No problem," Scott said.

"Walk with me?" Teddy asked me.

"Sure," I said, and he held my hand.

"Someday, I'm going to hand you the world," he said when we reached the front door.

"I don't want the world, Teddy," I reminded him.

"Well, babe, whatever you dream of." He kissed my hand, then said, "Peace."

"Good luck in the morning," I said, and he walked out the door toward the SUV.

Kyle embraced me and said, "I'll wave to you when we're on TV."

"Okay." I smiled.

I waved to them all before I shut the door, turned, and was startled. Carol and Scott stood behind me. Scott had his arms folded across his chest. Carol smiled wide as she stared at me. I stepped past them to clean. They didn't say anything but followed me into the kitchen.

"What?" I asked.

"I like your boyfriend," Scott said.

"He's not my boyfriend, but I bet you do. He played with your guitars and made them worth several thousands of dollars," I teased.

"I know. I bet I can sell them online. Man, I should have taken a picture with him holding them," Scott joked.

"You will not," Carol said and lightly hit his arm.

"Wait until he autographs them for ya," I giggled.

"What a great idea, but I bet I can get more if the whole band signs them," he said as we cleaned the kitchen.

"I'm telling them not to sign," Carol said.

"We're joking, Carol. Damn, girl. I wouldn't do that. I'll sell Beth to him for a few million." He laughed.

We completed the cleanup process then said our goodnights before I walked downstairs. I stopped at the guitar Teddy played, as it hung on the wall. I glided my fingers over the strings.

How could a relationship work with two people like Teddy and me? I would be in one state while he traveled the world. He was used to having someone by his side, and Carissa could travel with him. He needed a trophy girlfriend and not some dumb plain hick like me.

I set the alarm, switched off the lights, and laid in bed. I stared at the ceiling with my thoughts returning to Teddy and myself. My normal life would not fit into his or vice versa. He lived states away, in a different time zone, and that's not even mentioning the media issue or the threatening texts we faced. Tomorrow, we will go our separate ways with no more thought of us being a couple.

Chapter 13

"Are you up?" Teddy asked when I answered the phone.

"Yes. How are you?" I asked sleepily.

"Tired, but okay."

"Have y'all rehearsed?" I snuggled into the blankets.

"Twice. We have time for one more run. Carol and Scott are enjoying themselves, but I wish you were here."

"You'll do fine, Teddy. What time do you go on?"

"The 8:05 mark."

"Are you nervous?"

"No, but if I fall, will you continue to speak to me?"

"No. You're *The Teddy*. You don't mess up," I teased.

"Oh, yes, I do," he chuckled. "I don't want you to think any less of me if I do."

"I'll still speak to you," I assured with a laugh.

"I knew you liked me. You're a fan."

"Am not. Go wow your fan's here in Colorado. Good luck."

"I'll speak with you after the show," he said.

"Bye, Teddy," I said.

"Don't say that!" he exclaimed. "I don't want to hear that from you."

"What? Me saying your name?"

"No, I like that. It would sound better if you moaned it from pleasure," he said.

"I'll moan it if I have a stomachache," I giggled. "What do you want me to say?"

"Peace, babe."

"Peace, babe."

"No goodbyes from you," he said. "I'll speak to you later. Peace."

He hung up, and I smiled from him, being superstitious about a word. I crawled out of bed and dressed for the day. I turned on the TV and made the bed.

"Teddy Nafton and Five/Ten will join us after this. Stay tuned," an anchorwoman said.

The weatherman explained the day's temperatures when I stepped into the bedroom. I packed a few things when I received a text:

This is Shelly. They'll be on in 2. Wish you were here.

Me too. Wish them luck from me and please tell Teddy I said peace. - I texted.

I will relay.

I went into the entertainment room and sat on the couch. After the commercials, a shot of the anchorwoman, along with a male co-anchor, was shown.

"I met these guys this morning while they rehearsed," the woman said. "Teddy looks wonderful, and Five/Ten are sounding great."

"Without further ado, here's Teddy and Five/Ten," the gentleman introduced them.

The camera panned back and showed Teddy, and the band sitting around the table with the news reporters. Teddy sat next to the lady, Susan next to Teddy, and Kyle sat beside Susan. Mark and Thad sat on the other side of the gentleman.

"Thank you," Mark said.

The lady laid her hand on Teddy's arm and asked, "How has it been going?"

"Everything is good." He glanced at her hand then adjusted in his seat. "We're enjoying this beautiful state." He looked well-rested and dapper in his black and white silk shirt.

"Thank you. You sold out at the Pepsi Center Saturday night. Is that correct?" she asked, not letting go of his arm.

"Yes, ma'am. We had an awesome concert," Mark answered.

"Thank you to all who ventured out and showed your support for us," Teddy said confidently.

"Where are you guys going next?" she asked, letting go of Teddy.

"Seattle," Thad said.

The lady smiled, and the gentleman held the CD to the camera. He asked, "You released *Dance With Me*, two months ago?"

"Yes, sir," Thad said and pointed to the CD.

"Is Colorado your first stop of the tour?" he asked.

"Our third," Susan spoke this time.

"You guys check out our website. Tour dates are listed," Mark said.

"You're going to be busy playing twenty-eight cities in a few months. I hope you sell out everywhere you go," the gentleman said.

"They will. It's Teddy and Five/Ten." The lady giggled and replaced her hand on Teddy's arm. "Are you going to play something for us?" She batted her eyes at him.

"If it's okay with you," Teddy said.

"Please." She blushed, moved her hair behind her ear, and looked at the table.

They stood, walked a few steps to the instruments, and Teddy grabbed his guitar. He slipped the strap around his shoulder with his back to the camera while everyone got into position. He nodded to Susan, who played the melody for *Streams*.

Teddy and Susan's voices sounded smooth as the camera shot a close-up of Teddy. At the end of the song, he turned to Susan, who followed the melody with her guitar riff, and he sang *Reconcile*.

After they finished, the station went to commercial. When the show aired again, the anchorwoman stood next to Teddy. He held the guitar and slightly smiled at the camera. The band waited for their cue.

"We're returning with Teddy and Five/Ten. It's been a pleasure having you this morning," the woman said.

"Thank you," Mark stated.

"We thank you and feel your love, Colorado," Teddy seductively stated while he winked at the camera.

"Are you going to play one more for us?" she asked him flirtatiously.

"Yes, ma'am," he said, and she giggled.

Teddy gave her a side glance, and she stepped away from him. He looked at Mark, who played the piano with Kyle following on the drums. Susan and Thad joined next while Teddy walked to the microphone and sang *Dance With Me*.

Kyle waved to the camera before it focused on Teddy at the end of the song. Teddy kissed his two fingers and held them in a peace sign, which made me laugh.

The next set of commercials came on. I went into the bedroom and continued to pack, listening to the TV. When the show came back, the anchors spoke about Teddy and Five/Ten.

The anchorwoman bounced in her seat, and said in an upbeat voice, "He is a wonderful performer. Didn't they sound great?"

"They did," the man said. "The album is *Dance With Me*. Get your hands on it if you haven't already." Then they went to the next story.

I walked into the bedroom, then my phone rang.

"Hey," I said and sat on the bed.

"Hey, babe. What did you think?" he asked.

"I missed it."

"You better not have," he said.

"No, darlin', I watched it. The anchorwoman wants you," I teased.

"I don't want her," he said. "I have someone else in mind."

"The anchorman?"

"No," he laughed.

"I noticed the peace sign, kiss. Was that a jab at me?"

"I'm glad you caught that."

"Yeah, I caught Kyle's wave too. Please thank him for me."

"I will. Carol and Scott are on their way to the house, and we're going to the hotel. I'll see you in a little while."

"Carol and I are going to shop for souvenirs, then I have to finish packing before I catch the plane," I said since I wouldn't be able to see him before I leave.

"Carol, you, and Shelly," he corrected me.

"What are you talking about?"

"Shelly and Gene will take you and Carol to the mall, then we'll have an early dinner before I take you to the airport," he said.

"We're not playing this game again. I don't need a babysitter, and you can't take me to the airport. You have to get rest and prepare for *Blizz*."

"I need music sheets, and I'll see you before you leave," he said. Someone mumbled to him, and he asked, "Can you hold on a moment?"

"Yeah," I said and muffled voices, buzzed in the background, and a car door shut.

"You there?"

"Yes," I said.

"I had to put you in my pocket for a second. Cameras are everywhere, and I didn't want the chance of someone knowing I was speaking with you."

"I always wanted to put you in my pocket."

"Do tell."

"I wanted to put you there to hear you sing to me when I was sad. That was before the age of these smartphones," I reminisced.

He paused for a few seconds and asked, "You said that?"

"Yes."

"I knew you liked me."

"The verdict is still out on liking you," I said with a slight laugh.

"You're a funny one, Beth. I know you're a fan," he said.

"I am not, nor; will I ever be a fan of Teddy Nafton," I teased.

"We'll see if I can change your mind."

"Get some rest, Teddy."

"Don't worry about me. I'll see you later. Peace."

"Peace," I said and hung up.

After about an hour, I completed my packing and heard the door open.

"Beth?" Shelly asked.

"I'm here," I said as I folded a load of Carol's towels.

"I brought you a soda," she said and handed me the can.

"Thank you. You guys were up early. Did you get enough sleep?"

"Yes. Are you ready?" she asked.

"Almost. Is Teddy sleeping?" I asked as my phone from the bedroom sounded with a text.

"When we arrived at the hotel, he went into the bedroom and closed the door. I don't know if he's sleeping or writing."

"Hopefully, he's sleeping. Where's Gene?" I asked.

"Upstairs."

"They did a great job this morning."

"Oh, I have something for you." She reached into her purse, handed me a T-shirt from the news station, and I laughed. "Teddy wanted me to give you this, as well." She handed me another T-shirt, but it was from their new album. He signed it "Peace forever to my favorite fan. Teddy."

"Really?" I shook my head and smiled. "I can't believe him. I have to think of a way to get him back." I walked to the bedroom to pack them. I grabbed my phone as I spoke with her, "You have to help me get him, Shelly."

"I can do that. I like this game," she said.

I stopped at the door and read the text message from the unknown number:

Back off or you'll regret the choice to stay with him.

Go away. - I texted.

A few seconds later, I received a picture of Carol and Scott from this morning. Scott held a glass door open for Carol as they walked into the news station.

Chills raced across my skin. My stomach tightened from concern for my family. Anger built within me at whoever stalked them.

I called the number, but no one answered. I texted:

Who the hell is this?

The green bar slid as the text was sent. I jumped when the phone rang.

"Yeah," I blurted.

"Are you okay?" Teddy asked.

"What are you doing? You're supposed to be asleep," I scolded.

"I'm going to tell you something, but don't think I'm weird," he said.

"Too late," I smirked. "What?" I asked and walked to the couch while Shelly looked at me.

"A picture of you flashed in my thoughts. I asked what was wrong, and you said you were scared. I embraced you, and you were cold to the touch. Why are you scared, Beth?" he asked.

"This confirms you're weird, but everything is fine," I lied, trying to process what Teddy saw in his imagination.

"I know something is wrong," he said.

"Nothing is wrong. Your girl is here waiting on me, so I need to go," I said while Shelly held her hand out for the phone. "You can talk to her."

I handed it to her, then walked into the bathroom. I stared in the mirror and thought about someone watching my family. I won't tell Scott and Carol about the picture. I'm the family's protector, and no one will touch them.

I retrieved my makeup bag, returned to the couch, and sat next to Shelly. She stared at the phone before she held it out for me to take.

"You had a text while I spoke with Teddy."

"Thanks," I said and read the text:

I'm not going to answer so stop calling.

Have the balls to tell me your name. If you touch anyone, I'll come after you and I'm a damn good shot. - I texted.

Say Helper in your southern drawl. That's the only name you will call.

What the hell are you talking about? What name?

"I didn't mean to be nosy, but I saw the picture and read a few texts. I'm sorry," Shelly said.

"It's okay," I said and sent the text.

"Does Teddy know about this?" she asked and pointed to the phone.

"He knows about the ones from last night," I said and received another text.

If you leave him alone, everyone wins.

"Tell him about this NOW. Whoever this is, knew we were going to be at the news station," Shelly said with eyebrows raised. "What did that one say?"

I handed the phone to Shelly and said, "I don't want anyone in an uproar, and Teddy needs rest. There's nothing to worry about, so please don't say anything to Carol or Scott. Whoever this is, didn't send a picture of them here at the house. Maybe they'll leave them alone when I leave."

"I don't like this," she said. "We need to find out who the hell this is. I don't know if this shopping trip is a good idea."

"Maybe it would be better if you and Gene didn't go with Carol and me. You might draw attention to us, plus it's a fast shopping trip, and I will protect my own family," I said while I applied makeup.

"No," she demanded. "We'll tell Gene, so he can be prepared."

"Prepared for what? There isn't anything to worry about. Please don't tell him or Teddy," I said.

"You have to tell them, or I will," she said, and I stared at her. "Promise me, Beth."

"I will later."

"We'll go with you, but if one thing doesn't feel safe, we tell Gene."

"Fine," I said.

"Turn around and let me braid your hair. I'm a wizard." She placed her hands on my shoulder before she twisted me.

"What are you trying to do?" I asked.

"Being nice. You don't have many girlfriends, do you?" she asked.

"No. My life consists of kids and work. I have two close friends. We speak from time to time throughout the year, but we don't have girls' night out or anything."

I felt like a teenager while we sat on the couch and spoke. We shared life stories. It was nice to relax and talk even though I kept my guard up with her. We learned how both of us had trust issues.

"You and I are more alike than we care to admit," she said.

"I concur."

"You can trust me," she said.

"I'll try if you will," I said. "Can I ask you something?"

"Sure," she said.

"You were with Teddy when he brought me downstairs Saturday night, but did he see anything?" I asked.

"No. I was here more for his protection than yours. He stepped out of the room then I helped you out of your pants and shirt. You climbed into bed, and I covered you. You were out when Teddy went in and told you goodnight. He kissed you on the cheek, then we left."

"Thank goodness. All this time, I thought I undressed myself, but I wanted to make sure he didn't see me almost naked."

"He saw more of you in the towel than he did that night." She reassured me.

"That was embarrassing." I looked at my hair in the hand-held mirror. "You are a wizard. Thank you."

Shelly, Gene, Carol, and I walked through the mall, went into a store, and Shelly helped me find Teddy a T-shirt. She held it in the air for me to see.

It was blue with a cartoon drawing on the front. A man sat in a recliner and was dressed in a red flannel shirt and blue jeans. He had one arm wrapped around the waist of a big-breasted woman, who sat in his lap. She wore a matching red flannel bikini. The top barely covered her nipples. The man pointed to her breasts, and the caption read, "Her peaks are almost as good as Pikes."

We laughed at the stupidity of the shirt. I bought it for Teddy to remind him of how and where we met.

Carol helped find a few souvenirs before we checked out, then walked toward a toy store. On the way, Gene tried to grab the bags from my hand, but I held it tight.

"I'm capable of carrying these," I said.

"Fine. I'll stand in the background as though I don't exist," he pouted.

"You better let him help. He might cry," Shelly teased Gene.

I walked arm in arm with him for a few minutes before my phone sounded with a text. I let go and pulled it from my pocket.

Everyone stopped, except for me. I ran into Shelly while I read Teddy's message.

"I'm sorry, Shelly. Did I step on you?" I asked.

"Don't text and walk, Beth," Gene laughed.

"You bumped into me." She laughed as I held her arm and looked at her leg.

"You would know if she stepped on your foot," Gene said, and I lightly hit his arm.

"Shelly!" a woman exclaimed.

We looked to our right. Carissa and the tall, muscular gentleman walked toward us.

"What are you doing here?" Carissa asked as I stared at the beautiful model.

Gene tugged my arm and led me from them.

"What are you doing here? We thought you went to California," Shelly said.

"I needed a new outfit for the trip," Carissa said and looked at me.

"Keep moving, ladies," Gene said and pulled Carol and me further from them.

"Good luck with that," Shelly said and walked to us.

"Teddy looked great on the morning show," Carissa boasted, which made Shelly stop.

My phone rang, "Hey."

"Hey. I texted, but didn't get a response," Teddy said.

"Your girl is here," I said.

"I hope you're having fun."

"It's not me."

"Yes, it is."

"No. It's Carissa."

"What! Where's Gene?" he demanded.

"Hold on," I said and handed Gene the phone.

"You and Carol go into that store," Gene informed us as he took my phone and pointed in the direction, he wanted us to walk.

We didn't move, so I listened to his portion of the conversation. "Roger is with her." He paused for a second and said, "I will." He handed the phone back to me, gave me a shove in the direction of the store, and said, "Go. Shelly and I will catch up." Then he walked to Carissa, Shelly, and Roger.

"Yeah," I said into the phone.

"Please stay away from her and do what Gene says," Teddy said.

"We are," I said and went into the store with Carol.

"I don't understand why she's there," Teddy said.

"She needs a new outfit," I explained and felt betrayed by him. "I won't be played, Teddy. I told you I didn't want to come between y'all, so you and her need to talk."

"I'm not playing you."

"I think you are, and I don't want…" I said.

"Beth!" Carissa yelled.

"What?" I yelled as I spun on my heels, and Gene raced toward me.

"Aren't you going to speak to me?" she asked.

Gene stood between us, looked at me, and shook his head.

"It was nice seeing you, Carissa, but we have to go. Good luck in California," I said while Carol and I walked to the exit.

"You're not as friendly as you were at the concert," Carissa yelled.

"I'm sorry, babe," Teddy said.

"I'm not your babe, Teddy. Your babe is a beautiful model who is wanting to work things out. She's here, so call her and leave me be. I don't like drama, and I don't have time for anyone." I fumed.

"Don't build your wall and shut me out," Teddy said.

"No more. Go away, Teddy." I hung up the phone as we walked outside.

"Are you okay?" Carol asked while Shelly joined us.

"Yeah, but he needs to speak with her. I like my quiet, boring life, and I have a feeling with Teddy, comes drama," I said.

"You're wrong, Beth," Shelly said. "Roger confirmed they were shopping for an outfit. He said her shoot in California was rescheduled. She leaves tonight."

"Then why didn't she tell Teddy about the rescheduling or did she, and he's lying to me," I said.

"Teddy's not lying to you. He wants you," she said.

Gene held the car door open for me. I sat, stared out the window, and thought about Teddy. I liked him, but Carissa's presence reminded me of how our lives were different. I didn't want to be a part of the media or drama caused by an ex-girlfriend. I can't compete with her. It was fun hanging out with him and the others, but it's over.

Chapter 14

Teddy opened the front door and embraced me. Carol, Shelly, and Gene walked around us.

"Why are you here?" I asked.

"We need to talk," Teddy said.

"There isn't anything to say."

"Yes, there is."

He held my shoulders, guided me to the downstairs door, then opened it. We followed Gene, who carried the bags to my room. I stepped into the entertainment room then stopped fast. Teddy grabbed me around the waist and lifted me off the ground, so he wouldn't trip over me.

"What are you doing?" he asked and stood me up.

"Why are there instruments?" I pointed.

Music sheets laid on the coffee table. Teddy's guitar leaned against the couch. Drums, keyboard, bass, and another guitar stood in the room.

"Scott said we could rehearse for *Blizz*," Teddy said.

"Y'all are rehearsing here while I'm going home?"

"Yes. Unless you stay, and I take you home Thursday."

"You have a girl who needs you."

"You," he said, and I shook my head.

"I sat the bags on the love seat," Gene said and patted my shoulder before he ascended the stairs.

"Thanks," I said.

Teddy and I walked to the bedroom. Two teddy bears sat in the middle of the bed. They were approximately three feet tall and wore green, blue, and purple colored tie-dye shirts. A picture of Teddy, the band, and their tour name were printed on each shirt along with everyone's signatures.

One bear wore a tie-dye lace skirt around its waist with the same colored bow in its ear. The other wore a tie-dyed bow tie around its neck to match. Between the bears stood a vase containing five red and five white tulips.

"What are these?" I pointed to the bears.

"They represent us," Teddy said and wrapped his arm around my waist then placed his chin on my shoulder.

"Ha, ha. Seriously." I picked up the vase and smelled the flowers. "Why five?"

"One from each of us in the band and for your five kids," he said.

"Thank you, but what am I supposed to do with two bears?" I asked and sat the vase on the nightstand.

"They're our mascots." Teddy smiled at the stuffed toys as I held them. "I want something to remind me of you when we're on the road. They come with their own suitcases." He pointed next to the love seat. "I would like for you to name them and to borrow your perfume, please."

I squeezed the boy bear to my chest, closed my eyes, and smelled Teddy's sweet-scented cologne. He held my hand, guided me to the edge of the bed, and patted it for me to sit. He stood in front of me.

"You broke my heart when you told me to leave. I don't like the idea of us separated." He shook the thought from his mind. "I don't want to lose you."

I, too, was sad of us not being at arm's length. I felt a heavy heart of losing a friend.

"I'm not yours to lose," I said, and he sat next to me on the bed. "You need to go about the tour and your girl. That's what you were doing when we met, so that's what you're going to do now. When I leave, I have no problem if you want to call me, but it will be with the condition that Carissa knows we're speaking."

"You and I are meant to be together." He held my hand and stared into my eyes.

"No." I stood. "She's here waiting on you."

"I didn't know she was here," he said.

"She didn't tell you?" I asked with doubt.

"No, she didn't. She's been calling and texting me since the afterparty. I wanted her to leave me alone, so I called her last night and threatened harassment charges. I haven't spoken to her since, so it was a surprise that she showed at the mall."

I stared into his pleading eyes. What do I do? Do I trust him? Do I walk away and never look back? The strong connection between us was hard to escape.

"If you're playing me, I'll never speak to you again," I said infuriated. "I don't play mind games, and I need honesty. With friendship comes trust, so don't break that trust. I told you friends and…" I shifted my eyes to the floor, checked my emotions to make sure I could handle a friendship with him, and expect nothing more. I nodded and said, "Friends. It will stay that way."

"Why?"

"I like my life the way it is. It can get crazy, but it's the kind of crazy I know how to cope with. Drama is something I can't cope with, and I won't," I said, then Shelly appeared at the door.

"Food is on the table," she said.

"Did you have something to do with these bears?" I asked her.

"Yes." I hugged her, and she said in my ear, "He doesn't want anything to do with Carissa." She held me at arm's length. "Give us all a chance to become friends and trust. Remember?"

"I consider all of you as friends, so please call me. After the tour, come out and hang with us. Bring Carissa. I hope we speak between now and then, but if we don't, I understand."

"No Carissa and we will speak," Teddy said.

I stared between her, and Teddy then said, "Friends."

Teddy picked up the girl bear, and I left my room. I walked to the bathroom, grabbed my perfume, and took it to him. He sprayed the scent on the bear, smelt her fabric, and handed me the bottle.

"Thank you," he said.

"These are cute, but I don't understand the mascot thing." I took the bear out of his hands, squeezed her, and smelled my perfume.

"It's a work in progress." Teddy laid his arm around my shoulder and said, "Let's eat."

We walked to the stairs. I evaluated my feelings. Every touch from his fingertips made it difficult for me to deny how much I liked him. I relaxed being by his side.

We stepped into the living room. Scott pointed to the garage, and Teddy guided me to the table. Scott led us in prayer. We settled in for a delicious Italian dinner with great company and conversation.

"How did y'all escape the reporters?" I asked.

"Like they did last night," Teddy said, "Scott brought them here while Rick and I drove to the airport. Reporters can't follow us to the plane where Shelly arranged another car for us. It wasn't magic, but I do thank Scott. Poor guy has been driving us around for the last two days."

Teddy held my hand, kissed the back of it, and stared into my eyes. I smiled, then thought how I missed him today.

"I knew you would." He smiled.

"Would what?" I asked.

"Miss me."

How does he know what I'm thinking? Can he read my body language?

"Did you notice the wave, Beth?" Kyle asked.

"I did. Thank you. Did you see me wave?" I asked, and he laughed. "You guys were great this morning. I don't know how y'all stay pumped with so much energy."

"Sometimes we run on adrenaline alone," Thad said while we ate.

"Okay, girl. I want to know you so, why not eat meat?" Teddy asked as we passed the food.

"She's crazy," Scott said, and I shot him a look.

"You're an ass," I said to Scott then looked at Teddy. "I do it for the animals. I can lay my head on the pillow at night, knowing I didn't hurt one. It's sad that a cow or well, many cows gave their lives to feed you people."

"Yeah, but it sure is tasty," Scott said before he put another piece of steak in his mouth.

"You have a good heart, babe." Teddy patted my leg under the table.

"Thanks," I said. "I have a question."

"Ask," Teddy said.

"How did you guys come up with the name, Five/Ten?"

"If you were a true fan, you would know," Teddy teased, and I laughed.

"Five/Ten came from the fact, there are five of us, but each has different personas other than music," Mark explained. "Music is a big, big, and I mean, a big portion of our lives, but it's not the whole us. It makes up half of us, so ten represents our other half. Our different personas or attributes, so to speak. You explain," he said and looked at Susan.

"Great. We're back to this discussion," Teddy said, shook his head, and smiled at me.

"That's not the reason, but let's hear it, Susan," Thad said.

"Well, Mark is fantastic on the piano, but he also likes to play the stock market. He's our financial guru. Thad loves the bass, but he's also a motorcycle enthusiast and races them," she explained.

"I ride," I said.

"I can see you on a hog, packing a forty-five, riding down the road with your hair blowing behind you," Thad said.

Teddy gently rubbed his fingers down the length of my braid, and I said, "I do, but not a hog. I have a Honda. I also pack, but not a forty-five. I have a nine."

"You got yourself a biker babe, Teddy," Thad teased.

"Sorry, Susan, please go on." I shook my head at Thad.

"You get the picture. We have more to offer than music, and like Mark said, ten represents the different interests we hold," she said.

"That's not the reason," Thad said.

"Tell me about you and Kyle." I smiled at Thad.

"Kyle is artistically talented," she proudly said.

Teddy relaxed in the chair and twisted my braid around his fingers. "Kyle is good. He's designed the last four album covers."

"With help," Kyle said.

"I've seen them. The covers are good," I agreed.

"Thank you," Kyle said and blushed.

"What about you, Susan?" I asked.

"She's a fashionista and organizes our wardrobes when we go on stage," Kyle boasted. "Well, except for Teddy. What he wears is what he plays in."

"I look good in anything." Teddy boasted.

"Yeah, right," Thad said.

"And your interest?" I asked Teddy.

"He has many personas. Interest you would not believe," Susan said.

"I'm more interested that Beth rides motorcycles," Teddy said.

"Scott does too," I pointed to his motorcycle, which was parked in the corner of the garage.

"Yeah, we played with it today, but back to the name," Thad said. "You're saying Five/Ten is because there are five of us, and music makes up half of us. The ten is our other half, which represents our other attributes?"

"Yeah," Mark said.

"No. Teddy was the one who thought of the name," Thad said. "Tell them, Teddy."

"They would not shut up about it. They focused all their energy and time for several days to find the perfect name. It made me crazy. No one wanted to rehearse, so one evening we were in the studio, and the conversation started again. It was ten o'clock. Five/Ten was born, and it shut them up," Teddy said, and we laughed.

"That's ridiculous," Kyle said.

"That was lame, dude," Mark said.

"Maybe, but it's the truth." Teddy smiled.

"I thought you came up with the name Five/Ten because we're five talented people who have twice as much talent as anyone else in the world. Five times two is ten," Thad said.

"You're wrong," Mark said to Thad. "We put a lot of deep thought into this."

"Too deep." Teddy laughed.

We sat at the table, ate, spoke, laughed, and listened to a few stories Teddy and the band told. After dinner, we relaxed, and Teddy held my hand. He pulled it into his chest and stared at me.

"What?" I asked him with aching cheeks from the smile I held.

"You're cute. I'm glad you're here," he said.

"You're cute, and I'm glad you're here." I stared at his facial features. I didn't need to fall for him, but it was getting difficult, not too. I pulled my hand from his and stood. "I need to help clean."

He scooted the chair back, held my hips, and guided me into his lap. I straddled him while he ran his fingers over my braid once again.

"I like your hair," he said.

"Shelly did it." I gazed into his brown eyes and yearned for him.

"Good job, Shelly," he said quietly.

"I'm going to break your legs."

"You fit perfectly."

My eyes widened while I stared at him. I rocked my hips a little and smiled.

"You have a phone call."

"Yeah." He slightly smiled and held my hips while his phone vibrated in his pocket.

"You need to answer it," I said, but pushed my hips close to the vibration until it stopped. "Oh. They hung up."

"Maybe they'll call back," he said, not breaking eye contact with me.

Electricity ran through my body. I envisioned Teddy's hands moved up my sides and across my chest. I fantasized about his kisses being trailed from my neck to my breasts.

"Get up," he said and gently pushed me from his lap.

"I'm sorry," I blushed while I stood. "Friends don't do this, so no more. Understand?"

"You did nothing wrong, and friends or not, you can do that anytime."

We both took a deep breath to gain control. I shook my head from the thoughts of Teddy.

"I need to clean then finish packing," I said and gathered a few dishes as Scott came into the garage to help.

"I need to tell you something," Teddy said to me. "You don't have to be at the airport at seven. Shelly made a few calls, and…"

"What did y'all do?" I asked.

Scott stopped in his tracks and stared between Teddy and me. He bowed his head and carried a few plates into the house.

"I have to go home. Lucy is getting me." I sat the plates on the table and pulled my phone from my pocket to call her.

"You'll be there on time. No need to speak with her," Teddy said. "We'll have you home when you planned."

"I have to go through security," I said.

"You're not robbing me of an extra hour and a half to spend with you," he said. "Shelly took care of everything."

"I'm going to be pissed if I'm not on that plane by nine," I said and put my phone in my pocket.

"Everything is arranged," Shelly said and placed her hand on my shoulder. "I've taken care of you, so trust, Beth. This is one small step."

I looked between them and said, "Thank you, but I don't need anyone to take care of me." I picked up the plates, pointed at Teddy, and said, "Don't make me miss my plane."

"You won't." He smiled.

We adjourned to the back porch after the cleanup process. I walked to the band members and hugged each one.

"Thank you for the flowers and bears. I like 'em," I said.

"You're welcome, but do we have any names yet?" Mark asked.

"Don't cheat and look at a clock," Thad said and looked at Teddy while we laughed.

I shook my head, then Scott walked to me.

"Countdown, Beth," Scott said.

"In four hours, I'm out of your hair, if Teddy doesn't make me miss my plane," I said.

"I told her we had it covered," Teddy said.

"I told you to stay longer," Scott said to me.

"I love you, dear brother, but I'm ready to get home. I miss it so much, I've checked the cameras to make sure the house and business are still standing."

"What do you mean checked?" Scott asked.

"Let me show you." I pulled the phone from my pocket. "I love this system. I can monitor the office or the house from wherever I am."

I tapped the security app on my phone, logged in, and within a few seconds, the office cameras appeared on the screen. I handed it to Scott, and Teddy leaned in as they viewed the system.

"You can see everything," Scott said.

"I know. A pile of paperwork is waiting for me on my desk." I pointed to the screen.

"This is your office?" Teddy asked.

"Yes, sir."

"Who is your provider?" Teddy asked.

"Me. I'm not paying anyone to monitor my stuff when I don't have to."

We spoke about the details of the security system, and Scott asked about me placing one in his house. I retrieved my house to show him the resolution of the outside cameras when he pointed to the screen.

"Helen sent me a picture of the bench," Scott said. "I wish I could see the detail."

"Why does this family have to know everything?" I asked and shook my head. "I cut a few trees down several weeks ago, so I played."

Scott pulled his phone out of his pocket and found the picture to compare to the screen. It was a log about seven feet in length and four feet around. I used the chainsaw and made a small loveseat with an armrest then another seat out of its entirety.

"You better watch yourself around my sister. She's good." Scott showed Teddy the picture.

"You did that?" Teddy asked.

"It's a work in progress. I need a smaller chainsaw to add intricate detail. I can't maneuver my heavy saw like I want, but I'll figure it out. I have a few more trees to cut before winter, so I'll have more logs to practice on before tax season."

"You cut down trees?" Teddy asked.

"Only the dead ones, so they won't fall on houses or cars when it storms. I use the firewood for winter," I explained.

"You're a packing, bike riding, singing, dancing, chainsaw babe," Teddy chuckled.

"I'm many things, Teddy, but so is everyone in this world," I said.

"Except a person who likes to fly." Scott laughed.

"Shut up, Scott." I smiled. "I have to finish packing."

"Will we be in your way if we rehearse?" Teddy asked.

"Be my guest," I said.

"Let me know when you all are ready," Teddy said to the band.

"Let's do it," Mark said, then we went downstairs to the man cave.

I walked into the bedroom, looked at the bears, and names came to my mind. I stepped into the entertainment room with a slight smile. Teddy stood at a keyboard and looked at me.

"Beth has names for the bears." He announced to the others.

"How do you do that?" I asked, and he winked at me.

"Well?" Thad asked.

"Waldorf and Wilma," I said.

"How did you come up with those?" Teddy asked as everyone laughed.

"You can't say Waldorf and Wilma without smiling."

"True. I like the names, and it's better than Six/Nine or Eleven/Twelve," Mark said.

"Vote," Teddy said.

"You guys can change the names. They're only suggestions."

"I like it, so I say yes," Thad said.

"Me too," Kyle agreed as Susan nodded.

"Waldorf and Wilma, it is," Teddy said.

His graceful fingers moved across the keys and created a smooth slow melody while he held my stare. Pictures of he and I being together intimately, flashed in my mind. Emotional conflict played in my head and heart. I felt alive in his presence and anticipated his touch. When he spoke, excitement filled me. I could fall hard for him even though our lips have yet to meet. How do I stop these feelings?

"Excuse me for a moment." I walked into the bedroom.

I packed my belongings, listened to them practice, and received a text on my phone. I pulled it from my pocket. It was the unknown number again. I leaned against the bedroom doorframe and read:

With him comes lies, deceit, and mistrust.

I texted:

We're friends. Either explain yourself or drop it.

Teddy stared at me. I stuffed the phone in my pocket, walked across the room, and went into the bathroom. I shut the door behind me, stared into the mirror, and thought of Teddy. The music came to a stop. Footsteps pounded the stairs.

I checked the bathroom for my belongings and grabbed my makeup bag. I opened the door, walked to the bedroom, and added the bag to my carry-on suitcase.

"Where is everyone?" I asked and walked to Teddy, Shelly, and Gene as they stood by the keyboard.

"Break. Can I see your phone?" Teddy asked, and I looked at Shelly. "Dammit," he said and reached in his pocket.

He retrieved his phone, and I glanced at it. Carissa's name appeared on the top of the screen. I quickly diverted my eyes to the ceiling as it was none of my business.

"My threats of pressing harassment charges didn't shut her up. Please do something about this," Teddy said while Shelly took the phone, and it stopped vibrating.

"This makes the twelfth call, Teddy. She said she was leaving," Shelly said.

I didn't want to listen to the conversation, so I walked to the stairs.

"Where are you going, Beth? Did you receive another text?" Teddy asked.

I smiled at him and ascended the stairs. I overheard Teddy say to Shelly. "Why is she blowing up my phone? I told her it was over." His voice faded with every step I made.

Did she call when I sat on his lap? Was she behind the weird text messages?

I stepped outside onto the porch with everyone. I lit a cigarette, and Teddy joined us. He stood next to me and wrapped his arm around my waist. I stepped out of his arms and moved to the other side of the porch.

"Where are you going now?" He followed, and I didn't respond. "You're running from me because of Carissa."

I stared at him and tried to push the feelings I had for him, to the pit of my stomach. He held my hand and tugged me into the house as I put out my cigarette. We stepped into the den to be alone, but Shelly joined us.

"It's taken care of for right now. Carissa's insistent in speaking with you, so if she calls again, you're going to talk to her." She handed him the phone and looked between us. "Did you tell him about the earlier text?"

I gave her a stern look, and Teddy asked, "You received some this morning and a few minutes ago?"

I slowly nodded but stared at Shelly. She pointed at me and said, "Trust, Beth." Then she walked off.

"May I please see your phone?" he asked.

"You need to take care of your girl," I said and avoided the question.

"I'm trying. Just when we're making progress, you pull your emotions back and lock them tight. I can't crack the code, and it makes me crazy."

"We're not talking about me, Teddy. You know who I mean. You need to be with Carissa," I said.

"No, I don't. The crap she's pulling is a reason for me not to be with her," he said while his phone rang a soft melody. He pulled it from his pocket, turned it to silent, and said, "I'm sorry, but I have to take this one. Don't go anywhere." He tapped the phone and said, "Hey, sweetie."

How many women does he have? I gave him the same burning glare I gave Shelly then walked to the kitchen.

"We have the interview tomorrow afternoon, so I'm not sure if we're going to be able to stop in Wyoming." He watched me walk out the back door.

He paced the den floor and looked at me through the window. He gestured toward me while he spoke.

I walked to the railing, and my phone sounded with another text. I lit a cigarette and pulled the phone from my pocket.

"You're getting nervous. You're quiet and smoking a lot," Scott said.

"I'll be okay once I get home," I said, then read the text.

Let's play a game. Which lies are the truth? You two are meant to be together? He'll buy you anything? You can leave your life behind to follow him? Love, money, and fame is not handed to someone like you. Don't get comfortable with him.

Teddy emerged from the house while I texted:

Do you think I'm after those things? Give me your name, call me, and let's talk.

"Sorry," he said.

"It's okay," I said and stuffed the phone in my pocket.

"You got another one," he said.

"Quit watching me," I said.

"Was it your boyfriend or the kids? How do I know you're not playing me? Are you after my money?" he asked.

"Are you serious?" I asked him quietly. "I want you for your body and nothing else."

"You can have it anytime." He smirked.

"I didn't mean to say that." I blushed.

"Yes, you did," he said. "May I see your phone?"

"If you can retrieve it without getting hurt." I didn't want him to see the picture of Scott and Carol.

With my back against the rail, he pinned me with his body. "You don't think I would do it."

"Ninja skills. Remember?" I stared at him while he searched my eyes.

I needed to separate from him for our own good. It would be easier to push him away before I developed deeper feelings.

"Stop it," he said.

He grabbed my hand, led me into the house, downstairs, and to the first landing. He lightly backed me into the corner. Staring intently at each other, I thought about how bad I wanted him to kiss me or me kiss him. I wanted his lips against mine, one time, then I could let him go. Was there more between us than the feel of his touch? A kiss would prove there wasn't anything special.

"You're not ready," he whispered.

Did I say anything out loud? I questioned myself.

"No, you didn't," he said.

The door opened, and Shelly walked down the stairs. Teddy left me in the corner. My mind raced with thoughts of him.

"You look like you saw a ghost." She stopped in front of me.

I blinked a few times and received another text. Frustration came over me while I read the words:

> *Everyone is after love, money, and fame. You're no different. You're stupid if you think I'll call you. I gave you the one name you need to know.*

I shut the screen off and looked at the clock on the phone. I'll be out of Teddy's life soon. I descended the stairs.

"May I see your phone?" Gene asked.

"Whatever," I said and handed him the device.

"Thank you, honey," he said.

"Please don't tell Scott. This is not his concern."

"Why in the hell didn't you say something about this?" Teddy asked as he and Gene stared at the picture.

"They said no one would get hurt if I leave you alone. I leave within an hour, so everything will be okay," I said.

"We need to make sure Carissa is gone," Teddy said to Gene. "Have you heard anything from Paul?" he asked Shelly.

"No," she said.

"They're telling her a lot of crap," Teddy said. He looked to the floor for a second in thought then looked at me. "Helper," he said. He cocked his head, smiled, and said to me, "Say, helper."

"Helper," I said.

"Whoever this is, said to use your southern drawl," Teddy said.

I said it once more. 'HELPER.' Teddy, Shelly, and Gene smiled and watched me play with the word, then it hit me. "Who in the hell am I supposed to help?" They laughed, and Teddy took me into his arms. "What?"

"You're cute." He looked at Gene and asked, "You did say she was smart, right?"

I pulled back, lightly hit Teddy's arm, and said, "I'm nervous about flying, so it took me a minute."

"Yeah, babe. Help her," Teddy said.

"Who is HER, and who is Paul? Why are you talking to him about me?"

"He works for me, so you have nothing to worry about," Teddy said.

"I can take care of myself, Teddy," I said.

"I want to help protect your world, babe," he said, then Gene handed the phone to me.

"I don't need you to protect my world," I said.

Gene walked away from us with his phone pressed against his ear as Shelly followed. I tapped on my message app to text Helper.

"How am I going to get through?" Teddy asked.

I texted:

Help who? I need a name.

I then added the contact name Helper to my phone.

"Let me tell you something, Beth Chambers," he said and raised my chin, so our eyes met. "You don't have to let me into your home or your business, but you will let me into your life. We are a part of each other, and someday soon, you'll see it."

"I don't want love, money, or fame like the text said. I don't want anything from you," I said.

"You said friendship. You guaranteed that to me," Teddy said, and I shook my head.

"Please don't delete any of the texts, Beth," Gene said. "It's a given whoever this is, wants you two apart. We want to use your phone to ping the phone the texts are coming from and stop this."

"You don't need my phone to ping anyone. Everything is okay," I said.

"He has a good idea," Teddy said, then my phone rang back with another text.

Took you long enough.

"We need a real name," Gene said. "It was confirmed Carissa is flying to California, so she should leave you alone, Teddy. It doesn't mean that it isn't Carissa, but she isn't using her or Roger's phone."

"We need to find out," Teddy said.

"Please don't say anything to anyone," I said.

"You said you don't want anything from me, but you don't mean it." Teddy pulled me into his body and wrapped his arm around me. "I've seen it, babe. I'm not the confused one."

"I'm not either." I lied to myself.

He smiled and said, "You're stubborn." He traced his finger across my cheek and said, "We won't say anything to anyone. I got you."

"I don't need you to GET ME, Teddy. I got this all on my own." I stepped out of his embrace.

"I have never met anyone as stubborn as you," he said.

"I'm not stubborn. I'm determined."

"I'm determined to show you," he said and placed his guitar strap over his shoulder. He sat two chairs to face each other, sat in one, and patted the other. "Will you sit here?"

"Why?" I asked.

"I hope I can open your eyes." He played a soft melody and asked, "Do you know this song?"

"Yes," I said and sat in the chair.

"Sing with me."

"How are you going to open my eyes with a song?"

"Trust me," he said.

"It's hard to do that," I said quietly. His damn brown eyes held my gaze. "Fine."

He stopped playing and removed my glasses. "Let's take these off for a minute, but I need you to look at me and only me."

He started the song over, and I stared into his beautiful eyes. His sultry voice took the lead, and the words traveled through to my thoughts. In my vision, everyone disappeared from the room. I felt at ease, so I harmonized with him as we sang, *Stay*.

He smiled as our voices grew louder. I matched him word-for-word but never broke eye contact. In my imagination, he held me close and glided me across a dance floor.

The words were appropriate to our situation. Like the couple in the song, one person needed to pursue the other to stay, and also like the song, one left. They never spent their lives together.

We finished, but I couldn't pull my eyes from his. He played notes from another song I recognized. I daydreamed that he spun and guided me with his hips as we danced to his song, *White Flowers*. Pictures flashed in my thoughts of us, pressing our bodies against one another as electricity heightened my senses.

We completed the song, and he gently brushed his fingers across my cheek. My breath was sucked from my lungs while the intensity grew between us.

Clapping brought me to reality. I consciously blinked. Everyone stared at us, including Scott, Carol, and the band members.

"Perfect," Teddy said and held my hand.

"Did you know your sister could sing, Scott?" Carol asked.

"You two sounded good," he said.

"Yeah, they did," Thad said.

Teddy leaned close to me and whispered, "My Beth. I'm breaking through." He smiled and said, "Thank you for the dance."

"It's time, guys," Gene said.

Teddy stood his guitar in the stand. I stood to gather my suitcases. He grabbed my wrist, pulled me close, and spoke softly.

"I changed words and notes in the songs. You followed me to a tee. You didn't notice?"

I shook my head then looked to the floor for a second in thought. Did we read each other's minds? I looked at him, and he nodded a few times then released my waist.

My head felt dizzy, and my energy drained. I took a few steps from him. No two people could read one another's minds, so I shook my head to ward off the notion.

Gene loaded my suitcases into the car while I stepped onto the back porch for one last cigarette. I gazed out to the pond as my phone rang with another text.

You like games. Guess.

I stared at my phone until the screen went blank. I needed my head analyzed for even contemplating the idea of having emotions for Teddy. With him comes the media, drama, and being separated. Long-distance relationships never work.

I tapped my screen and texted:

No games. It's over.

"Are you okay, babe?" Teddy asked as he closed the back door.

"I'm confused," I admitted.

"I can feel it." He stood next to me.

"What does that mean?" I asked him.

"Have you ever felt something from someone and knew it was the truth?" he asked.

"Sometimes I can get a feel of people when I meet them. It's not everyone, but sometimes, I meet a stranger, and pictures pop into my thoughts. I can see if their intentions are good or bad or if they're sick or in danger. I can't pick who or what I see, and I'm not claiming to be a fortune teller." I smiled. "I'm not crazy. At least, I don't think I am, but do crazy people know they're crazy?"

He smiled, stared at the porch, and said, "That's weird, Beth. You can see all that, but you can't see us."

"Don't make a big deal of it," I said.

"I'm not, it's just that, you can't see us." He looked in my eyes. "Do you feel my emotions when I'm not touching you?"

"I don't know."

"There isn't anything to be confused about. I want you, and you want me, so bam. No confusion. We make it happen," he said.

"You're full of it. We don't want each other, and I'm not confused about us. I'm torn with the decision if I want peanuts on the plane." I smiled.

I didn't want to admit how I liked him. We needed time and distance from one another to evaluate our emotions.

"You're lame," he snickered.

He caressed my cheeks and stared intently into my eyes. This is it. This is our first kiss. His lips on mine would add to my confusion. It would be easier to leave him if he didn't kiss me, but my body yearned for his full kissable lips and electrifying touch.

"Are you ready?" Gene asked as he stuck his head out the back door.

"You are confused," Teddy said.

"I'm telling you. Peanuts are a big decision," I said with a smile.

"What am I going to do with you?"

"Be my friend," I said softly.

"That and much more," he said, then kissed my cheek.

Chapter 15

"You have a job if you want to come out of retirement," I said to my mother as we sat in my office.

"That isn't going to happen." She laughed and adjusted her thin black-rimmed glasses. She moved a strand of light brown hair from her forehead and said, "All of this is your problem."

"Great," I said with no enthusiasm. "Thanks for coming in for the last couple of days. You were a big help."

"No problem." She stared at me with a smile.

"What?"

"I had another dream about you," she said, and a twinkle came to her blue eyes. "This makes the second. It's serious."

"Nothing is serious unless you had a dream that we sold the place and comfortably retired." I giggled.

"No. You're doomed here forever, ha-ha," she teased. "Someone is serious about you. It could be a person from the SUV."

"Did you see someone?" I asked.

"Yes and no. You stood in the parking lot and stared at the door," she said and pointed out the window. "It was raining, and you held a blue umbrella. I flew over you, buzzed by your ear, and asked if you were going in, but you didn't hear me. A guy appeared out of thin air and stood next to you. The rain continued to fall, and you turned your attention to him. He was soaked with water, but you wouldn't share the umbrella. You smiled at him, and he outstretched his hand toward you."

"I yelled for you to take his hand, but you wouldn't move. He stepped under the umbrella, grabbed your free hand, and the rain stopped falling. He took the umbrella out of your other hand, and the dark clouds parted. He kissed you and guided you into the building," she said. "Whoever it is, belongs with you."

She patted my hand from across the desk and stood to leave.

"What did he look like?" I asked.

She thought a moment and said, "He kept his back to me, but he had black hair. I felt the love he had for you more than I saw his features. When I see him, I'll know. I'll point him out to you."

"Retirement has made you crazy." I smiled.

"No. I'm happy. I'll see you sometime this weekend. Love you, sweetie."

She walked out of the office and bid goodbye to my employees. I stared out the window, watched her get into the car, and pull from the parking lot.

Colorado felt like a dream with several days and distance separating Teddy and me. Not a phone call or text came to me regarding him. I reminisced of when Gene drove me to the airport.

Shelly joined us for the ride. Sadness left my heart heavy, saying goodbye to my brother and sister in law. I was quiet. Teddy held my hand while Shelly spoke about the tour, reporters, and Carissa.

"Are you okay?" Teddy asked me.

"I hate flying," I said.

"Is it your stomach or head that bothers you?" Teddy asked while Gene drove through a gated area behind the airport.

"Head," I said to Teddy. "Where are you going, Gene? You missed the turn. The front is the other way."

"You didn't tell her?" he asked Teddy.

"Tell me what?" I asked, and Gene parked the car next to a small aircraft.

"Sawyer and Lamar are taking you home," Teddy said.

"What?"

"They're my pilots. You're flying in my plane," he said as Gene and Shelly rose from the car and left us alone.

"No, I'm not," I said, but he smiled and nodded. "It's a waste of jet fuel, so you better get your guys a hotel. I'm not using your plane."

"You have no choice. Your plane has left," he said.

"Dammit, Teddy!" I exclaimed.

Gene opened the car door and said, "Things are loaded, so whenever you're ready."

Teddy held my hand and tugged me to follow him. I stood from the car, stared at the plane, while Shelly spoke with two gentlemen in uniforms. He guided me to the stairs as the gentlemen stepped to us.

"Hey, Teddy," one said and shook his hand.

"Hey, man. This is Beth Chambers. She's the reason you're going to Arkansas," Teddy turned to me. "This is Lee Sawyer and Herald Lamar."

I shook the tall ones' hand first and said, "It's nice to meet you, Mr. Sawyer." I then shook the other one's hand. "You as well, Mr. Lamar."

"Please call us Sawyer and Lamar," Sawyer said and held a smile across his plump cheeks.

"Beth doesn't like to fly," Teddy said.

"Why?" Sawyer asked.

"I don't like heights, and my youngest daughter is studying to become a pilot, which makes me nervous."

"I didn't know that," Teddy said.

"Yeah. She tells me about having to stall the plane and being a mom, I worry," I said.

"You and your family amaze me, Beth," Teddy said.

"We are who we are," I said.

"Stalls are hard." Lamar smiled and ran his hand through his black straight shoulder-length hair.

"You're in good hands. Lamar and I have been with Teddy for years, and we know about stalls," Sawyer chuckled.

"Let's don't do one," I nervously laughed.

"I'm going over the checklist, Teddy. When you're ready, Ms. Chambers," Sawyer said.

"Thanks," Teddy said.

"Thank you, gentlemen," I said.

"Shall we?" Teddy held his hand toward the stairs.

"I'm pissed," I said.

"I know, but you'll be okay," he said and grabbed my hand.

"I'll be glad to get away from you, Nafton."

"No, you won't," he said with a smirk. "Let me show you around."

Defeated again, I said, "I guess today is a good day to die."

"Not today, Beth." He led me up the stairs.

The plane was spacious, and Waldorf sat on one of the couches in the back. Several captain's chairs stood throughout the center. Small tables with gold-plated cup holders stood between the captain's chairs. Toward the front, was a big-screen TV, mounted on a wall. A few couches lined the walls, and a minibar stood on the left.

Teddy led me to the rear of the plane, took my bag and purse from my hands, and sat them on the couch next to Waldorf. He opened a back door to reveal a small bed then showed me the bathroom before he guided me to the couch, which contained my belongings.

"This is my spot," he said and drew the curtains closed.

"My spot is getting my ass off this plane. I can't believe you're doing this."

"You need comfort," he said and walked to the minibar.

"The plane is gorgeous."

"Thank you," he said and reached into the cabinet. He retrieved a few items, opened the miniature refrigerator, and plucked a soda from inside. He walked to me and said, "Remote to the TV, gum, and a soda. Make yourself comfortable. Within three hours, you'll be home."

"It's a waste. This plane is too big for one person," I said.

He sat the soda, gum, and the remote in a couple of the built-in cup holders on the couch arm. He held my shoulders and stared at me.

"It's not a waste for the love of my life, so get used to it." He commanded.

"I'm not the love of your life, and never again will I see this plane," I said, and Shelly stepped from behind him. "Trust you? You couldn't tell me about this?" I asked her.

"I agreed with Teddy on this one." She smiled. "You need comfort." She embraced me. "It was nice meeting you."

"You too, Shelly. I enjoyed our time together, until now," I said and looked at Teddy while I hugged her.

"It's payback for the spa." She laughed.

"Well played," I chuckled. "Call me if you need to talk."

"I'll do it," she said.

She left the plane, then Gene stepped in front of me.

"Thanks for running into me," he said.

I reached up, hugged him around the neck, and said, "You're my favorite."

"Your mine, honey," Gene chuckled, then kissed my cheek, and walked off the plane.

Teddy stared into my eyes. Nervousness, anger, confusion, and gratitude mixed my emotions. He didn't say a word but gently placed his hands on my cheeks. Butterflies increased in my stomach.

"Peanuts are in the cabinet," he said softly.

I slightly smiled before his lips touched mine. He kissed me softly and passionately. Some people described a magical kiss as seeing fireworks exploding, but for me, the kiss intensified the energy between us. Nerves in my body heighten, and a tingling sensation ran to the core of my womanhood.

My legs grew weak, but I stood strong. My body yearned for his touch. He embraced me, and the comfortable sensation returned as I hugged him, not wanting to let go. My heart ached for him to be near. I struggled within myself that I can't have Teddy Nafton.

He glided his finger down my cheek then walked to the stairs.

"I don't like you, Nafton." I smiled.

He looked at me, smiled, kissed his fingers, then held them in a peace sign before he disappeared from my eyesight. The stairs raised, which made the walls close in around me. I stood motionless until the door locked.

I was brought out of the memories when my employee, Lois, informed me that I had a call. I focused on work. After several hours sifting through paperwork and creating spreadsheets, the door chimed. Helen, my niece, and employee, came to my door. Familiar voices filled the office area.

"You might want to come out here," Helen said as I stood from the desk.

I rounded the corner. Teddy, Gene, Shelly, Rick, and the band members stood in the business entrance. They introduced themselves to Lois and my other employee, Irene. Helen stayed by my side, gawked at the famous people while I shook my head at them. Teddy smiled brightly, held my stare along with the flowers from Scott and Carol's house.

"Beth!" Lois exclaimed. "Do you know who this is?"

"Yeah. A stalker and a thief. Call the cops," I said and continued the staring contest with Teddy.

"My Beth," Teddy said and embraced me.

"What are you doing here?" I asked.

"You forgot the flowers, so I bought the vase from Carol," he chuckled. "I paid a lot of money for these." He handed me the vase.

"How much do I owe you?" I asked and smelled the flowers.

"You have a choice. A thousand dollars or you have to eat dinner with me," he said.

"Let me get my wallet." I smiled and sat the vase on the desk.

Shelly embraced me and said, "I couldn't get him to go to Michigan. He was going to board a plane by himself."

Gene took me into his arms and said, "We came straight here from the airport. He wouldn't let us go to the hotel."

"You aren't mad?" Teddy asked while everyone else hugged me.

"You gave me some time to cool off." I smiled. "I can't believe y'all are here."

"Rest before hell breaks loose," Thad said.

"Please take a seat," I said and pointed to chairs.

"Scott and Carol thought it would be okay if we came to visit. You did invite us." Mark reminded me.

"Anytime, Mark, but I thought y'all had to go to Seattle?" I asked.

"That's next weekend," Susan explained.

"I can't believe you didn't tell us about these people," Lois said.

"Gene, Shelly, Rick, and Five/Ten are awesome. There isn't much to say about Nafton. He's not all that." I joked.

"I beg to differ, Beth," Irene said, "I bought *Dance With Me* last weekend, and I love it."

"Thank you," Kyle said.

"I also thought you guys did a great job on *Blizz*," she said.

"What did you think?" Teddy asked me and swung our hands.

"They did a wonderful job," I pointed to everyone but Teddy.

"They couldn't have done a wonderful job without me." He smirked.

I couldn't stop smiling. I missed the electricity from his touches and his beautiful big brown eyes.

"Let me get a few things together, and y'all come to the house for dinner." I looked at my employees and asked, "Can you handle the rest of the day without me?"

"We didn't come to impose, babe. I want to spend time with you, in private, without reporters surrounding us. We're going to the hotel, so when you get off work, you meet us for dinner," Teddy said.

"No. The media will be called to your doorstep if you go to the hotel. We don't get many celebrities in Arkansas, so y'all are going to follow me to the house for dinner," I insisted.

"Go on, Beth. We have this," Lois said.

"Fine," he said, then looked at Shelly. "Please make the call."

"What call?" I asked.

"We'll take care of dinner," Teddy said.

I guided Teddy into my office. I showed him to a seat while I stepped around my desk.

"I don't mind feeding you people. I haven't been to the store yet, but I can find something to cook."

"No arguments, babe. I didn't come to inconvenience you." He leaned back in the chair and said, "I like the office, but why a pink and purple building?"

"The colors make me comfortable," I said.

I turned off the computer, gathered my belongings, and bid the ladies a good evening. I offered Teddy to ride the five miles to the house with me while the others followed.

"I hope you guys have fun and relax," I said to him in the car.

"I'm glad you're not mad that I'm here," he said.

"Not at all," I said as we approached my street. "I'll show you where my family lives. That will make you run fast and hard."

"I'm not running. Seeing you today confirms you and I are a thing."

"We aren't a thing." I smiled. Less than a mile, I pointed to the left and said, "My niece lives here, and my other niece lives next door. If you look to the right, my sister lives there while she's building her house."

We rounded a corner, and I pointed, "This is where my sister's house is being built. My nephew lives here next to her, and my mother lives in the brown house to your left. Lucy lives a mile behind us, and Danielle lives about two."

We drove to my brown brick house with woods surrounding us. I put the car in park.

"That's how close we are, Teddy. We call this Psycho Path Compound."

"It's secluded." He laughed.

My house sat two thousand feet from a dead-end road. Raw land of trees and scrubs sat on both sides and behind the house. The neighborhood road was visible through bare trees during the winter, but otherwise, you couldn't see the neighbors.

"Is this all yours?" Teddy stood from my old, beat-up Altima while Gene and Rick pulled in the other vehicles behind me.

Everyone emerged from the other cars, and I pointed to my right, "These twenty-eight acres of land belong to the neighbors, and we own four acres on the other side. Four more behind me and a few hundred or so of raw land, the government owns are next to these four. This is my sanctuary."

"It's gorgeous," Shelly said.

"Thank you," I said.

My dogs, Izzy and Olly, jumped at my legs when I walked into the house. I patted them on their heads and invited everyone inside.

"Let me show you around."

We stepped into the den, kitchen area. The living room was to our left. The kitchen and dining area were on our right. Those rooms were spacious as an island bar stood in the center of the kitchen. A bathroom separating two bedrooms were on the right of the kitchen. One bedroom was a playroom for the grandchildren with a toy box and a bed. Sadie called it her room.

"You need to see this, Teddy," Susan said.

He walked past me, peered into the bathroom, and asked, "Did you do this?"

"It took us about four weeks. Lucy drew while Danielle and I wrote," I said.

The bathroom consisted of two cartoon trees and characters, which were painted in bright colors. We wrote different inspirational sayings on the walls, in paint.

"Most people read while they sit on the toilet, so I'm helping them out." I smiled.

"It's creative," Teddy laughed while everyone read the words.

We walked into the kitchen. I pointed to my office area, and the washroom, which was off the kitchen, then walked into the living room. An open door off the living room led to a big exercise room, which contained two treadmills, a stationary bicycle, a large-screen TV, and a weight machine. The equipment lined the walls and left an open space in the center of the room.

Teddy walked to the back French doors and peered into the back yard. He then followed me while I walked through the living room into a small hall, which led into my room and bathroom.

A back door in my bedroom led to a wooden porch that ran the length of the house. A metal roof covered twelve-feet width, then another twelve was uncovered.

A hammock stand and firepit sat in the sun with a few chairs sitting around the pit. A fence surrounded the back yard for the dogs, then woods as far as the eyes could see. Water rushed in a creek down a small hill, behind the house, from the rain we had a few days ago.

"This is nice," Teddy said.

"Thank you. It's dirty and small compared to what you're probably used to," I said.

"I like this better than Carol and Scott's place," he said.

"Thank you," I said.

Noise from a car door shutting came from in front of the house. I opened the door for everyone to gather in the living room. We walked through my bedroom, but Teddy stopped me.

"Mirrors?" He pointed to the ceiling.

"I wanted the room to appear bigger, so we placed small mirror panels in the pan ceiling," I said. My ceiling had three tiers with a ceiling fan in the center on the last level. "You have to be lying in bed a specific way to see a little bit of anything. I need to take them down, but they're tied in the attic. That'll be next year's project." I smiled. "I hope you make yourself at home, Teddy. I want you comfortable."

Lucy's voice echoed from the living room, and the dogs ran to me. She, Ellis, Sadie, and Kara stood in the living room. I looked out the tall windows, and Danielle got out of her vehicle. Colby got Gabi out of a car seat then they walked to the door.

"What are y'all doing here?" I asked as the front door opened.

Lucy and Danielle shook everyone's hands with Colby and Ellis following. Teddy stood behind me, and I picked Gabi up from Danielle. Kara crawled to me, and I settled Gabi on my hip. I scooped Kara into my arms while Sadie held onto my hips.

"It's nice to meet you guys in person," Lucy said and held her hand out to Teddy.

"You too. Thank you for your help." He shook her hand, then Danielle's.

"Help?" I asked.

"We gave them addresses and directions," Lucy informed.

Teddy guided me to the couch, and I asked, "Why aren't you in school, and you two at work?" I nodded to Danielle, then the boys.

"We wanted to meet Teddy and Five/Ten," Danielle said then looked at Teddy. "How was y'alls flight?"

"What?" I asked.

"Scott didn't call until thirty minutes ago." Lucy ignored me.

"Y'all knew they were coming and couldn't tell me?" I asked.

"Yep. You said you didn't want to hear Teddy's name, so we didn't tell you," Lucy said.

"You didn't want to hear my name?" Teddy asked me.

"I was mad at you," I said.

"She was fuming about flying her home in your plane," Ellis said as he unpacked the playpen in the corner of the living room.

"Someone could have told me," I said while Lucy and Danielle took Gabi and Kara from my arms and sat them in the playpen.

"I knew you were mad, but not to mention my name?" Teddy asked.

"For the plane thing, yes, but I'm glad you guys are here. Y'all need to relax before things get crazy, but don't you want to go home?" I asked.

"Wife and kids aren't due in until Monday," Mark said.

"Rob and the kids are fine," Shelly said.

"Tabi is with her mother, until Tuesday of next week," Gene said.

"Can you tolerate me until Sunday night, or are you going to hold a grudge?" Teddy asked.

"They can stay as long as they want. I like them. You, on the other hand, make me crazy." I smiled.

"I can't believe Teddy and Five/Ten are sitting in your living room, Mom," Lucy said.

"Can I have strawberry milk, Mimi?" Sadie asked in my ear.

"Sure." She and I walked into the kitchen. I asked, "Would anyone like something to drink?"

"We're good," Teddy said.

"I can do it myself," Sadie said and retrieved a stool from the office.

"Do you know the song *Streams* we were listening to, Sadie?" Lucy asked.

I stood near Sadie. She stirred the milk and syrup in the cup.

"Oh, Mimi. I love that song," she said. "There's a girl singer and a boy singer. They talk about how happy they are and walk next to a stream."

"Do they?" I looked at Teddy, and he smiled at me.

"It turns sad because they don't get to see each other for a long time." Sadie continued.

She found the lid for her drink in a drawer. She twisted the lid on her cup, then placed the milk and mix in the refrigerator.

"Mr. Nafton sings the boy part, and Susan sings the girl part. Everyone else plays the instruments," Lucy told her.

Sadie grabbed my hand, walked me to the couch, and I sat next to Teddy. She took a drink and studied him for a few seconds.

"Are you serious? You sing the boy part?" she asked him.

"Yes, ma'am," Teddy said.

"What's your name?" Sadie asked.

"Teddy," he said.

"Momma, I don't think Teddy sings it," she said and looked at Lucy.

"Mind your manners, Sadie," Lucy scolded.

"Sorry, I mean, Mr. Teddy don't sing that song," she said in a little girl's voice.

"Please call me, Teddy," he said and looked at Sadie. "I do." He retrieved his phone from his pocket, and she stood a foot from him. He asked, "Do you want to watch?"

She looked at me then at him and crawled onto my lap. Teddy leaned into us, and we watched a video of their rehearsal. Sadie didn't blink until after.

"That girl, is you?" she asked Susan.

"Yes, sweetie." Susan smiled.

Sadie put one hand over her mouth, smiled, and said through her fingers. "I like that song."

"Thank you," Teddy said and winked at me.

"You guys have connected," Lucy said and pointed between Teddy and me.

"Mind your manners, Lucy," I said.

"I didn't ask if you had sex yet." She laughed along with everyone else.

"Do you have a guitar, Mr. Teddy?" Sadie asked.

"Yes. I may play a song for you later if your Mimi helps me sing."

"Oh, man. She didn't say she sang with you. We're sorry," Ellis teased, and I smiled. "I'm kidding, Beth. You can sing. That's where Sadie gets it." He walked into the kitchen and asked if anyone wanted tea.

"I do," Danielle said.

"Do you want one of the good glasses or what?" Ellis asked.

"I'm embarrassed. I didn't think about this, but I have four good glasses, plastic glasses, and the rest are mason jars," I said.

"We can drink out of plastic and mason jars, babe." Teddy smiled, then asked, "Do you guys mind eating pizza tonight?"

"I love pizza," Sadie said and hugged Teddy.

"I also love pizza, sweetie," he said and hugged her back.

"What time did you call in the order?" Gene asked Shelly.

"It should be ready," she said, then Gene walked out the front door.

"Where is it? Ellis and I can get it," Colby said.

Shelly looked at Teddy with wide eyes, and he said, "No, they can, but thank you."

Gene walked into the house and carried a few bags while Rick and Shelly walked out the door. Izzy laid between my feet and Olly between Teddy and me. Teddy patted Izzy on the head, and she wagged her tail.

"These are the famous dogs who are a part of your world?" Teddy inquired.

"Yes, sir."

"Could you please sit here, Gene?" Teddy stood and pointed at the couch to indicate for him to sit next to me.

"What did you do?" I asked Teddy, and Gene patted my hand.

Teddy reached in a bag and produced a few toys for the babies. He handed them to Lucy and Danielle. They thanked him, then he plucked two wrapped dog bones out of the bag and gave them to me.

"Thanks, but you didn't have too," I frowned.

He winked at me then looked at Sadie. He held a big bag toward her.

"This is for you," he said.

"Me?" She rummaged through the bag and pulled out an American girl doll. "She's beautiful." She smoothed the doll's hair and looked in the bag again. "Oh, my goodness." She pulled a horse doll from the bag and showed Lucy first then me. She walked to Teddy, hugged him, and said, "Thank you. Thank you."

"You're a sweet girl, honey," he said and looked at me while I glared at him.

"Thank you, Mr. Nafton, but you shouldn't have," Lucy said. "Mom spoils these kids as it is."

"Can I take these to my room?" Sadie asked.

"Yeah." I smiled at her.

"Please call me Teddy," he said once again.

"Or an ass," I said to him, but he smiled at me.

"Thank you for the toys, Teddy," Danielle said.

"You're welcome," he said.

Gene held my hand then reached in his pocket. He handed Teddy a few envelopes.

"You might want to hold her down for this one," Teddy said.

"What's going on?" I asked.

"I got you all something as well," Teddy said to the kids.

He handed Colby, Ellis, Lucy, and Danielle, each an envelope. He then stepped in front of me with his back toward me.

"Nice view darlin' but move." I lightly patted his butt.

He laughed, moved his hand in the air behind him, so I placed mine in his. He held it tight, took a step to the side of me as the kids opened the envelopes.

"I'm not trying to buy anyone, but you all hold pieces of Beth's heart. I hope someday I can share her with you," Teddy said.

"You did sleep with him," Colby said and stared at the card he held.

"If she did, he wouldn't be doing this," Ellis said, and everyone laughed.

Danielle looked at me with wide eyes. Teddy and Gene squeezed both of my hands tight.

"I'm not gonna hit y'all," I said.

"You might," Gene said.

"We can't accept these, Teddy," Lucy said. She and Danielle held the envelopes out for him to take. "Believe me, it's hard to say, but we can't."

"What is it?" I asked.

"Let Teddy do this," Gene whispered to me.

"Yes, you can," Teddy said. "You guys have these beautiful kids to raise. I want to help, so you can buy groceries, pay rent, or whatever you need. Buy something special for yourselves. I don't care what you do with it, just don't let your mom kill me."

Danielle walked to me, and Teddy looked at the floor. She showed me a credit card that had a $2,500 limit. Teddy handed out $10,000 in a matter of minutes.

"Wow," I said with wide eyes. "Teddy…"

"Beth, please," Teddy said and moved his hand to my shoulder. I think it was to help hold me down. "Like I said, I'm not trying to buy anyone. I wanted to do something nice for you guys, so enjoy it."

"Can I hug you?" Danielle asked.

"Anytime, Danielle," he said and embraced her.

Lucy followed then Ellis, and Colby shook his hand and thanked him profusely. He stepped back to me and reclaimed my hand.

"I need to speak to you, and the cards don't have anything to do with what I'm about to ask," Teddy said. "Maybe I should have done this before, but, oh well."

The kids gave him their attention, but I fumed with anger. He looked at me and smirked.

"I can feel it, Beth."

What the hell is he talking about? I didn't say a word as we stared at each other.

"I ain't scared, little girl." He smiled. "Maybe a little." He winked then faced the kids. "First, I wanted to thank you for keeping us off the social sites so, thank you. It means a lot to me that you would respect my privacy." He looked at the floor. "I can play in front of thousands of people at a concert and not be as nervous as I am right now."

The kids laughed, and Danielle said, "We're the nervous ones. You, guys, are intimidating."

"I don't think of us being intimidating. We're like you, well, except for Mark and Thad. They're snobby," he said, and I held his hand to help steady his nerves.

"No, they aren't." I laughed. "I know what the kids mean, though. We're hot dogs, and beer people, and you guys are champagne and caviar."

"We aren't champagne and caviar," Teddy said.

"I like champagne and caviar," Thad said.

"On those square crackers," Mark said, which kept the laughter steady.

Teddy smiled but gave them a stern look and asked, "May I continue?"

"Beth mentioned the champagne and caviar," Thad said.

"Sorry. Go ahead," I said.

"I'm going to stumble but, here it goes." He helped me from the couch and stepped behind me. He wrapped his arms around my waist and said, "I like Beth and hope we continue this thing we have."

"What thing do we have?" I asked.

He squeezed me tight, made me laugh, and said to the kids, "We have a strong connection, but she can't see it right now. All she's thinking about is killing me." He smiled. "What I've thought about the most since the first day we met is how I keep her, and you guys out of the media. I lost it at the concert, babe. I got caught up in the moment," he said and placed his chin on my shoulder.

"I knew I should have left the stage," I said and stepped out of his arms.

"No, you did everything right except I wasn't supposed to have moved you to sit next to me." He looked at the kids. "Sorry for getting off track. We filmed the concert if you want to watch, but that's a different story."

"Yeah, we need to," Lucy said with raised eyebrows.

I walked to the babies while he nodded and continued. "I wanted to bring a few things to your attention. I'm hoping to be friends with all of you, but it comes with a stipulation. If you don't like it, I'm out the door to never be heard from again."

"I don't like it," I quipped.

"You don't have a say, yet," Teddy said, and I smiled.

"What is it?" Danielle asked.

"No pictures of us together are allowed on social sites. I don't care if you take them, but nothing on the Internet with me being around the kids or Beth or even you guys. I need to keep you out of the media for as long as I can."

"Why?" Ellis asked.

"Privacy," he said seriously. "Look, I'm asking to be friends right now, and I feel like I'm nine, asking to play baseball with neighborhood kids. The media can be right on top of us since we started the tour. I want privacy, so I can get to know you all."

"Pizza's here," Sadie said and ran into the living room.

She opened the door, then Shelly and Rick walked inside carrying the boxes. They placed them on the counter, and Rick thanked Sadie for her help.

Shelly looked around the room and said, "Oh, the talk. I thought you were going to wait for me?"

"I hoped I could explain it better than a lawyer, but I don't know," Teddy said.

"We get it," Danielle said and looked at the other three while they nodded in agreement.

"Good," Teddy said, and his body language showed his relief.

"You gave them the envelopes, and you're still breathing?" Shelly asked, and I nodded. "You're slipping, Beth."

"Oh, he'll get his, but I'm trying to figure out why he's nervous. You guys talked on the phone, so why?" I asked.

"The phone is different than meeting face-to-face. We didn't speak about the stipulation," Teddy said.

"Scott told us no pictures and no social sites," Danielle said.

"What did he say?" I hoped he didn't tell anyone about Carissa or the guy in the bathroom.

"He said for us to keep Arkansas media free. He told us you liked Teddy, and we needed to give you two a chance to get to know each other without the hassles of reporters," Lucy said.

"Is that all?" I asked, and they nodded. "They need to relax before things get crazy." I smiled at Teddy. "Not one time did I see him get nervous when he performed."

"You should have seen him on the plane," Kyle said. "He paced back and forth and kept asking our opinions."

"We had bets on how long you were going to let him live once he handed out the envelopes." Thad laughed.

"I understand the privacy thing. Keep Arkansas media free, but are you telling us everything?" Lucy asked.

"Yes," I said quickly and glanced at Teddy.

"Does anyone have questions?" Teddy asked. The kids shook their heads no. "If you want to take pictures and post something online, talk to one of us first." He pointed around the room. "It's simple if we leave the communication lines open."

"We can do that," Danielle said and looked between him and me.

Ellis stood next to the couch, slapped the back of it, and said, "I'm hungry."

"Me, too," Colby said, then they walked into the kitchen.

"Hold up, guys." I looked at Teddy. "They aren't used to being civil and giving thanks."

"Then let's pray," he said.

After the prayer, Teddy and I sat on the sofa with the babies on my lap. Danielle and Lucy stepped in front of us. Teddy stood, but they looked between us with concerned expressions.

"Did anyone see you with him and ask questions? Where you in danger at any time?" Danielle shot off questions.

"No," I said and stood from the couch.

"I have a feeling that you're not telling us everything," she said and studied my eyes. "Why is that?"

"Nothing happened," I assured her so the girls wouldn't worry.

"All right," She faced Teddy and said, "The stipulation will work for me. I hope we can be friends." She hugged him once more then kept him at arm's length. "We want Mom to be happy, and if you do that, you have my support, but understand one thing." She gave him a piercing glare. "I don't care if you're homeless or a megastar. This country girl knows how to shoot damn good. If anything happens to…"

"I won't let anything happen to her or you all. You have my word, Danielle," Teddy said.

She took Gabi from my arms and stepped from him. Lucy embraced him.

"I feel the same as Danielle," Lucy said. "I'm grateful for the opportunity to get to know you, and we want Mom happy, but…" She, too, held his shoulders and stared into his eyes. "We know how to burn evidence, and we'll take you out if she gets hurt."

"I understand," Teddy said.

She took Kara from me then they carried the babies into the kitchen. Teddy held my waist.

"You passed initiation, but I'm pissed," I said.

"I know, but I had to buy my safety from your kids." He smiled and placed his hands on my cheeks. "All I have to do is open your eyes to break down your wall."

"I'm going to break you. We aren't a charity case, so the cards weren't necessary. I do thank you, but the kids will give them back to you," I said sternly.

"I won't take them," he said and embraced me. "They're raising families, Beth. Everyone who is starting a family can use money to help on occasion. I'll let you yell at me later."

Chapter 16

Dinner was pleasant, and conversations flowed. Lucy and Danielle were insistent on cooking for the group over the weekend.

"Let us get the food," Teddy said.

"Oh no, you don't. We'll take care of it," Lucy said.

"I don't want you spending the money I gave you, back on us. That's not what it's for," Teddy said sternly, and Lucy nodded. "How about leaving Saturday night open for us? I'll provide dinner and entertainment."

"No," I said quickly.

"Why?" Teddy asked.

"You guys are here to rest. I don't want y'all entertaining," I said.

"It's what we do," Mark said.

"He's not going to let us go a day without rehearsing," Kyle said.

"We're the best for a reason," Teddy said. "Saturday night will be ours unless you don't like my music."

"I don't," I said playfully, "Besides, I can't make it."

"Why not?" Teddy asked.

"I have plans."

"Yeah, with me." Teddy smiled.

"I might have a date."

"A date with me," Teddy said.

"I don't date thieves and stalkers," I chuckled.

He leaned close to me and said, "I don't date fans."

"I'm not..." I giggled. "I see what you did there." He snickered, and I held his arm. "I have a wonderful idea."

"What?" He moved some of my hair behind my ear.

"You guys stay here," I said.

"We aren't imposing."

"No imposition."

"That's a good idea, Mom," Lucy agreed. "I have a spare room, a couch, and an air mattress."

"I have two spare rooms," Danielle said.

"You're on my turf now. I have two rooms, a couch, and an air mattress as well. I have a big room for you to set your gear to rehearse. There's no need for you to go to the hotel and draw attention. I have to work tomorrow, but you're welcome to stay."

"Keep Arkansas media-free." Lucy reminded him.

"No way." Teddy shook his head.

"Remember the plane thing? As you wanted to help me, I want to help y'all," I said.

"It's not a bad idea," Gene said.

"Vote." I held my stare with Teddy.

"I don't want your family thinking any less of you," Teddy said.

"I don't care," Lucy said.

"It's fine with me," Danielle said.

"It's a no brainer. You'll have one side of the house, and I'll have the other." I looked between Gene and Rick and said, "We'll get the toys off the floor in the toy room."

The girls and I cleaned the kitchen while we planned sleeping arrangements, and Shelly canceled the hotel. I leaned against the counter and listened to the different conversations.

"Are you nervous about tomorrow night?" Lucy asked Teddy as she cleaned Kara's face.

"What's happening?" I asked.

"Potluck with the family," Danielle said, picking up Gabi from the highchair.

"I thought you guys were meeting everyone Saturday," I said.

"We spoke with Scott and Carol and thought it was best for them to meet the family as soon as possible. They can get the formalities out of the way and leave Saturday to relax," Lucy said. "You're going to get questioned with them being on the compound. Get it over with and introduce everyone."

"Y'all arranged everything for tomorrow and Saturday night?" I asked.

"We didn't know about Saturday night, so we didn't say anything to the family. We'll tell 'em at dinner," Lucy said. "Is it okay if we make it a BYOTBC for Saturday?"

"That's a great idea," Colby said.

"A what?" Teddy asked.

"Bring Your Own Tent, Booze, and Chair." Danielle laughed.

"Like the crawfish boil," Ellis said.

"You got it," Lucy said.

"Did Scott warn you about them?" Ellis asked Teddy.

"No," Teddy said.

"Go with the flow and everything will work out," Colby said.

"What?" Teddy asked.

"I don't want a full-blown thing, so let's keep the headcount to a minimum. They're here to rest, not entertain half of Arkansas, plus no pictures," I said.

"I don't mind being a bitch and telling everyone no pictures," Danielle said.

"That's for sure," Colby said, and Danielle lightly hit him.

"I want to get to know you, not take over your house, Beth," Teddy said.

"I'm not putting you guys on display, Teddy. You don't have to entertain, and we can keep it intimate with a family gathering. We can play cards or just hang out," I said.

"You're not putting us on display, babe," he said. "I didn't want to disrupt your life."

"Too late, you stalker. You've already disrupted my life," I said with a grin.

"We know how to keep a low profile," Danielle said.

"We'll protect your privacy. That's a guarantee," Lucy said.

"Beth runs these crazy people, so they'll do what she asks." Colby smiled, and I lightly hit him.

"That's bullshit," I said. "If that were true, there would be no family drama, and we all would be stinkin' rich." The kids laughed, then I said, "I'm stepping out for a minute."

"Can we put the babies in your room to sleep? I want to watch the concert," Lucy said.

"That's fine," I said.

I walked to the back door, and the band followed. A breeze swept through the air. A beautiful starry night and full moon illuminated the familiar tree line.

"This is crazy, Beth," Teddy said and shut the door behind him.

"What?" I asked and placed a few fold-out chairs on the porch.

"You and the girls planning things." He held me in his arms. "Thank you."

"Thank you for coming." I kissed his cheek, and the jolt of electricity between us intensified.

"Are we gonna watch the concert?" Sadie asked, walking outside to us.

"After Mom and Danielle put the babies to sleep," I explained and stepped out of Teddy's arms.

She waved her little arms in the air, and said as she walked to the door, "I wish those babies would hurry up and go to sleep."

"I like her," Teddy chuckled.

"Me too."

"Can I see you in here for a moment, Mom?" Lucy asked from my bedroom door. I walked inside, and she said, "I hate to ask, but we need to get a few groceries to feed them. Can I use your debit card to go to the store?"

"I was going to give it to you. I don't want Teddy spending any more money on us. The money and dinner were enough, and now he's emphatic about entertaining," I said and knew I would be the one to provide the food.

"Did you know about the cards?" Danielle asked.

"No. He surprised me again."

"I like him. Not because of the money, but the look on your face when you speak with him. You're happy," Danielle said.

"Y'all make a cute couple," Lucy said.

"We're not a couple. Long-distance flings never work. It ends when he leaves," I said.

"Give him a chance," Danielle said.

"We'll see." I handed Lucy my card, then we met everyone outside.

After we viewed the concert, we visited, and Teddy played the guitar. The late-night hours crept upon us.

The kids announced it was time to leave. I held Sadie in my arms as everyone stood next to the door to bid us a good night.

"I love you, my beautifulest wonderfulest, Mimi," Sadie said sleepily.

"I love you, my beautifulest, wonderfulest, princess," I said, then Ellis took her from me.

"Dishing the dirt on Mom tomorrow," Lucy announced.

"Y'all remember who gave birth to you." I laughed.

The kids thanked Teddy again for the money and promised to tell him my secrets. The band thanked me for opening my house to them, then they bid us a goodnight. The door closed behind everyone, and I turned to Teddy and smiled.

"Good kids, Beth," Gene said as he walked out the front door.

"Thanks," I said and went to the kitchen to tidy. Teddy leaned against the counter and watched. "What's wrong?"

"How do you know something is wrong?" he asked.

"You look deep in thought," I said.

"Kyle told me about him and Susan," Teddy said.

"I knew about them," I said.

"When did they tell you?" he asked as Gene brought in their luggage.

"Are you sure this okay?" Gene asked, pointing to the spare rooms.

"Yes," I said to Gene then looked at Teddy. "I saw them."

"What do you mean?" he asked.

"Remember when I told you about seeing people?" I asked, and he nodded. "I saw Kyle and Susan in my thoughts, then I asked them."

"In your thoughts?" he asked, and I nodded. "It blows my mind how you can see them and not us."

"I can't pick what or who I see, but they love you, so don't be mad at them," I said.

"I'm happy for them, but I can't believe I didn't see the signs."

"You keep your eyes closed." I smiled.

"Come here," he said and embraced me.

"Your things are in the far spare room," Gene said as he joined us.

"Thanks," he said, and I stepped out of his arms.

"Go settle in, and I'll finish the cleanup," I said.

"If you're sure," Teddy said, and I nodded.

The task of cleaning the porch and loading the dishwasher was finished. Gene was showering. I walked to the far spare room and knocked on the open door.

"Yeah," Teddy said.

"You okay in here?" I asked.

"I'm good." He sat in a chair, putting a keyboard stand together.

"I'm going to take a quick shower," I said. "Please make yourself at home. If you need anything, get it."

"Thanks. Let me know if you need help," he said, and I smiled.

While I showered, anxiety from Teddy being in my house, rushed over me. I reminded myself we were friends. I completed and dressed in my T-shirt and flannel pajama pants. I walked into the kitchen, and Gene stared in the refrigerator.

"I'm tired of pizza," he said.

"Let's see what else I have." I walked to the pantry. "Are you looking for something particular?"

"No. Don't worry about it," he said.

"You look and help yourself to anything."

Teddy stepped around the corner, laughed, and said, "Why does it not surprise me that Gene is looking for food?"

"I'm tired of pizza," he said, and I patted his back.

"I'm taking the dogs out one more time, so please excuse me," I said.

I opened the back door, and the dogs ran into the woods. I sat and lit a cigarette, then Gene and Teddy joined me. Gene found cookies and held one toward me. I smiled and shook my head.

Crickets chirped, and an owl hooted in the distance. A pack of coyotes yipped and howled through the woods. The dogs barked and moved as the leaves crunched beneath their paws.

"Aren't you worried something is going to get the dogs?" Gene asked.

"There isn't anything back here except raccoons and squirrels. Coyotes run, but if they come toward the house, the dogs let me know. Izzy stood her ground with a coyote once. Scared me to death. I hate the sound of their packs moving," I said.

The dogs jumped on the porch, wagged their tails, and bounced at my feet. I thanked them for protecting me and patted their heads.

"These are your babies," Teddy acknowledged.

"Izzy and I are closer than Olly and me. We've had dogs around since I was a little girl and when the kids were small, but Izzy is the first dog I got to pick out. She's a rescue from a puppy mill. I adopted her when she was six months old."

"Olly was abandoned at the veterinarian's office when he was a few weeks old. He was the runt of a litter, and the owner didn't want him. I do the vets books, so they called me to see if I wanted him. I got him to keep Izzy company when I'm at work," I said.

I told them stories about Izzy going to the creek and the adventures of taking them camping. Sometimes, I took them to the office, so my employees and clients knew the dogs.

"I have a rescue cat named Max. He's my buddy, but since I travel, I don't get to see him as often as I would like. When I get home, he finds me and lets me pet him for a while, but you know cats. They're like women. They choose when a person gets to love them," Teddy said.

I laughed, and Teddy picked up Olly. He held him in his lap while we spoke about the animals in our lives.

"Tell her about the horses," Gene said. "Girls are suckers for horses."

"Teddy having horses. That's funny," I said.

"Most people don't know, but I have nine right now."

"I did not see that coming," I said, and he smiled. "Gene's right. I'm a sucker for them. We had a few growing up. I love riding."

"Really?" Teddy chuckled.

"The horses," I laughed.

We all agreed on how animals can become a part of someone's life as if they were part of the family. After a while of enjoying the conversation, Gene yawned, which made Teddy, and I yawn.

"I need to get some rest," I said and placed Izzy on the ground.

"We all do," Teddy said.

He held the door open for me. I methodically moved throughout the house and locked the doors. Teddy and Gene stood silent in the living room.

"Sorry, guys. It's a force of habit. Come and go as you please," I said.

"We'll protect you, babe." Teddy held me in his arms.

I nuzzled my nose into his neck and smelled his scent. He turned me toward my room. He stopped us in the hall, gave me another hug, but held me longer.

"I'll be in the other room. Goodnight," he said and kissed my forehead.

"Night," I said.

Did I want him in my bed? I imagined us being intimate while I stared into his eyes. He gazed back for a few seconds, smiled wider, and I blushed.

"I'll see you in the morning," he chuckled.

"Goodnight," I said.

I walked into the bedroom, made sure the dogs were in their beds, and looked back at Teddy. He winked at me then shut the door.

I shut the lights off, patted the dogs' heads, and set my alarm. I crawled into bed, stared into the darkness, and my thoughts raced to Teddy.

I wish he would have thrown me across the bed and made love to me. I forced my eyes closed and imagined his lips on mine. My body tingled with the thought of us being together. I snapped my eyes open to stop my imagination.

How would I feel about being with another man? No man wanted me. No man should fit his life into mine, and I couldn't fit mine into someone else's. I concluded, Teddy and I needed to remain friends. My focus was on work and not an emotional relationship. I fell asleep, building a protective wall over my heart.

Carissa stepped next to Teddy. She intertwined her arms through his and glared at me.

"Leave him alone," she hissed.

"He's not mine," I said to her while Teddy kissed her neck.

"Back off, or I'll make your life hell." She pointed her finger in my face. Her beautiful perfect facial features became distorted. "He's mine and always will be."

"He's yours," I yelled. Teddy vanished from her side, and she pushed me against a wall. I screamed, "You're perfect for him."

She wrapped a cold hand around my throat and cut off my airway. With her other hand, she pulled a knife from the back waistband of her pants. She held it against my jugular. The wall behind me gave way, and a black hole was at my feet. Carissa laughed. I grabbed her wrist, so I wouldn't fall into the abyss.

I pushed her shoulders to break her hold on my throat. With a hard shove from her grasp, my feet slipped. I fell into the black hole. Her laughter grew faint, the further I fell.

Darkness surrounded me. I waved my arms in the air to find something to grab. I needed to stop from free-falling, but the walls were slippery. I jumped in my sleep.

A slight knock came on my door, and the dogs barked. I blinked a few times.

"Beth," Teddy called my name. "Are you okay?"

I turned on the lamp beside my bed, rose, and opened the door. Teddy stood in the hall, wearing a black and blue silk pajama set. He stood in the glowing light from the other hall light.

"Yeah. Do you need something?" I asked.

"No," he said and took me in his arms. "I had a dream."

"About Carissa?" I laughed and stepped from him.

"Yeah," he said seriously.

"Really?"

"Yeah." He stepped into the room and held me.

"What was your dream about?" I asked.

"It's late. We'll talk tomorrow," he said.

"Is everything okay?" Gene asked from the other hallway.

"Yeah, Gene. Sorry, I woke you. Go back to bed." Teddy walked to the door then looked back at me.

"Please tell me?" I asked and sat on the bed.

He hesitated, and I patted the mattress. He sat on the other side of the California King Size bed.

"I was arguing with Carissa when she pushed you into a hole. I appeared standing in the middle of a road. I looked up and watched you fall. I stood under you and tried to catch you, but…" He became silent.

"I tried to grab onto something when I fell, but I woke before I hit the ground," I said.

"You hit. I jumped out of my sleep," he said sadly.

"That's weird," I said. "Have you spoke with her today?"

"She's called a few times, but I ignored her," he said.

"How did you two meet?"

"A mutual friend introduced us four years ago. We spoke on and off for a few months then one day we played a concert in London, and she showed. We became companions for over a year. I met another woman and stopped seeing her. The other woman left, and Carissa came back into my life," he said, then continued.

"She's an amateur photographer, and she leaked a few pictures of us being together, which created *The Teddy and Carissa Watch*. We both got a kick out of the media, making us out to have a big romance when that was not true."

"She needed the publicity more than me, and that was okay. I wasn't seeing anyone serious after Jenna, and it became a game for us. There was not one time we left each other without arguing. Weeks passed without speaking to one another, but she would meet me somewhere and make a big production about getting back with Teddy Nafton. She would have one of her people call the media to give them scoops. I thought we could play together until one of us found our special someone," he said.

"You don't love her?" I asked, scooting up on the bed.

"I never did," he said.

"Who was Jenna? Tell me if I'm being too nosey."

"I'll answer any questions you have. I won't deceive you as the text stated," Teddy said. "I wasn't in love with Jenna, but she was great. The same mutual friend of Carissa's and mine introduced Jenna to me. We had a good time together before she split. She was a talented music producer with a bright future, until one day, something in her snapped. She left town, leaving a note behind."

"She could be your Ms. Right, and you didn't go after her?" I asked and laid on my side then propped my head up with my hand.

"She wasn't my Ms. Right, and no, I didn't. I let her go and haven't heard from her since. She spelled it out in her letter how we were not compatible. She didn't have family, and she cut all ties with everyone through letters. It was strange, but I do associate with weird individuals being in the entertainment industry," he said and scooted up on the bed.

"Sometimes I daydream about packing up and leaving," I said.

"Your kids wouldn't let you vanish. They would hunt you down with me leading the way, babe," I rolled my eyes. "Anything else?"

"What are your other interests besides music?" I asked.

"I like to read and learn about different subjects in life."

"What do you mean?" I asked.

"I know four languages and would like to learn more." He placed his head in his hand and laid on his side. "Does that impress you?"

"No," I laughed. He was a smart man, and maybe I should be intimidated.

"Not even a little impressed?" he asked, and I shook my head. "I told you to impress you."

I laughed, stood, and turned off the small hall light. I stopped in the doorway and asked, "Okay, sir. Which languages do you know?"

"English, Spanish, French, and Sign Language." He beamed.

"I know Sign Language. Why did you learn it?"

"Now, I'm impressed, but it's fascinating to me. I like to study language, art, religion, and politics. Different subjects in life. Why do you know sign language?"

"My mom had a friend who had a deaf daughter my age. For us to play together, the daughter taught me basic words. ABCs, 123s. I studied in college, then we used simple words when Sadie was little. It helped her to communicate with us. We're teaching the babies basic words."

"The girls know?" he asked.

'They know a little, but they're not fluent. I also learned that my Grandma Emma knew sign language. We visited her in the hospital when she was on her deathbed. I signed with Sadie, and my grandmother saw it. She got excited, but she could no longer talk, so she signed. She told me about her sister. My great aunt was born deaf. Grandma Emma was the only one who learned sign language and communicated with her." I slid a pillow to Teddy and found comfort on one. "What else do you like?"

"Writing and drawing, even though I'm not as good as Kyle. I also like to watch movies and sports."

"Are you a sports fanatic?" I asked playfully.

"Not a fanatic, but I like football and basketball," he said, and I offered him another pillow. "No, thanks. Why do you sleep with so many body pillows?"

"I love 'em." I slid two between us. "After the divorce, I bought one to have something in bed with me, but it wasn't enough, so I bought more."

I yawned, and he said, "I need to let you sleep."

"I'm okay. I want to build a wall between us, lay here, and listen to you. I'm getting a feel about who you are."

"Why build a wall?"

"Because." Pictures of his lips touching mine flashed in my head.

"You're all about walls, Beth."

"I admit I push people away," I said.

"That's how you protect yourself."

"Yeah. I have a lot to protect, and it's the only way I can," I said.

"It's okay to let your guard down. You may miss something great if you keep it up."

"You sound like the girls."

"Tell me about the divorce?" he asked.

"There isn't much to say. We were married, then divorced."

"Scott said you and Alan are friends."

"I wouldn't say best friends any longer," I said. "Don't lie to me or cheat on me. Those two go hand in hand, and he did both. I suspected it for a while, so when I confronted him, and he admitted to it, I was relieved. It was my way to escape."

"Did he make you happy?" he asked.

I flipped the blanket over me and settled in the bed. I played the last ten years in my mind.

"No. We were happy at first, then it turned into contentment. I was okay with taking care of him, but the days became systematic and mundane. I worked all the time, and our marriage became neglected, so we drifted apart," I said.

"Alan is a good man, dad, and grandpa, so I don't hate him. He and June are happy. That's all I ever wanted for him. He deserved someone who could dote on him. I wasn't the right person."

"Twenty-seven years is a long time to be with someone," he said and yawned.

"How long were you married?" I asked.

"Which time?" He pulled the blanket over him and settled in bed.

"How many were there?"

"Two. My first marriage was seven years, and my second was four. My first wife and I married young before the success. We were happy if we struggled, but by my second album, she was in it for the money. She broke us with everything I brought in, which caused the fighting, then it led to a separation," he said then continued.

"We tried to make it work, but I could see the love was gone, so it was divorce time. I feel guilty I created a gold digger. It makes me sick to think her life revolves around money. I don't think she'll ever change."

"You didn't create a gold digger. She had it in her, but it didn't come out until you guys had money." I relaxed.

"That marriage did teach me the word prenup. My second wife cheated on me with a roadie and a bodyguard in my dressing room while I performed a concert."

"What?" I asked in shock.

"I completed a set, went into the dressing room, and found her with two guys. She asked if I wanted to join them. I walked away from them and finished the concert with that scene playing in my mind. My emotions were all over the place, but thankfully, we only had two sets left," he said.

"That's cold," I said.

"Yeah. After her, I threw myself into writing and music but got sucked into the drug scene. The media caught me with girls going in and out of my life, but Shelly kept the drug world out of the publics' eyes."

"I'm sorry, Teddy."

"With all the trials and tribulations I've had in my life, I'm glad it brought me to you," he said. "We have something special, Beth."

I closed my eyes and said, "I don't know. It's hard for me to trust."

"That's why we take things slow. I'm not going anywhere if you'll let me stay in your heart," he said.

"Always," I said, and enjoyed him being in my bed while sleep took over my body.

Chapter 17

I jumped from sleep as my phone rang. The word *Office* appeared on the screen.

"Hey," I whispered.

"Good Morning," Lois said.

"I'm sorry I'm late." I looked at Teddy, who hugged a body pillow.

"Your appointment with Larry is at ten o'clock. Do you want me to reschedule?" she asked.

"I'll be there," I said then hung up.

I missed a text from Helper.

Tell him to leave.

I shook my head then responded:

Tell me your real name and what's going on. Honesty is best.

I went to the bathroom, brushed my teeth, and hair. I waited a few minutes for a response from Helper before I opened the door. Teddy wasn't in my room. The dogs barked at the back door, so I let them in and returned to dress.

In the kitchen, Gene and Teddy sat at the table, drinking coffee. I went to the fridge, and my phone sounded with another text.

You know my name.

I texted back.

Friend or Foe?

"I'm sorry, I made you late today, babe," Teddy said.

"That's okay. Go back to bed, gentlemen," I said.

"We'll take you to work," Teddy said and walked to the door.

"I'm supposed to meet a client," I said while my phone rang.

I didn't recognize the number. I stepped next to Teddy and showed him.

"It's a Reno area code," Teddy said and retrieved his phone. The number came up in his contacts. "How did she get your number?"

"Carissa?" I asked as the phone stopped ringing. "I'll call her back."

"Put her on speaker, but don't give her information about your location," Gene said and looked at Teddy.

"I got this." I tapped her phone number then speaker.

"Hello," she answered on the second ring.

"This is Beth. I received a call from this number." I looked at Teddy. "How can I help you?"

"This is Carissa," she said.

"Carissa?" I asked.

"Carissa Litkin. I was with Ted Nafton this past weekend. You know me," she said harshly.

"Yes. How can I help you?" I asked.

"Is he with you?" she asked, and Teddy shook his head.

"How did you get my number?"

"Ted gave it to me," she said, and Teddy's eyes widened. He used sign language and told me he never gave it to her. "Am I on speaker?"

"Yes, ma'am. I'm trying to get to work," I said.

"Sorry to bother you, but this won't take long. I have a few questions. Do you mind?" she asked.

"No, ma'am."

"Let's start with a proper introduction. I'm Carissa Litkin," she said.

"I don't like formality, so call me, Beth." I smiled at Gene.

"No last name, huh. Where are you from?" she asked.

"The south."

"Being vague, are we?" she asked.

"I'm sorry, Ms. Litkin, but I don't know why you're contacting me. Teddy and I…"

"Is he with you now?" she asked again, then Teddy's phone sounded with a text. "I guess so. I sent him that."

"I told you we were finished," he said.

"Ask him about Jenna and why she left. He lies, Beth," Carissa said. "Do I need to come to Arkansas and set a few things straight?"

"Hell no," Teddy retorted.

"If he doesn't want you, wouldn't that be a sign for you to leave him alone?" I asked and smiled at Teddy.

"Are you acting as his bodyguard? Gene is somewhere close, so you don't need to protect him. Hello, Gene," she said.

"You leave if someone doesn't want you, Carissa," Gene said in an irritated tone.

"You and I are no longer together. How did you get her number? It didn't come from me," Carissa was silent, and Teddy continued, "I'm going to ask you one more time, and I want the truth. Have you been texting her as well?"

"No. I need to see you face-to-face, Ted," she said.

"That's not going to happen." Teddy fumed.

"Are you two together now? The media might want to know. *The Other Woman Steals Teddy From The Supermodel.* That would make for a great headline," she said.

"No more *Teddy and Carissa Watch,*" Teddy stated.

"I don't know if I'll come back to you when she leaves like Jenna did," she said.

"We both know there isn't anything serious between you and me, so think of it as…you need to find your, Mr. Right." Teddy smiled at me.

"You are my, Mr. Right," she said.

"No, I'm not. I was a publicity stunt."

"You're more than that. Where are you?" she asked.

"Somewhere. Don't call Beth anymore."

"I want to see you for a few minutes, Ted."

"No."

"Ted…" she said.

"Bye." He took the phone from my hand and ended the call. He handed the phone back to me and said, "I'm sorry. I don't know how she got your number, but if she calls again, don't answer. If you get any more text, please let me know."

"I did this morning," I said and showed him the last message.

"What the hell is going on?" Teddy asked and handed the phone to Gene.

"We're trying to find out," Gene said. "You guys have to be careful. She commented about a headline, so she's searching for Beth."

"No one is to give her information," Teddy said to Gene.

"Do you have any social sites?" Gene asked.

"Helen takes care of one for the business. I don't have any photos of me linked to it," I said.

"Good. I'll check out the Internet when we return," Gene said.

"Well, I need to get to work," I said.

We walked to the car, and my phone rang once again.

"Don't answer. I'll take care of her," Teddy said, and I gave him a burning glare.

"I told you I didn't want to come between you two."

"You're not. Get in the car."

I looked at the new Caddy and said, "It's five miles away."

Gene looked at Teddy, and he nodded. Gene threw me the keys.

I sat in the driver's seat, and the leather hugged my butt. Teddy sat in the front seat while Gene sat in the back.

"Do you drive?" I asked Teddy.

"Yes," he said.

I placed the seatbelt on then started the vehicle. I could feel the newness of the car compared to my old Altima.

"This is nice, but it's big," I said with wide eyes and a smile.

I loved driving new cars, so I could get an idea of what I wanted once I saved enough money to buy one. I played with the buttons on the steering wheel to find out what they did while Teddy laughed. I told him how Alan got the truck, and I needed to find another one for the summer, so I could pull the boat to the lake.

"I'm rambling," I said, and Teddy smiled. "Thank you for last night. You opened up, and I enjoyed it."

"I don't think I've ever talked myself to sleep," he said.

I parked the car at the office front door. Teddy opened his door, and I grabbed his elbow.

"Where do you think you're going?"

"To walk you to your desk," he said.

"I have a client who will be here any moment, so shut the door," I said.

"Not going to do it," Teddy said.

Gene held my door open, smiled at me, and said, "I'm keeping track of who wins these arguments. Teddy is ahead."

"I know, right? He always gets what he wants," I said and walked to the door while Teddy held it open for me.

"No, I don't," Teddy said childishly as he smirked.

"Beth one, Teddy five," Gene said.

"She doesn't get one," Teddy laughed.

"She called the hotel issue. I give her one."

I laughed as we stepped into the office and told everyone hello. My phone sound with a text. I retrieved it once I sat at my desk and read the message:

Depends on your actions.

Real name? - I texted.

Helper

"Dammit," I said out loud.

Teddy took the phone, read the text, and closed his eyes for a second. He shook his head then called for Gene. He appeared in front of my desk while Teddy showed him the message. Gene tapped on his phone and walked out, speaking with someone.

"I hate this shit," Teddy said quietly. "I'm sorry."

"Everything is fine." I focused on typing the password into my computer. I sat back in my chair and stared at Teddy, who smiled at me but didn't say a word. "What?"

"I like seeing you in work mode. You're relaxed," he said.

"I'm not in work mode." I leaned forward and looked in his eyes. "Not until you leave. I have to concentrate."

"I distract you?" He leaned toward me and met my stare.

I thought to myself, hell, yes, you make me lose my concentration. You take my breath away and make me want things in your stare. A picture of him kissing my neck appeared in my thoughts. My smile widened from the idea of his lips on mine.

"Well, ma'am. I'll leave you to your thoughts." He stood, but stopped in the doorway, "What time shall we get you?"

"Six," I said.

He took a step from the door but stopped. He leaned in and said, "Oh, babe." I looked at him. "Just breathe." Then he was out the door.

What the crap was that about? I watched out the window. He sat in the passenger seat when Larry pulled into the parking lot. I was glad he left before Larry came inside. I didn't want to explain Teddy Nafton to him.

The meeting with Larry went smoothly, but productivity was slow on my part. Concentration was difficult to find as my mind wondered about Teddy being at my house, and I'm stuck in the office.

I focused my attention on the computer. I wanted to know more about his wild days, so I pulled the Internet up and typed in his name. His image flashed before my eyes.

I scrolled the list of sites he was associated with until I found his home page. I clicked on it, and a picture of his big brown eyes stared at me. Guilt set in, and I scolded myself for researching him. I pushed that aside and clicked on his history to read his background.

He was born and raised in Michigan, with his parents being farmers. He was interested in music from an early age and formed his first band when he was twelve. He played at church or school dances until he became older and played in bar settings.

Even though some of his band members quit and went on to other things, Teddy persevered and formed other bands. Five/Ten had been together for years, with Mark being the oldest member and Susan being the new kid.

I was involved in finding information when Irene stopped at my door, followed by Lois. They wished me a good weekend, then Helen walked into my office. She told me she would see me at the house.

Once they all left, my attention was returned to the computer. I searched through Teddy's information and found a few sites, which contained pictures of him and Carissa. Stories labeled, *The Teddy and Carissa Saga Continues,* or *The Teddy and Carissa Watch - Will They Reunite?*

The pictures were of them caught in a kiss or walking hand in hand toward a limo. One photo showed Teddy lying across a bed with sheets pulled to mid-chest. His arms were behind his head, and he stared at the camera with no smile. A full-length mirror was seen in the shot. It revealed Carissa took the picture. She wore a blue bra and panty set while she held the camera.

I scrolled and found a website, which consisted of interviews from people in his past. I read a few and moved on to another site, which showed him speaking to other stars at award shows.

His life was plastered on the Internet for the world to see. I wouldn't want everyone to know my business or my friends or cared what I wore. The guilt returned. I was no better than any of his fans. I scolded myself for spending the afternoon doing so, but it was an addiction I couldn't stop.

I clicked on his home page, then the underlined word Tour Dates, and read the list. The tour would go overseas to the UK, Japan, and Canada. I read the screen intently, then a knock rapped on the door-frame, which made me jump.

"Hi," Teddy said and leaned against it.

"Hi. Is it six?" I shut off the sites and was grateful the computer faced me on the desk.

"You were focused on something," he said sternly and gave me a disapproving glare. "Did you hear the door chime?"

"I wasn't paying attention," I shut off the computer. I walked around my desk, tried to pass him in the doorway, but he grabbed my waist.

"You weren't paying attention." He stared into my eyes.

"I'm sorry. I wasn't thinking."

He let me go and followed me around the office while I shut the computers off and locked the back door. Gene stood by the front door, arms folded while he looked at me and shook his head.

"I could have robbed you," Teddy said.

"I let my guard down for a second," I explained.

"A second is all it takes. Does this happen often? Do you focus so hard, you don't hear the door?"

"In all the years, I've been here, it's happened maybe a handful of times. It's no big deal. Nobody is gonna rob me."

"I don't give a shit if you're here two minutes by yourself. Lock the door if you're going to be alone," Teddy said.

"I get it, and I'm sorry," I said.

I walked into the office, retrieved my purse, and rounded the desk. He leaned against the doorframe again with a concerned look. I stepped in front of him, and he laid his hand on my hip.

"I want you safe, Beth. With the weirdness of the texts and dream, please meet me halfway and lock the door."

I nodded, then embraced him. His grip tightened around me as if he held on to me for dear life.

"I'll be more careful," I whispered.

Once he released me, he held my hand and led me to the front door. "Do you own this building?"

"I pay Mom rent to help with her retirement, but eventually it'll be mine. I hope not soon, but someday."

"What's next door to you?" He pointed to the vacant part of the building.

"We put that space up to rent. No takers, yet. Alan had his business there until the divorce."

"What kind of business?" he asked.

"A tobacco shop."

"That explains the smoking. Can I look at it?" Teddy asked.

"Right now?" I glanced at the clock.

"We have time," he said.

"Let me get the key."

I walked into my office, retrieved the key, and joined Teddy and Gene.

"The building was a small community grocery store when we purchased it," I told the history as if I were selling the location. "Alan decided to quit his job and open a tobacco store when we moved in. He eventually built the business to two stores, by the time we divorced. He just opened his fourth."

I turned the key to reveal a good size area with the smell of fresh paint and new carpet lingering in the air. Teddy and Gene walked around the massive room, noticed the bathrooms, and the back door.

"This isn't bad," Teddy said.

I walked to the back door, unlocked, and opened it to reveal a fenced-in backyard. A covered picnic area connected both sides of the building.

"Smoking hole." I pointed to the picnic table while Teddy looked outside. "I fenced in the yard, so I could bring the dogs with me, but I can divide it."

"It's nice," Teddy said.

"Thanks," I said.

I relocked the building then we left to go to the house. Teddy fell silent.

"Are you okay?" I asked as we rode in the car.

"I don't like you leaving by yourself," he said and held my hand.

"I've been doing it for years."

"January through April, it gets dark earlier, and you work later, right?" he asked.

"Yes, but a lady works with me part-time during tax season. I'm not here by myself much, and if I'm going to be, I bring the dogs for protection," I explained.

"Those dogs aren't going to do anything but lick a person to death," he said.

"You would be surprised."

"Maybe," he said.

"If it makes you feel better, I carry a gun. I don't keep cash around, so who would want to rob an accounting firm?" I asked.

"People are crazy. I know you need to work for a living, but I want you safe," he said.

"Do you shoot often?" Gene asked.

"Maybe once a month," I said. "Thank you, gentlemen, for caring about my safety, but I've survived for all these years. I can handle this."

"Just be careful," Teddy said.

Chapter 18

The house was a buzz with family members. I changed clothes, put my hair in a ponytail, and stepped out of my room. Teddy and my mother sat on the couch in deep conversation. I walked to the kitchen and stood by the table for a few minutes. Lucy held the oven door open, checked the meat, and looked at me.

"What can I put on this to keep it moist?" she asked.

"Add water and keep it covered," I said with a scrunched nose as barbecue baked in pans.

"She doesn't know meat," Ellis said as he leaned against the counter.

"I know it better than you." I laughed. "What do you suggest?"

"Cover it after you put water in the pans." He smiled.

"That's what I said, you ass," I said.

"Teddy, your girl, called me an ass," he yelled.

"She likes you," Teddy yelled back.

I retrieved tea for Teddy and me, joined him in the living room, then handed him the glass. Music came from the exercise room. I went to the doorway to investigate.

Kyle and Susan showed Sadie the drums. Teddy walked behind me and placed his chin on my shoulder.

"I hope you didn't mind us doing this," Teddy said.

"Not at all, but the equipment folds for more room," I folded a treadmill and moved it close to the wall. Kyle folded the other and moved it, then I unhinged the weight bars and folded them.

"Thank you, but that's good," Kyle said and looked at Teddy.

"We didn't want to take over your house," Teddy said.

"I know how to put things back." I smiled. "Was Sadie playing the drums?"

"Watch, Mimi."

"Hold on, girl." Kyle sat and lifted her to his knee. She hit several drums with sticks in a rhythmic pattern. "I showed her that twice."

"You did good, baby, but let's not bother Kyle. He has to practice."

"She's not a bother, Beth. She has talent. She's a natural." He smiled.

Teddy wrapped his arms around my waist and whispered, "I missed you today."

"No, you didn't." I felt the same about him. I looked at the equipment, saw the cramped space, and knew they needed to rehearse in a proper setting. "I'm keeping you from your life and adding obstacles in your way."

"Where would you get that idea?" he asked.

"What would y'all be doing tonight if you weren't with me?" I asked.

"We would be doing nothing different back home, except rehearsing in a studio," he said.

"A studio doesn't have people running around," I said.

He gently pushed me against the wall, wrapped his fingers in my ponytail, and said, "I like to hear the house move, Beth. We all do. Your kids have impacted us. They've accepted us for who we are, not what we do."

I ran my finger across his cheek, then Sadie said, "Watch again, Mimi."

She beamed with joy to be able to hit the drums as Kyle wanted. We clapped, then Teddy grabbed a guitar and sat in a chair. He strummed the instrument while Sadie played the drums.

"Do you have any hot sauce, Mom?" Lucy asked from the kitchen.

"Excuse me for a moment. You're doing good, Sadie," I said.

"Hot sauce?" Lucy asked when I walked to the cabinet.

I said hello to Shelly as she went to the refrigerator. I opened the cabinet. Food filled the shelves.

"Did you clean out the store?" I asked.

"We grabbed a few extra things," Lucy said.

"You and Danielle?" I asked and looked at Shelly, who froze in her steps. "Well?"

"I helped them," Shelly said.

"How much on the card?" I asked Lucy.

They fell silent. Teddy paid for the food after I asked him not too. I grew angry, snatched the bottle of sauce from in the back of the spice cabinet, and slammed it on the counter. I walked to the exercise room door while Kyle and Sadie sat at the drums. Susan strummed her guitar, and Teddy spoke with Ellis and Colby. Ellis drew Teddy's attention to me.

"Can I help you?" Teddy asked.

"The food?" I asked as Shelly stepped behind me.

"It's no big deal," he said, studied me, then asked, "Is this the look you told me about, Shelly?"

"Teddy!" I exclaimed. "It is a big deal. You cannot keep doing this crap. I told you we had this covered."

"I'm not going to stay somewhere for free," he raised his voice.

"If I couldn't provide you food, then I wouldn't have asked you to stay." My voice rose, then Danielle and Lucy walked in behind me. "You think you have to buy your way around me, and that isn't it at all. The cards, clothes, concert, plane, and now the food. I'm not a charity case. I'd appreciate it if you stopped thinking I am."

"I never said you are. You told me you put obstacles in my way, but it's the other way around. I am the obstacle, and it's only food. An extra bill you were not expecting," he said forcefully.

Everyone stared at us. He was concerned about adding an expense to me.

"Teddy!" I exclaimed loudly, "You're an ass."

"I'm in the ass club. Scott would be proud." He strummed the guitar and sang a silly song about ass people.

"She always tells me I'm one," Colby said.

Teddy threw that into his silly song. He stared at me while he sang crazy words about me being stubborn. He rhymed in a song how the people in my world were asses. Everyone laughed, except for me. I tried to keep from smiling, but it didn't work. He moved the guitar behind him and grabbed my waist as he sang.

He dipped me and said, "We need to work together on some things, huh."

"Thank you for thinking about me, but you need to talk to me," I said.

"We'll get it right," he said, then stood me.

I placed my hand on his cheek. "You're not an obstacle and never will be with me. My door is open to you."

"Beth two, Teddy five," Gene said from the doorway.

"No." Teddy laughed.

"I give that one to her. She said, don't do it, and yet you did," Gene said, and I laughed.

Teddy embraced me for a few seconds, walked to the chair, and Lucy handed me the card. I went into my room, put the card in my purse, and stepped on the back porch as the dogs followed me outside.

My phone sounded with a text. I leaned against the porch railing and lit a cigarette. Teddy joined me outside as I retrieved the phone from my pocket. I had two messages from Helper, but I didn't immediately read them. Instead, I smiled at Teddy to let him know we were okay.

"You make me crazy," I said to him.

"You make me crazy, but I don't think it's in the same way." He stood with his hip, touching mine.

"Stop spending money on us. I'm not after your money. I like you because you're funny, nice and…" I stopped the sentence. I wanted to tell him, he made me feel alive, energized, and sexy by his touch. His eyes made me feel comfortable and relaxed, but I couldn't bring the words to my lips, so I said, "You're not bad to look at."

"Did you get hung up on some words?" He smiled.

"I'm sorry I got mad but, when you drove me to your plane, it reconfirmed how I can't compete with your lifestyle. Look around. This is my world."

"I know," he said.

"When you STOLE the kiss from me, I knew then I'm not the right person for you." I looked at the phone. I didn't want to admit to him how I melted in his arms when he kissed me. "I like you, and… how do I say this? If you weren't in your profession, we might have something, but we live different lives."

"Your back on that," he said.

"It's true," I said.

"When I kissed you, it confirmed I was correct about us," he replied.

I raised my phone, looked at the messages, and said, "I'm tired of the games."

He looked at the phone and saw a picture of him and Carissa, lying in a beach chair. Her head on his chest and a sheet covered certain naked body parts. In the background of the picture, the beach sands glistened while the blue water lapped against the shoreline.

The text from Helper read:

Safety…not guaranteed. Continue…could be the end.

I texted back:

Is this a warning or a threat? Is this about Carissa?

"I can guarantee you're safe," he said, and I received another text.

Guess.

More pictures came to my screen. They flashed back to back before my eyes. Pictures of Teddy performing on stage while a beautiful, dark-headed female dancer, wrapped her arms around his body.

Another revealed Teddy in a recording booth with a young, blonde female, who kissed his neck as he tilted his head back, enjoying her lips. I glimpsed at one of Teddy laughing with twin brown-haired females. His arms wrapped around their waist as they held onto his shoulders while leaving a building.

"What the hell?" he asked, and I handed him the phone.

He studied the pictures when my sister joined us on the porch.

"Hey, sis. It's getting crazy in there," Nancy said.

"I thought so. Nancy, this is Teddy. Teddy, this is my sister, Nancy," I said.

"It's nice to meet you," he said and extended his hand.

"I can't believe it's Teddy. Do you know who you are?" Nancy asked and shook his hand.

"Sorry. Scott tried to flush her in the toilet when she was a baby." I smiled.

"You're, *The Teddy Nafton*," she said.

"He knows who he is," I said.

The pictures weighed on my mind. They confirmed how Teddy could have anyone at any time. I don't want to lose my heart over him. We needed to remain friends and nothing more.

She pointed at me. "You couldn't tell me you met him? No one said anything until I got here. Danielle smiled at me, not saying a word until she introduced me to the band."

"Sorry." I looked around to think of an excuse, but couldn't. I smiled and said, "This is my friend, Teddy."

"I know that now, dumbass," she said.

I pointed at her and looked at him. He smiled and asked, "Is Scott the only one who doesn't have ass people in the family?"

"He's headmaster," Nancy said, and I laughed.

"You're going to have a lot of people mad at you," she said to me then patted Teddy's arm. "Are you nervous about meeting the whole family?"

"A little," he said.

"Well, Mr. Nafton, if you need help with names or singing, I got your back," Nancy said.

"Thank you, Ms. Nancy," he said and placed my phone in his shirt pocket.

"We're loud and crazy when we get together, but you're gonna like us as long as you treat Godfather Junior, okay."

"Really?" I asked, and he smiled at her.

"Dinner will be ready in a few minutes," Danielle said from the back door.

"I'll help gather everyone," Nancy said and left us.

"Wanna get in the car and drive away?" I asked him.

"No. Danielle and Lucy went over the list of everyone with us. I feel intimidated with them all here, but I'm anxious to meet everyone. Also, we're more than friends."

"You caught that," I said, and he nodded. "First off, you don't get intimidated. You're, *The Teddy*. Secondly, don't feel anxious about seeing my world. There are times I don't like my world. And last, yes, we are."

"At least you admitted we're friends. That's progress," he said. "Is it okay if I slip Gene your phone?"

I nodded and held my hand out for him. We joined everyone in the house, and my family stood in groups. Lucy pointed at the head of the table for us to take our spots. Teddy moved his hand around my waist and squeezed me as I laughed.

"Hey, guys. We're going to introduce everyone before prayer. I'm starting with Teddy's group. There are less of them," I said.

"Where's the name tags?" Gibson, my nephew, asked.

"I thought the same when I met these guys," I said.

"It's Granny's fault. She had too many kids," Bryan, my other nephew, said.

"With four, I never imagined you people would produce offspring's like you did. Y'all are like rabbits," Mom said.

I introduced Teddy's group then continued to my family.

"Let's start behind us. This is my niece Cora and her children, Terry, Pam, Lynn, and Reed. Next, we have my other niece, Chastity and her daughter Haley and son Walt. Then we have Scott and Carols oldest daughter, Helen, and that is her son, Cullen. Nicky is Scott and Carol's youngest daughter." I pointed to each person.

"Then you have my mother, Coreen, and father, Lou. You guys know Lucy and her crew and Danielle and her crew, so next is my sister Nancy."

"Hey guys," Nancy said with enthusiasm.

"Gibson is her son and his daughters, Dakota and Lisa. Nancy's youngest son, Bryan, his wife, Roselyn, and their daughter, Stephanie," I said.

"And I'm Sadie," she said, and we laughed.

"That's everyone except Bub and Carol," I said.

"Why didn't you tell us you met these guys, Beth?" Cora asked.

"I wanted to respect their privacy."

"When Dad told me about them, he made me promise to let it be her decision to tell everyone." Helen looked at me. "If we weren't meeting them right now, you would have eventually said something. Right?"

"I don't know," I said.

"It's nice to meet you all," Chasity said.

"It's a true pleasure to meet every one of you," Teddy said.

"One more thing, guys. Tomorrow night we're having a Super Bowl party without the Super Bowl. It'll be a Five/Ten Bowl. I don't know. You guys are welcome to join us," I said, and looked at Teddy for confirmation as he nodded.

"But no pictures," Lucy said, "It goes back to the privacy thing. Keep Arkansas media free for them. If we post pictures on the social sites, the media could pick those up, then the freedom they have will be gone."

"We're trying to keep the headcount to a minimum, so keep that in mind, please. We'll have snacks, but I don't want to feed the world," I said.

"Well, I'm hungry now," Ellis said.

"You're always hungry. Teddy, do you want to lead us?" I asked him.

"I'm going to ask if Lou would like too," Teddy said.

Dad nodded and said, "Let's bow our heads," then led the prayer.

After prayer, I explained to Teddy, "You sit here, and I'll be right back." I went into the kitchen, made him and I a plate.

The house was loud with laughter and different conversations. The little kids ran back and forth from the kitchen to the living room picnic area as they grabbed more food.

"Are you guys touring?" Nancy asked Teddy.

"Yes, ma'am. You own a steakhouse, right?"

"Yes, sir. The best steak house in Arkansas. Most of the food you're eating came from my place," she said.

"The barbecue is good, but I find it ironic how you own a steakhouse, and you don't eat meat, Beth," Teddy said.

"Not everyone is close to perfection like me," I said playfully.

"Mrs. Coreen, how does it feel to have raised such smart people to be successful in their endeavors?" Teddy asked.

"It's a great accomplishment. I'm proud of my family." She glanced around the room and said, "Okay, proud of most of my family."

We laughed, and Teddy said, "I can't get over how you contacted everyone less than twenty-four hours ago, and here they are."

"They're here for free food," I said.

We visited with everyone while Teddy and the band got to know the family members. He answered questions about the album and how many songs he thought he had written over the years. He learned what everyone did for a living and became familiar with their names while we laughed at the stories the family told.

"How many times do you guys get together like this?" Teddy asked.

"Every holiday." I looked at the family for confirmation.

"But the best time of the year is July 4th," Danielle said. "Everyone saves their vacation to go to the lake."

"Do you want me to fix you another plate?" I asked him.

"No, thank you. I want to hear about the lake," he said.

"Little islands are in a big lake, a few cities from us," Gibson explained. "One of us with a boat will go reserve an island for the rest of the family."

"Then we all meet to camp, fish, and swim, tube, and ski. Woohoo, it's a ball. I love it," Bryan said excitedly.

"It's my favorite spot in the world," I said.

"Like you have any basis for comparison, Ms. I don't want to fly because I'm going to die." Nancy laughed.

"You have no room to talk. You haven't gone places. I bet laying in a hammock, looking at the water is the same scene no matter where you are," I said.

"I've been to places where the water is so clear, you could see ten or more feet under you. The glistening sand is so white, it hurts your eyes from the glare of the sunlight," Teddy said.

"Ha," Nancy said and smiled at Teddy.

He held my hand and said, "I hope you see those sites someday. They'll take your breath away."

"Not cool, Mr. Rhymer Guy," I remembered the picture Helper sent.

"Sorry, but that wasn't the place I was referring to." He smiled.

"Beth, Scott, and Carol were at your concert last week?" Cora asked.

"Yes, ma'am. We taped it if anyone would care to watch," Teddy said.

"Uh, yeah," she said.

"Go right ahead," Teddy said and looked at Gene. "It's in my computer bag if you will?"

After dinner, everyone settled in to watch the performance. The small kids laid in a line on the floor as they stared at the TV.

I walked outside to build a fire in the pit, but Keith was hard at work to get a flame burning. Teddy walked behind me.

"What are you doing?" he asked Keith.

"I started a fire," he said proudly.

"That's a sorry excuse for one," he said and walked to the pit.

Susan and Shelly joined us. We watched the men get a blaze burning. Teddy sat next to me and pointed to the fire.

"There you go," he said.

"You're so macho." I laughed when Mom and Dad joined us.

"We're heading home. Thanks for dinner," Mom said.

"Is the concert over?" I asked.

"Not yet, but I have something for you," she said and handed me a blue umbrella.

"It might not be him," I said.

"You are to share this, so pay attention. Listen to the music. Have fun, singing, and dancing." She winked at me and patted Teddy's shoulder. "Teddy, you and the others do a fine job on stage."

"Thank you, ma'am." He hugged her then shook Dad's hand. They left in the Kubota, and Teddy asked, "What's up with the umbrella?"

"It's nothing, but did Mom come up here today?" I asked.

"No. I met her when we came back from picking you up," he said.

"She's crazy," I said and placed the umbrella on the side table.

Gene and Rick emerged from the house, and Teddy met them at the door. He took a small wrapped package from Gene while Rick carried a bigger wrapped box. They placed the gifts on the porch in front of me.

"What is this?" I asked while Mark, Kyle, and Thad came out the back door to join us.

"Don't get bent out of shape, but we wanted to get you something. Open the big one first," Teddy said proudly.

"Teddy…" I said.

"Please?" he asked.

"It's a small token of our appreciation, Beth," Kyle said.

I shook my head then opened the big box. I unpacked a small, lightweight chainsaw.

"It's great." I laughed with excitement.

"Here." Teddy handed me the small package.

Different sizes of blades and chains for the new saw were in the box.

"Thank you. This is awesome."

I gave each a hug, and Thad said, "We want to see you in action tomorrow. Well, Teddy tonight, but us tomorrow."

"The bench is great," Teddy said.

I hugged him, kissed his cheek, then stared into his eyes. A peaceful, happy sensation rushed over me. These feelings over a chainsaw?

"Thank you for not putting up a fight," he said and brushed my cheek with his finger.

"Thank you." I faced everyone. "I'm excited. I can't wait to use it."

"I've never bought a girl a chainsaw," Teddy said.

"It's perfect," I said.

Everyone walked out of the house, which told us the concert was over. Colby held the small chainsaw, and Ellis picked up a blade.

"Man, Teddy. Flowers are supposed to work," Ellis said.

"I tried, but they made her mad," he said.

Nancy walked to me, pulled on my sleeve, and threw her head toward the corner of the porch. I joined her while everyone else spoke in different conversations.

"What?" I asked.

"What's he like in bed?" she asked in a low voice.

"I don't know. Why are you asking?" I asked quietly.

"You two have a connection."

"No, we don't."

"Yeah, you do," Cora said from behind me.

"Eavesdropping, are we?" I asked.

"Yeah, Beth. You guys had sex," Nancy said.

"No, we haven't. We're friends."

"She ain't gonna tell us," Cora said.

"There's nothing to tell, and if there were, you guys would know before I reached orgasm. You can't hide anything in this family." I walked to Teddy and the others.

"Beth, wait," Nancy said.

"No, Nancy. Nothing is going on," I said, embarrassed from the conversation.

I sat next to Teddy with aggravation because they wanted to know my business. I remembered how his life was on the Internet for the world to see. I stared at him while he spoke with Ellis, Gibson, and Colby. Nancy stepped behind me and leaned into my ear.

"Sorry, sis. We didn't mean to stick our noses in, but you two have a strong connection."

Teddy looked at me and smiled.

"See?" she asked.

"He heard you. I'm going to ignore you right now," I said in a low voice.

Teddy squeezed my hand firmly but continued with his conversation. We sat outside and spoke with everyone for hours.

I walked to the railing, lit a cigarette, and talked to Nancy. Teddy stood on the other side of the porch and spoke with Gene, Keith, and Colby. He and I would occasionally make eye contact and smile at one another.

Helen stood next to me and asked in a low voice, "What's the story with Thad?"

"What do you mean, darlin'?" I asked then they looked at each other. "There's nothing for you with him."

"Is he married?" she asked.

"Leave him alone, girl," I said.

She moved next to Nancy, and I glanced at Teddy. He set his drink on the railing and signed the word *what*. I signed Helen and Thad's names. He smiled and returned to his conversation.

"What was that?" Nancy asked.

"He knows sign language." I looked at Helen and said, "Please don't go after Thad. He's between five to ten years older than you."

"Teddy is older than you," she said to me.

"Y'all communicate through sign language?" Nancy asked.

"Please focus, Nancy. We're talking about Helen." I looked at Helen again. "Teddy is a few years older than me, but so was Alan."

"Are y'all talking about Thad and Helen? We saw the looks they give each other," Chasity said after she and Lucy joined us.

"I'm trying to stop it," I said.

"Just because you want to shut Teddy out doesn't mean everyone needs to be against love, Mom. I say go for it, Helen," Lucy said.

"You're not helping, Lucy," I said then looked at Helen again. "He's on the road, and long-distance relationships never work."

"We'll see," she said before she walked to Thad.

"So that's it. You're scared you're gonna get hurt again," Nancy said.

"This isn't about me. I don't want to be in the middle of her and Thad. I don't want anyone hurt," I said.

"This is more about you than you realize," she said.

I looked at Teddy, and he signed *you okay*. I nodded, but Lucy noticed the sign language.

"He knows it. Hey Danielle, come here," she said.

"He knows about a bazillion languages, Lucy. Leave him alone, please," I said.

"Teddy knows sign language," Lucy said to Danielle.

"Oh, wow. I told you we needed to learn more. They could be having sex talk right now, and we wouldn't know it." Danielle laughed.

"That's gross," Lucy said. "Please don't do that in our presence, Mom."

"We aren't, and we won't." I laughed.

After a few more hours, people dispersed. I gave out hugs. Teddy and I leaned against the railing and spoke with Nancy, Lucy, and Danielle when Helen approached us.

"I have an idea. Thad and someone else can stay at my house. That way, no one needs to take a couch."

"I don't like that idea," I said while Shelly joined our conversation.

"Nothing will happen. Cullen will be at the house to chaperone," she pleaded.

"It would be more comfortable for them," Lucy said.

"You're so not helping," I said to Lucy then looked at Helen. "I don't want to be caught in the middle, understand?"

"You won't." She promised.

"Y'all work it out," I said in defeat.

"We're going to clean the toy room for Gene, then we're headed out. We have a big day tomorrow," Danielle said.

I hugged everyone as they prepared to leave for the night, then I stepped in front of Rick. I extended my arms and reached around his neck.

"I know you don't like me, but thank you for all you do," I said.

"I do like you, but we're here to make sure Teddy doesn't get hurt." He hugged me.

"I hope he doesn't either," I said.

I stepped to Gene, and he said, "You have me tonight."

"I don't care." I embraced him and whispered in his ear, "You're my favorite. Thank you, Gene."

"Thank you for not getting upset about the present. He was worried that you would."

We said our goodbyes to everyone then I went into the house through my bedroom door. Lucy and Danielle left the TV on, so I glanced around to find the remote. I no more shut the back door and picked up the remote when Teddy joined me.

"Spill it about Helen," he said.

"I love my niece, but she can get wrapped up in guys," I said.

"Stalker issues?" he asked.

"Nothing like you." I smiled and turned the volume down on the TV. "I don't want to hear the, she said, he said, drama."

I let the dogs in then turned to Teddy. He sat on the edge of the bed with his hands folded in front of him.

"I agree with Nancy. Let things go as they should."

"You and my sister get along pretty good," I said.

"She's not you." He smiled. "Look, Thad is not the type of guy for a one-night stand. He's had those as we all have, but maybe he's looking for someone special and can find it in Helen."

"One-night stand," I said and straddled his knees while he looked at me.

"That's right. You haven't had one of those." He smiled.

"Nope. I would love to someday," I said.

"It's not what you think." He placed his hands on my hips. "There's an awkward moment when you leave, and you don't know what to say to the other person or even the person's name. It isn't fun."

"It could be. I could get a guy drunk, throw him across a bed, and take advantage of him. He wouldn't have to do anything but lay there."

I leaned into him, and without our bodies touching, he laid against the bed. I pinned him under me with my hands around his head and my knees around his hips.

"Afterward, I would hand him his clothes and say, 'Thanks. See ya.'" I smiled.

"I'm here if you need someone to practice your moves on." He laughed and scooted up the bed.

I crawled up the mattress on my hands and knees with him under me. I stared into his eyes.

"It wouldn't work with you."

"Why not?"

"You crossed the line by giving me a chainsaw." I visualized his lips on mine.

"I can return it," he said playfully.

My mind raced with images of him slowly kissing me while his fingers glided down my throat, toward my breasts. He quickly grabbed me, pulled me on top of him, and rolled me over in bed.

"You need to stop," he said while I laughed.

"I'm not doing anything." I wrapped my arms around his neck. "I wasn't even touching you. You were touching me."

He stroked my hair with both of his hands while he stared at me. He stood and held his hand out for me to take.

"Do you want me to end this thing with Helen and Thad?"

"No. Leave 'em alone, but I don't want any drama. I don't like drama." I stood.

"That's all you have with this family."

"That's true."

"I like them." He pulled me into his body. "It's rare you find a close family."

"That's what I've heard," I said.

I felt confused, yet I yearned for him. I wanted to feel his body, even if it was a one-time circumstance. Carissa and the other women appeared in my thoughts, and the realization struck me. I carried baggage, and he was scheduled to leave in a few days.

"You're arguing with yourself. You need more time," he said.

"No, I'm not." I lied. "I'm going outside. Care to join me?" I asked, and he nodded.

We sat next to the firepit, joined by Gene. The dogs ran past me, and Gene held the phone toward me.

"You received several more pictures and a new message," Gene said.

"Really?" I opened the app.

Four more pictures showed Teddy with different girls, backgrounds, and positions. I had one message after them.

"We think the pictures are copied from the Internet. Marcy is checking," Gene said.

"They were from my partying days," Teddy said and held my hand.

I read the message from Helper.
Warning for now because I like this game.
Carissa is not the only one to be named.

"There's a reason Helper sent them. I think this person is telling you it could be any of those women trying to come between you two," Gene said.

"But Carissa is the one who called," I said.

"Humm," Gene said in thought.

I texted:
If it's not her, tell me who.
I'm good at riddles, but can I trust you?
So far, you have not proven that I can.
Tell me your name or at least your plan.

I stared at one of the pictures to evaluate my emotions. A black-haired, scantily dressed woman hung on Teddy's shoulders as they walked toward a hotel door. It reminded me of Teddy's past with women and how they threw themselves at him.

"I don't want to look at these," I held my phone up.

"Don't delete them. I'll take them off your phone or forward them to me," Gene said.

"I have a confession, Teddy," I said and handed Gene my phone.

"What," he said.

"I was researching you when you picked me up tonight."

"Like a fan." He smiled. "Did you find what you were looking for?"

"I don't know what I was looking for, but you're all over the Internet, and I didn't see these pictures," I said.

"If you dig deep enough, you could locate them," Gene said.

"I guess," I said.

"Do you guys need privacy?" Gene asked.

"I need you to chaperone, Gene," Teddy said, then turned his attention to me. "You have questions."

"I felt guilty researching you, but you were a cute kid," I said.

"I might have been a cute kid, but now I'm a fine man, so what's your point," he said.

"You are, so fine, Teddy." I smiled, shook my head, and rolled my eyes. "I read the tour dates on your home page. I can't believe you skipped Arkansas."

"Would you have come?" he asked.

"Probably not." I smiled.

"Why not?"

"You're not Noah Parker."

"You would see him and not me?"

"Yeah."

"I'm telling you, babe. He would fit into your world. He's an ass," he said in disbelief.

I chuckled and said, "Keep Arkansas media free, Teddy. If you and the guys need a place to unwind, use this place. My door is open, but only as friends. I can't and won't compete," I said seriously and pointed to the phone in Gene's hand. "Not with those women nor the likes of Carissa."

"You're right. You can't compete." Teddy held my hand and stared into my eyes. "There isn't anyone who can compete with you. You're the best."

"I'm not ready for this." I pulled my hand from his.

"I deleted them," Gene said and handed the device back to me.

"You were online to find out my tour dates?" I shook my head, and he said, "I'm going to save you some time, babe. I was born and raised on a farm in Michigan. I lost my dad fourteen years ago, and my mom eight years back. I have one sister named Catherine, who I haven't spoken to in years."

"Wow. Why?" I asked.

"We're not like your family. We had a falling out and never reconciled."

"And you haven't seen her in years?" I asked.

"No. I see her around, but haven't spoken with her."

"How do you do that?"

"My hat's off to your mom for raising you guys close."

I got the feeling he didn't want to speak about his sister, so I asked, "Did you always want to be a musician?"

"Yes. I tried to be the good son and follow in the family business of farming, but it wasn't for me. I squeaked by in high school, so college wasn't in my cards. I left a few months after graduation to pursue my career. Once I made it passed the first wife, and a name for myself, I hired farmhands to help the folks. After they passed, my sister and I split the land. She lives on one side and me on the other with about two hundred acres between us," he said then continued.

"My first wife has the house in California while my second got the place in London. It was perfect for me to build in Michigan. What would you like to know now?"

"It's only you and Max in this big ol' farmhouse," I said.

"It's not a farmhouse, but something like that. I have people coming in and out, but when I lay down at night, it's just Max and me."

"What about you, Gene. What makes you stay with Teddy as his security personnel?"

"I told you we've been good friends for a while and he's family. It also doesn't hurt that he pays well." We laughed, and Gene continued, "We've had good days and bad, but this last week has been fun."

"It's been nice to relax," Teddy agreed.

"It's not hard to relax around my family. We're laid back and don't spy for people," I said.

"Spy?" Teddy asked.

"Gene and Shelly spying for you," I said.

"We told you we were watching you, but it wasn't spying. We were looking out for Teddy's best interest," Gene said.

"They have your back." I looked at Teddy. "It made me feel…" I searched for the word, then said, "Guky."

"What the hell is guky?" Gene asked.

"Gross and yucky. I don't like being spied on."

"We didn't. Teddy asked questions about you, and we answer. You blend well with this misfit group, so trust us to be friends," Gene said.

"You're calling me a misfit?" I smiled at Gene as my phone sounded with a ding.

"I didn't mean that. I meant you get along well with everyone," he said.

"I told them you would," Teddy said.

"I don't think Rick likes me," I said.

"Rick is a special kind of guy. He takes his job seriously, which there are times to be serious and times to relax. He hasn't learned how to relax," Gene said.

I looked at the text from Helper, which read,

I'm the only one who will be honest with you.

Prove it. Who am I supposed to help? Give me a name. - I texted.

"These have to be coming from Carissa," I said.

"We don't know whose phone she's using," Gene said.

"What would it matter if she had my last name? Teddy and I aren't dating. The pictures of these other women are accessible, and they're not famous. The media doesn't follow them, so how do you know they'll follow me?"

"You can research who those women were. They'll forever be known as the women who dated Teddy Nafton. If he were serious about one of them, they would have become household names. The reporters are after Teddy's life and the women who are special to him," Gene said.

Teddy tugged my hand to indicate for me to turn my attention to him. "Babe. Those women are from a long time ago before media access was at everyone's fingertips. Now it's a click of a button. That's how *The Teddy and Carissa Watch* began. Carissa and her people posting things online. She was in the public eye, so it didn't matter to me, but you're not. Carissa could draw negative attention to you. That's why we're trying to protect you, your family, and your business. I don't want your life turned upside down."

"Do you think she would use the media for negative purposes?" I asked.

"If she was pissed enough, she could. She knows how to play the reporters," Teddy said.

"Let's don't piss her off anymore, then." I smiled. "I'm going to clean." We stood to gather dishes off the porch, and I said, "You wear me out, Nafton."

"No, I don't, but I could," he said with raised eyebrows as he held the door open for me.

After the dishwasher was loaded, Gene settled in the recliner. Teddy and I sat on the couch. We stared at the black screen on the TV for a few seconds.

"You can turn it on," I walked to Gene and handed him the remote. He popped the legs out on the recliner, and I patted his shoulder. "You're my favorite."

"Hey," Teddy said to me.

I walked to him, straddled his legs while he looked at me with a smile. He held my hips. I bent over him and smiled.

"This also reclines." I pulled the handle, and the legs popped out, then I stood.

"Man," he said and let go of my hips. "I was hoping for something else."

The flicker from the TV in my room caught my attention. I went to my bed and found the remote. My phone dinged with another text, and I sat on the edge of the bed. I pressed the app to read the message from Helper.

No need to know. You will end this NOW!

The screen went black, and I thought about the different women in the photographs. I shook my head then stared at the carpet. Those women were beautiful, and I'm a nobody. I need to push him away, but how?

"Stop it, babe," Teddy said as he leaned against the doorframe. "May I borrow your phone?"

"Sure," I said and handed it to him.

He took it to Gene while I laid across the bed, stared at the mirrors and ceiling fan. I liked Teddy, but I didn't want drama. I need to listen to Helper and leave Teddy alone. He needed to focus on the tour and forget about me.

"No," Teddy said and sat on the opposite edge of the bed. I rolled to my side, looked at him, and he leaned into me. He ran his finger across my cheek and said, "Don't build a wall between us."

"You say I do, but I think it's you.".

He laid across the bed, stared at the mirrors, and said, "I think you, and I want the same thing, but I don't think now is the time. You're struggling with your emotions, but it's hard as hell not to touch you."

"It's not that difficult," I mumbled.

"More than you know," he said.

I turned to him as he did the same to me. Our bodies laid the opposite way across the bed. We were eye level with each other.

"I know what I want."

"What is that, babe?" he asked.

"You haven't been home, and you need to find out what you want. I'm not saying I want a relationship, but long-distance ones never work, besides Carissa could be standing next to you in a heartbeat. She doesn't have family crap hanging over her head, and she's used to the spotlight."

"You've thought about you and me being together?" He smirked.

"A little." I giggled.

"Before or after you met me?"

"After. Like just now." I laughed.

"Oh, good. I didn't want you to turn into a stalker. We're dealing with one too many as it is," he chuckled.

"I'm not even a fan, so how could I be a stalker?" I asked. "I'm not like you."

"I'm going to turn you into a fan," he said playfully.

"You know what scares me the most about you, Teddy?" I asked.

"What, babe," he said.

"You won't be truthful. You're hiding something."

"You feel that from me?"

"Yes."

"There isn't anything I can hide from you. With the text and Carissa's bullshit, you're guarding yourself and don't want to trust me. This is also why you need time. I like you, so I'm going after what I want," he said.

"A hamburger?" I asked.

"No. You're random." He laughed. "You're like a skittish animal. I get close, and you pull away. I see what you want then you turn your emotions off when you think I would be better with someone else. You had to learn how to take care of things on your own and build your wall for survival."

"I want to give you my heart, but I'm scared you'll crush it," I admitted.

"I'll do nothing to hurt you." He stroked my hair for a second, then said, "Get some rest."

I moved my hand close to him, and he held it. "I don't think we belong together, but I don't want you to leave either. That doesn't make sense to me."

"Trust me and let your heart lead," he said.

"It's hard," I said.

He kissed the back of my hand and bid me goodnight. I was grateful he left me alone lying across the bed. It will be difficult to watch him leave Sunday.

Chapter 19

I stared at the bench with chainsaw in hand. Teddy draped his arm over my shoulder.

"Let it speak to you." He smiled and pointed at the log.

"The thing is saying, please don't cut on me anymore," I chuckled and received a text on my phone. I pulled it from my pocket.

"It's dead, Beth. You can do this," he said.

"I'm going to try," I said then looked at the phone.

I can't stop the events which will unfold if you two don't separate. – Helper.

"What does that mean?" I asked Teddy, then I texted.

What events?

"Good luck," Mark yelled at me from across the yard.

He and the other guys were looking at my bike. Kyle nodded at me. Thad gave me a thumb up.

"Thanks," I responded and received another text.

Too much information being told. DEADLINE is coming.

Lose my number unless you give me details. I'm tired of this game. - I texted.

After a few seconds, I received:

You can't hide when someone knows everything about you.

Like what? - I texted.

"That's enough," Teddy said.

"Helper is finally talking, and you want to stop the conversation?" I asked, and my phone dinged.

"I'm also tired of this, Beth," he said.

Name, address, kids and business. Common things. – Helper.

Don't fuck with my family. - I texted.
You don't have a say. - Helper.

"Dammit," I said, but Teddy placed his hand over mine.

"This isn't getting us anywhere. Helper is trying to get you fired up. Don't give up on us," he said.

"There isn't a US like you think," I said.

"Yes, there is," he said. "I would like for Gene to log these texts. Is that okay?"

"Fine," I said and handed him the phone. "Don't walk up on me."

Teddy kissed my forehead, then stepped back. Nervously, I made the first cut, then I couldn't stop. I cut patterns, and my vision of the bench appeared before my eyes.

The chainsaw was light and easy to manipulate. I cut patterns in the armrest and on the back. I didn't notice the time or my surroundings.

I took the frustration of Helper out on the log. I stopped to refill the gas or bar oil, changed the blades twice to get the effect I wanted, and continued with my focus on the wood.

"Beth!" Teddy exclaimed behind me.

He held up a glass of tea. I shut the saw off and placed it on the ground.

"It looks good," he said and handed me the glass.

"Thank you." I examine the bench. "I feel liberated."

"It's a great feeling to see your creation come to life. I got a kick out of watching the wood fly around you."

I smiled and looked around the yard. People were putting up tents.

"When did they get here?" I asked.

"The kids arrived an hour ago and your nephews a few minutes ago."

"All you've done is watch me cut?" I asked.

"No." He pointed to the back porch. "We moved the equipment outside for tonight."

"Are you sure you want to play outdoors?" I asked, and he nodded. I handed him my glass and said, "I'm going to finish these last few cuts. Thank you for the tea."

I started the chainsaw once again. I made the cuts and became engrossed. I retrieved a hammer, chisel, and sandpaper from the shed. I was meticulous and wanted to perfect it.

I wasn't sure how long I worked, but being satisfied, I turned off the chainsaw. I gathered my tools, then stared at the piece. Who would need a bench made from a log? Everyone stood behind me and clapped.

"Y'all like it?" I smiled.

"I love it," Kyle said.

"Thank y'all again for this handy dandy light thing." I held up the new chainsaw.

"Thanks for the write-off, babe. It was wonderful entertainment," Teddy winked.

"I'm jumping in the shower," I said and patted his arm.

"If you need help, I'll volunteer," Teddy said.

I shook my head and put the tools in the shed. I went inside and showered. Soreness set in my arms. I smiled at the thought of throwing wood in the air like a lumberjack, but it was fun.

After I dressed, I went outside. A few more tents stood around the yard. Teddy spoke with Colby, and I joined them next to the railing.

"You guys tested the sound?" I asked.

"Yes. We're good," Teddy said.

Ellis jumped from his four-wheeler and joined our conversation. "Did you say something to her, Teddy?"

"Not yet," he said and looked at him with wide eyes.

"What?" I asked.

"I want to buy the bench," Teddy said.

"Not for sale," I said.

"Why not?" Teddy asked.

"What would you do with it, and how would you get it to Michigan?"

"I want it in my garden, and the guys said they would deliver it to me."

"Y'all are crazy. It's not for sale," I said.

"You could come to Michigan and make another one," he said.

"Nope," I said.

"Then let me buy this one," he said.

"It's not finished."

"Y'all talk about it and let us know. Colby, Gibson, Brian, and I can deliver it at Thanksgiving," Ellis said, then he and Colby left us on the porch.

"Please, explain," I said.

"I want to fly everyone to Michigan for Thanksgiving. You would have time to finish the bench," Teddy said.

"Thanksgiving is over a month away."

"Will you think about it, please?"

"Did you see the people here last night? Do you want them running through your house?"

"Yes," he said, then kissed my cheek and went into the house.

Teddy and I relaxed on the back porch. He strummed the guitar and sang in a low voice, a crazy song about today's events and the lumberjack in all of us. Friends and family gathered around us and laughed while they listened to the silly song. Mark joined us and played keyboards.

Sadie came outside, sat in my lap, and listened to Teddy. She buried her face in my shoulder when he asked her to sing a children's song he wrote for a kid's movie.

After some time, she relaxed and sang with him. Thad, Kyle, and Susan joined us and played. A few of the other children stood around them and sang several children's songs.

"I'm not a fan, Teddy," I said between songs. "I know the songs, but I had no clue you wrote those."

"I had to eat those years." He laughed. "I wrote songs for five children movies. I told you I liked kids. Did you see their faces light up?"

"I didn't know this was a kid's show," Colby yelled from across the yard while he laughed.

"It's pretty bad the parents knew the songs as well as the kids. I saw you, son," Teddy pointed at him.

The children begged Teddy to do one more, so he smiled and said, "Everyone in the yard, please." They ran to the yard while Teddy walked to the railing. "You have to dance to what I say. Can you do that?"

"Yeah," The kids yelled.

He sang a song he wrote about a lion who walked through the forest. The kids stomped their feet and roared while Teddy interacted with them. He took the lion on a journey to meet other jungle animals. The kids made sounds and walked as though they were the different animals the lion met. They danced and acted silly.

At the end of the song, Teddy said. "I need a nap. We'll sing more in a little while. Is that okay?"

The kids were disappointed but agreed. They laughed and recreated the song while Teddy walked to his chair.

"That was cute," he said and sat next to me.

"I'm impressed." I smiled.

"That impressed you, but me knowing four languages didn't?" he asked.

"Yes," I said. "It takes a lot to hold a child's attention, and you held twenty-five of them."

"And their parents, so are you impressed again?" he asked.

"No," I chuckled.

He kissed my cheek then joined the rest of the band. He faced everyone in the yard.

"Do you all wanna jam?" he asked as he held the guitar.

"Yeah," everyone said in unison.

He played with the same enthusiasm he had at the concert. While he entertained, people walked around in the yard. Some waved at me, pointed to Teddy, and held a thumb up.

I retreated into the house for drinks. I stepped into the kitchen. Lucy, Danielle, Helen, and Chasity were speaking as they leaned against the counters and ate a few snacks.

"Did Teddy talk to you about Thanksgiving?" Lucy asked me.

"A little," I said.

"What are your thoughts?" she asked.

"It's not going to happen," I said.

"Don't push him away," she said.

"I agree with Lucy. You two have something, and we want you to give him a chance," Danielle stated.

"Ellis' mom is coming to get Kara for the night, and the other kids will entertain Sadie. You can have time with him without worrying about the babies," Lucy said.

"The same goes for me. Colby's mom is coming to get Gabi. Relax tonight," Danielle said.

"Are y'all trying to play matchmaker?" I asked.

"With the kids here, you're going to focus on them instead of speaking with Teddy. I know you. Family first then Beth. He makes you smile and laugh. I haven't seen you this happy in years, and I like it. Please give him a chance," Lucy said.

"Is this because of what he gave you?" I asked.

"No. We like him for him," Danielle said.

"If he were a duck washer, you both would feel the same? You want us to date?" I asked.

"Yes," they both said.

"Plus, I like ducks." Danielle smiled. "He stood behind you when you worked on the bench today. The look he had on his face told us he likes you."

"Is everything all right?" Teddy asked as he walked into the kitchen.

"Yeah," I said and handed him a glass of tea.

"There are a couple of people looking for Lucy and Danielle, but take your time, especially if you're talking about me. Girls, you have my back, right?" he asked with a smile.

"Yes, Teddy. We gotchu," Lucy said.

We stepped outside. Ellis spoke with his mom, and Colby spoke with his parents. We visited with them, then I kissed and waved bye to Kara, Gabi, and the in-laws. Teddy retrieved his guitar, sat next to me, and strummed a familiar song as Nancy ran up the stairs to us.

"Where have you been?" I asked her.

"Got hung up at the restaurant," she said.

"Would you care for something to drink?" I asked her.

"Sure," Nancy said.

I stood to go into the house, but Teddy grabbed my arm. He looked at Gene and asked, "Would you mind getting a few drinks? I need Beth for a second."

"No problem," he said.

"Take my seat, Nancy," Teddy said.

I followed Teddy to the keyboard. He faced me and pointed at the porch.

"Stand here, please." I did, and he stood on the other side of the keyboard. "Do you know *Taking Time Back*?" he asked and played the music.

"Yes," I said.

"My eyes, Beth."

We held eye contact. People around us faded in the background. I harmonized with him.

In my imagination, he gently rubbed the sides of my body and rested his hands on my hips. His soft kisses moved across my throat and onto my lips. I wanted to stay in this safe place with him in my mind.

He grabbed my hand and guided me around the keyboard like he did at the concert. He completed the song and leaned in to kiss me. I pulled back and studied his eyes.

Butterflies danced in my stomach. I told myself not to get close, but my body yearned for his touch.

He smiled, gently held my face while we were in our own world. I physically felt his soft lips on mine and returned his kiss. He wrapped his arms around my waist and pulled me close to his body. Electricity escalated between us.

My nerves tingled from his touches. My thoughts turned to Carissa and the other women. I pulled my head back, gazed into his brown eyes, and felt confused.

"Don't do that, Beth. Don't think that you aren't good enough," he whispered.

"We can't do that again."

He smiled and said, "Yes, we can." He pulled me back to his lips and kissed me once more.

I wanted the passion, so I didn't hesitate to return the kiss. I wrapped my hands around his neck and held him gently to my lips. I loved his body next to mine. His heartbeat thumped against my chest. He held my hands while the band played a fast-paced song.

"The electricity is amazing." He smiled.

"Is it real?" I asked.

His smile widened. I brushed my finger across his cheek, to his lips, and he kissed the tip. I wanted him, but I couldn't have him.

I stepped out of his arms, and he said to the band, "Beth needs to go on the road with us."

"You're a funny man, Teddy," I said as my legs were weak from his touch.

Nancy grabbed my arm and said in a low voice, "I couldn't breathe watching you two. You've found you're, Mr. Right."

"I'm not looking for Mr. Right."

"He found you," she said.

"You two glowed," Shelly said as she sat next to my chair and stroked Olly's back.

"My baby sister's boyfriend is Teddy Nafton," Nancy teased.

"There's nothing between us," I said in denial.

The night went on with Teddy and Five/Ten entertaining us, while people danced and visited with each other. Nancy, Shelly, and I danced on the porch and sang. After another hour, I walked into the house to check on the little kids, and Shelly followed.

"It's going to be miserable dealing with him when you two are separated," Shelly said.

"No, it's not," I said and started a movie for the kids to watch on TV.

I walked to the kitchen and leaned against the sink, while people grazed over the food. Teddy, Mark, Keith, and Gene walked inside. Mark and Keith each carried a bottle of spiced rum. They spoke as they poured shots for people.

"Where did you get that?" Shelly asked Mark.

"We have a few bottles from Colorado. Last time to party for months to come," he said.

"It's back to work after tonight," Teddy said as he leaned against an opposite counter from me.

"Do you want some, Shelly?" Keith asked.

"Yeah," she said and stared at Teddy.

Teddy winked at her then walked to me. He placed his hands on the counter, pinned me against the sink, and looked in my eyes.

"You're going to be a bitch without her," Shelly said and patted his shoulder.

"Convince her to come with us," Teddy said.

"She won't. She's stubborn and will stay here to work," Shelly said then took a gulp from her cup.

Teddy kissed me, smiled, and walked out the back door. Shelly took her bottle and cup then followed the guys outside.

I replenished the snacks then went to the porch. Teddy and Five/Ten played. I danced my way to the yard. I stopped at the different groups of people to say hello and visited with family and friends. Some of the guys stood around a bonfire in the yard, so I visited with them for a few minutes.

I stepped onto the porch, and Teddy placed his guitar in the stand. He wrapped his hands around my waist, spun me while he sang, and I smiled. He let me go and returned to his guitar. They completed the song, then the band made fun of Kyle for missed beats.

"Aren't you tired of playing?" I asked Teddy when he leaned against the railing next to me.

"No. We're having fun," he said.

Mark went into the house while Teddy pulled me to him, with my back against his chest. A minute later, Mark emerged from the house and carried another bottle of rum.

Shelly stood in front of us, pointed her finger between us, and said with slurred words, "You two are some of my favorite people."

"Why the drinking?" I asked her.

"I like this stuff," she said, then gulped a shot. She pointed at us. "I see you two, and you remind me of someone."

"I told you to go home, Shelly," Teddy said.

"I'm not talking about Rob." She held my arm and asked, "Why don't you come with us?"

"I can't."

"We need to get together regarding the schedule. I don't want to deal with a bitchy Teddy, so please join us for a few concerts," she said.

I laughed, but now was not the time to discuss the tour. I shook my head, then she sat and took another drink.

"Is she always like this?" I asked Teddy.

"Nope. This is rare," he said and held me close. His body against mine caused a sensual sensation rush over me. "I want to stay like this forever, okay?"

Those words brought me to reality. I moved his hands, faced him, and said, "If it were different circumstances."

I walked from him and sat next to Shelly. Olly was in her lap.

"Are you stealing my dog?" I asked her.

"We've bonded," she said.

"We need to talk, Beth," Teddy said as I looked for Izzy.

"About what."

"I want you," he said and held my hand.

"It's not going to happen," I said.

"You're right. I want you when I can have all of you. Your mind and heart. I want your touch to feel the energy. Tomorrow night is approaching, and I don't want to think about leaving you," he stated.

"It's affecting me too, but the reality is, tomorrow will come. You and I won't work, so it's easier to end this now. You have your tour and life in Michigan. Look around darlin'. I have to take care of this," I said. "This is MY world. It wouldn't be fair to ask you to fit this into YOUR world, and I'm not giving this up."

"I like YOUR world and would never ask for you to leave it. You can't tell me you haven't felt the intensity of the energy we share." He leaned close to me. "I don't know how, but we're connected, and you know it."

"That spark isn't enough to keep us together. It's not reality. You know that US isn't going to happen. WE won't work." Now was the time to turn him loose. I stared into his eyes and said, "I don't want you, Teddy. We agreed on friendship, and that's that. I've enjoyed spending time with you, but we have to stop."

"Stop lying to yourself and me. I've seen and felt it from you. You won't let me get close to you," he said forcefully.

"I don't want you or the drama you carry. It's too much," I said to push him out of my heart.

I needed him to focus on his life and leave me. We would be better without one another. Less drama than trying to combine OUR worlds.

He stared at me, but I stood my ground. He walked to the bonfire and spoke with the guys. Mark passed the bottle of rum, so everyone could fill their glass. Thad handed Teddy a cup. Teddy looked at me, said something to Kyle, and drank the shot.

"What are you going to do?" Shelly asked while we watched him.

"Let him go before I develop stronger feelings for him," I said with a heavy heart.

I visited with people for a while then had my fill of watching Teddy take shot after shot of rum. I walked into the house to clean the kitchen when Gene helped Shelly walk past me. He pointed to the spare room, and I nodded.

"Why are you pushing Teddy away?" Nancy asked as she stood behind me and placed food in containers.

"It won't work," I said and washed a plate.

"It will if you let it." She leaned next to me.

"She's out," Gene said. He scooped some nuts into his hands and asked me, "How are you feeling, honey?"

"I'm fine," I said.

"Let me check on the others," he said and left Nancy and me alone in the kitchen.

"Go for Teddy. What do you have to lose?" Nancy asked.

"My heart," I said.

Nicky and Chasity joined us and stated they wanted to go to Teddy's for Thanksgiving. We spoke about it while they helped me clean the kitchen, then they were out the door after exchanged hugs.

I bid my goodbyes to Nancy, and a few other people then returned to the task of cleanup when Rick came to me.

"Gene needs to see you in your room, please," he said.

"How are you doing, Rick?" I asked and wiped my hands.

"Better than, Teddy." He smiled and walked with me.

He stepped in and helped Gene lay Teddy across the bed. Teddy mumbled something.

"What the hell happened? Where is everyone?" I asked.

"They went to bed in their tents. Thad, Keith, Mark, Kyle, and Teddy finished off the fourth bottle of rum," Gene said. "Helen put Thad in her tent, and Susan is helping Kyle in the tent they borrowed from Colby. We need to get Keith and Mark settled in yours."

"Go. I got him," I said.

They left, and I stood over Teddy. He opened his bloodshot eyes, and we held a staring contest. My thoughts turned slow, and my head spun like I was drunk. Words came to my mind as they had before when we sang, but they were distorted and fuzzy.

"Babe." He reached for me.

"What?" I asked and placed a pillow under his head.

"You're everything to me." He slurred his words.

"Sleep." I took his shoes off him, then covered him with the blanket.

"Why don't you like me?" he asked.

"The problem is, I do," I said and made sure he was covered.

"Well, I don't care what Carissa says. She's not going to get to you." He rolled to his side. "You and I are going to be together." He hugged the body pillow, then a moment later, he was asleep.

Chapter 20

"You bitch!" Carissa yelled.

I stood in the brightly lit white, cubed room. I scanned the walls but saw no doors. Being trapped with her, I gathered my strength and stood firm. She lunged toward me, grabbed my shoulders, and shoved me against one wall. I struggled to break her grip, but the wall gave way. I glanced behind me to the left. The endless black hole was at my feet.

"You're dead," she screamed and shoved me to the edge of the floor before the drop.

I grabbed her arm, pushed my weight into her, and made her take a few steps back. I gained traction and drove her to the opposite wall while she struggled against me.

A black cloak draped tall silhouette appeared behind her. I couldn't see this person's face.

"Destroy her," a man's deep, graveled voice yelled.

She held tight to my shoulders and looked in the direction of the voice. No wind blew, but the silhouette dissipated into tiny particles, drifted into the air, and disappeared before my eyes.

"Why the hell are you mad?" I yelled at her.

"I told you to stay away. We have to dispose of you." She faced me.

"Whose we?" I asked.

"Die," she shrieked and wrapped her hands around my throat.

She pushed me against a wall. I broke her grip from my jugular and punched her in the jaw, which sent her to stumble back a few steps. She regained composure, stared into my eyes, and pulled a knife from her belt loop. She devilishly smiled, turned the sharp object in the air as the light beamed across the blade. She thrust the knife toward me. I moved to the side, sent her into a wall, and took a stance.

"You fucking whore. Why don't you die?" She ranted.

"I did nothing to you," I growled.

She rushed and pinned me against the wall next to the black hole in the floor. I wrapped my arms around her wrist as she held the cold, steel, blade against my throat.

I swallowed hard. I stared into her emotionless blue eyes, tightened my grip on her arm, and she shrilled an evil laugh.

"Time's up," she said, and the knife glided across my throat before she pushed me into the black hole.

My body jerked, and I sat up in bed. Dazed and trembling, I placed my hand on my throat and made sure I wasn't cut or bleeding. Teddy grabbed me into his arms.

"Are you okay?" He embraced me.

"Yeah. How about you?" I asked and held onto him.

"You're shaking," he said and laid us against the mattress.

"It was vivid. I felt the…" I said.

"I know, babe." He stroked my hair.

The dream left me unnerved, but I was safe in his embrace. We didn't exchange words. We laid in bed with my head on his chest. I listened to his heartbeat, heard his labored breathing, then I drifted into darkness.

Small footsteps pitter patted the hardwood floor outside the bedroom. Sadie stood in the doorway.

She looked at Teddy then at me. I motioned for her to come to me. She quietly crawled into bed and laid in my arms. Teddy stirred. I placed my first finger to my lips to indicate for her to be quiet. She snuggled under the blankets into my side.

"I'm hungry," she whispered.

"Me too," Teddy said in a low voice.

He smiled at us but didn't raise his head. Sadie's eyes widened, and she looked at me then at Teddy.

"Good morning, Teddy," she said.

"Good morning, sweetie," he said and scooted in bed, to be close to us. "Good morning, babe."

"Morning," I said.

"Can we have waffles for breakfast?" Sadie asked.

"What about cereal?" Teddy asked.

"I need waffles," she said.

"Where are the other kids?" I asked.

"They're watching TV in the living room."

"Find out what they want while I get dressed."

"Okay, Mimi." She jumped from the bed.

"I'm sorry to have woke you," I said to Teddy.

"I felt the bed move," he said.

I threw the blankets off me, but as I stood, he grabbed my wrist. He pulled me back onto the bed.

"I'm sorry about last night," he said.

"It's okay."

"No, it isn't. Please forgive me?" he asked, being sincere.

"Forgiven," I said.

"I feel like an idiot."

"You are an idiot." I smiled and pulled my wrist from him. I walked to the back door and let the dogs outside. "How's your head?"

"Hurts." He laid his arm across his forehead.

"Good." I walked to the foot of the bed, smiled, and stared at him.

"What?" He looked at me from under his arm.

"Does this make you want to throw up?" I jumped in the middle of the bed.

"Stop it," he said while we bounced and laughed.

I sat still, stared at him, and he smiled at me. He moved a strand of hair from my forehead.

"What did you dream last night?" I asked.

"It was a bad one," he said. "When she slid the knife across…" He stopped in mid-sentence, held my hand, and rubbed my fingers. "I don't want to see that nightmare again."

"I can't believe it's the same dream," I said.

He kissed my hand and said, "When I leave, I'm going to call, so get used to the phone ringing. We'll pick out a good ringtone."

"As long as it's Noah Parker. I may not answer, so I can hear his voice." I laughed.

"Oh yeah?" He laughed.

"How many times are you going to call before you'll quit?" I asked.

"Enough to where your whole family will change their numbers."

I gazed into his brown eyes. Sadness filled my heart. I didn't want him to leave. Words formed in my head: *I don't want to.*

"I'll get you a cup of coffee, stalker," I said.

"Come with me." He sat up in bed and held my hand. "Get on the plane with me tonight and let me take care of you."

"I can't. My life is here." I kissed his forehead, stood, and walked to the closet to retrieve clothes for the day.

"Shelly took your bed in the spare room," I said before I shut the bathroom door.

Teddy made the bed before he left the room. I walked to the back door and let the dogs inside then went into the kitchen. Sadie joined then asked me to help make breakfast.

I told everyone good morning, as they migrated into the living room or kitchen area while we prepared food. Shelly joined us, sat at the table, and I stepped to her.

"How are you feeling this morning?" I asked and sat a cup of coffee in front of her.

"I don't ever want to drink again," she said.

I laughed and returned to the task of pouring the waffle batter ingredients into a bowl. I prepared breakfast for everyone then retreated to the back porch.

I was alone to smoke my morning cigarette. The dogs sniffed the ground where the tents once stood. Less than twelve hours and Teddy would be gone. I've developed feelings for him, but he needed to move on with his life. Helper would be happy to know we separated.

"Thank you for breakfast, honey," Gene said, which made me a jump out of thought.

I placed my hand over my heart and said, "You're welcome. Did you get enough to eat, or did the vultures devour everything?"

"There's plenty of food. How do you cook for an army?" Gene asked.

"I'm used to it," I said when Teddy joined us. "Did you get enough to eat?"

"Yes. Thank you," he said. "You guys put our instruments in the house last night?"

"Beth was the one who thought about the morning dew," Gene said and pointed at me.

"I screwed up," Teddy said.

"I got your back," I said.

"That you do." He held my hand, but I pulled it back.

People migrated to the back porch. They thanked Teddy for the mini-concert, then hugged and thanked me. The back yard was tent free.

Ellis and Colby parked the four-wheelers. Ellis laid his guns on the porch railing. He asked if I had ammo, and I confirmed I did. The guys wanted to target practice, as discussed at last night's bonfire meeting.

Gibson, Colby, and Ellis placed targets in the tree line. We had fun in the late morning sun, target practicing. Everyone took turns shooting, then we wrote our names on the target sheets to see who shot the best.

"How are you comfortable with guns?" Teddy asked me.

"Born and raised with them," I said and compared the targets. "I would only use one if the kids were in danger. Don't fuck with my kids, and everyone lives." He looked at me with wide eyes. "I don't mess around when it comes to my babies."

"You know how to handle that thing," he said and pointed to my gun.

"I know how to handle a lot of things." I smiled, and he smirked. "You did better than me."

"Not by much," he said.

I left the guys outside to discuss the targets. I went to the kitchen and prepared the dough for the dumplings. Shelly helped, and we spoke about family.

Teddy came into the kitchen and stood behind me as I placed dumplings into the pots. He leaned further and further into my back and pushed me forward.

"What are you doing?" I laughed.

"Take a ride with me?" he asked.

"You want me to ride what?" I smiled.

"Not with a houseful of people. I bet you're a moaner." He snickered.

"Like you could make me moan," I said sarcastically.

"I could have you calling my name within a minute," he whispered into my ear and sent a shiver down my spine.

"Oh man," I said to stop my desire for him.

"Yeah. Like that, except you would exaggerate my name."

"Stop. Four-wheeler or bike?" I giggled and blushed.

"Four-wheeler," he said and laid his chin on my shoulder.

"I drive?" I asked.

"For a little."

"Okay," I said and finished the dumplings. He walked out the back door, and I washed my hands. "Wanna come, Shelly?"

"He wants it to be the two of you," she said.

"Gene won't allow that, and I don't want to be alone with him. Please?" I asked again with my hands folded as I begged.

"Fine," she said and wiped her hands.

"Thank you. I need to get him on the plane without doing something I'm going to regret," I said while we stepped outside. Teddy waited by the four-wheeler. "We're ready. Are you going to lead the way, Ellis?" I asked, so more people would join us. Teddy expressed a disappointed look in my direction.

"Where to, Beth," Ellis said.

"The Stones."

"Danielle and I will get the kids in a bit," Lucy said.

"Can you please make sure the dogs stay in the pen? I don't want them muddy," I said.

"Sure thing. We'll keep an eye on the dumplings," Lucy said.

Teddy and I sat on my four-wheeler, while Shelly and Gene rode one, then Kyle and Susan took another. Mark and Keith used Gibson's, and Rick sat on the back of Ellis'.

"I hope you don't mind mud," I said to Teddy.

"Show me," he said, and I started the four-wheeler.

"Be careful, Beth. He's my meal ticket," Gene yelled.

I was raised in this area and knew every mud hole, rock, tree, and bump. We weaved around turns on the path as mud splashed our legs to our waist. Once we came upon the hill and stopped the four-wheeler, I told everyone about the stones.

The old rock quarry consisted of three big water cliffs. Brush and trees grew on the sides, but the gravel was intact around the holes.

As kids, we jumped off the cliffs and swam on hot summer days. We walked to our favorite water hole and threw rocks from the cliff. I explained how a few neighborhood kids jumped and broke their necks. Once, a kid jumped into the water and got tangled in steel from a bulldozer left in the water. It took a week for the authorities to find his body, which caused the place to close to the public.

"I can't thank you enough for these past few weeks," I said to Teddy as we walked by ourselves. "I've enjoyed getting to know you."

"It's you and your family we need to thank. I've had fun getting to know everyone, but you're my favorite." He shoulder bumped me.

"How sweet, kind sir." I smiled and picked up pebbles from the ground. I threw the stones into the water, and asked, "What would you be doing if you weren't here right now?"

"Rehearsing in the studio. What about you?"

"Working or cutting trees."

"Let me hire someone for you," he said.

"I'm capable and can do it for free."

"Oh, I know. Look at the bench, which you need to let me buy."

"How much?" I smiled.

"$2,500."

"After the hard work, I've put into that thing?"

"How much, Beth. Name the price, and it's yours. I'll hand you the world if you would take it from me without a fight."

"I don't want anything, Teddy. It's yours."

"Are you serious?" He took my arm and spun me to face him.

"Yeah, but I need to finish it, so it'll be a few weeks."

He hugged me tight, as though I told him he won the lottery.

"Thank you."

"You're welcome."

He held me at arm's length. "What about Thanksgiving, or am I pushing it?"

"You're pushing it." I turned from him and threw a few rocks down the cliff. "Who knows? You may get home and forget about us hicks down here."

"There is no way Elizabeth Chambers. Your name is burned into my heart forever."

"I'm not a song, Teddy." I gave him a side glance.

"You would make a great one," he said and held my hand. "Please think about Thanksgiving. I have enough room for everyone, and the kids will have a great time swimming and riding horses."

"Swimming? You got one of those cement ponds," I said in a hard-southern accent and pulled my hand out of his.

"Inside cement pond," he said in his best southern accent, and I laughed. "I have a pool table, foosball table, ping-pong table, and all kinds of toys in my man cave. I would love to show you our world. Promise you'll think about it."

"Don't make plans. You need to go home and focus on the tour. Last night, you said Carissa wouldn't get to me, so that tells me you two are talking."

"Did I say that?"

"Yeah. How much does she know about me?"

"Not a lot," he said. "In the last few texts, she said if I choose you, then she would do everything she could to expose you. It's the same bullshit she said in Colorado. She doesn't have your last name or your exact location, and we'll keep it that way. I got to see your world. I know what you need to protect. Believe me, I'm protecting you and everything in your heart," he said, and we stared at each other. "I don't want her or the publicity. I want you."

"WE won't work. You're in the public eye, with or without her. I don't want that for this family. I don't want the kids to be on display or scrutinized. You're who you are, and we don't mesh."

"The kids won't be, and we can make this work." He held my hand again.

I pulled my hand from him, and said, "I don't want this Teddy, so friends and only friends we will be. Nothing else between you and me."

He smiled and said, "You rhymed, and that was cute, but we are more, so don't dispute. We'll be together, now and always, so join me for the Thanksgiving holidays."

"That was lame." I laughed.

"It works." He laughed.

"Are you guys ready?" I asked everyone loudly.

"Whenever you are," Ellis shouted.

"Let me think, Teddy. Once you and I are back to our own lives, we'll see how things go. I'll give you one day at a time, but if we fade from each other…"

"We won't." He smiled. "I'm driving."

I nodded and sat on the four-wheeler. I wrapped my arms around his waist.

"If I go, you go," I said, and he smiled, then took off to the path.

We arrived at the house. He leaned back on my chest.

"That was fun," he said.

Everyone was muddy to our waist. Lucy, Helen, and Danielle joined us with the babies on their mother's hips.

"It looks like you guys had a great time," Danielle said.

"My driving is better than Teddy's." I shoulder bumped him, walked to the porch, and took off my shoes.

"I don't think so. I got in a few good splashes," he said.

"I thought you two were going to kill yourselves," Gene complained.

"You can't keep up, old man," Teddy teased.

"I'm showering," I said. "Someone can use the other one."

"You can, Shelly," Teddy said.

Once I showered and dressed, I walked to the back door and told Teddy the shower was free. I went into the kitchen to complete an early dinner. Shelly came out of the bathroom and looked refreshed. She helped me prepare side dishes while Gene took a shower in the spare bathroom.

"It's going to be sad when y'all leave. I've enjoyed you guys being here," Lucy said as she and Danielle helped set the table.

"We've enjoyed being here," Shelly said and stared at me. "How do you feel about us leaving, Beth?"

"Teddy and I need time apart," I said.

"What are you afraid of, Mom?" Danielle asked.

On cue, Teddy walked through the living room with a towel around his waist. My mouth gaped opened. I stared at the sight of his sculptured body.

His chiseled, tight stomach muscles, and biceps, along with his olive skin, glistened from the steam of the shower. Inappropriate thoughts danced in my mind. I wanted to trace my lips from his neck, down his stomach to the edge of the towel while my fingers smoothly rubbed…

"Mom!" Lucy exclaimed and broke my concentration. "You can close your mouth now."

Teddy chuckled and looked at me, "I'm glad she got your attention." He stood next to me and said, "Your Mom isn't afraid of anything, Danielle." He kissed my cheek and explained, "I didn't want to get mud through your house. My clothes are in the spare room."

"Okay," I said, or I think I said.

He walked to the spare room. I closed my eyes to burn a detailed image of Teddy in my mind.

"Damn, he looks good," Lucy said.

"Has he always looked like that?" I asked Shelly.

"As far as I know, yeah." She laughed.

I pointed in Teddy's direction, looked at Danielle, and said, "I'm afraid of that. Oh, my goodness."

"You haven't seen him like that?" Lucy asked.

"No." I sat in a chair at the table.

"He looks nice," Danielle said.

"How do you feel now?" Shelly asked.

"I love you, Shelly, but you have to take him away." I liked the image of that scrumptious man in my memory, but I needed to stop picturing him in my bed. I said out loud, "He is beautiful."

"Thank you, ma'am." He rejoined us in the kitchen.

Shelly laughed loudly. I blushed and buried my head in my hands.

"I can't work out like I want on the road, but I do what I can," Teddy said and placed his hand on my head.

"I can't believe you heard me. I'm embarrassed," I said.

He drew my head unto his hip, and I closed my eyes. I deeply breathed in his fantastic cologne and pictured him in the towel once again. I stood, smiled, and stared into his eyes.

"I'm sorry, Teddy. You shocked me, but thank you for the view," I said.

"Say the word, and I'm yours." He winked at me.

He walked to my room, carrying the towel in his hand. I walked to the bedroom as he came out of the bathroom. He tackled me to the bed.

"I'm going to miss you." I smiled.

"Not as much as I'm going to miss you." He leaned in to kiss me, but Sadie ran into the bedroom and jumped on the bed.

"That's yucky," she said and looked at me.

Teddy moved to my side and said, "Your Mimi is yucky."

"No, she isn't," Sadie said and laid next to me.

I kissed her forehead and said, "Perfect timing. What do you want, little monkey?"

I tickled her, and she squealed. Lucy came to the door.

"I thought you were going to tell them to come and eat," she said to her.

"Come here, Lucy," I said and scooted close to Teddy. He wrapped his arm around my waist, and I yelled, "Danielle. Southern Therapy."

"Let me get Kara," Lucy said.

Danielle, Gabi, Lucy, and Kara joined Teddy, Sadie, and me in bed.

"This is Southern Therapy?" Teddy asked.

"You have a lot to learn, Teddy," Lucy said.

"It's my favorite thing. Lay in bed and listen to my girls speak about their lives. Many problems have been solved this way," I said and squeezed Sadie.

"Bubble wrap," Danielle said, and we laughed.

"What?" Teddy asked.

"When we have Southern Therapy, I want to bubble wrap the bed to protect everyone who holds my heart," I explained.

Teddy kissed my cheek and whispered, "Are you happy?"

"Get the dogs up here and bubble wrap. We can live like THIS forever," I laughed while the babies crawled on top of us.

Shelly came to the door with the phone pressed against her ear. "I need a time, Teddy."

"Come on, Shelly. Southern Therapy," I said.

"I don't want to be in the same bed as Teddy," she laughed.

"Once you had a piece of me, you wouldn't want to get out of bed," he said, and we all laughed.

"Time, please," she said.

"Late as possible," Teddy said and nuzzled his nose into my neck.

"You don't have a particular time to be at the airport?" Danielle asked as Shelly left the room.

"It's a private plane, so we leave whenever we want. When you get your pilot's license, you can fly us," Teddy said and hung on to me.

"No, she can't. She's not allowed to fly over rocks, mountains, or land." I explained.

"What about water?" Teddy asked.

"She knows how to swim." I smiled.

"That doesn't make sense," he said.

"If she crashes on anything but water, she won't survive." I theorized. "She knows how to swim."

"The plane can explode in water, babe," Teddy said.

"No, it can't." I snickered. "I know the dangers, but I don't like thinking about it. I want to live in this bed."

"I'm hungry, Mimi," Sadie said.

"Come on. Let's tell everyone dinner is ready," Lucy said, and the girls stood from the bed.

Danielle stopped in the doorway, pointed at us, and said, "Leave this door open."

"Okay, Mom," I said and rolled my eyes.

Teddy and I held each other close. The front door opened, and voices filled the house. I stood from the bed, then held my hand out to him.

"Let's get you something to eat," I said.

He sat up, grabbed my waist, and pulled me into him. He laid his head on my stomach and said, "Come with me."

"You know the answer," I said and stroked his hair with my nails.

Chapter 21

Sadie and the babies sat at the table and ate cake while the girls, Shelly, and I cleaned the kitchen. The band retreated to the exercise room. Teddy walked from the spare room with Wilma and Waldorf in his hands.

"Can I see the bears?" Sadie asked.

"After you wash your hands," Teddy said, then looked at me. "May I borrow your perfume before we leave."

"I'll give you mine if you'll give me yours." I smiled.

"You can have anything of mine." He winked.

"Your cologne will be enough," I blushed.

"Will you join me in the other room, Shelly? I have an idea I want to discuss," he said.

Danielle scooped Gabi into her arms as Sadie washed and dried her hands. Helen and Cullen followed Lucy and Kara into the other room, then Sadie, and I joined everyone.

"What do you all think about using the bears to market the tour?" Teddy asked as he handed Wilma to Sadie.

"She smells like you, Mimi," Sadie said, and I nodded.

"Give me ideas," Shelly said.

"Wilma can show the world the tour from behind the scenes. Post her on social sites being our eyes," Keith said.

"Wilma and her lost love. We can take pictures of her on stage or looking toward the crowd. She could be rehearsing or lying in a hotel bed, pining for Waldorf," Susan suggested.

"Are you all going to hold her during the concert?" Shelly asked as she took Waldorf out of Teddy's hands.

"We can, or we can sit her on the piano or somewhere on stage. She needs to be recognized by the audience." Teddy laid his arm on my shoulder. "Show fans how we miss family, friends, and even them when we travel. She'll be our other half."

"We can show how we bring the music to the public," Kyle said as Sadie sat in his lap with Wilma.

"Beth will be taking pictures and sending them to me of Waldorf. We could use them as a storyline," Teddy said.

"Order smaller versions to sell. Something like little Wilma's," Mark said.

"Get some of Waldorf and promote them as a set. We could package them with the CD or sell them throughout the rest of the tour. We could split the profits and create another educational trust for these kids. Like the ones you and Marcy did for…" Teddy stated enthusiastically and pointed around the room.

"What kids?" I backed away from him.

"I shouldn't have said that out loud. I was on a roll and didn't think about you standing…" Teddy said.

"I know you're not talking about the kids in this family."

"I want to know what you think of the marketing idea," he said.

"It's good, as long as y'all interact with her. You could build this up and sell plenty," I said with a piercing look.

"It's the trust you don't like," he said.

"It's the trust you won't do," I said.

"It's a great idea," Shelly said. "Interactive Wilma the bear. I'll call Marcy and the people who handle the social sites. *True Love* comes to life."

"I want the cost and sell comparison before Wednesday. See how soon you can get the sets. Hopefully, we can push these by California." Teddy looked at her.

"With no trust," I said.

"I vote yes on the trust," Thad said and laid his hand on Cullen's shoulder.

"Me too," Kyle said.

"I agree." Susan nodded.

"So, do I," Mark confirmed.

"It's an awesome idea," Keith stated.

"Wonderful. We split it like the merchandise sales," Teddy said, and I shook my head.

"These kids are going to need an education, Beth. You know that better than anyone in this room next to Shelly. You two are the ones who have completed college thus far. Education is not cheap, and these kids could benefit from this," Kyle said.

"What about the millions of other children in this world, Kyle? I don't know what the future holds for these babies, but I'll work my fingers to the bone to make sure they have an education," I said.

"This will make the funds easier to come by," Mark explained. "My portion is going to an educational trust for my kids, Shelly, and Marcy set up."

"As far as other children go, we donate to different educational charities as it is," Teddy said.

I stared at him. My family became one of his projects and charity cases. I didn't want him or the band members to care for the people who are my responsibility.

"Excuse me for a minute." I walked to the back porch to control my anger.

I lit a cigarette, and Gene followed me outside. He, too, lit a cigarette.

"Teddy's done this for all our kids and others. This is who he is," Gene said as he stood next to me.

Pride took hold of me. A single tear ran down my cheek. It was not his responsibility to take care of my babies.

"It bothers me," I said.

"You're a strong woman, honey," he said and laid his big hand on my shoulder. "Along with all your other wonderful traits, you're also humble. Turn around and look at those kids, Beth. This is about those people."

I watched them through the glass doors. The kids laughed and took pictures with everyone while Shelly, Teddy, and Kyle huddled in the corner of the room. Shelly drew something on her tablet, and Kyle pointed to it as he spoke with her. Teddy looked out the window. He patted Kyle on the back then joined us on the porch. I turned my back to him.

"I made you cry," Teddy said and embraced me.

"She's a different one," Gene said, then laid his hand on my head. "You'll be okay, honey. You're a B minus with me." He left us and rejoined everyone in the house.

"Thank you for the thought of my family, but I don't want this." I composed myself and stepped away from Teddy. "If the bears sell, donate that portion to others. Please?"

"You think this is a handout."

"I can take care of my own," I calmly said.

"Your own." He cocked his head while he stared at me. "You're my Wilma. Therefore, you deserve this. I knew you wouldn't take the money outright, so I thought of the trust. If we don't sell any, then no big deal, but if we do, think of what you could offer the kids. Financial help for a good education."

"You guys would be offering them. Not me," I said.

"Do you have to control everything?"

"No, but we're not a charity case. I've raised these kids to stand on their own two feet, which includes taking care of their babies. Sometimes they stumble, but I'm a pretty good catcher," I informed him loudly.

"Who catches you?" he asked. "Did Alan share any of your burdens? Did you make all the decisions without him backing you?"

"I'm asking you to leave us out of the trust. It's no big deal." I lowered my voice. "I owe you a lot as it is, so no more."

"Why are you keeping up with that?"

"I won't owe anyone. I have to make payments to you for the cards alone, so there is no way I can afford to pay back a trust," I said.

"You don't owe me a damn dime," he said offensively. "I wouldn't be here if I didn't want to be." He held my shoulders. "What was your marriage like? I know he didn't physically abuse you, but was he a part of your life?" I blazed a glare at him as he studied my eyes. "He didn't support you at all," he said as a matter of fact.

I jerked away from him and said, "Alan never took an interest in the decisions I had to make. I'm the one who works long hours to make a buck to pay for this house. I'm the one who comes up with the money to help make Sadie's tuition or cover an extra expense if the kids can't. I make sure everyone has food on their table, and their rent paid. Nancy and Scott do the same damn thing. We work together to help provide for the entire family."

"We aren't rich by any means, but we survive. My job is to make sure we can. It's not yours, and it wasn't Alans." I stepped into his personal space and backed him against the railing. "I can take care of my own family, so I don't need any handouts or sympathy from anyone."

"You think this gesture is a sign of weakness," he said and stared into my eyes. "Your strong and carry the weight of the family on your shoulders." He grabbed my hands and held them against his chest. "Life is not a burden for you alone to carry. You can share it with me."

"We haven't spent enough time together to know one another," I said.

"I'm learning about you. I know where this wall comes from," he said.

"Am I nothing but a challenge to you?" I snapped and pulled my hands from his. "I let you in, Teddy. I let you see my world and came close in giving you my heart, then you do this shit, making me feel like a needy person."

"You're not. I need you to trust me enough to lean on me and me on you," he said. "You don't know how to let anyone take care of you because you're too damn busy taking care of others. This is why you're deemed, Godfather Junior. You don't shop for yourself or take time out for you because you don't know how. You worry about everyone else, but yourself."

"I added to this wall last night, and I'm sorry. It was another time you had to take care of someone. I got aggravated by how you won't open your eyes. I don't want to think about leaving you, so I found a bottle to relieve the idea of you not being in arms reach. I should have connected the dots, but it took, until now, to see it. Never again will I put you in a situation where you will have to take care of me. I want to be here for you, but I need you to let me," he said.

"I don't need help from you or anyone," I grumbled.

He stepped into my space, placed his hands on my cheeks, and held my gaze. He leaned in to kiss me, but I pulled my head back. I wanted him out of my life, so I wouldn't feel the heartache of losing him. I didn't want or need his support, the media, or even to fight with Carissa for his affections.

"You're not running from me," he whispered, and his soft full lips touched mine.

My heart stopped for a second. The electric charge coursed through my body as chills ran down my spine. My anger softened, and my yearning grew. I wrapped my arms around his waist, pulled our bodies close, and gave in to his passionate kiss. I wanted to melt into his heart and give him mine, but I was scared.

"I won't break your heart," he said.

He kissed me once again and held me tight. I closed my eyes and wanted to stay in his arms, but my thoughts snapped me back to reality.

"I can't," I said.

"That's the damn wall, Beth. Forget about everyone and everything for a second." His embrace tightened around me. "How do you feel?"

I pushed him back and asked, "What about Carissa and the other women? Helper and your control issue? We don't blend."

"You won't let it go. You analyze everything. What will it take for me to convince you that I want you?"

"I don't know," I said. "I can't give you what you're looking for, and I'm not going to hold you back."

"I've been looking for you. I don't care about Carissa or the other women. We'll find out who Helper is and stop the texts. My control issue is as bad as yours, but we'll work through it."

"I don't want the drama or hand-outs," I said.

I searched his brown eyes again. I felt like he reached deep into my soul and begged me to hand him my world. My heart told me to give Teddy a chance, but my head said, stop. No more. I struggled with myself. Do I want to give him a chance and hand him my heart?

"One day at a time, Teddy," I said and gave in.

"Deal." He smiled then kissed me again.

He guided me into the house. Once we opened the door, all eyes were on us, which made me blush.

"I thought the earth moved," Shelly smiled.

"I want to thank everyone for the kindness you guys have shown to us. The educational trust is a wonderful gesture, and I hope y'all sell the crap out of those bears," I said in defeat.

"That's the plan," Teddy said and embraced me.

"Beth four, Teddy seven," Gene said.

"He gets no more," I said, and Teddy laughed.

"Why didn't we think of this before… Teddy bear?" Shelly asked.

"You're funny. It's not like I hadn't heard that before," he said.

Danielle leaned into me and said, "I saw you, Mom. You two were glowing."

"Danielle's right," Lucy said.

"Leave me alone, guys," I said.

"My mom is dating, *The Teddy*," Lucy said.

"Are we?" Teddy asked and smiled.

"No. Not officially," I said. "Maybe I should have hesitated in thought before I answered."

Everyone laughed, then Gene said, "I hate to break up the fun, but we need to pack and load."

"I want to show Beth something before we go," Teddy held my hand.

"Oh, I bet," Mark said.

"You two keep the door open. We leave in twenty minutes," Shelly said.

"It's been a while for Teddy. All he needs is two," Mark teased.

"That's what Ginger says about you," Teddy said to him then led me into the spare room.

My three guitars stood in the corner. He reached for one.

"I thought you wouldn't have these unless you wanted to learn to play, so I restrung them. They're ready," he said.

"Thanks. I wanted to learn but never had the time," I said.

He played one to show me they were in tune.

"Sit on the bed for a second." He handed me the acoustic guitar, held the electric, and sat next to me. "I know your busy, but I'm going to teach you to play. You have talent, so you need to learn."

"Show me," I said.

"These are three standard cords. Strum these for fifteen minutes a day. By next weekend, you should be able to move from cord to cord fluently." He sounded like a teacher.

"Okay," I said and played the cords for him.

He smiled while I moved my fingers against the strings. I messed up.

"I'll get it."

"I know, babe." He sat the electric guitar in its stand.

I laid the guitar on the bed and stared at him. My heart broke with the idea of him not being near.

"You stalked your way into my life." A knot formed in my throat as he embraced me.

"You sound surprised," he said.

"I am. It's hard to watch a friend leave," I said.

"We're more than that," he reminded me. "We'll speak every day, and you and the family come to my house for Thanksgiving."

"I'll think about it," I said.

"No thinking, Beth. Tell me you will," he said.

"Sorry, but we need to be going," Gene said, standing in the doorway.

Teddy and I walked out of the room and the house, arm in arm. We walked to the vehicles, and I stepped out of Teddy's grasp.

"Will we see you Thanksgiving?" Thad asked.

"You might," I said.

"If you need a job as a singer, come join us," Mark said.

"I'll keep my day job," I said and hugged him. I embraced Susan and said, "If these guys get out of line, call me."

"I might take you up on the offer," she said.

"Anytime, Susan," I said.

"Take care of her, Kyle," I said then embraced him.

"Thank you, Beth. I'm glad Teddy found his happiness," he said then kissed my cheek.

I walked to Rick, held my arms out, and said, "You can celebrate leaving after you give me a hug."

"I'm not going to celebrate." He lightly hugged me. "You're a nice lady, Beth."

"I like you, too, Rick." I smiled.

The group and my kids hugged and shook hands with one another. Helen stood in Thad's arms while Cullen spoke with them. I walked to Shelly then, we embraced.

"Call me, even if it's to blow off steam. I'm here for you," I said.

"It's not bye forever," she said.

"Not between us," I said.

"Shopping at Thanksgiving?" she asked, which made us laugh.

I walked to Gene, hugged him, and whispered, "You're my favorite."

He squeezed me tight and said, "You're mine, honey. Thanks for running into me."

Teddy held Sadie and spoke with Lucy and Danielle. Gene led me to him. Teddy stood Sadie, but Kyle quickly grabbed her up and made her laugh. Teddy took me in his arms, squeezed me tight, and swayed us.

"Get in the car, and I'll buy you anything you want or need. No packing, no anything, just come with me," he said.

"I can't," I said.

He stared into my eyes for a minute and said, "Thanksgiving then."

"Call or text me to let me know you made it, okay," I said.

He nodded, and we walked to the car, arm in arm. Everyone sat in the vehicles and waited for him. He spun me to face him, placed his hands on my cheeks, and studied my eyes.

"I met my best friend," he said then kissed me hard before he let me go. "Thanksgiving." He kissed his fingers, held them in a peace sign, and sat in the SUV.

The cars pulled away, then we went into the house. The girls helped me finish the cleanup process. We visited until the babies, and Sadie grew tired. I bid my goodbyes, exchanged hugs, and shut the door after them. I leaned against the door, looked at the dogs, and listened to the silence, fill the house.

I showered and crawled under the bedsheets with Izzy and Olly by my side. I turned on the TV, and my phone rang.

"Hey," I answered.

"Hey, babe," Teddy said but sounded different.

"What's wrong?" I asked.

"I miss you," he said.

"Bull," I chuckled. "Did you just get in?"

"I've been here long enough to unpack, shower, and now lying in bed," he said.

"What are you wearing?" I smiled.

"Sheets."

"Are they green with yellow duckies?" I asked.

"No. They're white with blue bunnies," he said with a laugh, then repeated. "Man, I miss you."

"I'm right here," I said. "Have you seen Max?"

"Yes. He's curled up at my feet."

"Pet him from me," I said.

"When I unpacked, I found a T-shirt among my things. Shelly said she snuck it in there for you. Thank you."

"You're welcome. It's lame, but it's hard to shop for a person like you."

"I can think of other places to hide in a bikini," he said.

"I bet you could," I said, recalling me writing on the shirt *a bikini didn't have pockets*.

"I could with you wearing one," he said and made me nervously chuckle. I felt better with distance between us. "I have an idea."

"You want to go race car driving?" I asked.

"That would be fun, but no, Ms. Random," he laughed. "You could fly to Seattle, Friday evening after work. Stay with me until Sunday, then back to work on Monday."

"No, I can't," I sang the words. "The guys are coming Saturday to help me cut trees, and I have a bench to finish before Thanksgiving."

"Are you coming?" He sounded like a little boy.

"If you want me to."

"That's great," he said excitedly. "Thanksgiving can't get here quick enough."

"This will give us time to figure things out, but it's okay if you feel the need to forget about me."

"And the control is back," he said.

"You know I'm right."

"I don't want to talk about this right now. Let me hold on to the idea, I'll see you in November."

"Maybe," I said, missing him.

"Remember that I will be calling you."

"I might not answer," I teased.

"You will, but I need to ask a favor from you."

"I won't sleep with you for a million dollars, Teddy. Quit beggin." I smiled.

"You wouldn't accept a million dollars. If you would, I can be back in Arkansas in two and a half hours with my checkbook," he said.

"What do you want, Nafton?" I laughed.

"For you to call me every day when you leave the office, then when you get home."

"I won't be watched like a hawk," I said.

"How about text when you leave the office, then call me when you get home."

"That's still being watched like a hawk." I laughed. "We sound like adolescents having to keep track with one another." I shook my head at the thought of being sixteen again.

"It's either that or I hire someone to sit with you," Teddy said.

"You're being paranoid, or you're not telling me something. What is it?" I asked.

"She texted other people to persuade me to leave you alone. She's pressing everyone for information about you." He sounded upset. "They said they wouldn't talk, but the dreams also concern me. What do they mean?"

"They don't mean anything. I'll be okay, and we aren't together anymore. That should make her happy," I said.

"It doesn't make me happy. You need to be by my side," he said sadly.

"Can't," I said. "Now that we're apart, the dreams will stop. We'll be okay."

"I hope your right. We have a life to build together," he said.

"As friends," I said.

"For the time being," he said, then we spoke to one another until early-morning hours.

Chapter 22

Teddy and I spoke to one another, several times a day as if we were never separated. It relaxed me to hear his voice. He kept me informed about the rehearsals and how Shelly found a company to make the bears for the tour.

I sent him pictures of Waldorf lying in bed with the dogs or him sitting on the back porch. Whoever ran his social sites and web page, created a love storyline between the bears and used a few of my snapshots.

Saturday arrived, and I thought about Teddy's performance. I wanted to be there to enjoy the music, but I was stuck at the house to cut trees. I reluctantly pulled myself out of bed and let the dogs out for their morning routine. I changed into old black sweat pants and a gray T-shirt.

I retrieved my chainsaw, filled it with bar oil and gas. I waited for Ellis and Colby, but after a few minutes, I was antsy to get the trees cut. I walked into the woods with chainsaw in hand, and the dogs followed. The machine vibrated as the chain whirled, and I cut a tree.

After it fell, Mom and Dad arrived on the Kubota. Dad yelled at me for cutting by myself. Ellis drove his four-wheeler with Colby on his and met us in the woods. We weren't far from the house, so we left the first tree lying on the ground and walked to the next.

The second tree was thirty feet from the back shed. The guys and I spoke about which way I was to cut, and my phone rang. I pulled it from my pocket.

"Good afternoon," I said.

"Hey, babe," Teddy said.

"You sound sleepy."

"I haven't slept well this last week."

"It's the late-night rehearsals," I said.

"I'm used to those," he said sadly. "What are you doing?"

"Cutting trees."

"Do you have someone with you?" He sounded concerned.

"Yes. Ellis, Colby, Mom, and Dad."

"My lumberjack, Beth."

"I have three to finish before dark, so please call after the party tonight, and we'll talk," I said.

"No. Call me when you finish," he said.

"You'll be performing."

"I don't care. Call me."

"Explain that to thousands of people. You would be on stage in the middle of a song when your phone rings. You would say, 'Excuse me thousands and thousands of people, but I have to take this call.'" I smiled.

"Don't think I wouldn't," he laughed. "They would wait for me. I know how to bring people to their feet and show them a good time."

"I know, baby. I've seen it," I said.

"Did you call me, baby?" he asked.

"Crap," I said. "I meant darlin', honey, sugar, or anything else."

"Yeah, right, babe. You like me," he sang.

"That was a slip of the tongue," I chuckled.

"I like that…and the word," he snickered.

"You better stop." I blushed.

"Why aren't you with me?" he asked.

"You know the answer," I said.

"MOOOMM," Lucy yelled from in front of the house.

"Can you hold on for a moment?" I asked him. I held the phone from my ear and yelled, "WHAT?"

"MOOOOMM!" Lucy screamed.

"Lucy is yelling, so we're headed to the front of the house. I'll call you back," I said, and we walked in the direction of her voice.

"Is she okay?" he asked.

"MOOOOMM!" Danielle joined Lucy and screamed.

"Now Danielle is screaming," I said.

I stepped around the corner of the house. Lucy was crying and standing next to Danielle, who was bent over in front of the car. Olly sat next to her.

"Come quick. Run," Lucy shouted through tears.

I gripped my phone, ran to them, and Danielle looked up at me. A white fur pile laid next to Lucy's tire. I dropped the phone and landed on the ground next to Izzy.

"I'm sorry, Mom," Lucy said hysterically. "She appeared out of nowhere."

"Oh, my God," I exclaimed.

Izzy raised her head, looked at me with her dark coal eyes, and I placed my hand on her chest. She tried to stand but fell.

"It's her back legs," Danielle said as she stroked Izzy's face.

"What time is it?" I asked.

"1:20," Ellis said and hugged Lucy while she cried.

"Danielle, call Dr. Wilton. Tell him what's going on and ask where I need to take her." Danielle made the phone call, then I said, "Lucy, please go in my room and get her blanket. It's the red and white one in her bed."

Ellis and Colby got the kids out of the car. I held Izzy's head in my lap, stroked her fur, while tears came to my eyes. I spoke with her while Dad scooped Olly into his arms.

"Teddy doesn't want to hang up until he speaks with you," Mom said and held my phone toward me.

Lucy ran full speed out of the house with the blanket, and Danielle said, "Let's go. Dr. Wilton is waiting."

"I'm coming with you," Lucy said, handed me the blanket, and took my phone from Mom.

I covered Izzy, then gently picked her up, which made her whine with pain. She wrapped her front legs around my arm as if she hugged me. She licked my arm while I settled her against my body.

"Somebody drive me," I said.

"Get in my car. Ellis and Colby can stay with the kids," Danielle said in an ordering tone.

We loaded in the car. Izzy laid in my lap and whimpered. I looked out the back window and made sure Sadie and Kara were with Ellis on the porch. Colby held Gabi while Dad held Olly. Mom stood next to Dad as we drove off. Lucy handed me the phone.

"I'll call you back, Teddy," I said.

"Don't hang up. I'm staying on the line until this is over."

His words brought tears to my eyes. I wished he was next to me. I needed his strength.

Lucy pet Izzy on the head, leaned into her, and said, "I'm sorry." She looked at me with tear-soaked eyes, and Izzy licked her hand.

"It's okay, sweetie. It was an accident, and she's going to be fine," I said as tears rolled down my cheeks.

"Do you want me to speak to Lucy? Maybe I can calm her," Teddy said.

"Please." I handed the phone to her.

I'm Dr. Wilton's accountant, and he's been my family's veterinarian for thirty plus years. He and his wife, Mary, the receptionist, knew both dogs and me well. Olly came from them.

Danielle drove to the front door of the clinic, where Dr. Wilton waited. He ran to the car, and I stepped out with Izzy in my arms. He guided me toward the door into the clinic.

"I don't want to move her much, Beth. Bring her back here," he said and led me to a room with an x-ray machine.

He helped me place her on the metal table. Mary came to my side and patted my shoulders to console me.

"I'm going to sedate her, so we can x-ray. I'll let you see her in about ten minutes," Dr. Wilton said.

"Fix her, Peter. Please?" I asked as tears streamed from my eyes.

"Go with, Mary," he nodded at me.

She led us into an examination room, shut the door behind her, and left us alone. Lucy handed me the phone.

"Hey," I said.

"I can leave…" Teddy said.

"You can't go anywhere." I snapped. "I'm sorry, Teddy. I need Izzy well. She needs to be home with me. Why didn't I put them in the pen this morning? They usually don't run from me."

"This was an accident," he said.

"Cars went in and out of the driveway for days, then today. Why today? What the hell have I done to deserve this?" I blamed myself.

The other door opened. Peter stepped inside, and I handed the phone to Danielle. He motioned for us to follow him to the x-ray room. Izzy laid motionless on the metal table. Blood stained a patch of white fur on her shoulder. I placed my hand on her head and stared at her chest until her side rose and fell.

"I gave her something to ease the pain, so we can move her to take x-rays. The majority of the damage is in her back legs, but I won't know the extent until I see inside. She'll need stitches on a few small cuts here and here." He pointed to several places on her body.

Izzy didn't lift her head but searched for someone with her big dark coal eyes. I came face-to-face with her and kissed her head as tears fell from my eyes, onto her face. I wiped them off her while the girls gently pet her, then I said a prayer for her.

"I'll meet you in the examination room when I have the film developed," he said and laid his hand on my shoulder.

"Okay." I kissed Izzy's head.

The girls led me to the room. I looked at my sawdust-covered pants.

"I'm stepping out for a minute and brush this stuff off," I said.

Danielle handed the phone back to me, and the speaker button was pushed. I forgot Teddy was holding, so I took him off speaker, and opened the door.

"I can't believe you've been on the phone this whole time," I said to him.

"I'm not going anywhere," he said.

"I'm going to step out and get this dust off. Did I track it in?" I asked Mary as I walked to the front door.

"You're okay. I'll get you when Peter is ready for you," she said.

I nodded, walked outside, then around to the side of the building. Images of Izzy's dark coal eyes, being scared and searching for someone, stayed in my mind. I held the phone to my ear and cried.

"I need to be there, Beth," Teddy said.

"No, you don't. She's just a dog, Teddy. At least, it wasn't one of the kids, but why in the hell am I this upset? I can't stop crying," I said.

"She holds a piece of your heart," he said.

I pulled cigarettes out of my pocket and lit one to settle my nerves. My left knee burned when I wiped the sawdust from my pants. I dismissed my injury and thought of Izzy.

"They usually stay near me when I'm in the woods. Why did I screw up and not lock them in the pen? It's my fault," I said.

"This was an accident," he reiterated.

"What the hell are you doing on the phone with me? You have a concert tonight and don't need this on your mind. Focus on the people who paid good money to see you," I became angry at him for caring. "Thank you, but go away, Teddy. I can take care of this on my own."

"Let me worry about the concert. I need to focus on you right now."

"No, you don't. Get your head in the game. We got this." I put my cigarette out and walked into the clinic.

"You're not mad at me, but the situation and I'm not leaving you," he said sternly.

Mary smiled while I walked past her and entered the examination room. I mustered a smile for the girls, but tears lightly fell from my eyes.

"I'm sorry. I appreciate you caring, but now I feel like crap how you're listening to this instead of doing your job."

"I care about you and the kids," he said. "Put me on speaker."

I hit the button and looked at Lucy, who sat in a corner chair. I tightly embraced her.

"I'm sorry, Mommy."

I smiled at the thought of her calling me mommy when she thought she did something wrong, or she wanted something.

"It was an accident. I should have locked them up, so don't blame yourself," I said.

"You're bleeding." Danielle gasped and pointed to the floor.

"What?" Teddy asked from the phone.

A few drops of blood were on the floor. I raised my black pant leg.

"I'm okay. I scraped my knee on the gravel," I said.

Danielle handed me tissues. I cleaned the floor then she handed me more. In the middle of road rash across my right knee cap, an inch long, deep gash, seeped blood. It streaked my shin, stained my white sock, and dripped on my tennis shoe before it reached the floor.

"You people are going to turn me gray," Teddy said.

"Hey, guys," Shelly said from the phone. "I'm sorry about Izzy. Any word?"

"You told her?" I asked.

"Yes, and I just told Gene," he said.

"Hey, honey. I'm sorry," he said.

"I can't believe you, Teddy. It's not that big of a deal," I said, and the doorknob turned. "Hold on."

Peter walked into the room. "We have the x-rays." I held a tissue on my knee with one hand and cleaned my leg with another. "Let me see, Beth."

"I'm okay. What about Izzy?" I asked with wide eyes.

"Let me look at your knee," Peter ordered.

I raised the tissue. He walked out of the room then returned with peroxide and a few bandages. He guided me to a chair and placed my leg over a trash can. He poured the peroxide on the cuts, and it bubbled.

"Great. Now you're going to charge me for this, huh."

"Six hundred bucks for a Band-Aid. Isn't that the price of my taxes?" he asked sarcastically and walked to the sink.

I snickered as he wet a paper towel, placed it on my skin, and applied pressure on the wound. He glanced at my phone, which laid on the examination table.

"Can you hear me okay, Mr. Nafton?" Peter asked.

"Yes, sir," Teddy said.

"Damn it," I exclaimed.

"Too much pressure?" Peter asked.

"No. I didn't think you needed to know about Teddy," I said.

"Hold that on the cut."

He moved my hand onto the paper towel. He walked to a wall box, flipped a switch to turn on the light, and placed two x-rays side by side.

"She took the brunt of the hit in her back legs. Her left leg is fractured, but she has a crushed right leg." He faced me. "She needs a few stitches in her chest and shoulder, but I'm worried about her back leg."

Tears streamed down my face once again. He removed the paper towel from my knee and replaced it with a fresh, clean one. He held it on my wound and looked me in the eyes.

"I don't see any internal bleeding, and her organs look intact, but she's badly hurt." He continued. "I can amputate her leg, and we can fix the fracture. I can't guarantee she'll survive even if I do the surgery, but it might be worth a shot."

"I don't give a shit if you take all her legs, and she lives, Peter. Please fix her."

"You need a few stitches in this knee." He patted my leg, left the room for a second then returned with ointment. He applied it to my wound, and asked, "How much are you willing to spend to save this dog's life? It could get costly."

"How much are we talking?" I asked while he placed a gauze bandage on my knee.

"We aren't worried about the money, Dr. Wilton. When can you do the procedure?" Teddy asked.

"No, Teddy." I snapped.

"For argument's sake, it will be a loan to you, Beth," he said forcefully. "Dr. Wilton?"

"Please call me, Peter. I need to get her stitched and remove the leg within the next thirty minutes."

"What's the percentage of her making it?" I asked with hope.

"I don't know. If she were my dog, I would say to take the leg, and let's see what we have. It's a good sign, I don't see internal bleeding," he said and wrapped more gauze around my leg.

"Thank you." I lowered my pants leg and asked, "How long will she stay here?"

"She could go home by Monday late afternoon if everything goes well. You'll need to watch Olly around her for several days. She'll be on pain medicine and needs rest. You'll have to help her up and down the stairs until the cast on the other leg comes off, which would be about four weeks," he explained.

"I can help her," I said.

"Let's get her through surgery and see what we have. Keep in mind, this is not a guarantee. We need to get her through recovery as well," he said.

"I'll carry her in a papoose if I have to," I said.

"You guys talk about it, and I'm going to see Mary for a minute. Let me get you an estimated price on all this," he said.

He closed the door, and I immediately said, "You're not paying for this, Teddy."

"We'll work out payment arrangements on this. Let's focus on saving her," he said.

"I'm scared of the interest you're going to charge."

"You should. How's your knee?"

"It burns, but it'll be okay," I said.

"How are you feeling, Lucy?" Teddy asked.

"I'm sorry for all this," she said.

"It was an accident, and it's a good chance she'll make it," I said.

"Danielle? How about you, sweetie?" Teddy asked.

"Fine," she said and wiped her eyes.

"Danielle has been our rock through all this," I said and hugged her.

"I've been listening. You have some strong women, babe," he said, then Peter joined us.

"All right, guys. It's not going to be cheap, but we can barter some of it," he said.

"What does 'not cheap' mean?" I asked.

"Twelve to fifteen hundred. That's with a discount because of you being you."

"Do it, please," Teddy said.

"I wish we could have met under better circumstances, Mr. Nafton," Peter said.

"Me too, sir. Take care of our Izzy," he said.

"I will," he said into the phone. "Beth, go home, wash the knee, and if it's still bleeding, get stitches. I'll call you after surgery to let you know how she did. Do you want to see her before you leave?"

"Yes, please," I said.

We three followed him to the x-ray room, where she laid in the same spot. Her eyes were closed, but I bent to her. I came nose to nose, rubbed my hand across her soft, white, fluffy body, and cried again.

I whispered in her ear, "I love you, my princess." I kissed her black nose and laid my head on hers. "You're my sunshine, and I'll love you always, with three legs or four. You come home to me in a few days."

Danielle and Lucy rubbed their hands gently across her body while I stroked her face. More tears fell from my eyes. I kissed her again, walked out of the room, and took my phone from Danielle.

"I'll call you in a few hours," Peter said and patted my shoulder.

"Thank you for what you do, also for fixing my knee." I smiled at him through tears.

We walked to the front. Mary embraced me.

"We'll take care of her, Beth."

"Thank you, Mary," I said.

I placed the phone to my ear after I took it off speaker. "All right, Teddy. Please focus on the concert."

"I will later. How's your knee?"

"It's fine. My heart hurts worse over a dog," I said.

"I'm sorry I didn't have bubble wrap the other day."

"It'll be okay, right?"

"Yes. You can take her everywhere you go. You'll bring both dogs when you come to my house. We'll get them little suitcases for their bones and blankets." He tried to encourage me.

"I forgot her blanket. Lucy, call Mary and ask her to put Izzy's blanket with her," I said.

"Okay," she said and reached for the phone.

"Thank you, Teddy," I said.

"What can I do for you to make this easier? I want to help," Teddy said.

"There's nothing except, is it stupid to pray for a dog?" I asked.

"No. We've all been doing that since we heard."

"She'll be okay," Shelly said.

"Thanks, Shelly. I feel silly I'm this emotional," I said.

"We've all suffered over something or someone we love. It doesn't matter if she is a dog, she's a big part of your life, honey. You, Olly, and her roam that house. They are who you come home to at night," Gene said.

"Thanks, Gene," I said. "Please focus on the concert now. Teddy, get some rest and Shelly, get your tablet ready. Gene, protect him, and please get him to focus."

"Call me as soon as you speak to Peter," Teddy said as Shelly and Gene chuckled.

"I will."

"Love you, Beth," Shelly said.

"Love you, Shelly," I said.

"Bye, honey," Gene said.

"Take care of Teddy," I said.

"I'm good," Teddy said. "Beth?"

"What, baby," I said.

He exaggerated a deep breath before he said, "Call me."

"I will. Peace," I said as we arrived at the house.

"Peace," he said, then hung up.

"What's he doing here?" I asked and pointed to the familiar blue truck.

"We called Dad when you went outside. We thought he would want to know about Izzy. He spent time with her, Mom," Lucy explained.

I rolled my eyes with the thought of seeing him then said, "Before y'all get out, I want to thank you both for being with me today. It means a lot to me that you guys were by my side."

"I never meant to hurt her," Lucy said.

"I know. I don't blame you. I've accidentally hit a few animals in my time," I said. "Have y'all said anything to your father about Teddy?"

"No," Lucy said.

"I haven't, but I can't guarantee the guys haven't," Danielle stated.

"Okay," I said.

We walked into the house, and Olly jumped on my legs. I petted his head and glanced into his eyes, which brought tears to mine. Izzy should be here to jump on me. Will she be able to do that with three legs?

"Hey, Beth. I hope you don't mind me coming, but the girls called. They said you were cutting, so I thought you would need help," Alan said.

He stood from the table. He wore jeans, which had a few holes in the legs and an old rusty red T-shirt. His dark blond hair fell to his shoulders and shook as he spoke.

"Thank you, but we can manage," I said.

"How is she?" Colby asked.

"I'm waiting on Peter to call after surgery," I said.

I plugged the charger into the phone, then walked to the front porch. I lit a cigarette, then Alan joined me. He lit a cigarette and stared at the tree line.

"I like Izzy. She slept at my feet, on the couch, when you worked tax season," he said.

"I caught you two several times."

"I'm sorry this happened," he said.

"Thanks, but can you speak to your daughter? I don't want her to feel guilty. I tell her it was an accident, but she's carrying weight, I can't take off her shoulders," I said.

"Maybe you're not supposed to take it," he said.

He looked at me with a side glance as he squinted his deep-blue eyes. I almost said something, but Sadie joined us on the porch.

"Where's Izzy?" she asked.

"At the doctor. They have to remove one of her legs," I explained.

"That's what Mama said." She hugged my hips.

"We'll help Izzy when she comes home. Right?" Alan asked.

"Right, Pop," she said.

"Can you draw her a pretty picture?" he asked.

"I sure can," she said and bounced into the house.

He looked at me and said, "I'll talk to Lucy, then cut the other trees if you want to work on the ones from this morning."

"Okay," I said.

He retreated inside and shut the door. That moment, my feelings changed for him.

He was a good man, a wonderful father, and grandfather. I cared and respected him, but knew I wasn't in love with him any longer. He was a friend, but I was happy to live my life without his disapproving glares.

I walked inside. Danielle and Lucy sat next to Alan while he played with Gabi and Kara. Sadie laid on the floor and drew. I stepped over her to check the charge on my phone.

"Whenever you guys are ready," I said and unplugged the phone.

I walked outside as everyone followed. Alan pointed to the log bench while I checked the gas in the chainsaw.

"When did you do that?" he asked.

"Last weekend." I gathered the bar oil and gas.

"Let me look at this thing," he said.

He walked from the porch to the yard and examined it. I rolled my eyes and waited for the negative statement to come from his lips. After a few minutes, I was not disappointed.

"Didn't you take too much off this one seat? It's not level," he complained, then pointed. "It needs to be sanded."

"It's not supposed to be level for rain run-off, and I'm not finished with it," I smirked and thought he would never change. He criticized everything I did.

"You gonna sell it?"

"She already did," Lucy said and handed out glasses of tea.

"No, I didn't. I gave it away," I said.

"I guess it's okay," he said.

My phone rang, and I answered, "Hey. How is she?"

"Hey," Peter said. "She made it through surgery, and she drank a little water. Her left leg is in a cast, and her right was beyond repairable, so I took it. I'm going to give her another hour of recovery then she's coming home with me. I can watch her better at the house."

"Thank you, Peter. I appreciate everything you've done." I felt relieved.

"We aren't out of the woods, Beth. I need her to eat, drink, and use the bathroom before I let her go home. I don't know how she's going to do overnight, but she'll be with me. I'll call you on Monday to give you a progress report. No news is good news tomorrow," he said.

"I hope I don't speak to you until Monday. Thank you, Peter," I said before we bid our goodbyes.

Everyone waited for me to tell them about her. I explained what the doctor said, then stepped from the group and called Teddy.

"Well?"

"She made it through surgery," I said, relieved.

"Good. Now what?"

"If he doesn't call tomorrow, and she shows improvement, I get her Monday. No news is good news, so I hope I don't hear from him."

"Me too, babe," he said.

"Are you ready?" I paced the far end of the porch, away from everyone.

"Yeah. I'm putting you on speaker."

"Hey," everyone said.

"Hey, guys. Are y'all ready for tonight?"

"About as ready as we're going to be," Thad said.

"We're sorry about Izzy, but she'll be all right," Kyle said.

"Thanks, Kyle, but she's just a dumb ol' dog," I wanted to keep the mood light for them.

"No, she isn't. She's your baby, but she'll be okay," Susan said.

"Don't ever think of Izzy as a dumb ol' dog," Mark said.

"Thanks for the support, everyone. You guys are awesome. Please have a wonderful concert," I said.

"We'll be thinking of you," Kyle said.

"Thank you," I said.

"Hold on," Teddy said. I waited for a second, and his voice became clearer. "How are you doing?"

"I'm good. How are you?" I asked.

"I want to be with you," he said.

"You were, and I thank you," I said.

"Not like that, but I'm always here for you," he said.

"Alan's here," I blurted. "The girls called him about Izzy. He came out to help finish the trees. What it boils down it is, he and June want firewood."

"You two have a lot of history, and he'll always be a part of your life," he said.

"I know, but I looked at him differently today," I said. "A few weeks ago, he was an old lover. It hurt when I saw him with June, but today, he's only a friend. I have no feelings left for him except respect for being a good father and grandfather."

"Does he know about me?" he asked.

"If he does, he hasn't said anything."

"I'm going to have to meet him," he said.

"No, you won't. Are you going to call me before you go on?" I asked.

"Yes, ma'am."

"Good," I said.

"I don't want to hang up."

"You have to go to work, so peace, baby."

"Peace," he said.

I sat by the firepit with my energy drained. I drank the last of my tea, and Alan pointed to the small chainsaw.

"Where did you get that?"

"Friends," I said.

"Friends buy you chainsaws, huh." He sat next to me and looked at the kids. They didn't say a word, but went into the house at the same time and left Alan and I alone, "Was this friend Teddy Nafton?"

"They told you?" I stared into the woods, numb from today's events.

"Sadie told me bits and pieces of Teddy and the band members. When she said Teddy, I knew it was Nafton. You've been a fan of his since I've known you. The kids confirmed it was Five/Ten. How did you meet them?"

I told him a vague version of how we met then explained they left a few days ago. I came to my senses and asked, "Why am I telling you this?"

"You and I both know you can't shit in this family without everyone knowing. I was going to find out, but I'm amazed its' Teddy Nafton. He has models and superstars falling all over him, so what would he want with a country hick from Arkansas?" he asked, and I gave him a go-to-hell look. "Where is Romeo now? Was that him, you were talking to a few minutes ago?"

"Yes, and he's in Seattle. We're only friends."

"I'm glad you recognize that. It would be like mixing peanut butter with caviar. You being the crunchy nutty peanut butter." He smiled.

I rolled my eyes at him, stood, and said, "I need to cut trees before it gets late."

"Yeah. We only have a few hours of daylight," he said.

Chapter 23

The sun shone, and alarm buzzed. I let Olly outside and stammered into the bathroom. I looked in the mirror and rubbed my puffy, swollen eyes. I washed my face, dressed for church, and was out the door within thirty minutes. The kids met me, then after service, we all returned to my house for breakfast. My spirits rose with each passing minute for Izzy to come home.

After breakfast and clothes changed, we adjourned to the back porch. We spoke about the trees. Tires crunched the gravel driveway, which indicated a car pulled up to the house. A few minutes later, the back door opened, and Alan stepped outside.

"I hope you don't mind, but June came with me to help," Alan said.

"I don't care," I said numbly.

"I figured you wouldn't," he said.

"Hey, Beth," June said.

"Hey," I said. "Are you guys ready?"

"We're going to watch you work for a little while, then Danielle and I will make dinner," Lucy said.

"Thanks," I said.

We walked to the woods, and everyone watched me cut another tree. We trimmed the limbs when I thought my phone rang. I shut the chainsaw off and pulled it from my pocket. I shook my head in disbelief, and my eyes teared.

"What's wrong?" Danielle asked.

"Peter," I said and held the phone out to her. "No news is good news."

My phone rang once again, and his name reappeared. My stomach knotted. I slid the bar on the screen and held it to my ear.

"Hello?" I squeaked.

"Beth, it's Peter," he said.

"No news is good news. I don't want to hear this," I said nervously.

"I'm sorry," he said. "She passed this morning while we were at church."

"No, she didn't, Peter," I said in disbelief, and sat on a log. I placed my hand on my chest and said, "No. I'm supposed to get her tomorrow."

"I'm sorry," he said again.

I cried hard, dropped the phone, and ran into the woods. My stomach gurgled as the vomit taste rose to my mouth. I shook with grief. Danielle ran up behind me, held my phone to her ear, and rubbed my back.

"I'm sorry, Mom, but Dr. Wilton needs to know what you want him to do with her," she said.

I looked at her as tears fell. "Make it to where she'll come home." She walked away from me and spoke with Dr. Wilton.

Lucy placed her hand on my shoulder and said, "Teddy's on the phone."

I didn't want to speak to him. I couldn't be upbeat, and I didn't want him to be concerned about me. I waved her away, sat in the leaves, and buried my face in my hands as I cried. Sadie wrapped her small arms around my neck and squeezed me tight while the others stood around us.

"I'm sorry, Beth. She was a damn good dog," Alan said and patted my shoulder.

Olly jumped on my knee, but I pushed him back and yelled, "Get away from me."

Danielle scooped him up and pulled him to her. I rocked back and forth and held Sadie. I stared at the leaves and thought of Izzy's dark eyes, searching in fear when she laid on the table.

Colby picked Sadie up out of my lap, helped me off the ground, and led me to the back porch. I sat in a chair as everyone followed. Lucy, Danielle, and the babies sat on the porch with me while June brought me water. The chainsaws echoed through the woods, and Olly laid at my feet.

I cried nonstop. In my memories, Izzy ran through the grass, to the woods, then the creek. I imagined her walking toward me, carrying a crawdad in her mouth as if she wanted to provide for me.

A picture came to my mind of us lying in bed, and our noses almost touched while we stared at each other. Her dark coal eyes, black nose, and puffy white, hair stayed in my mind's eye, whether I had them open or closed.

My phone rang, and Danielle handed it to me.

"Hey," I answered through tears.

"Hey, babe. I'm sorry," Teddy said.

"Thank you, but how was the concert?"

"Always thinking of others. How are you?"

"I don't want to bring you down with this crap. It's not your problem," I said.

"Your burden is my burden, and I know you hurt, so talk to me," he said.

"How do I stop crying?" I asked calmly.

"She was part of your fabric, and it's okay to cry," he said.

"Peter said I could bring her home in the morning. I need to find her a good place, and you need rest. I know you're tired, so please sleep. I'll call you later."

"Okay," he said, and we bid our goodbyes.

"What did Peter say?" I asked Danielle.

"He thinks a small blood clot reached her heart," she sadly explained.

Izzy returned to my thoughts, and I sat immobile on the porch. Life continued without my baby dog. Birds chirped, and squirrels ran through the trees while the sound of chainsaws hummed in the distance.

When the girls were small, we had several dogs. Alan always became angry with me when I cried over the loss of one. He said I was silly for getting attached to animals, and he couldn't understand why I became a vegetarian.

I went inside the house, washed my face, and stared at myself in the mirror. I closed my eyes, but images of my life without her flooded my thoughts. I retrieved a roll of toilet paper, went back outside, and Olly jumped at my feet. I didn't want to touch him.

I stared at the white dog. How am I going to come home to only him? She was our protector and barked at the strange armadillos and raccoons, which strayed to the porch. Olly was still a baby and didn't know how to protect me.

I looked to the tree line to think of a beautiful resting place for her. I retrieved a shovel and walked to the little hill, which led to the creek. A small clearing to the right of the rushing water would be perfect. I dug a hole and cried with every shovel of dirt.

She loved the water and often swam in the creek. If I stood on the porch and called for her, she would slowly walk up the hill, covered in mud, and dripped with water. Her head cast down, but she would stare at me with her dark eyes. She hated baths, but she never fought me when I gave her one.

"Let me do that." Alan found me in the woods.

"You have trees to cut," I said.

"We have two left, but the guys wanted to know how big to leave some logs. They said something about you carving," he explained. He stared at me and asked in an aggravated tone. "You still crying?"

"I can't stop the tears," I loudly said in a defensive voice.

"Tell the boys how big you want the logs," he said and took the shovel from my hand.

I reluctantly walked up the hill as Ellis and Colby met me at the top. I explained how big and where to place the logs then walked back to Alan. He dug for a few minutes and hit a rock. I sat on my knees, pulled the rock out of the earth, and worked with him until a deep hole was visible.

Being covered in sawdust and dirt, I stood, and Alan pointed to my gray pants leg. "You're bleeding."

Darkness loomed over our heads while night approached as we walked to the house. Alan put the shovel away while Lucy came to me.

"Can Dad and June stay for dinner? She helped cook, and I didn't want to be rude and tell them to leave."

"That's fine. I'm going to take a shower."

"You look tired." She hugged me. "I'm sorry about Izzy. Do you want me to get you another dog?"

"No."

"I get that this was my fault. I didn't mean to hurt her or you," she said as tears came to her eyes.

"No, it isn't your fault, so not another word. I love you," I said and embraced her tight as tears fell from my burning eyes.

I walked into the house, peeled my clothes off, and stepped into the shower. I unwrapped the bandage from my knee and blood poured from the cut. I reopened it while I dug rocks from the ground.

Warm water hit my wound and made it burn. Sore muscles in my back and arms made my nerves jump with shooting pain. I cried while I stood under the pulsating water, and wished this day never happened.

I tied a hand towel around my knee, dried, and hobbled into the bedroom. I dressed then walked to the porch, where Colby was building a fire in the pit.

I sat, placed my knee on the other chair, and untied the towel. Blood ran from the wound, so I wiped it when Colby went into the house. A minute later, Danielle was by my side.

"You need stitches," she said as she looked at my knee.

"No. I need a butterfly band-aid, and I don't have any," I said.

"I'll call Granny," she said.

Mom appeared on the Kubota within a few minutes of Danielle's call. She said, "I'm sorry about Izzy."

"Thanks, Mom," I said as tears streamed down my face. "How does a person have so many tears?"

"Let your body morn, Beth," she said and placed a bandage across the cut. She stared at me for a minute, then mumbled, "It begins."

"What?"

"You and Teddy. You two have been speaking and growing close."

"We're friends," I said.

"You're more." She shook her head, patted me on the shoulder, then said, "Get some rest."

"Thanks, Mommy," I slightly smiled through tears. She hugged me then left me alone on the porch.

I retrieved the phone, texted Helen to inform her I wouldn't be in the office tomorrow. My swollen eyes and tears, which lingered, blurred the letters. A few seconds later, she texted a response and admitted she knew about Izzy. She expressed her condolences and assured me she would take care of the office.

I received text after text from family members who comforted me with words of sympathy. Nancy and Scott called to console me while I cried into the phone. A person who didn't know the family would think we lost a member.

Alan joined me on the porch and stirred the fire. He asked, "How are you doing?"

"My heart hurts," I said.

"I was mad when you brought her home, but we soon bonded," he said.

"Man, I miss her." I blew my raw nose as the back door opened.

"Hey, man," Alan said.

"Hey," Teddy's sultry voice said from behind me.

I jumped to my feet and ran into his arms. I buried my face into his shoulder and cried. He held me tight and stroked my hair.

"What are you doing here? You're supposed to be going to Sacramento," I said in a muffled voice.

"I need to be here with you," he said softly.

He kissed me, and we tightly embraced. The back door opened, and voices filled the air. Gene, Rick, Shelly, and Five/Ten stood around Teddy and me.

"You can let her go," Mark said, then grabbed me from Teddy's grip and embraced me. "I'm sorry, Beth. I know how you feel." He held my hand and said, "I had a mutt named Rocky. I found him in the park. I put posters up to make sure he didn't belong to anyone, and after a few days, I was glad no one claimed him. He was mine."

"Every time I sat at the piano, he would sit or lay by my feet while I played. We would jam, and he watched the crowd, being my own personal bodyguard. I had him for eight years." He moved his arm to my shoulder and guided me to the porch railing as we leaned against it.

"He died a few months after we discovered cancer. The ironic thing is, I married his doctor. That dog's death affected me. I had a heartache from hell and felt like the world collapsed around me. I imagined him sitting next to me while I played and sometimes, I think he's there. He didn't want to leave until he knew I would be okay, so he introduced me to the woman, I am to spend my life with."

"I know when you look around, you see her and your heart breaks into a thousand pieces. Izzy wasn't just a dog. She was part of you. Time will heal your heart." He hugged me.

Thad took me from his arms, embraced me, and said, "Okay, Mark. I listened to your Rocky story a hundred times. It's my turn." He looked at me. "I don't have a dog story, but I've lost a few cats in my life. It's just as hard, and I'm sorry for your pain."

"Thank you, both," I said and wiped my tears.

Susan walked to me and said, "You're dealing with a group of people who sing for a living." She hugged me. "We know what you're going through, and besides, what else are we going to write songs about? Love between others, lost love, and love we give."

Kyle stood between Susan and me. He placed his arms around our shoulders.

"I never had a dog, but I asked Mom to catch her when she got to heaven. You'll see her again," he said and hugged me.

"I know, Kyle. Thank you," I said through tears.

Gene held me in his big protective arms. "Hey, honey. I'm sorry your heart hurts."

"Thank you, Gene," I said.

Shelly stood behind him but didn't say a word. She wiped her eyes, and I embraced her while we both cried. She felt more like my sister with each passing day. We let go of each other, and she wiped a tear from my cheek.

'I'm sorry.' She mouthed.

I hugged her again and asked, "Why did you let them come?"

Teddy held my shoulders, turned me to him, and embraced me once again. "My turn, you crazy people. I told them what was going on, and they said they were coming."

I kissed his cheek, turned, and faced everyone, then faked a smile. "Thank you all, but you do need rehearsal time."

"One hurts. We all hurt." Kyle laughed with everyone.

Rick stood next to Gene. I walked to him and embraced him. He melted and hugged me.

"Were you forced here?" I asked.

"No, ma'am," he said. "I'm sorry. I know what you're feeling."

I looked at him and asked through tears, "What? There's a heart in there?" He smiled as his expression softened.

Teddy grabbed my hand, led me to a chair, and guided me to his lap. I laid my head on his shoulder, and the tears fell from my eyes.

"Y'all are exhausted. How long are you staying?" I sniffled.

"Tuesday morning," he said, and everyone else emerged from the house.

"Nine o'clock," Shelly said. "And I mean nine. Not nine-fifteen, not nine-thirty, but nine."

"We get it," Teddy said and stroked my hair. "I hope I don't make things worse being here then leaving so quickly."

"You made it easier, Teddy. Thank you." I squeezed him.

"I'll do anything for you," he whispered.

Thank you," I said then kissed his neck. With a muffled voice, I asked, "Did you meet Alan and June?"

"Not formally," he said.

I looked at Alan, who glared at me. "Alan, June, this is everyone. Everyone blah, blah, blah." I laid my head back on Teddy's shoulders. "Was that okay?" I snuggled into his neck and smelled his cologne.

"Yeah." He reached around me and shook their hands.

"Did Lucy and Danielle know you were coming?" I asked.

"Yes, and sleeping arrangements have been made." He squeezed me.

"You say I'm a control freak," I said.

He laughed and asked. "How's your knee?"

I sat from him, raised my pants leg, and said, "My mommy fixed it. See my boo-boo?"

"Blood is coming through the gauze." Teddy pointed.

"She needs stitches," Danielle scolded.

"She'll duct tape it and move on," Alan said, and everyone agreed.

"I'll be okay," I stood and reached for the toilet paper. I blew my nose and said, "Sorry, I look like crap, but I've had a bad day. I soaked you with tears, Teddy."

"I'm not worried about that, but you look tired. Have you eaten?" he asked.

"No, she hasn't. Dinner will be ready in a few minutes," June said.

"Do you want me to fix you a plate?" I asked.

"No, but I'll make you something," he said.

"I can't eat," I said.

Sadie bounced out of the house. She gave everyone hugs, then stood next to me.

"Momma told me to leave you alone," she said.

"You're okay." I hugged her.

"You're sad because Izzy died?" she asked.

"Yes," I said and stroked her hair.

"Let's get you something to eat, Sadie," Lucy said.

"It's okay, Lucy. If she has questions, she needs to ask." I sat next to Teddy as Sadie climbed in my lap.

"Where is Izzy now?" she asked.

"Her body is at the vet's office, but her spirit is in heaven," I said.

"Can I see her?" she asked.

"No, princess."

"I'm sad because you're sad, Mimi," she said.

Tears formed in my eyes once again, and I hugged her tight. I looked at Teddy and said, "Sorry."

"Don't be. You feel what you feel. Don't suppress your feelings," he said and held my hand.

"Everyone, get in here and eat," Danielle said from the door.

Sadie jumped from my lap, followed everyone inside except for Shelly, Teddy, and I.

"I'll get you something, Teddy," Shelly said.

"Thanks," he said.

I walked to the railing, lit a cigarette, and stared into the darkness. I imagined Izzy walking up the hill, and I cried softly.

"I can't stop the damn tears," I said.

Teddy stood behind me and asked, "Where did you decide to place her?"

"By the creek." I pointed. "I'm grateful you guys came, but you need to focus on the tour. You wasted money on fuel, and you're tired."

"You're not blind, Beth. Add it up." He held my hand. "You of all people have an idea of know how much I make."

"You never wanted to be rich and famous?" I asked.

"Music is my first passion, but the money and fame came with it. I learned how to turn that into a business," he said.

"Teddy." Shelly walked outside with a plate of food and asked, "What would you like to drink?"

"Is there any tea?" he asked.

"Yes. Beth, what would you like?" she asked.

"Bourbon and coke," I said.

"You can't drink this away," Teddy said and sat in a chair.

"I can make it go numb tonight. I'll get our drinks," I said.

"No, you stay and make sure he eats. He hasn't been eating well since we left," she said.

"You haven't?" I sat next to him.

"Not much of an appetite," he said.

"You tell me to eat, but you don't," I said as Alan and a few other people joined us on the porch.

"I can do that." He smiled, then took a bite of green beans.

"No, you can't. Practice what you preach," I said.

Danielle walked out and handed us glasses. I smelled the bourbon in the cup. I took a big gulp, and it hit my stomach hard.

"How long are you touring, Mr. Nafton?" June asked.

"Please call me, Teddy. Eight months. Shelly has more dates."

"How many?" I asked.

"Ask her. I go when she says, well, except for today. It was funny, babe. Those guys couldn't pack fast enough to come back. Keith was upset, he couldn't join us, but he needs to get everyone settled in Sacramento."

"I understand. How was the concert? Did you bring them to their feet and make them laugh?" I asked.

"Like always," he said with a smile.

"I told you, Beth. Peanut butter and caviar." Alan reminded me.

"What?" Teddy asked.

"Nothing. Where are you headed?" Alan asked.

"California for two, then Utah." Shelly joined us.

"How many venues did you schedule?" I asked Shelly.

"It went from twenty-seven to thirty-three with more coming together. I believe the lowest venue is 15500."

"Did y'all sell out last night?" June asked.

"Yes ma'am, and the afterparty," Teddy said.

"How many are you trying to fit in?" I asked.

Shelly looked at Teddy and asked, "The maximum is what, forty? Those are the big venues. I'm not sure how many small performances."

"Are you extending the time frame?" I asked.

"We don't know," Teddy said.

"You're gonna kill yourself," I said to him.

"He doesn't want lag time," Shelly said.

"Why so many?" Alan asked.

"Beth has tax season, and I need to stay busy while she's focusing on her work. Also, this is turning into a big tour," he said.

"Are you retiring?" Alan asked.

"No. I don't know what the future is going to hold, so we'll ride this as far as we can," he said and held my hand.

"Want me to get you another plate?" Shelly asked him.

"No, thanks," he said and handed the empty one to her.

"Let me freshen your glass, Teddy," I said and took the plate from Shelly. "Anyone else need anything?"

After everyone shook their head, I walked into the house to get another drink. The band members gathered around the food, engrossed with conversation.

I mixed my drink, and Thad said, "Whoa buckaroo. Take it easy."

"I am," I said.

Mark stood by my side, laid his arm on my shoulder, and held my cup. He smelt it and said, "You're going to pass out."

"I hope so," I said and retrieved my cup from his hands.

"Teddy hopes not," he said and squeezed me into his side. "He likes you. That boy has not eaten nor slept much since we left. He writes all the time."

"Make him sleep. He's running on fumes. Last night's performance was spot on, but you could tell the fire wasn't there," Kyle said.

"It was because of me," I said sadly. "The audience didn't catch on, did they?"

"They can't tell when *The Teddy* is off, but man, we could," Mark said.

"I'll talk to him, but he's stubborn," I said.

"Thanks, Beth. Also, ask him about Wilma," Mark said before I walked out the door.

I handed tea to Teddy and asked about Wilma.

"I'll show you." Teddy reached for his phone then pulled up the pictures.

"Who is Wilma?" Alan asked.

Teddy handed the phone to me, guided me into his lap again, and explained the concept of Wilma and Waldorf. I scrolled through his pictures but went the wrong way.

One of me kissing Izzy on the nose while I was at the vet, showed. My eyes watered. I scrolled in the same direction and saw one of me laying my head on hers as she laid on the x-ray table. Teddy took the phone from me.

"Danielle sent them to me. I'm sorry," he said and squeezed me.

"It's okay, but can you send me those? I know it's morbid, but I want them," I said.

He hugged me tight and slid through the pictures. Alan and June moved behind us to see.

"These are the ones."

I focused my sight on several pictures of Wilma sitting atop the piano on stage with the crowd in the background. He explained the photos then scrolled one too many. Me, carving the bench shown on the screen. He smiled, then turned off the phone and hugged me.

I rose from his lap, and he stuffed the phone in his pocket. He explained how people followed the bear's story on the Internet. Shelly scooted her chair close to me. She showed us a social site where the story began of Wilma and Waldorf.

"People are trying to find out who Wilma represents. They're guessing different celebrities." She showed a picture of Wilma waving goodbye to Waldorf from the car in my driveway. "During the set breaks, they moved her to different instruments. The crowd went crazy when the band took turns holding her toward them for a second after the set. Smaller versions should be waiting on us in California."

Alan glared at me. I diverted my eyes from his and tried to comprehend what I did wrong. I closed my eyes and knew I wouldn't understand him. I lightly shook my head, pushed it out of my mind, and took a big drink from my cup.

"I'll have a copy of the concert for you before we leave. You can watch it and tell me how wonderful I am," Teddy said to me.

"You're not all that," I said. "You're more."

"I knew you liked me." He moved a strand of hair from my face.

"I'm still not a fan," I teased.

"We're going to go crash," Thad said as people emerged from the house.

"Yeah. It's been a long day," Teddy agreed.

I hugged and thanked each one. I reminded Danielle and Lucy, I needed to get Izzy in the morning. They said once everyone woke, they would cook breakfast at my house.

"If you guys need a place, we live fifteen minutes from here. We have a spare room," June offered.

"Thank you, but if I need to, I'll take the recliner," Gene said.

"Beth slept there after her breast surgery. She and Izzy curled up in that chair and sleep the day away," Alan said sadly.

"Remember how she cussed me out when I got her from the groomers?" I smiled.

"That was funny. That dog would look at you, and I swear she talked with her grumbling," he said.

"Alan threw a fit when I brought her home. He stomped around saying how much he didn't want a girly dog, but I wanted one like Izzy. It was love at first sight."

"I thought she was girly until we took her camping the first year." Alan smiled. "I'd go fishing, and she would help me bring 'em in. I feared I was going to hook her a few times, then you would kill me." He grew quiet for a second, then said, "I'm sorry, Beth."

Tears welled in my eyes, and Teddy put his arm around me.

"It's okay, Alan. I'm sorry, too. I can't believe she's gone," I said.

"Well, you still have this little guy." Shelly picked up and hugged Olly.

"I don't know what's wrong with me. I look at him, and I'm mad. I love him, but we never bonded like Izzy and me," I said.

"The bond will come," Shelly said and rubbed his head.

"We're about to go." Alan stood. He shook Teddy's hand and said, "It was nice to meet you, but you need to run like hell from this family. They're crazy."

"That's what Scott said," Teddy said.

"He should know. He helped create these monsters." Alan smiled.

"Thank you for helping me today," I said to Alan.

"No problem, and Teddy… Beth needs control," he said, and Teddy smiled.

Alan and June walked into the house. I took the last drink from my cup.

"Does anyone need a drink refill?" I asked.

"I could use more tea, please," Teddy said.

"I'll get them," Gene said.

"Bourbon and Coke, please." I handed him the cup.

"Alan is nice guy," Shelly said.

"He's negative when he comes to you." Teddy squeezed my hand. "Has he always given you reprehensible glares?"

"That's what they are." I turned Teddy's hand in mine. "I can't tell if he disapproves of me or is disappointed in me. I got tired of doing things wrong. No matter what I cooked, it wasn't right, or what I cleaned, it wasn't good enough, so he landed in June's arms."

"I can't understand why. You're awesome." Teddy leaned his forehead against mine.

"I'm new," I said while Gene handed us the drinks. "Thank you, Gene."

"New?" Teddy asked quizzically.

"You could say one man's trash is another man's treasure. I like how Alan put you and me. Peanut butter and caviar," I said.

"You are not, nor ever will be trash, and I don't get the peanut butter thing," Teddy said.

"He said I was the crunchy nutty peanut butter and can't mix with caviar, like you," I said.

"How do people come up with this stuff?" Shelly asked.

"I don't know, but it's true. How many people do you know likes peanut butter and caviar?" I asked.

"You always refer to caviar," Teddy said.

"Your prestigious, elegant, and awesome," I said to Teddy. "I'm just a country hick who cuts down trees."

"You're more than that. Alan doesn't know me, Beth. He hasn't been around us, so he doesn't know," Teddy said.

"I agree with Teddy. You two have a connection I've never seen. This morning when Teddy couldn't get a hold of you, he banged on my door. When I opened it, he was speaking with Lucy, and she told him about Izzy," Shelly said.

"I dreamt about you," Teddy said and rubbed my fingers. "We were sitting on your couch, speaking, then suddenly you grabbed your heart. I sat up in bed, wide awake, and tried calling. When you didn't answer, I knew something was wrong. I jumped from bed, threw my pants on, and ran toward Shelly's room. I felt bad that I woke her, but she threw the door open when Lucy said you were physically getting sick. My heart hurt, and I knew it was what you were feeling."

"He looked at me and said, 'I'm leaving.' He told me to get Sawyer and Lamar to the plane and ready to be in the air within thirty minutes. I called them while packing," Shelly explained.

"I threw my clothes in the suitcase, went to Kyle's room, and woke them," Teddy said. "I gave them a short explanation as to why I wanted to come back. Kyle banged on Mark, Thad, and Keith's doors and told them. Gene and Rick were the last to know. Several hours later, we arrived."

"Y'all are crazy, but I'm grateful," I said.

"Crazy for you, babe." He kissed my forehead.

"I have to go to bed," I announced as the bourbon mixed with my emotional drain and made me exhausted.

"I bet you do," Teddy said.

"We all do," Shelly said.

"Y'all don't feel like you have to on my account. Make yourselves at home," I said.

"We need sleep, Beth," Gene said.

We walked into the house with Shelly and Gene bidding us goodnight. Teddy and I walked into my bedroom when he stepped into the bathroom. Teddy's bag laid in a corner.

How did I feel about him sleeping in my bed? He emerged from the bathroom wearing green silk pajama pants and no shirt. I stood in front of him, placed my hands on his chest, and felt his heartbeat.

"I hope you don't mind me staying in here with you."

"Not at all," I said with a smile.

"Pants will stay on." He held my hands.

I nodded and went into the bathroom. Teddy's shaving kit sat on one side of the sink. I liked him settling into my house as he has my life.

I washed my face, brushed my teeth, and rubbed lotion on the end of my nose. I dressed in my blue cotton pajama pants and shirt, then walked out of the bathroom.

"Where's Olly?" I asked.

"Let me look outside." Teddy opened the door.

Olly ran inside as the door cracked enough to let his body through. He stopped short of me, backed up a few feet, and jumped into my arms. I gave him a funny look and held him.

"Put him between us," Teddy said and patted the bed.

I laid him in his bed, which was next to Izzy's. My eyes filled again with tears.

"I don't want him right now, Teddy." I sat on the edge of the bed, looked at the white dog, and his tail wagged. I looked at Izzy's empty bed and cried. "She's never going to sleep here again." I petted Olly's head and turned off the lights.

Teddy slid his knee between my legs and spooned me. He reached across me and patted the bed to call Olly. The dog jumped up and curled next to my stomach.

"You can't be mad at him," Teddy said.

"I don't want to feel this ever again. I don't want another dog, as long as I live," I said.

"You don't mean that right now. Give yourself time," he said, then held me tight while I cried myself to sleep.

Chapter 24

My nose was sore and dry. I rubbed my swollen, burning eyes to relieve the itch. My body was stiff, and my muscles ached. My knee hurt when I moved. I rolled over in bed, and Teddy cuddled with a body pillow while Olly laid on top of it.

I studied Teddy's facial features and couldn't believe a man like him was in my bed. I loved what he stood for and how he made me feel as a person. He stopped his life to console me, which meant the world to me. Alan's words came back to my mind: peanut butter and caviar. Teddy and I are too different to have a relationship.

I rose from bed, tiptoed into the bathroom, and brushed my teeth and hair. I walked to the nightstand, picked up my phone, cigarettes, and Olly. I carried Olly out of the room and shut the door as softly as I could. I tiptoed to the kitchen, retrieved a soda, and snuck out the front door. I placed the dog on the ground, then lit a cigarette. Clouds formed near the tree line.

After eight, I called the office, and Lois answered, "Hey, Beth. Helen told us. I'm sorry. We loved Izzy."

"Thank you. Do I have anything pressing today?"

"No. You have a few appointments tomorrow, but we'll handle today," she said.

"Thanks again. I'll be in around ten or so in the morning," I said then bid my goodbye.

I walked into the house with Olly at my feet. I opened the bedroom door and peered in. Teddy was in the bathroom. I made the bed, went to the closet, and retrieved clothes as my alarm sounded.

"Morning," he said, coming from the bathroom, already dressed.

"I wanted you to sleep. I can do this myself," I said sadly.

"You're not going to." He embraced me. "How are you doing?"

"I'm tired and want this over."

"Get dressed while I get coffee." He kissed my forehead and left the room.

I put my hair up, washed my face, dressed, and walked into the kitchen. Teddy and Gene sat at the table.

"Let me smoke before we leave," I said, and Teddy nodded.

I stepped out as Gene followed. "Tough day ahead."

"Yeah." I stared at the gray sky.

"Those are rain clouds," Gene said.

"It looks like how I feel."

"Damp and stormy?" Gene asked, trying to lighten my mood.

I smiled, laid my head on his bicep, and said, "Yes, Gene. I'm damp."

We smoked in silence, then Shelly and Teddy joined us. Teddy made Olly stay inside.

"Y'all need rest, and I can do this myself," I complained.

"You aren't," Shelly said.

We drove to the clinic as Shelly directed Gene to the location. Teddy held me as I laid my head on his shoulder. I wanted the pain in my heart to stop, but the closer we got to the building, the more my heart ached. Gene pulled into a small parking lot in the back of the building.

"Why here?" I asked.

"Dr. Wilton told us to park in the back in case customers were in the waiting room," Shelly said.

Mary held the door open for us as we stepped out of the car. Shelly, Gene, Teddy, and I followed Mary into an examination room. She shut the door behind us then embraced me.

"I'm sorry, Beth. My hopes were high when Peter got her to eat. I can't believe we lost her," she said.

I thanked her, turned to Teddy, and introduced everyone as they exchanged pleasantries.

"Let me get Peter," she said, then left us.

Teddy held me tight as we waited. We were in the room for a few minutes, then Peter joined us.

"I'm sorry, sweetie," he said and hugged me.

"Thank you," I said and fought back my tears.

Teddy introduced Gene, Shelly, and himself. I stared at the collar Peter held in his hand.

"Do you want this on her?" he asked as he noticed I stared at the object.

I swallowed hard, and a knot tightened my voice. I nodded. I wanted to be strong, but I struggled to keep the tears from falling.

"Since we lost her, the bill isn't going to be as high," Peter said.

"We aren't worried about that." Teddy looked at Shelly before she left the room.

"Let me get her," Peter said.

"Can I hold that for a minute?" I asked with my shaky voice.

He handed me the collar, and I smelt her musty dog sent. I cried and gave it back to the doctor before he left. Gene handed me tissues, and Teddy held me in his arms.

"I'm sorry, guys," I said.

"I don't want you to say that again, Beth. This is hard for me to watch. I can only imagine what you're going through," Teddy said.

The door opened behind us, and Shelly walked into the room. Teddy nodded to her, and she rubbed my back.

The door in front of us opened, and Peter carried Izzy's body, wrapped in her blanket. My tears flowed heavy, and Gene reached to take her. I pushed his hands away and took her into my arms.

"I left the cast on her left leg, and the other is missing," Peter said.

I held her close to my chest, choked back tears, and said, "Thank you for all you did. I know you tried."

"I wish it were different," he said.

Teddy and Gene guided me out the other door while I carried my precious Izzy. I was grateful for their guidance to the car. I couldn't see a thing while tears flowed from my eyes.

I sat next to Teddy, rocked my dead dog in my arms, and cried over her. I moved the blanket to reveal her face and stroked her fur. Shelly reached behind her from the front of the car and handed me tissues while Teddy rubbed my shoulders.

"My precious little one," I said to Izzy.

She looked like she was asleep, but she was cold to the touch. Teddy laid his hand on her head while Shelly watched us from the front seat.

"Hey, Gene!" I exclaimed.

"Yes, honey," he said.

"I'm glad I'm not driving today." I pulled Izzy close to my chest.

"We all are, Beth," he said.

We arrived at the house, and a few four-wheelers along with Lucy and Danielle's cars were parked in the drive. Gene and Teddy helped me from the vehicle. Gene offered to carry Izzy, but I shook my head, so he backed off. They helped me into the house and out the back door.

Olly followed and sniffed the air. He jumped to my waist to see what I held. Teddy guided me to a chair and sat across from me with our knees touching. He picked up Olly then held him in his lap.

The dog sniffed Izzy then nudged her with his nose as if to wake her. Lucy and Danielle cried. Susan and Shelly sniffled and handed us tissues.

I rocked Izzy, stroked her face, and cried. I needed strength, so I glanced into Teddy's watery eyes. He placed Olly on the porch and walked away from me. He leaned against the railing with his back toward me.

"Take your time, babe," he said.

Danielle and Lucy sat in front of me, stroked her face while we cried together for a few minutes.

"My glorious sunshine. Why didn't you stay with me?" I asked.

Everyone placed their hands on my shoulders, and I rocked her lifeless body. I drew her close to my heart once again, then something snapped inside of me. I stood with her in my arms, regained my strength, and carried her off the porch.

"Can you grab the shovel, Danielle?" I asked.

"I have it," Gene said.

I carried her down the little hill. Teddy and Kyle helped me as everyone else followed. I knelt in the dirt, brought her to my chest, and hugged her tight. I kissed her cold nose and placed her in the ground.

"Sleep, my baby love. I'll see you again." I covered her head with the blanket then said in a panic, "I need her duck."

"I'll get it," Lucy said and ran to the house.

A minute later, she appeared with Izzy's favorite toy. I placed it next to her in the ground as a light mist fell from the sky. I stood and reached for the shovel.

"I can do this, Beth," Gene said.

"So can I, Gene. Please?" I asked and cried hard.

He handed the shovel to me, and I placed dirt over the red and white blanket. My eyesight blurred from the tears, but I focused on filling the hole. After a few minutes, my body strength faltered. I grew shaky, and Lucy grabbed my shoulder to stop me.

"Find rocks and let me finish," she said through tears.

Teddy took the shovel from my hands and said, "Get rocks, Beth."

We walked in the woods, found rocks while Teddy shoveled the dirt into the hole. I knelt in the mud next to her grave and placed rocks on the mound of dirt. I didn't want them dropped on her, so everyone handed the stones to me, one at a time. With the rocks lying over her grave, I sat in the mud, as rain pelted the ground.

"Y'all get inside. I don't want y'all sick." I ordered and turned the stones on top of the dirt.

"Are you coming?" Shelly asked.

"I need a moment," I said and rubbed a rock. They left except for Teddy and Gene. "Go, guys. I want a few minutes. Please?" Teddy rubbed my head with his hand, walked up the hill, and left Gene and me at her grave. "Don't stay with me, Gene."

"You hurt. We hurt, honey," he said while Danielle returned and handed him an umbrella.

The rain fell harder, but I wanted the dirt washed off the rocks. I sat in the mud and continued to rub them. I don't know how long I was there, but Teddy joined me in fresh clothes and carried the blue umbrella. He stood over me while Gene went up the hill, into the house.

"Come inside," Teddy said and placed his hand on my shoulder.

I looked at him as tears streamed down my face. He held his hand out for me to take. I showed him how muddy and wet I was, but he grabbed my hand and helped me to my feet. He wrapped his arm around my waist, and I laid my head on his shoulder. We walked to the house as the rain stopped.

On the porch, I took my shoes off and walked to the bathroom. I sat on the floor, leaned my back against the bathtub, and let my tears fall freely. Teddy came into the room, sat on the floor next to me, and placed his arm around me. I laid my head on his shoulder and cried.

After a few minutes, I said, "That's enough. I'm done." I wiped my eyes, stood, and left Teddy on the floor.

"You turn it off like that." He stared at me with wide eyes.

"No, but I have to find my strength and stop being vulnerable." I fought the tears. "No more, Beth. No more," I said to myself and tried to stop crying.

"Why do you think you have to be strong? Why can't you lean on people?" He stood next to me.

"I don't have to," I said, then blew my nose.

"I don't want you sick, so take a hot shower, babe," he said.

He kissed my forehead and left me standing in the middle of the bathroom. I turned the water on, undressed, and pulled the mud-soaked gauze from my knee. I needed to wash the dirt from the wound, but blood poured down my leg as my knee burned.

I held a washcloth on it as I stepped into the shower. Blood mixed with water while I washed my hair and body. I rinsed, wrapped my hair in a towel, then stepped out. I held my knee as blood ran between my fingers. I tied a hand towel around it and wrapped a towel around me.

"Danielle," I yelled and hobbled to the bed.

"Yeah." She walked into my room. "What are you doing?"

"My knee won't stop bleeding, and I need another band-aid." I sat on the edge of the bed. "Can you call Granny and get me one?"

I wiped the blood from my leg without much success. As soon as I cleaned a streak, another stream ran from under the towel.

"Are you okay?' Teddy asked as he came to the door.

"Let me see, Mom," Danielle said and unwrapped the towel from around my knee.

"It's okay, guys." I struggled to cover myself with the comforter and hold a rag on the wound. "I need another rag and a stupid band-aid."

"Let me see, Beth," Teddy said and stepped close to me. "I've seen you in a towel before. Move your hand, please."

I moved the washcloth, which was blood-soaked while Danielle retrieved another rag and said from the bathroom, "There's blood on the floor."

"I know," I snapped.

"You need stitches," Teddy said.

"A butterfly will do," I said.

Teddy made sure I was covered, walked to the doorway, and asked, "Can you come here, Gene?"

He joined us while I cleaned the sticky red substance from my shin. Danielle moved the fresh rag for Gene to look.

"Yep. You need stitches," Gene said."

"Or a damn band-aid." I felt angry no one listened to me. "I'll get the stupid thing." I threw the blankets off me.

"You're stubborn," Teddy said forcefully and covered me.

"You're going to need more than one. I'll run to the pharmacy. It's right down the road," Danielle said.

"I'll drive," Gene said.

"I just sit here until you guys come back?" I asked in an aggravated tone.

"Yeah," Gene boomed before they left.

Teddy retrieved a towel, placed it on a pillow, and slid it under my knee. "Lay back." He laid another rag on the wound and said, "You need stitches."

"I'm not going to a hospital," I said, sat up, and cried softly.

Lucy came into the bedroom, "What's going on?" Teddy removed the washcloth, and she said, "You need stitches."

"I need a stiff drink." I wanted the pain in my heart and body numbed.

"You need food," Lucy said and towel-dried my hair.

"Let's get you bandaged, then you can eat something," Teddy said and placed pressure on my knee.

Lucy carried the towel into the bathroom and said, "There's blood all over the floor."

"I'll clean it in a few," I blurted loudly and closed my burning eyes.

"I got this," she said.

"Why are you mad?" Teddy asked.

"It hurts," I said.

"You reopened it," he said.

"I'm not referring to my knee," I said.

"I know, babe," he said calmly. "This day got to me. I don't ever want to feel that again."

Lucy went into the bathroom with the mop. Teddy pushed me to lay on the mattress, then he laid his head on my hip. He held pressure on the washcloth while I laid my arm over my burning eyes.

"Are you okay?" Shelly asked from the door. Teddy raised the cloth, and she said, "We need to take you to the hospital."

I shook my head, and Teddy asked, "Can you call Gene and ask him to get peroxide?"

"Here's some," Lucy said, then handed the bottle to Teddy after she cleaned the bathroom floor.

"Would you mind getting Beth a warm cloth for her eyes?" Teddy asked Shelly.

"They're in the first cabinet next to the shower," Lucy said and left the room.

"Y'all can stop fussing over me." I snapped.

"No, we can't. You're going to let us help, so stop being stubborn," Teddy said.

I sat up the best I could, looked at him, and said, "I'm not stubborn, and I don't need your help, Teddy."

"You are." He grabbed the back of my neck with his free hand and pulled me to his lips. He gave me a hard kiss then said, "I know you hurt from the inside out, but babe, learn to let us help."

"I don't know how," I whispered as my eyes filled with tears.

"You had to be strong and do things yourself, even though you had Alan. That was him, but now you have me," he said.

"She has us, Teddy." Shelly laid the warm cloth on my eyes.

Gene and Danielle came into the room as Lucy followed. Danielle retrieved another towel and placed it under my knee. She poured peroxide on the cuts. The bubbles fizzed. I sobbed from everyone doting on me, but I enjoyed the relief of the washcloth on my eyes.

"I'm putting the bandage on a few scratches, so it may hurt," Gene said.

Shelly rubbed my arm while he pulled the skin together and placed a big bandage over the small ones. That didn't bother me as much as my burning eyes. It felt like glass cut the inside of my eyelids.

"Done, but if it gets worse, please have it stitched," Gene said.

"I will. Thank you." I rolled to my side and held Teddy's shirt.

He held me in his arms while I laid next to him with the rag on my eyes and my head on his chest. His arm moved in the air before he laid it on my shoulder.

"You've had a hard morning, so rest," he said. I listened to his heartbeat, and the door clicked shut. He rubbed my arm and said, "I wish I could take your pain."

"You don't need this pain," I said. "I also didn't mean to get angry, but I'm tired of hurting."

"You'll heal with time," he said.

"Well, if you want to run, do it now. You've seen me at my lowest," I said.

"Stop trying to push me away, Ms. strong control girl." He pulled me close and kissed my forehead.

Chapter 25

Tapping water from rain hit the metal roof of the covered back porch. I closed my burning eyes and pressed my head into the pillow. I stretched my sore body, and the bandage pulled the skin on my knee. I rolled to my side. I opened my eyes then tugged the sheets over my naked breast.

Teddy cuddled with the body pillow and slept peacefully. I moved slow. I outstretched my left arm and felt under the blankets to locate the towel. He stirred, so I laid motionless as not to wake him.

He moved the pillow and rolled on top of my arm with his back against me. The sheets separated our skin from touching, but I was trapped. He reached behind him, felt for my free arm, so I handed it to him. He held my hand, placed it on his chest, and I felt his heartbeat.

"How long have you been awake?" He faced me and blinked.

"A few minutes," I said. How am I going to get out of this?

He smiled and asked, "How are you feeling?"

"Better."

"Hungry?"

"No, but I bet you are."

"I want to stay here." He nuzzled his nose into my neck.

"How are you?" I stroked his hair.

"Better with you next to me." He squeezed me tight with one arm. He popped his head up and studied my eyes. "You look sad. I can see a hole in your heart. I can't help heal it."

"I'll survive," I said.

He kissed me, rolled away, and said, "Okay. Get dressed, and let's eat." I hunted for the towel again, but he quickly sat up. "Let me see your knee." He raised the blanket off my leg. "It's bled. We need to change the bandage."

"I'll be okay," I said and focused on locating the towel.

"Come on, get up." He smirked, laid on his side, and propped his head in his hand.

"You know full well I laid down with nothing on, but a towel," I said as he stared at me.

"I know." He raised his eyebrows.

"Really?" I asked, and my phone sounded with a text.

"Really," he said in a daring attitude.

"A challenge." I smiled.

We held a staring contest as I talked myself into standing from the bed. I threw the blankets off me, stood, and fumbled in the sheets. I found the towel, pulled it free, and stared at him. I dragged the towel on the floor behind me and walked to the closet.

"I didn't think you would do it." He smiled and looked me over.

I winked at him, then retrieved clothes from the closet, and went into the bathroom. My hands shook when I shut the door. I dressed and brushed my hair, then walked back into the bedroom.

Teddy laid in bed with a smile. He raised his hand for me to take. I did and laid next to him.

"Lucy and Danielle said you don't use the L-word unless it's with them or the kids."

"Why are you talking to them about that?" I asked.

"We were only talking."

"Stop. I haven't had a reason to use it with anyone other than family," I said.

"We've only known each other for a short time, but I really, really…like you. Are you comfortable with that?" he asked.

I closed my eyes, laid my head on his chest, and said, "We have to quit. I can't offer you what you need."

"You already have." He rubbed my arm.

I hugged him, sat up, and said, "You're the second man in my life who has seen me naked."

"Really?" I nodded, and he said, "I'm privileged. You look good."

"How many women have you been with?" I asked.

"I'm clean if that's what you need to know. I've recently been checked."

"Recently, huh," I smirked.

"Last week."

"You told me we needed to wait, so you could get checked?" I asked.

"Yes and no. I wanted to get to know you. I've never taken so much time in getting to know a woman, but you…" He pointed his finger at me. "You're different. You're everything. I want to make sure we're safe, so when we arrived in Michigan, I got checked."

"Glad to know, but that's not why I'm asking. I want to know how many women you've been with."

"I don't know." He looked at his hands.

"That tells me, we're different." I stood from the bed and retrieved my phone. "You're everybody's dream and can have anyone you want, so why me?"

He stood, placed his hands on my hips, and said, "Look in my eyes."

I stared into his big brown eyes and saw into his soul. A slow-motion picture played in my thoughts of him standing in the darkness, lost, and alone. Sunlight streamed through clouds, and he basked in its warmth as he pulled me into his side. Happiness replaced his lost feeling. I blinked and stepped out of his hands.

"You saw it," he said in a low voice.

"I'm tired, Teddy. I'm on an emotional roller coaster, so I don't know what I see."

"I was lost, then you found me, and gave me light."

I shook my head, dismissed what he said, and looked at my phone. A text from Helper appeared on the screen.

Force him to leave or everything will be revealed.

I rolled my eyes and texted:

Not in the mood for games today. Leave me be.

After I hit send, Teddy took the phone from my hands, smiled, and said, "I'll handle Helper."

He sat on the bed, looked at my phone, and I walked to the kitchen. Gene sat in the recliner and watched TV with the volume low. Shelly sat on the couch and typed on her tablet.

"Where is everyone?" I asked.

"They left to get rest. How are you?" she asked.

I nodded and walked to the kitchen. I poured a glass of tea for Teddy and mixed a drink for me. I walked into my room, handed Teddy the glass of tea before I walked to the back porch. Teddy, Gene, and Shelly followed me outside.

The sky was different hues of oranges and reds as the sunset. Teddy stepped behind me and laid his hand on my shoulder. I set my cup on the small table, lit a cigarette, and slipped on my shoes.

"I'll be right back," I said.

I walked to her gravesite to make sure the rushing water of the creek didn't near her resting place. I stood in front of the rock pile and stared at the brown, freshly dug earth.

"Goodnight, sweet princess." I blew a kiss and walked up the hill.

"Everything okay?" Teddy asked as I stepped on the porch.

"Yes," I said and picked up my cup.

"You need food, not alcohol, babe," Teddy said.

I sat and held out my hand for him to take as he had with mine. Instead of his hand, he placed the phone in it, which made me smile. I stuffed it in my pocket, held my hand out once again, and he took it.

I led him in front of me, pulled him into my lap, and hugged him tightly. He smiled, rose, and sat next to me while Shelly and Gene sat next to him.

"Today was the saddest thing I witnessed," Shelly said.

"Let me tell y'all something." I stared hard at the three. "I could not and cannot make it through this day without you all being by my side. I don't know how to thank you. I'm indebted to you all." Light tears fell from my eyes. "I'm sorry for getting angry earlier, so will you please forgive me?"

"It's okay," Teddy said and squeezed my hand.

"We're good," Shelly said.

"You're my favorite." Gene smiled.

"I wish I could stop this mess." I wiped my cheeks.

"It'll stop with time." Teddy brought my legs up to rest on his lap.

"I need to cook. I know y'all are hungry."

"We can order anything you would like," Teddy said.

"I have what I want right here." I held up my cup. A few minutes later, I stood and said, "If I don't move, I'm going to hurt worse, so I'm cooking."

I walked into the kitchen while they followed me back into the house. As I washed my hands, the skin on my palms burned. Teddy stood behind me while I snickered at the few deep scratches on my right palm.

"Let's order out," Teddy said.

"No." I walked to the freezer, opened it, and studied the contents. "Do you know how to grill, Gene?"

"Yeah. Do you want me to fire it up?"

"Please?" I asked.

I peeled potatoes while Shelly defrosted the hamburger meat and chicken. Teddy leaned against the sink. I faced him, pressed my breast into his chest, and reached for the cooking oil and paper towels on the side of him. I slowly kissed him and smiled. I retrieved a giant pan and continued preparing dinner.

I cut potatoes into fries, and Teddy leaned against my back. His phone rang. He kissed my neck, stood behind me, and answered.

"What's up?" He moved to the opposite counter. My phone rang, and Teddy quickly said, "Don't tell her anything."

I concentrated on the potatoes while Teddy reached in my pocket. He grabbed my phone and asked, "How in the hell did she find out where we're staying?"

Shelly stopped patting the hamburger meat, stepped to the back door, and spoke to Gene.

"Is she there?" He paused, looked at Gene, who joined us, then Teddy said, "Whatever you do, don't tell her anything, Keith. Keep everyone there. I'll call you back with a plan. Thanks."

"She's in California?" Gene asked.

"Yeah," Teddy said and studied my phone. "She called Beth." I shook my head at the thought of her. "She showed in the hotel lobby when they were going to the arena for set-up. She asked Keith about me. He told her I wasn't with him, and she became insistent for him to tell her where I was. He told her he didn't know and left her standing in the lobby. I guess she called Beth to see if I was here." He looked at Shelly and asked, "Can you discreetly change our hotel?"

"Yeah, but it's getting more difficult to back her away," she said.

"I didn't hear from her last week when we weren't together," I looked at Teddy. "I told you I didn't want drama."

"We'll stop this," he said then looked at Gene. "Beth received a few texts from Helper. Whoever this is, used the term WE in the last one." He read the text between Helper, and I then said, "Helper texted: We're in control, so get in the mood."

"Carissa has inside help," Gene said. "Someone told her where you were staying."

"How do we know Helper isn't Carissa? There were other women in the pictures. It could be one of them," I said calmly.

"She's right," Gene said in thought.

"I want to hire someone for you, Beth. This is getting crazy," Teddy said.

"I don't want anyone." I wiped my hands on a towel.

"Would you please help me convince Ms. Stubborn to let me hire a bodyguard for her?" Teddy asked Gene.

"It's not a bad idea," Gene said to me.

"Are reporters at the hotel?" Shelly asked.

"Keith didn't say," Teddy said.

"I'll call him," Gene said and stepped out of the back door.

Teddy stood next to me, stroked my hair, and asked, "Please let me hire someone for you?"

"Leave me alone about this." I looked at him. "I'll handle my own, and you worry about your own."

"I'm trying to take care of my own, Beth." He wrapped his arms around my waist.

I kissed him then said, "Nothing else can be handed to me right now, so please don't put anything on me. She isn't coming after me, so there is no need for a bodyguard."

He stared into my eyes for a second and said, "The pictures, the dreams, the texts, and now Carissa showing concerns me. The dreams have a meaning. I don't know what, but they're intense and make me unsettled."

"I'm okay." I placed my hand on his cheek.

He laid his hand on mine and said, "If it continues, I'll hire someone whether you like it or not."

I pulled my hand from his face and said, "You're an ass, Teddy."

My phone rang again with Carissa's name appearing at the top. The front door opened. Danielle, Colby, Rick, Mark, and Gabi came inside. Danielle handed Gabi to Colby, then gently pushed Teddy out of the way of the sink to wash her hands.

"Excuse me, sir," she said.

Teddy smiled, but he and I continued our staring contest while my phone rang. He stuffed it in my pocket.

"I'll leave it to you ladies," he said.

He joined Colby in the living room, grabbed my electric wood guitar, and plugged it in the amp. He strummed the strings and created a beautiful melody. We stared at one another, and Shelly stepped next to me.

"It relaxes him," she whispered.

Teddy was in his element with some form of instrument in his hands. I'm the klutzy person who cuts her hands by moving rocks or gets covered in sawdust, cutting trees. We are peanut butter and caviar.

He shook his head at me as Lucy, Sadie, Kara, Ellis, and the others walked through the front door. I returned my concentration on dinner and drank while I cooked.

I wanted to stop the pain in my heart and body. I pushed the thought of Carissa to the back of my mind and didn't pay attention to the conversations which surrounded me. Once food sat on the table, we said grace. I made Teddy a plate and mixed another drink.

"Aren't you going to eat?" he asked while I stood next to him.

"Later," I said and kissed his cheek.

I walked to the back porch and dragged a chair to the railing. I faced it toward the tiny hill and stared into darkness. I waited for Izzy to run to me. I looked at the boat and envisioned her, lapping at the air while she sat between my legs when I drove. I was in deep thought, wiped my eyes, and wished I grabbed either tissue or toilet paper.

The door opened, then closed behind me. After a few minutes, the door opened again, then Shelly handed me a box of tissue.

"You think of everything. Thank you." She patted my shoulder, sat next to me, and I asked, "Did you get enough to eat?"

"Yes, but you need food," she said.

I shook my head, and we sat in silence. After a minute, a few tears streaked Shelly's face, and I handed her a tissue.

"I can't get the image out of my head of you holding her. It broke my heart. I wish I could do something for you."

"I am sorry for being short today. You guys came all this way to help, and I was hard on you. I thank you for everything you've done. I'm grateful and honored to call you, my friend, Shelly."

"You're my sista," she said with a smile.

"Please don't let Teddy buy me a damn dog." I smiled.

"That's funny. He told me to find you one when we were on the plane. I told him to wait and see what you thought."

"I figured. Why do guys think they need to fix things all the time?" I asked.

"I don't know. I'll call Rob to tell him about my day, and he tells me how to fix my problems," she said, and we laughed.

"Alan used to do that except most of the time, my problems were caused by something I did wrong. Men. They have to be Mr. Fix It's."

"But what are you going to do. You like him, and he has fallen for you," she said.

She put her arm around me, and we laid our heads together. I was grateful to have met this woman.

"What are you doing?" Teddy asked as he shut the door.

Shelly and I looked at each other and laughed.

"I'm getting drunk," I said.

"I can see. You haven't eaten anything in two days," he said.

"Trying to fix me there, spanky?"

"I'm trying to help." He laid his hand on my shoulder.

"You could help by coming over and sitting down," I said.

He did, and I stared at the hill once again. Images of Izzy lying underground, wet, and scared flooded my thoughts.

"Is there anything I can do for you?" Teddy held my hand.

"Can you bring her back to life with all her legs and place her in my lap?" I wiped my cheeks.

"You know I can't," he said.

"Then I'm going to get drunk to help ease the pain," I said in a strong southern accent.

"Has Carissa called anymore?" Teddy asked.

"No. Has she called you?" I asked.

"Several times."

"Do you want me to call her back?"

"Not with the kids around," he said.

"They're not back here." I pulled the phone from my pocket.

"I want to hear the conversation," Teddy said.

"I'm not going to put you down." I smiled.

"I know. I'm good at everything," he said with confidence.

I rolled my eyes and said, "Turn your phone off. I don't want her to text you like she did the last time."

He held the button on his phone while I tapped her number. I placed her on speaker.

"Hello," she answered on the third ring.

"Hey, Carissa. This is Beth," I said.

"Am I on speaker?" she asked.

"Yeah, sorry. I'm getting a few things done before I go to bed," I said with no enthusiasm.

"Is Teddy with you?" she asked.

"Wow. Not a how are you or anything."

"Dammit, Beth! Is he there?" she loudly asked.

"What would it matter?" I felt aggravated that she would not leave him, nor I alone.

"I'm trying to find him. He's supposed to be in Sacramento, but he's not."

"Are you?" I asked.

"Yes. I need fifteen minutes of his time, but he won't return my calls."

"I've told him your better for him than me, but how you're acting, I can see why he doesn't want anything to do with you." I stared at Teddy. "How did you get my number? I know it didn't come from him."

"I overheard him call you, Babe. I looked at his phone and saw the word as a contact. He doesn't call anyone else that, so I added your number to my phone and hoped it was you."

"Babe, huh," I said, and he smiled.

"I don't know how you caught his attention so fast. I know it's not your looks. Maybe you stalked him and planned that meeting in Colorado."

"You've lost it. I didn't stalk Teddy. He stalked me," I chuckled.

"He wouldn't touch some plain ugly country girl like you," she said.

"Us plain ugly country girls are the best in bed. We don't worry about smearing our lipstick when we please our man," I said sarcastically.

Teddy opened his mouth to say something, and I shook my head at him. He signed, 'I haven't been with a country girl, show me'. I smiled and rolled my eyes at him.

"He's not worried about what goes on between the sheets. He's worried about his reputation in the public eye. He needs to a pristine, glamorous beauty, like me, by his side," she said.

"Every man has a motive of sex when it comes to a woman who catches his eye. It's human nature," I said.

"Not with you. You're not his type," she said. "I know you're after his fame and fortune. I'll get him to see you're a gold digger. I'll protect him with everything I have."

I laughed at this conversation. "Me a gold digger. I'm far from it, but if you can convince him, go for it. I'm glad you're protecting him, but you don't have to from me."

"Don't lie. You're the one person he needs protection from," she snarled.

"You're full of it. I don't want Teddy for his money. Maybe his body, but not his money." I winked at him. He held his fist over his mouth and chuckled. "I sure as hell don't want the fame, but I'll tell you what I do want."

"What?" she asked.

"I want you to leave him alone. His happiness comes before anything. He needs to figure out his own life without influences."

"You would be okay with him choosing me over you?" she asked.

"I've been telling him to go to you. You could offer him more than me." Teddy gave me an evil glare, then Gene and Rick joined us outside. Shelly met them at the door to keep them quiet. "I'm on your side, Carissa."

"You're a lying bitch. All women want a piece of Teddy. You're no different. No one will come between us," she said.

"I don't scare easily, so is that a threat? Choose your words carefully." I took a drink, and she fell silent for a few seconds. "Well, it was nice speaking with you. I wish you happiness."

"Beth."

"Yes, ma'am."

"If you don't leave him alone, I'll ruin your life."

"Oh yeah, a stalking gold digger. You're back to that," I said. "Good luck and take it easy, Carissa." I hung up and shook my head at the thought of our conversation.

"I know you're after my body." Teddy smiled. "I'll get the lipstick."

"You're funny." I smiled. "She's not going to let you go without a fight, and I don't fight, bud."

"This isn't your fight, babe," he said and turned his phone on.

"She texted you?"

"She did."

"I thought so," I said and finished my drink.

"What did she say?" Gene asked.

Teddy explained what Carissa said while I stared in the direction of the hill. I didn't pay attention to their conversation. Olly ran into the woods, toward the creek. Is Olly searching for his best friend?

I pushed back tears as a knot formed in my throat. I didn't like the silence in my mind. It brought thoughts of Izzy dying, and I remembered the pictures on Teddy's phone of her and me.

"Beth!" Teddy exclaimed.

"What." I looked at him.

"Rick said you might want to change your number. Are you okay?" he asked.

"Yeah. Sorry. I don't want the hassle right now. This number is on my business cards."

"Business card," Teddy said. "Do you still have it, Gene?"

"Let me check," he said and pulled his wallet out of his pocket.

"She doesn't need your last name or address. If she got it, she could bring the media to your doorstep," Rick said.

"Yeah," Gene said and waved it in the air. "Rick's right. No one needs to speak with her."

"I'm not looking forward to going to Cali," Teddy said.

"Doesn't your first wife live there?" I asked.

"Yeah."

"You could meet with both her and Carissa. Have yourself a good ole time." I smiled.

"That would not be a good time."

"He won't. I'll make sure of that," Gene said.

"You don't see any of your exes?" I asked.

"Where is this coming from?" Teddy asked, and I shrugged my shoulders. "I have no contact with those two. I don't have a reason like Alan."

"Why are you talking about my daddy?" Lucy asked as she stepped outside.

"I told Beth, you guys are the reason Alan has to see her," Teddy explained.

"Y'all are talking about Dad?" Danielle asked as she followed Lucy.

"You're in trouble, Teddy. I'm not allowed to say anything about Alan," I laughed.

I sat my drink on the railing and held my arms out to take the babies. Lucy and Danielle placed them in my lap, then I kissed and hugged them close.

"How many times have you been married?" Lucy asked.

"Twice," Teddy answered and told them about his ex-wives.

"Can y'all take the babies for a second? I need another drink," I said, hugged them, then the girls picked them up from my lap.

"I'll get you one, but not as strong," Shelly said.

"Thank you, Shelly." She walked into the house, and I said, "Gene!"

"What, honey?" he asked.

"You're losing your status with me, son. Shelly is moving up the ladder." I laughed and felt numb.

"So, she's your favorite." He stood over me and rubbed my shoulders.

"Yep. I don't know what you're going to do to regain the status of favoritism."

"You've had enough. You need to eat," he said, and Shelly returned.

"She's back, plus more," I said as people followed her outside.

"Feeling good, babe?" Teddy asked.

"You know it." I reclaimed my drink from Shelly. I nodded to her, took a sip then asked, "Where's my princess?"

"Mom's drunk," Lucy announced.

"Am not," I said.

"Sadie is playing with Cullen," Susan said.

"Kids come, and Mimi gets shoved out," I said.

"That's not true. You're her beautifulest, wonderfulest, Mimi," Lucy said.

"I love that kid." I smiled and thought about Sadie's smile.

"Have you seen this woman drunk before, Teddy?" Lucy asked.

"Once," he said.

"I'm not drunk. I just feel reeeaaall good." I moved my hand through the air.

"I've seen her this way a handful of times in my life, and here's some advice. When she sings, you have thirty to forty-five minutes before she passes out. Remember, Danielle?" Lucy asked.

"Yeah. The night the divorce was finalized, she called us to say how sorry she was for letting us down. Lucy and I had to put her to bed," Danielle said.

"I am sorry, guys." Teddy stepped in front of me, laid his hand on my shoulder, and I said, "Y'all love your Daddy, and I made him go away."

"We aren't children. We love the both of you, but we saw you two were growing apart," Lucy said.

"I'm glad you're here, Teddy. You have your work cut out. Mom protects her heart as much as she can. It's a survival mechanism, I guess everyone has, but hers is strong," Danielle said.

"Do not," I needed to argue my point.

"Are too. And she's stubborn," Lucy said.

"Am not," I said.

"Are too," Teddy said.

"You people don't know me," I wrapped my arms around Teddy's hips.

"She's about to sing," Lucy said.

"Am not. Teddy is the singer," I said.

Ellis and Colby walked from around the side yard and handed Rick a few fold-out chairs. I took another drink from my cup, which held the secret to my pain.

Teddy kissed my neck and said, "How can anyone not like this."

"I don't know. How?" I smiled.

He laughed and went into the house for a few seconds. He returned with my acoustic guitar and sat next to me.

"Let's test her," he said.

"I don't mean this disrespectful, but it's hard to picture you as a megastar, Teddy," Lucy said.

"I'm taking it as a compliment coming from you," he said and strummed the guitar. "I hope you all can join us on the tour."

"That would be awesome," Susan said.

"I'm down," Lucy said.

"I have school, but could probably get away for a few days," Danielle said.

"Wait a minute." I laid one hand on the guitar to stop the music. Everyone stared at me, and I asked, "You people would join them, leaving me here to work my ass off and watch the babies?"

After a moment of silence, Danielle said with a smile, "Well, yeah."

"Oh, okay. I'm dooowwwnn," I said, and everyone laughed.

"Where are you going?" Teddy asked as I stood.

"Bathroom." I swayed and focused my sight on the porch floor.

"You don't need to take your drink, babe," he said.

"I might get lost." I smiled.

"I'll help her." Shelly laughed.

"I know how to do this myself, Shelly."

We walked into the house, and she turned the bathroom light on for me. I held my cup toward her.

"One more?"

"Fine," she said.

I closed the door, sat on the toilet, and my head spun. Olly sat in the bathroom with me. I finished then sat on the bathroom floor. We stared at each other, and he wagged his tail.

"You're not her, you know." I was aggravated at him.

Shelly knocked on the door. "Are you okay, Beth?"

"Yeah. Come in. Have a seat." I patted the floor after she opened the door. "Look at him." I pointed at Olly. He jumped into my lap, and I held his face softly between my hands. "His eyes aren't as dark as hers."

"I know, but let's go outside," Shelly said.

"I will in a minute." I ran my hand the length of his back. "Why wasn't it, him? I liked her better."

"That isn't true. You lost something special, so you're mad," she said.

I hugged him close, cried softly, and missed our little trio. Teddy came in and took Olly from my hands. He handed the dog to Shelly, wrapped his arms around me, and I hugged his neck. I buried my face in his shoulder and sobbed while he helped me to stand.

"I'm sorry, Izzy. I'm sorry I left her with Peter. Teddy, she died because she thought I wouldn't love her with three legs."

"No, she didn't," he said.

"I let her down." I waved my arm in the air. "I let you down, the kids down, and everybody down. I'm a piece of shit. I'm no good for anyone."

"Don't say that." He turned me toward the back door. "Let's get some air."

Shelly softly cried and held the door open for us. Gene stood and helped Teddy guide me to the chair. The girls stood as if they were going to help, but Teddy shook his head.

"We have her. She had a minor setback," he said and asked me, "Are you hungry?"

"No."

Shelly handed me the drink and asked, "Do you want him?"

"No," I said.

She sat with Olly on her lap and wiped her eyes with a tissue. She pet him while he stared at me. Tears filled my eyes once again while Teddy played a soft melody on the guitar.

"That's sad," I said and shook my head.

"You want this then," he said and played a fast riff.

"Yeah." I smiled.

"Here we go," Danielle said to Lucy. "Forty-five minutes."

Teddy sang an old song called *Rocking On A High Note*. He must have written it during his drug induced days. The upbeat melody was popular like many of his others. Halfway into the song, I felt better as the tears stopped, so I sang with him.

"Countdown begins," Lucy said.

"What countdown?" I asked.

"Nothing," she said.

"Did you guys hear that?" Thad asked and pointed at me.

"She's damn good," Teddy said.

"Hey. Not dead yet. No talking like I'm not here," I said.

"Mom sings that way when she's drunk or cleaning the house or when she doesn't think anyone is listening. We try to talk her into singing at church or karaoke, but she won't," Danielle said.

"I don't like crowds, and y'all are full of shit. I suck, but tonight I don't care. Let's everyone sing," I swayed to the rhythm in my thoughts.

Teddy played another old song, the kids, and I listened to when they were little. The memories of us dancing made me smile.

"Do y'all remember that song?" I asked the girls, and they both smiled.

"That was a lifetime ago," Lucy said.

"You're twenty-eight, sweetie. You haven't experienced a lifetime ago," I said.

"It feels that way," she said.

"What was the name of the song she sang when she put us to bed?" Danielle asked Lucy.

I thought a moment, then it hit me. *Happiness Is Forever* was a soft ballad that Teddy wrote.

"That's it," Danielle said and rocked Gabi as I sang.

I continued to sing, and Teddy played the guitar. I ended the song and stared at the porch.

"That brings back memories," Lucy said.

Teddy stared at me, and I asked, "What?" He didn't respond. "I'm sorry I killed your song, but I remembered these two being little, lying in bed while I danced, sang, and laughed. That song meant a lot to me. Thank you."

He leaned into me. With his finger, he guided my chin to face him. He kissed me softly, smiled, and played another song.

"You're a fan," he said.

"Am not," I argued, then took the last of my drink, and swayed when I stood.

"Where are you going now?" Teddy asked.

"I want one more then off to bed, I go." I held the cup over my eyes to see if the liquid drained from a hole in the bottom.

"I'll get it. Sit down my favorite," Gene said and guided me into the chair.

"Ass kisser." I smiled.

He took the cup from my hands, kissed my forehead, and smiled. "Yes, I am."

"Oh, Gene made a funny," I said, and everyone laughed.

"I want to hear one more. This is a new one, so tell me if you know it," Teddy said.

"She knows it," Danielle said.

"I might not." She laughed, and I listened to the melody for a few seconds. "Well, crap."

"You don't know it?" he asked.

"Yes," I said.

Gene handed the drink to me when I sang *My Heart Is Yours*. Teddy joined me. I took the lead, which made him laugh.

"I can't change one note unless you're looking at me," he said.

"Hate to cut this fun short, but my two kids have to get to bed. Sadie has school tomorrow," Lucy said.

Everyone stood except me. I held my arms out, and Lucy handed me, Kara. I kissed her little fat cheeks. Lucy told Kyle and Susan how she would be awake for a while if they wanted to stay.

I hugged Lucy, held her hand, and said, "Thank you for being with me today."

"I am sorry, Mom. I never meant to hurt her or you," she said softly.

"I know. There will be no more talk about it." I hugged her once more then she took Kara from my lap.

"Susan and I are going to head out with them. We have an early day in the morning," Kyle said while Teddy hugged Lucy and kissed Kara's head.

"Yeah, we're going as well," Danielle said and handed me Gabi.

"We're leaving at nine in the morning," Shelly said. "Not nine-fifteen or…"

Everyone joined and said at the same time. "Nine-thirty. It has to be nine."

We laughed, and Danielle took Gabi after I gave her kisses. I hugged Kyle. I kissed his cheek, then did the same with Susan. Mark, Rick, and Thad. Teddy made sure my butt landed in the chair before he bid his goodnights.

Once everyone was gone, Shelly, Gene, Teddy, and I stayed on the back porch. Teddy sat next to me, strummed the guitar and hummed while I closed my eyes and swayed.

"How do you come up with this stuff?" I asked.

"Sometimes I can crank a song out in a matter of minutes, and others stump me. I'm writing a few now, I can't get the sound I want, but it'll come to me," he said.

"I would love to hear them," I said.

"Not yet," he said. "You have talent, Beth."

"Thank you, but I'm an accountant and forever will be."

"You're much more," he said.

"Whatever, but I have a question for you," I warned.

"I'm ready," he said.

"Who did you write *True Love* for?" I asked.

He looked me in the eye and said, "You." I rolled my eyes at him, and he said with a smile, "Stop checking for spiders."

"Sorry," I said.

"I would like to know that answer. He tells me he just wrote it one day," Shelly said.

"I did. I wrote part of it after my second divorce. I don't know why I didn't finish it, but I put it in a drawer. I forgot about it until years later. I was in the studio, listening to playbacks and stumbled across it. I spent two days rewriting the music. Walla, *True Love* was born."

"You had nobody in mind when you completed it?" I asked.

"Nope. Is that your favorite?" he asked.

"No. My favorite is *Lion Who Walks*." I smiled.

"It's *True Love*." He laughed.

"I have several and hate to tell you darlin', but some are from different artists," I said.

"There isn't anyone better than me."

"Skyler Bray, Tom Kranic, Jumper, or Rachelle. Don't forget about Noah Parker, Tye Kravens, or Janis Hex. We can go back to the oldies or even talk about bands. Depends on what style or decade you want to discuss. I have favorites from the past forty years," I said.

"But I'm your favorite of all time. Right?" He smiled.

"Nope," I smirked.

"I like country," Shelly teased.

"Now, you tell me. I can sing country," he said.

"My life is a country song," I said.

I put my cigarette out, drank the last drop from my cup, and stood. On wobbly legs, I held onto the back of a chair.

"Off to bed, I go." I looked at Olly and said, "Come on, you, ol' scroungy dog." I looked at Teddy, Shelly, and Gene. "Goodnight, guys."

Olly ran into the house while I walked to the bathroom. I washed my face, brushed my teeth, and dressed for bed. I stared in the mirror, and my thoughts led to Izzy.

"Goodnight, my sweetie," I said out loud.

I hit the sink with my hand, spun on my heels, and opened the bathroom door. Teddy, Shelly, and Gene walked inside.

"Y'all didn't have to come in because I'm going to bed," I said.

"We need to leave…" Shelly said.

"At nine," Teddy, Gene, and I said at the same time and laughed.

"Goodnight, Beth." Shelly hugged me.

"Thank you for being here for me today," I said.

She smiled and walked out of the bedroom. Gene hugged me.

"You'll always be my favorite," I said in a little girl's voice.

"You're mine, honey. Goodnight." He kissed my cheek.

He told Teddy he would lock the house, then he pulled the door closed behind him. Teddy held my shoulders, guided me to the bed, and sat me on the edge.

He walked into the bathroom, and I laid on the bed. I stared at the mirrors on the ceiling for a few minutes, then the bathroom door opened. I sat up as Teddy walked past me.

I quickly grabbed him from behind. He turned in my arms and held me tight. I ran my hands across his bare chest, over his stomach muscles, and kissed his shoulder.

"No way. Shirt will go on, or I'll take the couch," he said and held my hands.

"Are you sure you would take the couch?" I asked in a small voice.

"I'm sure. This is difficult, but you're emotional. I'm not doing this unless I can have you as you. No alcohol. I want you free from fuzzy."

He led me to bed, patted the spot next to me for Olly to jump up. He kissed my forehead and turned the lights out. The bed moved while he laid next to me.

"Teddy," I said and held his hand.

"What, babe?" he asked.

"Thank you for picking me up off the ground today. I needed you, and you showed. It means a lot to me."

"Goodnight, Beth," he said.

Chapter 26

TEDDY LAID ON HIS SIDE, away from me. He hugged the body pillow. The blankets covered him from the waist down. I smiled with the thought of how I came alive when he kissed me. His back muscles were tight, and a small scar embedded his skin on his left shoulder blade.

Olly raised his head as he laid next to Teddy. I pet the dogs face until he laid still. I climbed out of bed and tiptoed into the bathroom. I brushed my teeth, stared into my swollen eyes, and touched my red nose. I brushed my hair, washed my face, and returned to bed in my pajamas.

Teddy rolled onto his back with his eyes closed and asked, "Why will you not wake me?"

"You need to sleep."

"I felt you staring at me earlier." He smiled.

He walked to the bathroom and left Olly and me alone in the room. I let Olly outside and curled back under the covers. After a few minutes, Teddy returned, let Olly inside, and slid in behind me. He wrapped his arms around my waist and spooned me.

His phone sounded with an alarm. I straddled him, reached for the phone then turned off the noise. He squeezed me tight, and I laughed.

"Be careful," he said. I kissed his neck while he held me. "Okay, girl. Get up."

I sat up and seductively moved my hips against his. My nerves jumped as his manhood grew. He held my hips and stopped my motion.

"I mean it, Beth. Get up."

I gazed into his eyes. Sparks of light danced in them. A yearning rushed over me, and my body tingled. Pictures of us making love played in my thoughts. I wanted him, but could I give myself to him?

He sat up, kissed me softly, then said in a low voice, "We don't have to do this. I want to, but we'll wait until you're comfortable with the idea of us."

"I'm nervous," I said.

"I will do nothing to hurt you." He wrapped his arms around me. "You don't owe me anything, and I don't want you to do this because you think you do."

"I want you, baby," I said and ran my nails through his hair.

He laid against the bed. "I can feel it." He smiled, stroked my hair, and asked, "Can you? I'm not talking about this." He held my hips and pushed his into me.

"Yeah," I softly said as my nerves jumped.

He moved my hair over my shoulder and ran his hands the length. He stopped at my breasts, and we continued to gaze into each other's eyes. Peace and comfort returned to me.

"I want you forever. No others. Are you comfortable with that?" he asked.

I thought about the question and realized it didn't matter how many women slept with Teddy. I trusted him. Maybe I was selfish or gullible, but I yearned for him. I closed my eyes. Chills coursed down my spine. Electricity raced through my body. I opened my eyes and studied his soft gaze.

I pulled my shirt over my head as my hair fell over my breasts. He gently pushed it over my shoulders and exposed my nakedness. He placed his hands on my hips while his eyes skimmed my body. Butterflies fluttered in the pit of my stomach. He sat up, laid his head over my heart, and squeezed me tight.

He rolled me in the bed and kissed me passionately. His tongue slipped between my lips, and I tasted the mint from his mouthwash. He gently rubbed from my breasts, down my sides, then to the edge of my pants. He slowly traced my waistband.

I glided my figure nails across his spine, stopped at his waistband, and slipped my hands under the material. I squeezed his hips. He looked in my eyes and words appeared in my thoughts, *Are you okay?* I slowly nodded, as his electric touch stimulated my skin with the intense energy heightening between us.

He smiled then slid his pajama bottoms off. The pulse in my body rose along with the heat in the room. I pulled my pants down my legs. My body screamed with desire when his naked body laid on mine.

We held eye contact, and he thrust his hips into mine. A jolt of energy took my breath away. He lowered his head to my neck and trailed kisses to my shoulders.

I quietly moaned from the marvelous sensations and electricity in the air. His pace quickened. I trailed my fingernails across his back, squeezed his hips tight, and loved the feel of his skin next to mine.

I tilted my head back, held my breath, and my body tensed. I released myself along with the air in my lungs, then melted from the energy which drained my body. He smiled, moved his hips back and forth a few minutes longer, then quickened his pace.

He took me on an excellent ride as ecstasy built within me. I quietly moaned as I reached the peak for the second time. He tilted his head back and squeezed his eyes shut. He softly moaned while he exhaled. He kissed me and slowed his motion.

He snuggled his nose into my neck, and I wrapped my arms around him. I kissed his cheek, and he raised his head. He looked into my eyes and four letters, *l-o-v-e*, flashed in my thoughts along with the words, *peace and happiness*. I loved every second of what we shared, but the reality was, we could never do that again.

"Don't leave me, Beth." He stared at me.

I loved being in his protective arms, but he needed someone who could stand by his side. Someone who could handle the drama the media caused. I wasn't the right person for him.

"And you're gone," he said out loud.

"I'm right here." I smiled.

"That's not what I mean. You were there. You felt it."

"I felt something several times." I smiled.

"That's not what I mean." He smiled. A soft knock rapped on the door, and he said, "Go away."

"Are you awake?" Shelly whispered.

"We'll be out in a few minutes," he said.

"You better," she said in a louder voice.

"You were with me," he said.

"I'm here with you," I said.

"I love to hear you say that," he said then kissed me. He stroked my hair. "It didn't last long, did it?"

"It's been a while for me, but it was perfect." I smiled and moved a strand of hair from his eyes.

"You're perfect. The intensity between us is strong."

I thought about our reality, then kissed him, and said, "Get in the shower before Shelly breaks through the door, dragging your butt out of here."

He grabbed my left leg, lifted it around his hips, and I placed my right leg around his other. He moved my arms to wrap around his back.

"I'm home right here, Beth Chambers." He kissed my chest and said, "This is home."

"You fit perfectly." I smiled.

I squeezed him until he raised his head with laughter. I released my legs and ran my nails across his back.

"You need to get ready, so shower now," I said.

"Fine, but you sound like Shelly." He rolled off me.

He stood, and I pointed to a scar on his left hip. "What happened?"

"You're not the only one with scars," he said, referring to my surgery. "A horse kicked me, tore my hip, leg, and shoulder. I had my knee replaced." He showed me a long scar on his left leg.

"It's good to know you have life's battle scars as well, now get in the shower, sexy." I smiled.

I laid in bed for several minutes and listened to the water run in the bathroom. I liked Teddy. I could love him. Olly pawed the side of the bed, and I rose. I let him outside as Teddy walked out of the bathroom.

His skin glistened from the steam. I stood in front of him and kissed his neck. I trailed my lips down his chest to his belly button, and he placed his hands on the back of my head.

"You better quit, or my mom is going to catch us," he said.

I stood face-to-face with him. "To be continued then. Yes?"

"Oh, yeah." He smiled.

"I'll bring the lipstick," I said.

He kissed me then I walked into the bathroom. I stepped into the shower and washed. I walked out of the bathroom in a towel, and Teddy tackled me to the bed. He laid on top of me while I laughed. He kissed me softly, and it was that moment, I gave my heart to Teddy Nafton.

We laid in one another's arms for a minute as I basked in his touch. He stood, held his hand out for me, and I went into the bathroom. I dressed for work in maroon slacks and a white button-down, fake silk shirt.

"You look nice," he said and embraced me again.

"Thanks. My nose and eyes are dead giveaways I've been crying," I said.

"Are you okay?"

"I miss her, and I hurt, but I physically can't cry," I said, and a louder knock rapped on the door.

"Ten minutes, Mr. Man," Shelly said, and I jerked the door open. "Sorry, Beth. I didn't mean to wake you." She tilted her head, furrowed her eyebrows, and stared at me.

"What?" I asked with a slight smile.

"No, no, no, no, no," she said and pushed me into the room. She shut the door behind her, pointed her finger between Teddy and me, and said, "I couldn't keep him focused before you two had sex. How in the hell am I going to keep him focused now?"

"We didn't." I smiled, not wanting her to know.

"You come with us, Beth. You can be Teddy's toy to keep him entertained on the road trips." She grabbed my hand, sat on the bed, and I laughed.

Teddy laid his hand on her shoulder and said, "I'll be okay. We have the phone, or we could Skype. It's five weeks before we're back together."

"It's five weeks of you being depressed because you can't see her. We just went through this, and it was only a week," she said.

"You're crazy," he said.

"You see, Beth. I now have to kidnap you." She let go of my hand. "Get your stuff and come with us."

"We'll be okay," I said and looked at Teddy.

"The story must continue. That thought alone will get me through five weeks." He wrapped his arms around my waist.

"Oh, God. This is going to be the longest tour of my life. Having to deal with a bitchy, Teddy." She hugged her clipboard and tablet to her chest.

We laughed as she opened the door, and we walked to the living room. I moved faster in front of him to retrieve a few travel mugs for coffee.

"Thad," Mark said and pointed at Teddy and me.

"I see it," Thad said and shook his head.

"What do you see?" Teddy asked.

I raised my eyebrows at them, and Thad asked, "How far is Thanksgiving?"

"You two little evil boys need to stop and tell us what you're talking about." I pointed at them.

"It's great. It's about freaking time, but that's what, five or six weeks until you two see each other intimately?" Thad asked.

"Do I have it tattooed across my forehead or something?" I looked at Teddy.

They laughed, and Thad said, "You're glowing, and this man can't wipe the smile from his face. I've never seen this smile thing on him."

"It's because they're in love," Susan sang the words.

"I don't use that word with him," I sang like Susan.

"She doesn't. We like each other…*a lot*." Teddy smiled and emphasized the words *a lot*.

I handed him a cup of coffee. I looked at the clock then at Shelly and asked, "Does anyone else want coffee to go? I have plenty of travel cups."

"Yes, ma'am," Gene said.

"I have a few more if there are any other takers," I said.

"I'll take one," Mark said.

"You may be late, so sorry, Shelly," I said.

"It's okay. I knew this would happen. That's why I said nine. We do have to be at the airport by ten, so you guys have twenty more minutes to kill," she said.

"Seriously? I could have laid in bed with the most beautiful woman I have ever seen in my life, for another twenty minutes?" Teddy asked and wrapped one arm around my waist.

"Then he woke and saw me," I said, and everyone laughed.

"You always make us late. I knew today would be no exception, especially you being with Beth," Shelly said to Teddy.

"I'm at fault?" I pointed to myself.

"Yes, Beth. Yes, you are." Shelly smiled.

"And you, ma'am." Teddy pulled me into his body. "Are the most beautiful woman I have ever had the pleasure of knowing. You hold my heart."

"I'll carry it with care." I smiled.

I moved out of Teddy's arms, gave Gene his coffee, and placed Mark's cup into the coffee machine. I leaned against the bar and looked at each person.

"I wanted to thank you all for being here. I appreciate each of you guys for helping me with Izzy. You guys made it easier, so thank you from the bottom of my heart," I said.

"No more tears," Kyle said.

"They're there, but I physically can't cry right now," I said.

Teddy moved me to stand in front of him while he leaned on the counter. He placed his chin on my shoulder, and I closed my eyes. I relived this morning in my memory until the coffee machine dinged.

I moved out of Teddy's arms, handed Mark his cup and asked, "Anyone else?"

"No. We're good," Thad said.

Teddy took his coffee, held my hand, and Gene opened the front door. Olly ran inside. Teddy stopped, let go of my hand, and pet Olly.

"See ya, buddy. Be good for your mom," he said, then shut the door behind us.

He wrapped his arm around my waist, and we walked down the porch stairs. I moved from him, but he grabbed my hand, pulled me into his arms, and I laughed.

"I want to tell everyone, bye."

"Wave to them." He joked.

Kyle stepped to me and whispered in my ear. "One happy family."

"You know I know," I said into his ear and hugged him with one arm. Teddy would not let go of the other.

"I know," he chuckled.

Susan, Mark, Thad, and even Rick hugged me while I stayed in Teddy's grip. When Shelly stood in front of me, I looked at Teddy, and he let go of my hand.

"Thank you, Shelly. I love you, girl." I embraced her.

"I love you too," she said.

"You'll say it to her, but not to me?" Teddy asked.

"Well, yeah. She's not you." I smiled. "She's like my sister. You're…well. I don't know what you are."

"Let's start with what makes you comfortable. How about, boyfriend?" he asked.

"Not official," I said.

"Lover?" he asked and raised his eyebrows.

"One time doesn't count." I smiled.

He pulled me tight into his body and said, "Best friend in the world."

"I like that," I said and wrapped my arms around his neck.

"We made progress today, Ms. Chambers. The next session will be in five weeks," he said as we held each other's waist and walked to the car. He leaned his forehead against mine and said, "I'm going to miss you."

I closed my eyes and said, "You have my heart, Teddy."

"I'll protect it with my life."

He kissed, then embraced me. I placed my hand on his neck and whispered in his ear, "I like you *a lot*." And emphasized the words *a lot*.

He stared into my eyes and said softly, "I like you *a lot*" and emphasized the words *a lot*.

I hugged him for another second then kissed him passionately. I gently pushed him back, and he smiled. He kissed his two fingers, held them in the air, and formed a peace sign.

Once he sat in the SUV, Gene shut the car door.

"Thank you, Gene," I said and embraced him.

"You come first in his life. If you need us, we're here for you, honey," he said, then sat in the vehicle.

I waved as they drove away, but Teddy wouldn't look at me. I walked inside the house, and Olly jumped at my legs. He backed a little, ran, and jumped into my arms. I caught him in the air, and he buried his head in my chest while I rubbed my hand along his back. The two of us were left to roam the quiet house, and my heart ached.

Chapter 27

I FOUND REFUGE WITH THE thought of being in Teddy's arms in a few weeks. Our nightly conversations and daily texts made me miss him with each passing day.

He was in Arizona. I arrived at the house and was about to call him when my phone rang.

"Hey, Shelly."

"Hey. Have you spoke with him, yet?" she asked.

"Not since this morning. What's up?"

"He's having a hard day, and he's about to lose it. Something went wrong with the sound, and they're trying to correct it, but he's as bad as you. He has to control everything and make sure tonight's performance goes smoothly." She sounded stressed. "He's not sleeping well, and now the sound guys are getting on his nerves."

"I don't know what I can do," I said.

"Try to calm him. You're a business person, Beth. You know it's Teddy, we sell. I didn't mean for that to come out as it sounded. I love Five/Ten, but you can't have them without Teddy."

"I get it. You protect your most important asset, and you can't have the leader of the team in a tizzy," I said.

"It's a sold-out show. I need him relaxed and focused. My life is easier when everyone plays nicely together."

"I'll call you after I speak with him," I said.

"Thanks," she said.

I smiled at the thought of Shelly's daily calls. She informed me of schedule and hotel changes along with venting about her day. I loved Shelly and learned she genuinely cared about Teddy and the Five/Ten members.

I called, and he answered, "Yeah."

"Yeah, to you too. What's going on?"

"Take a break, guys." He waited for a second and said, "Hey, babe."

"Are you okay?"

"You called fifteen minutes late," he said.

"You time me?" I asked.

"To a degree. I want to make sure you make it home safely."

"Quit worrying about me," I said.

"We need to talk, Teddy," An unfamiliar man's voice said in the background.

"Can you excuse me for a second, Beth?" he asked.

"Yeah," I said.

His voice muffled, and he said, "I'm on an important call. We'll speak once I'm off the phone." His voice cleared, and he said, "Sorry."

"If you need to go…" I said.

"No. This is our time," he said quickly.

"Why are you stressed?"

"Everyone knows when you call, they are to wait until we're finished. It's a good break time, and when we're doing sound checks, we keep our conversation short, but they still patiently wait. Not interrupt." He complained. "These people are pulling me in fifteen different directions, and everything anyone touches falls apart. I'm to go on in a few hours, and we can't get the sound correct."

"You being tired and sexually frustrated can make for a stressful situation." I smiled.

"Sexually frustrated, huh?" He questioned.

"You caught that, did you?" I asked.

"Yeah," he said.

"Sexual frustration has nothing to do with you being stressed?"

"Could be, Ms. Chambers."

"Seriously, Teddy. Y'all are tired, so give them some space and let someone else help. I promise everything will go smooth."

"I miss you," he said.

"Twelve more days, baby," I said playfully.

"Oh, man," he said.

"What?"

"By then, my sexual frustration will be through the roof." He laughed.

"I'll bring lotion."

"You would. I can see it now. You walk into my house, hand me a bottle, then disappear to avoid me for several days."

"I just need to know your favorite kind," I said.

"You," he said.

"Go make pretty music before this conversation gets heated." I blushed. "I like you *a lot*, baby."

"I'll call at prayer. Peace, babe," he said.

"Peace," I said.

I sat on the back porch, and the cold breezed through the air. I thought about the one-time Teddy, and I made love. It was special to me. I missed him madly, but I'll be in his arms soon. My phone rang and brought me out of my thoughts.

"Hello." I sang.

"Thanks, Beth. You put a smile on his face," Shelly said.

"I didn't do anything, Shelly. I know you're a busy woman running around with your clipboard and tablet, but can you do me a favor?" I asked.

"Sure, sweetie. What?" she asked.

"Can you get a bottle of lotion, and wrap it with a big bow? Set it and two red calla lilies on his nightstand with a note attached?" I asked.

"I'm scared to ask what you want the note to say." She giggled.

"From, Beth," I said. "Give it to him after the party. Please?"

"I have an idea of the meaning, but don't say it out loud," she said.

"Thank you, darlin'."

"Thank you, sista," she said.

"Call me if I can do anything to help."

"I will," she said, then hung up.

That evening, Teddy called for the before concert prayer. They corrected the sound problem, but I could tell he was exhausted.

I laid across the bed, watched TV, but my mind drifted to Teddy performing in front of thousands of people. I fell asleep and dreamt of Carissa in her chair on the side of the stage as she waited for him.

My phone rang early in the morning. I answered in a panic state, "What's wrong?"

"I shouldn't have called, but I wanted to thank you for the present, and flowers," he said with laughter.

"Present," I said and gained my thoughts. "Oh, the lotion." I smiled. "How did it work for you?"

"I'm waiting on you to try it."

"Not much longer."

"I'm assuming these are your favorite flowers?" he asked.

"Yes, sir. How was the afterparty?" I asked.

"Fine," he said. "Did you ask Shelly to do that?"

"Yeah." I smiled.

"I bet she thought you were crazy."

"I'll get it," Gene said in the background.

"Thanks. Somebody's knocking on the door at this hour," Teddy said.

I sat up in bed as it hit me. Pictures of Carissa knocking on the door flashed in my mind.

"It's Carissa."

"No, it isn't. I haven't spoken to her since…" he said then yelled, "What the hell are you doing here?"

"I'll talk to you later," I said and hung up the phone.

Now was the time to let him go. Carissa wanted him, and he needed her. Their encounter gave me the excuse to back away from him gracefully. I found happiness for a short period of time. It would break my heart to never see him again, but, for his sake, I would fade from his life.

Chapter 28

My alarm sounded, and I woke from the dreams of Teddy. He told me our relationship was over, and he no longer wanted to associate with me. In my mind, his voice repeated the words, *'stay away'* and my heart sunk to the pit of my stomach.

I glanced at my phone. I had a missed call from him. I didn't want to disturb his sleep nor hear the words, so I didn't call him. I convinced myself to turn off my emotions and relearn how to function without him. No more long phone calls. No more electrifying touches or dancing light in his eyes. It's better to end it now than later.

Olly and I walked into the office. I turned on the computers as Lois, Helen, and Irene joined us. The girls and I spoke about our weekend plans, which delayed the morning start. Lois planned to go to a few new restaurants, and Irene was going to shop for Christmas, which led us into a conversation about this year's new hot toys for the kids.

Reluctantly, I went into the office, sat at the desk, and pulled my phone out of my purse. Five missed calls from Shelly appeared on the screen.

My computer screen caught my attention. I clicked on the Internet symbol. A picture of Teddy and Carissa headlined the entertainment section. I forgot about Shelly and became focused on the top story.

Teddy and Carissa - Back Together Again

"Beth!" Lois said and stepped into my office.

"Yeah." I stared at the picture. Teddy's draped arm hugged Carissa's shoulders while they walked past a hotel door. "I see it."

"I'm sorry," Lois said.

"Don't be." I clicked on the picture to open the story.

"Teddy and Carissa are back together, spending a romantic night in Arizona." Helen read out loud. "I know that's bullshit. Thad said Teddy is miserable without you," she said while I focused on the words.

Irene continued. "She was in Vegas doing a bikini shoot for a summer magazine then met Teddy at his concert in Phoenix. Who goes to Phoenix for a romantic night?"

"A jealous supermodel," Lois said as she sat at her desk.

I clicked through the pictures. In one, he smiled as he spoke to her and leaned against an open limo door. In another, she gazed at him as they stood next to the car. I clicked on another, then my phone rang.

I retrieved it and hit the decline button. I didn't want to speak with Shelly. I wanted to see if this was real, so I clicked back to my home page. I typed in several more sites, which showed the same headline under the entertainment section. I clicked those to see if I could find more pictures of him from last night, and my phone rang again.

I grabbed it, plucked a lollipop from a bowl, and with Olly at my feet, we walked to the back patio. The phone stopped ringing by the time I unlocked the back door and stepped outside. I tapped my phone app, but it rang again.

"Hey," I said.

"They aren't real, Beth. She and Teddy aren't together," Shelly whispered in a soft panicked voice. "Teddy hasn't seen them yet. Gene is with him now."

"It's okay, Shelly." I wanted to calm her even though I was confused.

"She showed last night, and he and Gene walked her to the limo. They never published pictures of her leaving by herself. Please believe me," she pleaded in a low voice.

"It's okay," I assured her. "How much sleep have you had?"

"A few hours. The guy at the front desk recognized her to be Teddy's girlfriend from *The Watch* and led her to the room. Teddy nor Gene would let her inside, so they walked her out together to the car."

"Everything will be fine," I said and wanted to be her support.

"Teddy is going to shit when he finds out. We're trying to get the story pulled. I tried to call you this morning to warn you. You're his main priority, and I didn't want you to see the pictures and assume it was true. I'm sorry, Beth."

"Sorry about not answering. How did you find out about the pictures?"

"Marcy called."

A door slammed in the background, and Teddy yelled, "What the fuck, Shelly? You guys couldn't stop this? Has anyone spoken with Beth?"

"I'm speaking with her now," she said.

"Beth!" Teddy exclaimed and took the phone from Shelly.

"Good morning." I wanted to keep my cool until I figured out what happened.

"No, it isn't." He snapped. "These damn people, I pay good money to protect me, screwed me over. They couldn't stop the pictures from hitting the Internet. Did you see them?"

"Yes," I said.

"I promise nothing happened. Carissa and I are not together. That bitch threatened to expose you if I didn't leave you alone."

"She's been saying that for a while."

"She knows your full name and got pissed when I didn't tell her your exact location. She's one step closer in finding out where you live."

"It'll be okay," I said.

"You're on borrowed time," he said and raised his voice, "Get the pictures on the screen, Shelly. I haven't even seen the damn things."

"Calm down, baby," I said.

"The first fucking story?" he yelled. "Why is my life so damn important? She did this to get back at me. Don't believe the headline, Beth."

"What happened?"

"I was speaking with you and…" he said.

"And she knocked on the door." I completed his sentence.

"How did you know it was her?"

"A picture of her flashed in my thoughts," I explained as my phone buzzed with a call. "I also dreamt you told me it was over, and we were through. You kept repeating we were through. You didn't care who I told, but we were no longer together."

"That's weird," he said. "Once I saw it was her, Gene and I guided her into the lobby. Reporters took pictures of us through the windows, so Gene, Carissa, and I went out the back door. A reporter waited behind the hotel and snapped pictures as I opened the limo door for her. I wanted her taken to the airport or hell or wherever she came from."

"I tried calling you back, but you didn't answer. Nothing happened, so I didn't want to keep calling to wake you again. I knew we would speak about it today, but not like this," he said. "You dreamt what I was telling her. I said those things to her, not you."

"That explains everything. It's not as bad as you think," I said and believed him.

"Beth," he said calmly. "While Gene and I walked her out, she told me she knew your full name. Please understand it's a matter of time for her to expose you, whether it's positive or negative. She knows how to play the reporters. She's a ticking time bomb."

"It'll work out," I said, and my other line rang again. I pulled my phone from my ear and saw Carissa called, but I was not going to say anything to Teddy.

"She could cause your life to become a three-ring circus. If she does, I can't keep you out of the media."

"I live in a three-ring circus." I smiled.

"I'm serious, babe."

"I can disappear," I said.

"No!" He exclaimed.

"It might be for the best, Teddy. Get through the tour, and I'll complete tax season. We'll see if we still speak afterward," I explained, and my heart pounded. I didn't want to lose him, but I would sacrifice my happiness for his.

"No. I'll be damn to wait," he said forcefully before he spoke in a louder tone. "Shelly, I want to know how she found out where we're staying. I need to know how she got Beth's last name and what information she has on her. What story did she tell the reporters to bring them here? I want that information now. Not in an hour, but now."

"Teddy!" I exclaimed. "You're asking for the impossible. Carissa isn't going to talk."

"There has to be a way, Beth. We had a few reporters before and after the concert, but they doubled in numbers. She had to have told them something."

"You're tired and need to rest. You can think clearer once you sleep. Everything will be okay." I reassured him. "We'll take things as they come, but can you do me a favor?"

"Anything for you," he said.

"I want to speak with you in your room," I said.

"I need to get this stopped now," he said.

"Please?"

"Fine, but I don't know how this is going to help," he said to me then, "Shelly, when I get back, I need those answers."

"Wait, Teddy. You have her phone." I laughed.

"Oh," he said, "I'll call you right back."

I read my text.

Back off or you'll meet your worst nightmare. - Carissa

Teddy called, and I answered, "Are you sitting on the bed?"

"Yes, but I want to punch Carissa out."

"You can't. Are you alone in your room?"

"Yeah, but my ass needs to be in the other room getting information," he said.

"Before you answer, I want you to think about this next question."

"Okay," he said impatiently.

"Why are you mad?"

"The damn pictures," he said in a lower voice.

"What do those have to do with anything? Are you playing me, or do you want her?"

"No," he said and paused for a moment. "I don't want to lose what we have, and I didn't want you to think the story was real. Nothing happened. I'm not playing you, and I don't want her to come after you with the media."

"Close your eyes."

"Beth…"

"Please, Teddy?"

"Fine, they're closed," he said.

"I'm sitting in the smoking hole, sucking on a lollypop. I haven't had a cigarette in a week and a half," I said.

"That's great!" he exclaimed.

"Eyes closed," I said.

"They are."

"The sun is shining, and Olly is lying in the grass. Can you picture me?"

"What are you wearing?" he asked.

"Whatever you want me to, baby," I said in a low voice and closed my eyes. "Do you see me?"

He and I took a deep breath at the same time. I imagined him searching for me in the darkness. The sun suddenly shone, and Teddy walked around the side corner of the building, wearing a white coat, silver silk pajama pants, and matching silver tennis shoes.

"Hi," he said as he shut the fence gate.

"Hi," I said. "I miss you."

"I miss you so bad, it hurts," he said.

"I'm glad to hear you say that," I said. I imagined I stood and embraced him. "Can you feel my arms around you?"

He hesitated for a few seconds and said in a sad voice, "I can see you in my arms, wearing a button-down orange shirt, black pants, and flat, black shoes, but I can't feel you."

"How did you know I'm wearing that outfit?" I asked, perplexed.

"I see it in my mind," he said.

"What are you wearing?"

"Silver silk pajama pants. No coat and no tennis shoes. I do have shoes, which would match," he chuckled. "Our connection is getting stronger."

"It isn't possible for you to know what I'm wearing or thinking," I said.

"Yes, it is. We share a connection like no other," he said.

"Nope. It's not logical," I said to dismiss it.

"Not everything is rational, Beth," he said.

"I am."

"Why do you deny what we have?"

"We have a friendship, and if all you're worried about is losing that with me, then there is no reason for you to be mad. I'm not going anywhere unless you tell me, too," I said.

"This is more than friendship. I like you, a *lot,* babe." He emphasized the words a *lot.*

"I like you, a *lot,* too," I said in the same manner.

"I don't want you going anywhere, and I'm sorry I got angry," he said calmly.

"You don't have to apologize to me, but you need to apologize to Shelly later. I don't want you talking to her right now. I'm going to tell her if you say one word, she is to barricade herself in her room. If I have to come to Phoenix, everyone is going to be in trouble."

"I promise to give us space, but then again, I might stir up trouble, so you do come." He laughed.

"Teddy…" I wanted to say I loved him for thinking I needed to be protected.

"What?" he asked.

"Nothing. I'll talk to you in a little bit. Go to sleep," I said.

"Okay. Peace," he said, then hung up.

I tapped Shelly's number.

"What did you do to him?" she asked when she answered.

"I didn't do anything, but if he comes out of the room and says something to you, walk away. Even if he comes to you to apologize, turn, and go into your room."

"Why?" she asked.

"You all need to rest before you speak with each other. It takes one piece at a time to solve a puzzle, and you guys can't see the pieces because of how tired y'all are," I said.

"I can't believe those doors haven't opened."

"I'm sorry he got angry when it wasn't you who caused this Internet mess. Everything will be okay."

"Thank you, Beth. It's been a while since I've seen him that mad. I think he scared Gene." She snickered.

"Gene can take him out. That's for sure." I smiled. "Can I speak with Gene for a second?"

"Sure. Hold on."

"I love you, Shelly, but go to bed," I said.

"Love you, girl. Bye," she said and handed the phone to Gene.

"Hey, honey. I don't know what you said to him, but wow," he said.

"You need to get rest, but I wanted you to know, Carissa texted then called me when I was speaking with Teddy. I don't want to tell him right now. I'll call her and tell him later. He needs time to cool off."

"Will you forward me the text? Also, let me know what she says. Whatever you do, don't tell her your location. She's crazy, and we want to keep you safe."

"I'll be okay. Get some sleep."

"I will after you call me," he said.

"I'll talk to you in a few minutes then," I said before we disconnected from each other.

I wanted a cigarette. I ate my lollipop, so I looked at the stem. I smiled with the thought of how marvelous it would be if I could smoke a lollipop. I chuckled to myself, tapped Carissa's number, and she answered on the second ring.

"Did you get my text?" she asked.

"Hello to you too."

"Beth!" she exclaimed.

"Yes." I raised my voice. "I don't know why you think you could be my worst nightmare, but threats like that is no way to make friends, Carissa."

"Fuck you, Beth. We aren't friends," she blasted.

"What did I do to you? I'm not with him," I calmly stated.

"I know you aren't. I've been with him. We're back together, so leave him alone. If you don't believe me, check the entertainment section on the Internet."

"Oh, I saw it and had a good laugh. The story online doesn't tell me shit," I said. "Teddy said, he and Gene escorted you out of the hotel."

"We reconciled then made love. The pictures were taken when he walked me to the car this morning. I have business in Reno then I'm to meet him in a few days for Thanksgiving. I guess you and he are finished. I win, so leave him alone. No fame or fortune for you," she said.

"You're to meet him for Thanksgiving?" I asked.

"Yes," she said.

"How did you know what hotel they were staying in?" I asked.

"He called me to meet him."

"Is that why you called the reporters? *The Teddy and Carissa Watch*?"

"I let it slip we were reconciling, so they wanted a few pictures of us together," she said.

"You would think they needed a shot of you two in a kiss, but I guess you don't like to show affection in public." She was silent, and I continued, "I don't like games, but have a happy Thanksgiving."

"Beth!" She yelled. "If you pursue him, I'll expose you to the media for being a stalker."

"The media could give a shit less about me," I said.

"The media will do what I say, and I'll make your life hell." She threatened.

"Bye, Carissa." I hung up on her.

This woman was crazy. She couldn't thrust me into the media spotlight. The big question which plagued my mind was Thanksgiving. Who was lying? Her or Teddy? Maybe I should cancel the Michigan trip. Was Carissa right about last night? Did Teddy play me?

My phone rang, and I said. "Hey. You're supposed to be asleep."

"What's wrong?" Teddy asked.

"Nothing," I said, and my phone rang with another call.

"I dozed off for a second, but in my mind, you walked away from me. You wouldn't answer when I called your name, nor would you look at me, so talk to me."

"Go to sleep, Teddy. I need to get some work done, and we'll talk after you rest."

"I can't sleep without you next to me."

"Please try. Everything is fine."

He hesitated for a few seconds, then said, "Fine."

We hung up. Carissa was the one who called. I didn't want to speak to her, so I contacted Gene. I explained to him what Carissa informed.

"That's bullshit, Beth. She wasn't left alone with Teddy."

"I have my doubts, and a part of me is questioning if I need to come to Michigan. Maybe we need to wait until she calms before…" I said.

"You will be with us for Thanksgiving," he interrupted. "We are expecting you and the family. You don't want all of us standing at your doorstep to drag you away, so get your butt on the plane."

"Yes, sir," I said, and a text binged on my phone.

"She's determined to involve the media. We can protect you better in Michigan and hopefully find out who is feeding her information," he said.

"Thank you, Gene." I smiled and felt protected.

"Please let me know if you receive any more calls or texts. I want to stop them as much as you and Teddy. You two deserve peace and happiness," he said.

"You're my favorite," I said.

"You're mine, honey. I'll speak with you later," he said, then we bid our goodbyes.

Helper sent the message:

Your fate and destiny have revealed your
demise. To change your path, stay away
to stay alive.

I stared at the screen until it faded to black. I stood at a crossroads. To the right, I could leave Teddy and resume my normal hectic life. The crazy texts and calls would fade into the background and leave us media free. To the left, I could give Teddy my heart and fight for him. Am I willing to go through the drama? I evaluated my emotions, slightly smiled, and typed:

Can't stay away.

The End

CPSIA information can be obtained
at www.ICGtesting.com
Printed in the USA
FSHW020954110720